A
LITRPG NOVEL

SKY REALMS

ONLINE

GRAYHOLD

TROY OSGOOD

AETHON
BOOKS

GRAYHOLD

©2019 TROY OSGOOD

Print and eBook formatting, art provided by Jackson Tjota, and cover design by Steve Beaulieu.

Published by Aethon Books LLC. 2019

All characters in this book are fictitious. Any resemblance to actual persons, living or dead, is purely coincidental.

PROLOGUE

"Sorry, guys. This lag is killing me tonight," Redfire said as his hit points dropped to zero, and his avatar disappeared from the screen. His image on the group bar grayed out, joining the two others that were already grayed.

It was killing everyone, the worst it had been in a long time. There was always lag. The servers could only handle so much and with millions playing at the same time, there was bound to be some lag but what they had been dealing with the last hour had been horrible.

They would have canceled the dungeon raid if they had known it was going to be this bad. No one wanted to deal with it, even with their high-priced VR rigs. But by the time the lag hit they were already halfway through the dungeon and doing pretty well. They had run this same dungeon before, they knew what to expect and were feeling on top of their game.

Firefrost Mountain was home to the Jotuns, a race of blue-skinned giants. It was also home to a special set of Artifact Armor. Each of them had pieces, and they all wanted the rest. There was better armor in some of the newer dungeons but they were all completists. They wanted the achievement of completing the Firefrost Armor.

Now only two of them would get pieces.

Two Jotun Sentries lay to the sides of the Firefrost Throne Room. Their bodies were sparkling, indicating there was loot to be had. But first, they had to deal with the Jotun Chieftain himself.

Dravogr The Icebane swung his greataxe, the head as tall as a human. It slammed into the icy ground of the room that was carved from the mountain itself, the two characters jumping to the side. Cracks formed in the ground; such was the giant's strength. Sparks flew across the ground, blue lightning streaks erupting on impact. The axe had a debuff. Besides the high damage taken from it the debuff would cause a slowing effect that lessened the character's attack speed and power, it also caused a lightning-over-time damage.

Getting hit by the axe was not recommended.

And they were down a healer.

But Groven and Hall knew they had this fight.

Even with the lag.

Having Redfire the Bodin Shaman in the fight would have helped.

"We got this," Groven said over the voice chat.

"Hell yeah," Lysandra yelled out.

The Elven Druid, their healer, had been killed just before Redfire. The lag had been especially bad for her. The connection she had was always bad, her VR rig wasn't as good as the others, but she was good at her class and they all liked her. Some other groups would have ditched her a long time ago, but the Dragon Riders were not like that.

A close-knit group of friends even though none had met in real life.

"I just hope the Duelist gloves don't drop," Darkdagger muttered.

Hall ignored them all, concentrating on what he was doing. His job was that much harder as he was the only DPS.

Groven, as the Warden tank, was using his threat abilities to keep Icebane busy and distracted. If Lysandra had still been connected, Groven would have been standing still and taking most of the hits. A stationary target was better for Hall's abilities. There was also no way that Hall could take a hit from Icebane's axe, called Frostbite, one of the rarest drops in the game. Being a Skirmisher, Hall was limited to only leather armor. He needed to be able to move quickly. High Agility kept him from being hit, most of the time, but the low armor meant he couldn't take any big hits.

He especially couldn't risk taking a slow debuff.

From behind Icebane, Hall crouched low and pushed himself up using his *Leap* ability, one of the Skirmisher's Class Abilities. As he jumped into the air, he stabbed out with his spear using the *Leaping Stab* ability. Once, twice, three times. With each hit, there was a sharp explosion of light, and Icebane roared. Hall glanced at the health and energy bars that hovered over the giant. The attack had done a lot of damage. Icebane was down to a quarter of his health.

He landed on the giant's shoulders, wishing that Screech, his dragonhawk companion, was still alive. The companion's bonus attack would have been helpful.

From the Jotun's shoulders, he stabbed with his spear. A normal attack but still pretty effective with all the bonuses stacked from the weapon itself and the buffs he currently had applied. The timers were in his favor on all of them. None would fade before they should have had Icebane defeated.

Hall leapt off the giant, flipping backward, and used his *Flying Aim* ability to throw a javelin. Icebane was turning as the weapon hit. The end quivered from where it stuck out of Icebane's eye. Hall landed about fifteen feet from the fight, watching the bonus damage from the successful attack disappear from Icebane's health bar.

"Good shot," Darkdagger said, slightly mumbling.

"Are you eating?" Lysandra asked, her voice disgusted.

"Sorry," Darkdagger replied. "Eating the leftover candy. Didn't get many trick or treaters this year."

Even though their characters were all dead they were still able to watch as none would have hit the respawn button. They wanted to see this fight.

Hall stood up, watching Groven charge in. The Firbolg Warden swung his war hammer at the Jotun's chest. The hammer's head was on fire, green flames dancing around the carved silver head.

Pulling another javelin from the quiver on his back, Hall ran toward the fight. He drew the javelin back to throw it when he felt the world slow down. Everything started to stutter and slow. Groven's hammer seemed to skip as it swung toward Icebane. Hall felt his arm creep forward, his fingers releasing the javelin. It was like he was running through water.

"Lag spike," he said through the group chat, and even that was stuttering. He could hear a strange feedback through the channel.

The world shifted. That was the only way to describe it. Everything seemed to completely freeze and shake. He saw multiple images of Groven and Icebane, each seeming to slide out of sync with the others.

"What the hell!" Lysandra exclaimed. "Never seen a lag spike like that."

"I'm disconnected," Redfire cursed.

"Me too," Darkdagger muttered.

"Same," Lysandra growled.

"Come on," Groven said. "This last blow should do it. Come on," he continued, repeating the words.

Hall tried to talk but he couldn't. He could barely hear the others through the feedback. It hurt his ears, a strange humming and squawking. The words of the others echoed, repeating themselves and duplicated. Out of sync.

Then, it stopped.

Everything sped up to normal speed. Better than that Hall realized. He saw the javelin streaking toward the target. Saw the bright light, flames spreading across Icebane's chest as the hammers damage-over-time effect was activated.

Icebane's health bar dropped to nearly zero. The javelin struck and took it a little lower.

"We got this," Hall said excitedly.

He waited for Groven to respond, for any of them to say something, but his words were greeted with silence. His voice didn't sound the same either. There had always been something a little mechanical about his voice through the chat but now it sounded normal. Like it did in real life.

Weird, Hall thought as he gripped his spear, ready to deliver the final blow to Icebane.

Then, he stopped. Something was wrong.

Groven was frozen, still somehow stuck in the lag spike. The avatar did not move. But he did not look like he was stuck in lag. No shaking or stuttering. All the details of the avatar were tight and defined.

And Icebane was moving.

The Jotun Chieftain was pushed back by the hammer's strike, green flames spreading across his body but he recovered quickly. Too quickly. With a growl the giant raised his axe high with two hands. Angered, Icebane swung at the frozen Groven. The blow struck, and Groven just exploded.

He didn't fade from the game like normal when a character was killed. He just exploded into thousands of lights, little pixel-shaped pieces. They spread everywhere into the air then settled to the ground in a small pile before they quickly faded from existence.

"What the hell?" Hall said in the voice chat.

Or he thought he had. Icebane turned like he had heard Hall speak.

"Groven?" Hall asked skidding to a stop as the weakened Jotun completely faced him.

Icebane's health bar was still shrinking as the damage-over-time effect worked but he was still dangerous. There were no slow or attack debuffs on him. Not now. He was at full speed and strength, and one blow would end Hall and this raid.

"Guys," he asked taking a couple steps back from the advancing Icebane. He really needed some encouragement from the others right now. "Guys?"

Silence. Why weren't they responding?

They were all disconnected. All four. Which was weird. Even if they were disconnected from the game servers the chat was on a separate server. It still should have been active.

Cursing he leapt out of the way of a swing of Frostbite barely in time. Only his class's high Agility and *Evade* skill kept him from getting hit. He ran around behind Icebane and leapt up. Three times his spear hit the giant, three bright explosions.

And three wounds that leaked blue blood.

"What the hell?" he exclaimed again as he landed on the icy floor, slipping a little.

Another oddity, as never before had he slipped on the throne room floor. The icy look had just been graphics, not a game element. At least, not in this raid.

"Guys, are you seeing that?" he asked, watching the blood leak down the giant's side and splatter on the ground.

When did creatures in the game bleed? There was no gore setting to adjust.

Icebane stumbled, falling to his knees. He still held his axe but had no more strength to get up. The green flames started to fade but the damage had been done. Hall saw burn marks across the giant's body. Fresh and raw.

"Was that some kind of patch?" he asked, standing up, not really expecting an answer but it was habit.

He advanced on the weakened giant. Icebane's still visible health bar was very low, barely any red showing.

Hall leapt up into the air, spear pointing down. None of the others would see the cool finishing move, one of his favorites, but he did it anyway.

The spear struck, bright lights erupting as well as a fountain of blood. Hall saw it hit him, felt drops hitting his check where his leather helmet didn't cover the skin. His feet landed on either side of the spear wound, driving the spear in deeper.

Icebane's health bar blinked rapidly, indicating it had gone to zero.

Hall was breathing heavily, leaning against the spear shaft.

Breathing heavily. Breathing. He was breathing.

Not breathing in real life. His avatar was breathing.

"What the hell?" he said again.

This encounter was so strange.

Icebane's body was not shimmering. Neither were the Jotun Sentries. Something was wrong. There was always loot to be had. Icebane was a guaranteed drop. At least one piece of the Artifact green-level armor would drop with each kill. Random drops, but there were always drops. The Sentries were good for at least some gold, maybe getting lucky with an orange-level item drop.

But nothing. None of them had any loot.

The mountain started to shake, pieces falling from the ceiling above. Stone crashed against stone, large cracks appearing across the ground.

Hall stumbled as he landed, jumping off the giant's body.

More and more stones fell, ice chunks flying.

He felt the sting as a shard cut across his cheek.

"Damn," he cursed and reached up.

The cut was stinging, and the gloves came away with blood on the tips.

He was bleeding. His avatar was bleeding, and he felt the cut.

The shaking intensified, great blocks of stone falling and crashing, sending larger and larger chunks of ice through the air.

He had to get out of there.

Reaching into his pouch, Hall pulled out his Townstone. He ran his fingers over runes that started to glow a bright blue. The world around him seemed to grow foggy, graying out as the magic took hold.

He felt weird, a great weight against his body. He started to shrink, everything around him growing larger and fading.

Where was the black screen? When the timer on the Townstone's activation ran down the thirty seconds, the screen would go black and then come back, and he'd be where he had last set the stone.

Everything around him faded away, and all he saw was white, a bright white. Then that changed to a solid black. Dark.

Hall felt no more.

PART ONE
A NEW BEGINNING

CHAPTER ONE

THE BLACK FADED AWAY, AND HALL COULD SEE COLORS. Indistinct, foggy, at first. They quickly became more substantial, and he could start to see familiar details.

His Townstone had been locked to Timberhearth Keep for a long time now, Hall's favorite town on the zone of Edin. The inside of The Green Craobh Inn's Portal Room was not as he remembered. Thick log beams stacked tightly on top of each other, the three walls featureless with an open arch in the other. It was similar but not the same. Something was different.

And the room was empty.

He couldn't remember the last time the Green Craobh's Portal Room, or any Portal Room, had been empty. There were always avatars in the room. Some just teleporting in, others kneeled down and resting.

He heard a sound behind him, a slight whooshing, and turned only to be pushed against the wall.

"Hey, look out," someone said roughly as they walked through the arch.

Hall could hear the footsteps walking down the stairs and into the common room. What he found odd was that someone had bumped into him. The VR rigs allowed for people to run into each other and the avatars to feel the effects, but the Portal Room was one of the few spaces where that feature was deactivated. They were so busy with incoming traffic that no one would be able to move because of the constant bumping.

He leaned against the logs and tried to calm down.

There was just so much weird.

And he still hadn't heard from any of the others. They should have logged back in by now. His guildchat was empty as well. Where was everyone?

Hall passed through the arch, running his gloved hands along the familiar wood. He could feel every crack, every knot. The texture felt so real. He knew what logs should feel like, and that was what the walls felt like.

There wasn't much noise as he descended the wooden stairs. Normally the Inn's common room was full of talking, always a level of noise as people talked out of chat and the random background noise the game generated to make it feel like a crowded Inn in a vibrant frontier town.

Wanting to check something he tried to pull up the User Interface by double clicking his right thumb and forefinger together, the VR rig equivalent of a mouse click. Nothing happened. Odd, he thought, trying to picture what the Interface looked like.

As soon as he thought about it, the Interface appeared as an image in front of his eyes. Normally the UI was a large square that took up the entire screen. The size was still the same, basic look, all the options still there, but it was faded and translucent. He could see the walls of the stairwell through the Interface, foggy and blurry. Using his eyes, moving them up and down, he scrolled through the options to the audio tab.

He tried to double click, and nothing happened.

"Seriously, what the hell?" Hall said aloud. His voice still sounded strange to his ears.

AS he concentrated on the audio tab, it opened, and he looked through the options. Background music was still turned off. He thought about it, and a checkmark appeared in the box. Exiting the User Interface, he waited for the music.

He enjoyed the game's music but for the most part kept it turned off. The continuous loop of the same four-or-five-minute sequence could be very annoying.

Hall waited, listening, and heard nothing.

He brought up the Interface again, double checking the music was on. It should have been playing but there wasn't any.

Just another thing that was odd. It could have been that weird patch earlier, if that was what it was. That had happened sometimes. A patch to fix one thing sometimes messed something else up. There would be a hotfix in a day or two.

At the bottom of the stairs he paused and looked out into the common room. It was not the Green Craobh. He studied the room and finally placed it, an Inn he had not been to in a very long time. The room was wide open, with wooden planks running vertical along most of the walls, covering the logs. A bar was set along two walls in an L shape, another arch opening to stairs to the sleeping rooms above. A stage was set in the corner and a pair of double doors that led out. He knew what Inn this was. The Laughing Horse was the first Inn to which anyone could bond a Townstone.

It was a low-level room in the first zone, Cumberland, in the kingdom of Essec, located in the town of Grayhold. The beginner's town.

Why had his Townstone returned him here? Another glitch from that weird patch.

There was a decent mix of people in the Inn, PCs and NPCs. Almost a dozen of each. The computer-controlled characters were positioned around the room, dressed in the current fashion for Essec. NPC barmaids walked the room, serving drinks. PCs sat at the tables and the bars. They all looked just as confused as Hall felt, and most were wearing the beginning armor for their classes. He saw what looked like level-one Firbolgs, Bodin, Dwarves, and Elves; races that should not have been starting off in Grayhold as they had their own starting zones.

He noticed something else immediately. It was hard to tell the PCs from the NPCs. Usually the computer-generated characters were less detailed, a little faded in coloring with the PCs being brighter. But now, they all looked the same. The same level of detail, the same coloring. The NPCs looked the same as the PCs, just differences in armor and clothing. With some of the PCs wearing cosmetic clothing, non-armor with no stats, and starting level clothes it was even harder.

Shaking his head, he walked over to the bar and leaned against it.

"What can I get ya?" the barmaid asked, coming over.

"Nothing," Hall replied. He continued to look out over the room, studying everything.

He had never understood the idea of drinking in the game. The character got debuffed, and he never got to enjoy the aspects of intoxication through his VR rig. It was the same for the cosmetic outfits. Lots of Players enjoyed walking the towns in their outfits, but he didn't get the appeal. It was just clothing. He worked to get the ones he wanted achievements for but that was it.

A couple other people walked down from the Portal Room, a couple from the rooms upstairs and even some from outside. They all had lost looks, confused. Some were seemingly talking to themselves but Hall figured they were trying to voice or group chat and getting no response.

It made him feel better that he wasn't the only one experiencing this weird patch update.

This was the buggiest one yet, the worst the game had ever had, and he'd been there since beta testing.

An icon flashed just at the edge of his vision. An envelope. He'd gotten an in-system mail. Judging from the reactions of the others in the tavern, they had gotten it as well.

Good, Hall thought, *an explanation.*

Opening the mail window, he saw that it was from Electronic Storm, the makers of Sky Realms Online. He mentally clicked on the message, and a new window opened up, hovering in front of him. He started to read.

To All Our Players,

The day is January 3rd, 2047. We understand there might be some confusion, and we will do our best to alleviate any of your concerns. Please understand that this is a trying time for us as well, and communication is somewhat difficult.

Hall had to read the first paragraph a couple of times. He couldn't believe what he was reading. The year was not 2047, it was 2045. The raid on Firefrost had been October 31st, Halloween. Why was this press release dated in the future? He remembered using the Townstone to exit the mountain's Throne Room and next was appearing in an Inn just as expected, but back in Grayhold. Two years? What did that even mean? He had expected a message explaining about the patch and what it meant, not this.

On October 31st, 2045 the game servers of Sky Realms Online experienced what can only be described as an attack.

We still don't know everything about the attack and are still researching what exactly happened. As a result of this attack, some characters and players were disconnected from the servers. Others could not be disconnected and found themselves victim to neural feedback through the VR rigs. They were killed instantly.

Hall paused in the reading, looking around the tavern. Everyone had the same vacant looks as they read the in-system mail. There were a lot of mumblings, and some crying was starting. Everyone looked shocked and scared. He was almost afraid to continue reading, able to tell from the expressions around him that it was not good.

If you are reading this then you are among the rest that were not disconnected or outright killed. We do not know how, but your consciousness was transferred out of your body and digitally into the gameworld. You now exist as your avatar. You are alive as your avatar.

What that means? We do not fully know at this time. We recommend everyone to be careful. The game environment is still on and active. At Sky Realms Online we pride ourselves on the realism of the game, and now that realism is the world you exist in.

What did that even mean? They were alive in the game? Hall raised his hand up to his cheek, the wound from the ice shards still raw, no longer bleeding. Exist?

The attack caused the servers to receive information, not send it. Your consciousnesses uploaded to the game server and combined with your avatar. Once this occurred we took down the game servers until we could assess the damage and try to reunite you with your real bodies. We were unable to do so, and your bodies were all put into suspended animation.

Hall was numb. He wasn't alive anymore? He was in the game? He felt like himself. Well, not himself. In the real world he was a thirty-year-old, slightly overweight American male named Sam that worked a desk job in front of a computer all day. In Sky Realms he was a healthy, strong Half-Elf Skirmisher named Hall who completed quests and fought for the Realm of Essec.

The decision was made to turn the servers back on and allow you to live your lives in the game world. We will continue to provide expansions and keep the servers running. We will provide further updates when, and if, we can. No new Players will be allowed into the gameworld.

The world of Sky Realms Online is now yours to fully explore and influence. Good luck.

Thank You,
* Electronic Storm*

Silence filled the tavern. No one talked. The NPCs continued their rounds, confused as to why none of the patrons were responding.

"This has to be a joke," someone yelled out, standing up abruptly. There was a shrill note to the voice, on the edge of panic.

The speaker was one of the Dwarf avatars. A Warden judging by the armor.

"We're trapped in the game," the Dwarf exclaimed.

Normally, Hall kept the names turned off while in town. Too much clutter, but he thought about the User Interface and brought it up. He searched through the menus, noticing that some were grayed out. Anything that affected the VR output was inaccessible. He found the box to turn on the floating names and checked it.

Above the Dwarf the name "Roxhard" appeared in green with "Paradise Gangstas" under it. He'd never heard of either the Dwarf or the guild.

"I can't be stuck in the game," the Dwarf, Roxhard, said. He was on the verge of panic, starting to cry. It was odd seeing the thickly-built Dwarf, standing three-and-a-half-feet high and looking like he was carved from stone, with a deep and gravelly voice sniffling and snuffling the tears back. Hall didn't think the player could be more than thirteen or fourteen. How had this kid convinced his parents to let him play an M-rated game like Sky Realms? The minimum age was eighteen. "My mom. Oh god. What am I going to do?"

Roxhard was crying heavily now. He sat on the ground, hands against his face.

People ignored him, lost in their own thoughts or trying to somehow log out. Hall had looked for the exit option already. It had been grayed out.

"Everyone," someone else shouted, catching all their attention. "Look at your Character Sheet."

Hall did so, pulling up the Interface, wondering why he hadn't done it earlier. He rarely did. He knew the stats by heart and rarely got a piece of equipment that changed them. He'd been wearing the same armor for a while now. They all had. A new patch was supposed to be coming soon with new content and levels. Currently, they were capped at one hundred. Questing was Hall's favorite part, and he had been looking forward to more.

Graphically, the Character Sheet looked the same. A small picture of his character. Half-Elf with grayish brown skin that was the color of trees, medium length black hair hanging loose and beard, both streaked with green, light green swirling tattoos in circles and runes around the lines that ran up his arms and over his chest and shoulders behind his sleeveless leather chest and shoulder armor. His ears were slightly pointed, and he had brown eyes. Aside from the ears and slightly elongated eyes, the features were his but more so. Looking younger and stronger than reality. A fantasized version of his own face. Handsome but not in a way that stood out. More rough than fine.

Along the side were small icons of all the armor, necklace, rings, and trinkets that he wore. His weapons were shown on his avatar, their stats along the bottom. The right-hand side had other tabs that would open more information.

NAME: HALL
RACE: HALF-ELF
CLASS: SKIRMISHER
LVL: 1
XP: 0 | **NEXT LVL:** 200
UNASSIGNED STAT POINTS: 5

STATS:
BASE ADJUSTED TOTAL:
Health
20
0
20

Energy
20
0
20

Vitality
14
0
14

ATTRIBUTES:
BASE ADJUSTED TOTAL:

Strength

10

0

10

Wellness

12

0

12

Willpower

10

0

10

Agility

14

0

14

Intelligence

10

0

10

Charisma

10

0

10

Attack Power

0

0

0

Spell Power

0

0

0

Protection

2

5

7

Attack Speed

-2 sec

0

-2 sec

Spell Resistance

0

0

0

Carry Capacity

25

0

25

ELEMENTAL RESISTANCES:

Air

0%

Fire

0%

Earth

0%

Water
0%

CLASS ABILITIES:
ABILITY RANK:

Evade
1

Leap
1

The first thing he noticed was the armor. It was not the set he had been wearing. He barely recognized it. Each piece of armor, including his weapons, had their names in white. Basic. He had not had a single piece of basic equipment in fifty levels. All his gear had been Epic or Artifact, orange or green. Now he was wearing nothing but Basic. And his rings, necklace, and trinkets were gone.

His eyes moved to his health and energy bars. The numbers were nowhere near what they should have been. They were so low, similar to when he had just started the character. With a sinking feeling, he looked for his level.

Level One.

CHAPTER TWO

"Level one?"

It was a cry echoed by almost everyone in the tavern. Hall had just assumed that everyone in the Inn had been low levels, beginners, since that was the armor they were all wearing. He hadn't thought to check himself to see that he still had his level 100 gear. The patch had deleveled him? All of them?

All the PCs were level one now.

"This has to be a joke."

Electronic Storm was known for their elaborate practical jokes, but usually only on April Fool's Day. It wasn't like them to pull something like this randomly. Why would they reset everyone level to one? It made no sense.

But then nothing was making sense now.

"You seem calm," a voice next to him said.

He turned to the newcomer. A Witch. Human. Gael from the look. She had very fair skin, blond hair with purple streaks. Her hair was short, a pixie cut, and had large gold hoop earrings through her ears. Pretty, with vibrant blue eyes. She wore a dark blue halter top with short sleeves lined in gold trim and a skirt that ended just below her knees, cut high on the sides. Runes were etched down the sides of the skirt.

He glanced slightly above her head. Sabine. No guild.

Hall shrugged.

"I don't think panicking would help anything," he replied.

"True," Sabine said and leaned against the bar.

The barmaid immediately came over, and Sabine ignored her.

Roxhard was still on the ground, openly crying now. He alternated between saying "out" and "mom." The words started to blend together into one long sob.

"What do you think of all this?" Sabine asked.

Hall shrugged again.

"Not sure yet," he said. "Lots of odd going on, but to be actually stuck inside the game?"

Sabine nodded.

"It's a scary thought," she said quietly.

"There's some appeal," Hall said. "Back in real life I was a nobody. Dead end job, no girlfriend, lonely apartment. But here…" He gestured at the walls, meaning the world beyond. "Here, I was something."

"And now, apparently, you can be," Sabine said with a smile. "We all can."

Hall was tempted to ask if Sabine was really female. There were so many males that played female avatars that sometimes it was hard to tell. It could usually be figured out through conversations and mannerisms. Hall had a feeling that Sabine was truly female.

He chuckled.

She looked up at him, and he shook his head, not wanting to share.

Sabine settled in next to him, apparently comfortable in the silence. Hall liked that. He wasn't one to talk, only when needing to. In a social game, it was an odd stance to have.

"Enough," one of the patrons said. He stood up. An Elf. He was tall, a foot taller than all the others. Long green hair, part of it pulled up in a top knot, clean shaven face as Elves did not grow facial hair. He had the grayish-brown skin of that race and bright green eyes. Light blue tattoos covered his exposed arms and swirled around his eyes.

The level one armor indicated he was a Duelist. "No more moping. I joined this game for the fun and adventure. If I'm trapped inside it, then that's still what I'm going to do."

Silence greeted his statement. The text above his head said his name was Cuthard with no guild affiliation.

"They said the game was real now," one of the others said. "You could die."

Cutfast paused, seeming to think about what the other had said.

"I'm inside a game," he said finally, smiling. "I'll just respawn. Besides, it just can't be true. It's all a joke. I'm going to have a little fun."

With that the Elf Duelist jumped off the table, pushed open the doors, and ran outside. Everyone watched him go, none getting up to follow.

"He could have a point," Sabine said. "They said the game downloaded our consciousness. Does that kind of tech even exist?"

"No idea," Hall replied. "He's probably right…" he trailed off.

"I sense a *but*."

"But I don't think he is."

———

Grayhold looked the same as always but there was a subtle difference. More vibrant maybe, more detailed. More real, Hall forced himself to admit. He didn't want to use that word.

Real. Using it made it true, and he wasn't quite ready to accept that yet.

The small town, deep in the Green Flow Forest on the edge of the Gray Dragon Peaks, was the first bit of civilization in the floating islands that made up the Kingdom of Essec. It was also a questing hub for the southern half of the zone, the starting area for new Human and Half-Elf characters that were of the Gael subrace or had chosen alignment with Essec.

Sky Realms Online, the game, was the name given to the world of Hankarth. Long ago, or so the lore said, the world had been torn asunder, the continents splitting into much smaller sections of islands, called Realms. Each of these sections was tossed into the void of the world and left floating, some higher, some lower. They defied all known laws of physics but Hankarth was a world of magic, and somehow, that magic kept them floating.

The edges of the floating islands were sharp cliffs, rough and jagged. They appeared as one would expect, like pieces had been broken off. There were towns and castles ripped in two, roads that ended in a sheer drop to the nothingness below.

No one knew what was below the islands. No one had ever tried to go down that far. The theory was that the coders hadn't designed anything. If you fell off the edge, which was possible, you would fall a distance and then respawn. People gave up trying to see if there was a bottom, there was no real need, plenty of adventure was found in the floating islands of the Sky Realms.

Each was unique and varied. It was the perfect way to expand the game. New Realms were found floating in the air whenever an expansion was launched. Airships and portals connected them. A world that was ever growing and expanding.

There were many factions on the world, but five were the strongest: The Kingdom of Essec, The Storvgardians, The

Arashi Kingdom, The Highborn Confederacy and the Draco Legion. Players choose their starting faction; fighting for either Essec, Storvgarde, or Arash if they were Human and a couple different ones for the other races. Along the way, as they leveled, they would meet and perform quests for dozens of lesser factions. Eventually, the players could change their allegiance.

Hall had done so by joining the Greencloak Rangers, a lesser faction aligned with Essec. Timberhearth Keep was the nearest city with an auction house, all the other basic services, and the Rangers headquarters of Greencloak Hall. It was where Hall spent most of his time.

He had not been to Grayhold in a very long time. There had been no need.

Grayhold, all the buildings, were made of logs. Three high walls surrounded the many buildings that made up the Keep. The sheer face of a mountain formed the fourth. The town's small Lord's Keep was raised up on a low hill, putting the three-story structure over the rest of the buildings.

In real life, Hall lived in a city and hated it. He had grown up in the woods, and in the game, he had made his character into a woodsman. That was why he liked Timberhearth so much. Deep in the wild woods, it was an untamed land. Grayhold was a little tamer but not by much, still in the woods. That was what had ultimately led him to choose Essec as his kingdom of allegiance over Storvgarde, which was mostly frozen plains, and Arashi, which was open grasslands bordering a desert.

He made his way through the nearly empty streets of the town, his thoughts scattered. Did he really believe what the message had said?

Sabine had left, gone off to explore and discover on her own. She had promised to message him if she found anything. He wondered if she would.

Everything he checked indicated they were now in the game world. The interfaces were all the same but activated by thinking about them instead of hitting buttons with the VR equivalent of clicking. He had tried some of his level one abilities, including the Class Ability *Leap*. Instead of having to hit a button or activate a command, he just thought about it, and the ability worked. He could feel his Energy Pool draining when he used the ability. It was an odd feeling, similar to getting tired after working out in the real world. Not that he had ever worked out much.

All the interfaces, anything that connected with the VR rig or anything else out of game did not work. Some options were missing, the others grayed out. After trying a couple other abilities that came with his level one character's starting Skills, he just wandered the town, trying to determine what to do.

They were all level one. None had any money or Craft Skills of any kind. Not at this point.

Their bank boxes were empty. A couple different people had come into the Inn before he had left, complaining that all the items they had set aside in their bank boxes were gone now. Disappeared. No gold, no items. Nothing. Extra slots that they had bought were gone. Everything reverted back to what a level one, first day character had.

Which was next to nothing.

Hall was not looking forward to having to relevel -- if that was what he needed to do.

He held out some hope that this was all a joke. Even a dream. But part of him was beginning to think it wasn't. His new state of being just felt natural. His VR rig had been decent, not top-of-the-line but good, and no matter how immersive the game or how good the sensory input of the rig, he had always been able to feel a disconnect. Even when there was no lag. He always knew he was playing a game.

Now that feeling was gone.

Stopping outside the two-story structure that was the bank, he looked up at the double doors that led inside. Three steps up, banded in iron, the doors were thick. He turned away from the bank, not ready to face the empty boxes. He had some good gear stored there, plus some fun items. Next to the bank, in a much smaller building, was the post office.

Hall looked up at the bank once more before heading into the post office.

Inside there was just a single counter and an NPC standing behind it. The man was a Gael, fair-skinned and red-haired, as were most of the people in Essec. His red hair was short, bald on top, with a moustache. A name appeared above his head: Garrett. Below it read "The Postmaster."

"Can I help you?" he asked.

Hall paused. Normally he would activate the Action Cursor and hover it over the NPC he wanted to interact with, bringing up the NPC's menu. But would that work now?

He thought about the cursor, hoping to bring it up. The Postmaster just watched him, waiting, acting like confused adventurers was an everyday occurrence.

"I'd like to mail a letter," Hall finally said, feeling a little silly.

"Of course, sir," the Postmaster said. "Who would you like to send it to?"

"Redfire," Hall replied, surprised that speaking to the Postmaster really worked.

The Postmaster's head tilted his eyes going vacant as he thought.

"I'm sorry but that person does not exist," Garrett the Postmaster finally said.

Hall tried a different name, getting the same response.

He ran off the list of names from his friends list, not having to pull it up. He had done so already and had seen all the names grayed out. There hadn't been that many of them. He started with the other Dragon Riders, his guildmates. The Postmaster said the same thing each time he spoke another name.

"I'm sorry but that person does not exist."

There was one name left to try.

"Groven."

"I'm sorry but that person does not exist."

Part of him had expected that answer. It would fit with everything else he had learned. He remembered seeing Groven's avatar destroyed. Not just killed and faded away like normal. It had been destroyed, exploded. He had still been connected when the patch, that was not a patch, had hit. Did that mean Groven was one of those that the Electronic Storm message had said were killed by neural feedback?

He hoped not. Groven was a good friend.

"I would like to send a letter to Sabine," Hall said, picking the name at random.

"Certainly, sir," the Postmaster said almost instantly. "What would you like the message to say?"

Garrett pulled out a piece of paper, quill pen, and bottle of ink from underneath the counter. He set them on top and spread the items out. Hall stared at the items, unsure what to do. Had he ever actually written a letter with a pen? Even in real life, everything was typed. Reaching for the pen, he started to write his message.

Sabine,

This is a test. I tried sending mail messages to people on my friends list. None of them
exist or can be found. I haven't found out anything else.
Hall

"Very good, sir," Garrett said once Hall was done writing the message. "This will be delivered shortly."

Garrett took the message, folded it carefully, wrote Sabine's name on front and put it below the counter. He looked up at Hall, smiling.

"That will be 1 copper," Garrett said after a couple seconds of staring at Hall and waiting.

Mail had always cost money, and a single copper was a good price, but Hall wasn't sure what to do. The money would normally have been automatically subtracted from his total but that had not happened. Garrett just smiled pleasantly. On impulse, Hall reached into the small pouch on his belt and thought about taking out a single copper coin. He felt the object appear in his hand and retracted it, holding a copper coin, which he placed on the counter.

"Will there be anything else?" Garrett asked, taking the coin and making it disappear below the counter.

"No thanks," Hall said and exited the building.

Now what? he thought looking both ways. There were less people in the streets now, probably having realized the same things he did. He needed money, and there was only one way to get it.

It had been a long time since he had done the beginner quests offered in Grayhold. He hoped he could remember where the quest givers were located.

CHAPTER THREE

Hall walked the hard-packed dirt of Grayhold's streets. How many hours had he spent in his VR rig virtually walking these same streets when first starting out? He had been so impressed by the game's interface, even with having to buy his first VR rig. Just an hour into the game during the beta test, he had fallen in love with it. The story, the gameplay. He had spent almost one hundred levels in the game, years of his life.

But now, everything felt different.

He couldn't tell how, exactly. There was more life to the place, but even that failed to describe it. There was less pixelization to the buildings and the NPCs. No lag. He could feel his boots against the dirt, feel a light breeze against his face, hear the small sounds that normally were never heard. Creaks of leather harnesses, the neighing of horses.

The game had always been immersive but there had been limits imposed by the quality of the VR rigs, the connections, and the available technology. But now, those limits seemed to be gone.

Walking past a blacksmith's shop, he paused. The sound of hammer against anvil rang out, and he could see the smith pounding on a long strip of metal against an anvil. A counter was off to the side with two bored-looking NPCs behind it. By concentrating, Hall was able to see the names of the three and their occupations. One of them was listed as the 'Black-smithing Trainer'.

Skill Gain!
Identify Rank 1 +.1

He almost missed the prompt as it was not anything he had expected. Names of players and NPCs, which showed their level, Class, or Profession; was always visible or shown by concentrating on the Character. There had never been a skill involved.

Now there seemed to be. The same basic information was available from the NPC, so Hall wasn't sure the purpose of the Skill.

He shook his head, pushing away the distraction. There would be time to figure it all out later.

Thinking about his Character Sheet, it opened up in front of his vision, and he went to the Professions tab. All his recipes were gone, as were the three Professions he had spent so long learning. Each character could learn any combination of three gathering and crafting skills, but needed at least one of each. Two gathering and one crafting was the norm. Being a Skirmisher, Hall had gone for Leatherworking, Skinning, and Logging. He could make his own armor from the leathers he skinned and sell the logs he collected. It had made him a decent amount of gold.

The Professions even looked different. A couple new ones, a couple missing.

Crafting:

Alchemy

Blacksmithing

Cooking

Leatherworking

Tailoring

Woodworking

Gathering:

Herbology

Lumberjacking

Mining

Skinning

Hall knew he was a bit odd in how he had played the game. Always more interested in the questing and the lore behind it, he had never been a min/maxer, a powergamer. He used the best gear he could get, did the raids with friends, but was content with not being one of the top players. He wasn't rich by game standards, and he was okay with that.

He had fun and played his way.

Closing the Character Sheet, he pulled up his inventory. Most of his bag slots were gone. He was left with the starting bag of twelve slots as well as the bonus four he had received for being a beta tester and one of the first sign-ups for the game. All the other bags, almost fifty slots worth, were gone.

He was back to his starting equipment as well. All of it without a name and labelled in white.

SPEAR

Attack Power +1

Damage 1d6

Durability 6/6

Weight 5 lbs.

LEATHER CHEST

Protection +1

Durability 6/6

Weight 5 lbs.

LEATHER LEGGINGS

Protection +1

Durability 6/6

Weight 3 lbs.

LEATHER BRACERS

Protection +1

Durability 6/6

Weight 1 lbs.

LEATHER GLOVES

Protection +1

Durability 6/6

Weight 1 lbs.

LEATHER BOOTS

Protection +1

Durability 6/6

Weight 2 lbs.

JAVELIN

Attack Power +1

Damage 1d6

Range 30 Yards

Durability 6/6

Weight 2 lb.

DAGGER

Damage 1d4

Durability 4/4

Weight 1 lb.

The lack of gold was going to be the issue. He had a handful of Copper. Not even enough to learn Skinning, the quickest and easiest gathering skill to gain some coin. At the higher levels, mining and herbology were the best money makers. But early on, there was always an abundance of animals to skin for hides.

Making the screens disappear, finding he was liking this new way of interfacing, he continued down the street toward the East Gate. Grayhold was on the southwestern edge of Cumberland, the farthest south of the three islands to which Essec Kingdom laid complete claim. Essec itself, the largest of the islands as well as the capitol, was to the north. Wales was just to the east and farther north a little bit from Essec. Just because Essec laid claim to them did not mean the islands were safe. Far from it.

While not at war with the other factions, there were always groups rising up against the King. Nobles plotting against him, robbers on the highways, raiders and the various monsters that made the islands home.

There was no such thing as a peaceful and calm land in the Sky Realms.

The Gray Dragon Peaks ran from the south to the east, spreading north a bit on the western side, almost ringing in the Keep, which lay in the shadows of the mountains. Beyond the peaks was nothing, the end of the island. The Green Flow River, that gave the forest around it the name, came from far to the north and east where a water fell from the island of Edin a couple hundred feet farther up in the air. Edin was an unclaimed land. There was an Essec outpost there as well as one belonging to the Highborn Confederacy. The only way to get to Edin was by airship out of a large city on the northern edge of Cumberland, Land's Edge Port, which was also the only way off the island and to the other realms for low levels.

The waterfall was a sight to see. The designers had gone wild with it. The river was wide where the water hit, a large pond. It fell and splashed against the rocks, making a huge roar that was audible for miles around. The water itself was a torrent, falling with force, a sheet only a couple feet thick.

Some days, Edin could cast a shadow over the northern parts of Cumberland.

Hall looked up and to the north, barely able to make out the dark shadows that were the rocky underside of Edin. It was a level twenty to forty zone, while Cumberland was level one to ten. The other Essec Islands were levels thirty to forty for Wales and a mix of low level and high level on Essec itself. The largest island was really three smaller zones, while Cumberland and Wales were each a single zone.

The East Gate was a wooden arch covered in runes. It stood high above the log wall with ladders on either side leading to the walkway attached to the walls. The tops of the logs that formed the walls were sanded smooth, some higher than others forming crenellations. Large doors made of slats of thick wood banded in iron hung open. They were hinged to open out, making it harder for the many enemies of Essec to ram them open. The walls and gate were a common feature in all Essec towns and cities.

The hinged open feature of the gates had come in handy during one of the World Events a couple years ago. One of the most fun in Hall's opinion, but that had not been shared by the larger community. The Essec Revolution had seen the King's once thought dead older brother return to try and take over the kingdom that he thought he rightfully should rule. The Prince had raised an army of monsters and bandits, along with a few nobles that supported him. One of the pivotal large-scale battles had been at Land's Edge Port, the enemy trying to get at the airship at the Keep's dock that would bring them directly to Spirehold, the capital city of Essec.

Parts of the related event quests had brought players to Spirehold to prevent an assassination attempt against the King. It had been an Instanced Event, Hall and his group having their own instance of that attack while other players had their own. They had saved the King and been granted titles of minor nobility in the kingdom.

There had been a moral and ethics element to the event, not just killing mobs for rewards. The older brother did have a legitimate claim to the throne, and part of the event was the players choosing a side between the brothers. The younger and current King had his record on his side. While not a great King, he was decent and mostly kind to his subjects. Essec had prospered under his rule. The older brother had a claim by birth but had been missing for years and returned with an army of questionable allies.

Hall had always hoped for more events like that but chatter on the forums from other players had most likely pushed developers into going in the other direction for more straight forward events.

He wondered where in the game's timeline they were now. The developers of Sky Realms Online had tried to keep a progressive timeline for the game, each world event and expansion adding to it. There were some retcons, of course. Any game of the size and scope of Sky Realms Online would have those. The most common was NPCs that had died showing up alive again. But because the story was so deep, those things were mostly overlooked. Really, most players did not care. They played for the raids and the loot, not caring about the story too much.

Hall cared. He enjoyed those aspects the most. Which was

why he had enjoyed the Essec Revolution so much. It had been a very story-heavy event.

Guards patrolled the wall, some standing at the gates themselves. They all had names and occupations of "Grayhold Guard." Each was level two hundred, a level that players would never get to and meant a guard could insta-kill any player.

Or they were supposed to be, Hall thought as he looked at them. They looked like they should still be that high level. Each wore the standard armor of Essec. Chainmail shirt with light green tabard bearing the kingdom's symbol, a flowing river in front of a stone tower. Metal plates on the leather arms, shoulders, and leggings. Open faced helmets with flared bottom edges. A couple carried long spears, while others had sword and shield.

But they were only level twelve, Hall realized.

Skill gain!
Identify Rank One +.1

City guards had always been level two hundred, no matter what town or city. These guards were killable.

Off to the side was a small shack. The front was open to the city with only side walls and a roof. Inside was a desk and a firepit. At the desk sat another guard, this one an officer, with no helmet. Hall had to concentrate, getting another *Identify* gain, to get the prompts over the guard's head, which was the name "Henry" and "Captain of the Guard." There was something different about him compared to the other NPCs. Hall couldn't figure it out, some instinct just telling him that this person was special.

Henry the Guard Captain was a quest giver.

Hall approached him, stopping just outside the shack.

"Greetings, Hall," Henry said, standing up.

That was one feature that Hall had never agreed with the

developers on. They had coded all NPCs to recognize and use the player characters names. They said it added to the immersion. It detracted to it in Hall's opinions. A Guard Captain should not have instantly recognize a level one character with no reputation. That made no sense. The character should have earned some reputation with the area before being recognized.

As the Guard Captain talked, Hall saw a flashing icon of a book at the lower edge of his vision. Concentrating on it, a new screen opened up. Graphically it looked like a book opened to the middle. The leather covers could just be seen, with pages stacked on either side. On the open pages, Hall could see Henry's speech being written. His Journal was still being updated. A tab on the bottom led to the quest log.

"We're having a bit of trouble," Henry continued. "Seems there have been some aggressive wolves in the area harassing travelers. We could use some help in thinning the numbers. Scout Jacobs has also reported seeing some Goblins in the forest. My guards are a bit busy, could you go and meet with Jacobs and see what this is all about? Jacobs can normally be found patrolling just north of the bridge over the Green Flow River."

Before Hall's eyes, a new screen appeared. It was solid, blocking his view of everything behind it. Colored like parchment, the ends rolled up, most of what Henry had said was transcribed.

Guard Captain Henry would like your help thinning out the aggressive wolf population.

WOLVES OUTSIDE THE HOLD
Kill Green Flow Wolf 0/8
Reward: 50 copper, +100 Essec Reputation, +50 Experience

ACCEPT QUEST?

Guard Captain Henry would like
you to seek out Scout Jacobs.

GOBLINS AMOK I

Find Guard Scout Jacobs.
Reward: +100 Essec Reputation, +50 Experience

ACCEPT QUEST?

Hall concentrated and accepted each quest. The book icon flashed again. He knew it meant the quests were now in his log but opened it anyway. There they both were, listed under Essec and Cumberland in the tabs. He noticed the other Realms tabs were missing. Were they there before, or only added when he got to the realms? He couldn't remember.

He double checked the Experience rewards and was surprised they were so low. It didn't take much at the beginning to gain levels but those numbers still seemed very low.

Closing the screens, now being ignored by Henry, Hall walked out the gate. He pulled up his Character Screen and allocated the five unassigned points. One to Strength, two to Agility and two to Wellness.

———

Green Flow Forest was thick with trees. Tall and wide. Pines, oaks, and maples. Leaves fell, birds flew through the branches. Small bushes dotted the ground. The dirt road continued through the forest, as wide as he was tall. Hard packed, with ruts. Fence lined the sides for about fifty feet outside the gates. He could see the random small animal running through the forest, across the green grass.

As thick as the trees were, there was still space to move between them. Enough space to fight or ride a horse. As real as the developers had tried to make the world, there were some concessions that needed to be made. It was a game, after all.

Or had been, Hall amended. If that mail was right, this game was now his life.

He thought of the others in the Inn, how some had been panicking, not believing. Very few had appeared like the Elf Duelist, Cutfast. He had seemed eager to embrace this new life. Hall wondered how many were like himself? He had always been practical, trying to only care about things he could control. He couldn't log out of the game, that was out of his control. The only thing it seemed he could control was his actions in the game.

So why not just do what he would have been doing?

Play the game.

If this was a joke, it would end soon enough. If not a joke, he had a new life to live so might as well get started.

Hall walked casually down the road. For the most part, anywhere there was a road was safe to travel. Only those areas related to specific quests were dangerous and then only to those under the quest.

As he passed the last bit of fence, he paused and looked at a small rabbit in the forest. It was busy chewing on a plant. Thinking about it, a green arrow appeared above the rabbit and pointing down at it, along with another *Identify* gain. The creature's name, Green Flow Rabbit, appeared below the arrow. The name was a light gray, indicating there would be no experience from killing it.

But the deer that had just appeared beyond it, that name was in white.

Pulling the javelin from the special holder on his back, Hall took aim. Drawing his arm back, he let the short spear fly. It streaked through the air with a slight whistle, the ends moving up and down. He heard a thud as the missile hit the deer. He saw the health bar appear with the hit and quickly disappear as the creature was killed in one blow.

SLAIN: *Green Flow Forest Deer*
+25 Experience

Skill Gain!
Thrown Rank Two +.1

The corpse was glowing, a thin and low line of light around it. Not the sparkle effect he remembered but it still indicated loot. He quickly ran to the corpse. He felt his booted feet hit the hard ground, felt the uneven forest floor. Roots, rocks, sticks snapping under his steps. And when he got to the deer, he found he was breathing heavy.

Vitality - 2

He stared at the message that hovered in front of his eyes. That was new. He pulled up his stat sheet and saw a new bar below HEALTH and ENERGY that was labeled VITALITY.

Health: 20/20
Energy: 20/20
Vitality: 12/14

The number quickly climbed back to 14, and he was breathing normally.

Interesting.

Hall wondered which of his Attributes controlled the Vitality regeneration. Most likely Wellness and Strength.

He wondered how eating and sleeping, or lack thereof, would affect that number as well as the others. Those were things that had never been considerations before. Would they be things he would have to think about now?

Looking down at the glowing deer, he concentrated on it to open up the looting window.

Nothing happened.

Even if there was no loot to be had, a corpse still had the looting window.

How did it open now?

Staring at the deer, he tried to mentally will it to give up the loot. Nothing happened.

Feeling like an idiot, knowing he looked funny and it wouldn't do anything anyway, Hall reached out and touched the deer.

As he did so, a new message appeared before his eyes. The words were written on an open scroll, nothing to indicate who had supposedly written it.

Congratulations on your first successful kill.

Like before, some creatures drop loot.
Unlike before, it is now up to you to discover what that loot is, figure out how to collect it, and how to harvest any possible materials.

Hall made the message disappear, he'd worry about who wrote it later, and studied the deer. He tried to remember what loot a deer dropped. They were common in almost all of the forested zones in the Realms, and all had relatively the same loot. The animals only dropped one item. A gray item, *Deer Antler*, good for only a few coins. With the right skills a *Venison Steak* could be carved from the meet as well as *Leather Hide*.

He reached down and pulled at the antlers, trying to pull the bone growths off. They did not budge, he just lifted the dead deer's head up and down, thumping it against the ground.

There had to be some trick, he knew. The answer was probably simple, easy to figure out.

Hall tried to reason it out. If the game was real, then some aspects that had previously been taken care of by the game mechanics would now be real. That was what the message had hinted at, he realized. With a sigh, he drew his dagger and began cutting at the antlers where they jutted out of the deer's head. After some time and work and blood, the antlers came off.

You have gathered:
Deer Antler, value = 5 silver

The buck had been an eight pointer. Not the largest set of antlers, but they were still wide and spread out. He wondered what he was supposed to do with it now. There was no way he could carry the antlers, and they were essentially worthless, so why bother? That's what the gathering message had said; the antlers were gray and worthless.

But it hadn't. He hadn't bothered to read it that closely, thinking he knew what it said. But now something nagged at him, something he had glanced at but not registered.

He quickly pulled up his Journal, and there it was. The *Deer Antler* was now a white item and had a pretty decent value for a level one creature.

Collecting the antler was worth the time and effort, it seemed, but he still wasn't sure how he was supposed to carry it. All he had was his small belt pouch, the same bag that all characters had. The pouch never changed size on the outside, just the inside getting bigger. Everything fit inside, it had the appearance of a small leather bag attached to the character's belt, the design changing to match the characters style

Could the antlers fit inside?

Worth a try, he thought as he opened the pouch.

In the past, the *reaching into the pouch* action pulled up the inventory screen, and he picked the items he wanted. That put the item into his hand as he withdrew it from the pouch. Reaching in, he could feel a giant empty space, much larger than what it should have been. The pouch wasn't big enough to hold the sixteen slots worth of items he could currently carry but then it had never been physically big enough to hold all the items he normally carried.

Shrugging, he placed the tips of the antlers into the bag. He could feel a pulling against the antlers. He pulled them out, closing the pouch.

"What the hell?" he said aloud and looked around to see if anyone was near. He had this section of forest to himself.

Opening the pouch, he pushed the antlers in. The pulling was there again, but now he realized it was helping him. The antlers fit into the pouch, disappearing inside. Outside the pouch, they were the same size but he saw a strange distortion at the point they touched the shadowed opening of the pouch. They seemed to shrink down to nothing. Opening his inventory screen, he saw a small icon of the antlers appear in the first slot. Concentrating on it, the name and value of the item appeared.

Five silver would be a good start, he thought as he crouched down and studied the dead deer. He had a feeling that finding someone that would buy the antlers would be harder than collecting them. The days of being able to sell everything to the General Goods Market was going to come to an end, most likely.

The deer was big and heavy. Dried blood had leaked from the wound made by his javelin.

He drew his dagger and took a deep breath, having no idea what he was doing.

...Figure out how to collect it, and how to harvest any possible materials...

The line from the message was key. How to harvest. That meant he had to figure out how to get the hide and meat from the animal if he wanted it to sell or salvage anything.

Taking a deep breath, Hall drew cut a long line down the deer's chest. Blood leaked out the wound, getting on his dagger and his gloves. The smell was what got to him and made him turn away, gagging. Never before had he experienced smell in the game. There had been no need, but now the smell was overwhelming.

It made him want to puke.

Slowly, getting his breathing under control, Hall went back to work. He tried to breathe through his mouth only, and it helped. Some. The dagger shook in his hand, not making a straight line. He pulled and tore at the hide. Getting to the rear of the animal, he cut a line up the side and then back to the front before cutting down to his original point.

He was left with a large square of deer hide and the exposed insides of the deer.

He could see the muscles, the organs, blood leaking out everywhere.

Success!
You have skinned: Tattered Deer Hide

Skill Gain!
Skinning Rank 2 +.2

Skill Gain!
Survival Rank 2 +.2

Another new feature? What was *Survival*? What did it

mean? And he had learned *Skinning* just by doing? Without training? That was handy. The hide didn't appear that tattered, not to his eye, but he was new at this skinning, apparently.

There should have been blood and guts, or something, hanging off the hide but it was pretty clean. It looked like the icon that was normally in his inventory, when he knew there should have been more he needed to do. At least, there would have been if this had been done in the real world.

It was going to take some getting used to. A lot of getting used to. Some of the game mechanics were still in effect, most of them. But others had been changed to make the realism that much more. And some, like the hide, seemed to be somewhere in between.

Stuffing the hide into the pouch, he started to cut a hunk of meat off the deer. He held it in his hand, looking at the raw meat.

Success!
You have harvested: Venison Chunk

Skill Gain!
Survival Rank 2 +.2
1:00

The timer was counting down. He had less than a minute. But to do what?

Unlike the hide, the meat needed to be prepared, and he had no idea how to do that.

Cursing, Hall threw the chunk of meat onto the deer. That was useless. He'd have to figure out how to harvest meat from the animals it seemed, trying to remember where the nearest Skinning Trainer was located. There was one in Grayhold. Or, at least, there had been. He hoped the trainer was still there. But taking the meat had not brought a *Skinning* prompt but a

Survival prompt. The new Skill had something to do with harvesting meat from animals. He would need to figure out what that was and soon.

Standing up, wiping the blood off his glove as best he could, he turned around and headed for the dirt road. Something else nagged at him, and he turned back. His javelin still stuck out of the deer's side. It had been more than a minute, at least ten or more. The javelin's cooldown was done, and it should have returned to the holder on his back.

Walking back, he grabbed it and wiped the blood off on the deer. He examined the weapon again.

JAVELIN
Attack Power +1
Damage 1d6
Range 30 Yards
Durability 6/6

The Special Ability of the javelin was missing. Before when he had thrown it, the weapon would appear back in his shoulder harness after a minute, ready to throw again. But that, apparently, was gone now, nerfed out of the game. When he had first looked at his equipment back in Grayhold, he hadn't realized the Cooldown and Return Aspect of the weapon had been missing. Another thing he was used to seeing that it had become background.

Cursing, he vowed to pay more attention to every detail now. Replacing the javelin back in the holder, Hall started walking again.

There was a lot more to get used to now.

CHAPTER FOUR

He tried to move quietly, from tree to tree, avoiding the many sticks and leaves on the ground, but animals still ran before he neared them. Rabbits, squirrels, and birds along with random deer. His new *Stealth* Skill helped a bit but not enough. The first time he had actively tried to move quietly, the prompt had appeared for the Skill. He was gaining slowly, only having gotten .3 total in gains.

Hall headed toward the river, remembering that was where the wolves had been. He was glad that his first starting experience had been in Cumberland. It had been years, but he still remembered most of the island's layout.

Thinking about it, he brought up the local map. It only showed the areas he had been, everything else not revealed. He had hoped that the whole map would have been shown, he had been through all this before, but no such luck.

Distances seemed greater. He remembered the walk from Grayhold to the shores of Green Flow River as only taking about fifteen minutes in game time, much less once he had received his first horse. He had been walking for over an hour now and was still a good distance away.

If the distance from Grayhold to the river was now any indication, it would take days of walking to get to Land's Edge Port. Maybe a full week or more.

That was crazy to contemplate.

Was a month even a concept anymore? A day?

A sound off to the side pushed the thoughts from his mind. There was a rustling in the bushes to his right followed by a low growling.

He turned, holding his spear in both hands.

The wolf stepped out, growling deep in its throat. The animal's coat was a light brown. It stood about three feet off the ground, heavily muscled. Blood coated its long fangs.

It took one step toward Hall.

Circling him, Hall pivoted and watched the wolf warily.

It was not behaving as it should have been. The wolf was an aggressive monster; it should have instantly attacked him the second he stepped into its aggro range. Instead, it was almost stalking him, waiting for him to make the first move.

AGGRESSIVE GREEN FLOW FOREST WOLF

The animal's name was in Blue. He had expected as much. It was a quest mob, after all. It put the animal at least one level ahead of his level one. The creature's level should have shown, and he didn't get an *Identify* gain, which told him he needed the Skill higher to get even that much information about the Wolf.

"Come on," he said, tired of waiting.

Answering him, the wolf crouched low and leaped high into the air.

Hall leaned back, stabbing up with his spear. He missed and pivoted to the side, avoiding the landing of the heavy wolf. He swung out with the weapon, catching the wolf on the side.

The red bar above the animal's head diminished. It gave a yelp and snapped at him, growling.

Using his *Leap* ability, he jumped into the air. Pointing the spear straight down, he slammed into the wolf. The tip of his weapon skewered the animal, pinning it to the ground. Letting go of the weapon, he pushed off and landed a couple feet to the side of the wolf.

It turned and tried to rush him, unable to do so. Its life blood dripped out onto the ground, growling and whining in pain, the spear sticking out of its back. Hall drew his javelin and advanced on the wolf, which was now mad with pain and bloodlust.

Hall stabbed out with the short javelin into the wolf's throat. It gave one last whimper and lay still.

Messages popped up in front of him, translucent and foggy until he concentrated on each.

SLAIN: *Aggressive Green Flow Forest Wolf*
+30 Experience

Skill Gain!
Polearms Rank 2 +.1

WOLVES OUTSIDE THE HOLD
Kill Green Flow Wolf 1/8

Each faded after he read them.

The dead wolf was held upright by the spear. The head sagged, blood still dripping from the wound in the neck and chest. Putting his foot against the wolf, Hall pulled on the spear. It was a struggle, fighting against the wolf's legs that would not bend, but he got the weapon out, and the animal fell to the side.

There was no glow from the corpse.

No loot.

Or was there? Hall thought, setting his spear on the ground and crouching next to the wolf. He pulled out his dagger, making a mental note to get a true skinning knife at the first opportunity, and started to carve the wolf's hide.

Success!
You have skinned: Tattered Wolf Fur

Skill Gain!
Skinning Rank 2 +.3

Skill Gain!
Survival Rank 2 +.2

Like the deer hide, the wolf's came off cleanly. He had taken his time and done it with more care, and somehow that had earned him an extra point in the skill. Standing up, he stuffed the piece of fur into his pouch.

One wolf down, seven more to go.

Spear in hand, he continued his walk toward the river. He kept his eyes moving, watching the bushes and the trees, listening for anything that would indicate another wolf was stalking him. As his eyes scanned the ground and the bushes, things started to jump out at him.

They weren't shining or glittering, and none had a large arrow pointing at them; but some of the plants stood out. It was odd, Hall thought, as he stopped and crouched down next to one. It was green like the others, nothing overtly different, but it just called to him.

So, that's how it works now, he thought as he recognized the plant as a *Sagegrass*.

The plant, long green fronds with sharp edges tinged in yellow, was useful in numerous recipes. Herbalists were able to gather it and sell for use in alchemical recipes. When trained, players had a *Herbology* skill that would provide markers for various plants to find. Now, it appeared that they would just find them naturally.

Reaching down, he grabbed it by the roots and pulled.

Success!
You have harvested: Sagegrass Pieces

Skill Gain!
Herbology, Rank 2 +.2

Sighing, Hall dropped the useless pieces of Sagegrass to the ground. He wondered how many times he'd have to try to dig up a plant before getting something useful. Looking around on the ground, trying to find more, something else caught his eye.

Barely noticeable under a bush, he could see what looked like an imprint in the ground. Bending down, he saw that it was a track. Crouching next to the print, he ran his fingers over it, tracing the shape.

A wolf print.

Success!
You have discovered a track: Wolf

Skill Gain!
Tracking Rank 1 +.1

Another new skill. Unlike *Survival*, this one was pretty easy to understand. It would probably come in handy.

Listening, trying to make sure he was alone, Hall pulled up his skills menu. It was organized in four parts; Combat, Magic, Professions, and Character, or roleplay as the gamers called it. The last was where the skills that helped round out a Character were put; the immersion skills, the ones that didn't add to the fighting or magical strength of the character but added to the role-play elements.

There was a fifth section now.

Environment.

And Character was now called Activity.

What did that even mean? he thought but filed the it away for later. Right now, he had a quest to finish. Mentally closing the Skills Menu, he started looking for the next track.

Pushing aside the lower branches, he saw another print not far away. Looking around, he found a couple more, not as deep as they were on harder ground. Hall moved forward, following the tracks. They turned toward the east, away from where he had been walking, away from the river. Looking through the trees, he thought he could see some hills in the distance.

He saw more plants along the way as he walked but avoided them, focused on the quests. It had been years since he had done these starting quests, and he couldn't remember if this was the way to the wolves or not. Something about it seemed off. He could have sworn that most of the wolves for the quest were closer the river.

Shrugging, he followed the tracks.

It took over an hour of slow going, stopping, and making sure he was still on the trail, as well as listening for wolves or other threats in the bushes. His tracking skill was low but gaining. He had lost the trail a couple of times, having to backtrack and find it again, but was making progress.

Slow progress.

He was getting tired. Concentrating on the tracks and on his surroundings was wearing him out. The sky was also getting darker. Night was falling. He looked up at the sun, trying to gauge the height and how long before full night fell, but the branches were too thick to get a good look. *Not a big deal*, he thought as he continued to track the wolves. The night cycle in the game didn't amount to much. Just darker, but still able to see. It wouldn't hinder his progress.

The developers had talked about making the night cycle into a true cycle. Shops would close, and it would get too dark to see. But there had been a lot of backlash from the players who didn't want to be limited to just the daylight hours for adventuring as most of them did their playing at evening in their respective time zones which could be day or night in the game.

Another hour later, Hall found that another thing was different.

True night was falling.

The ambient light was gone, the sun setting with the thick canopy of trees, making the ground impossible to see. Dark shadows on darker shadows. With his meager *Tracking* skill there was no way he could still follow the tracks. He could barely see the world around him, the stars and moon blocked by the thick canopy of trees

But as he concentrated, trying to make out the various objects around him, some started to come into focus. There was more definition. Not just black on black but shades of gray. He heard a noise, a squirrel chattering in the trees, and looked that way. He easily saw the little creature in branches high up in an oak tree, close to the trunk. The shadows were thick and he saw the squirrel as shades of gray, different from the rest of the night. He saw it as just shades standing out from those around it, giving it some definition and basic shape. There were limited details, just enough to know it was a squirrel.

It was odd, he thought, turning around and taking it all in.

Congratulations!
You have unlocked Racial Ability: Limited Night Vision

A new Racial Ability?

Sky Realms Online had a mixture of races that players could choose from. There were the basic Humans with a couple of subraces; Arashi, Gael, and Nord. Playable Elves were similar to the more traditional elves from other fantasy games and books, but wilder and less civilized. Dwarves lived in their mountain homes, again similar to the traditional Dwarf. Bodins had a sophisticated culture, living in neat little homes in the sides of hills, about the same size as dwarves but not as stocky, combining features of Humans and Elves. And then there were the Firbolgs. Tall, strong, covered in a light fur. Each race had a set of racial abilities that helped define that race and set it apart from the others. Mostly, those racial abilities were focused around benefits to skills. Bodins got a bonus to Intelligence while Elves got a bonus to Agility. Not great bonuses, but enough for min/maxers to have specific races for their perfect character builds.

When the game had launched, Electronic Storm had created two additional races for beta testers and early players. Half-Elf and Norn. There was nothing special about the races; they had the same starting Attribute bonuses as Humans and Bodins for game purposes. It was just a way for the betas to proclaim their status. Other games had given special titles or cloaks, Electronic Storm had gone one better with Sky Realms Online.

Until the non-betas and late coming min/maxers complained. They were stuck with Bodins over Norns for the race with the best stats for Shamans or Witches. In response, the developers had buffed the Bodin race to make it more enticing.

For the players like Hall, it was all cosmetic. Until now, apparently, as it seemed he was getting a benefit of being a Half-Elf character.

Even with the vision he was not able to follow the tracks of the wolves.

He looked back the way he had come. It was a dark tunnel between the darker shadows of the trees. It would be difficult and even slower going. Opening the map, he studied the distance between his location and Grayhold. Four or five hours of normal walking, he figured. He searched for the familiar clock that had been on the map, not finding it. Which meant he had no idea how late it was.

Feeling a pain in his stomach, Hall realized he was hungry.

Shelter and food.

Something he had never expected to need in the game.

He wished he had access to his Townstone. He could have returned to Grayhold for the night but the Stone only became available at level five and had an eight-hour cooldown. Useful for when you were Realms away from your Bind Point, not so useful when in the same Realm. Originally the Stones had a twenty-four-hour cooldown, forcing the players to ride or walk most places. It added to the immersion but players had complained, and the Stone had been nerfed down to eight hours.

Making the map disappear, he retraced his steps. There was a cluster of boulders that he had passed about ten minutes ago. That could serve as shelter for the night.

It took twenty minutes to find it, and Hall was starting to fear he had gone the wrong direction and gotten lost. The night vision was useful, but the lack of detail was hard to get used to. Most things looked similar, especially in a forest. But he found it. Three large and two small boulders nestled together with a small opening on the side.

Approaching it slowly, he tapped his spear against the side. It made a solid hit, echoing through the night. Nothing seemed to move from within so Hall deemed it safe enough. A slight wind had picked up, and the rocks blocked it.

"This will work," he muttered to himself, already wishing he was back in Grayhold and the Inn.

Now for food.

He thought it safe to assume that his Vitality and possibly his Health would go down if he didn't eat.

The nocturnal sounds had picked up. More and more animals waking up for their evening. He crept out from the boulders and listened. It was too dark to try to find nuts or berries, and meat would require a fire, which he thought he could make. But even if he could make a fire, it wouldn't do any good without meat to cook.

A nice rabbit would do. Even a squirrel.

He could hear small animals moving in the underbrush. To the left, to the right, and then straight ahead.

Moving slowly, carefully, he shifted his spear and held it out at its full six-foot length. He moved a step at a time, pausing, another step. Hall crept closer to the bushes in front of him. He could see some of the leaves moving, rustling as something chewed on them from within the protective growth.

Hall could see the movement of the small animal within. Barely.

Taking a deep breath, Hall jabbed forward with his spear.

Luck was with him.

There was a small squeal that ended quickly.

Pulling the spear carefully out of the bushes, he saw a small rabbit stuck on the tip.

Setting it aside, he grabbed some small twigs and branches along with some thicker limbs. With an armful and the spear held awkwardly, he returned to the boulder pile. Laying the spear against the rock, he arranged his wood into a small pile. Adding some leaves from the ground, he drew his dagger.

He struck the side of the dagger with a rock. Small sparks flew off the steel, falling onto the leaves and twigs. He kept at it, throwing more sparks onto the pile. A small wisp of smoke curled up from the pile, an orange glow around the edges of a leaf.

Leaning down, Hall carefully blew on it. A little bit at a time, causing the spark to grow. The smoke got thicker, the orange glowed a little brighter. Slowly, with great care, Hall started the fire. He sat back and watched the small flames, feeding some twigs into the fire, satisfied with the result.

Success!
You have created: campfire

Skill Gain!
Survival Rank 2 +.2

"Just like camping as a kid," he said quietly, watching the flames hungrily consume the wood.

Taking the dagger, he started carving a point onto a long and thin stick. Satisfied, he pulled the rabbit from the spear. The fire didn't provide much light to see by but holding the small rabbit close to the flames he was able to pull away the animal's hide.

Success!
You have skinned: Tattered Rabbit Pelt

Skill Gain!
Skinning Rank 2 +.2

The pelt was small, only a couple inches long and wide, but Hall stuffed it into his pouch anyway. Starting out he had no items, now he had four. *Not a bad first day*, he laughed to himself.

Pushing the sharpened stick through the rabbit, he held it over the flames. Holding it close to the fire, which he had to keep feeding wood onto, he turned the rabbit around trying to cook it evenly. He had no idea how to tell when it was done.

There would be some risk to eating it, but he knew he needed to.

Without knowing how long it had been, Hall decided he was hungry enough to eat it. Holding the charred rabbit close, he took a bite. Grease ran down his chin, and the taste was more burnt than meat but it was food.

Quickly, he ate as much of the small rabbit as he could. It wasn't much, biting bone more often than meat. Turning the rabbit around, using the fire to examine it, he thought he'd gotten as much from it as he could.

Walking outside the boulder pile, Hall removed the rabbit carcass and threw it as far into the woods as he could. Having it in the boulders with him would have just attracted scavengers. He didn't need visitors in the middle of the night.

Grabbing a couple more sticks, he headed back inside the rocks and stocked the fire high. Smoothing out ground as best he could, removing some more sticks and small rocks, he laid down on his side wishing he had a cloak to use as a pillow, or better a blanket. Even with the fire and the somewhat enclosed walls of the boulders, it was still cold.

With the spear within easy reach, Hall closed his eyes and settled in for what he was sure would be a miserable night.

CHAPTER FIVE

IT WAS.

Hall woke cold, hungry, and tired.

He had tossed and turned all night, never comfortable. The smallest noise would wake him. And there was a lot of noise. He had gone camping as a kid and had forgotten how much ambient sound there was at night. The meager fire had died down, giving off no warmth. He had no blanket, nothing. At least when he had gone camping, there had been sleeping bags and a tent.

Status Update!
You did not have a restful night.
Vitality - 2 for 12 hours

Grumbling, Hall sat up and rubbed his hands together, trying to get some warmth back into his fingers. The sun was just barely creeping up on the distant horizon. He hoped it would bring some warmth to the cold morning.

There was no way he could spend another night like that. He didn't want to go back to town. Not yet, at least. He had some items to sell for money and could buy some supplies, but that would be almost a day wasted and another just getting back.

He had quests to complete.

No need to make the decision right away, he decided as he struggled to stand up. His body was stiff, aching. He stretched to work out the kinks, yawning.

A couple minutes of movement and he wasn't feeling as stiff.

Picking up the spear, he left his little shelter between the boulders.

The day promised to be a good one. The sky, what he could see of it, was clear. Concentrating, he pulled up the map, studying where he was now to where he had been. He had not come that far off course last night when looking for shelter.

Good way to start off the day, he thought as he headed back to his end point.

Once there, he searched the ground looking for the tracks. He knew they wouldn't be as fresh, might even be gone with the new day.

He spotted a decent track, a large wolf, to the side.

Success!
You have discovered a track: Wolf

Skill Gain!
Tracking Rank 1 +.1

Knowing it was pure luck, his tracking skill was not that high yet, he followed the first track and quickly found the other, and another after that.

An hour later, he came to the end of the trail.

A hill rose above him, grass covered sides with exposed rock faces at the top. Boulders grew out of the sides with a few trees. Around the side, where the tracks led, he could see the mouth of a large cave. A slight crack in the face of the hill, one needed to approach from the right side to find it. He never would have seen it if he hadn't been following the wolf tracks.

Bones and bits of hide littered the ground outside the entrance.

He couldn't hear anything. No noises of any kind. No way of knowing how many wolves, if any, were inside.

Hall found a small clump of bushes growing at the base of a wide oak. He crouched down behind them and studied the cave entrance. A new message flashed across his vision, startling him.

Success!
You have successfully hidden yourself.

Skill Gain!
Camouflage Rank 1 +.5

A handy skill to have and another without training, he thought as he shifted his weight to a better position.

He waited a couple of minutes and still nothing happened.

Can't wait all day, Hall told himself as he stood up holding a large rock.

Pulling his arm back, he threw the makeshift projectile as hard as he could. It slammed against the stone face of the cave before clattering inside the cave itself. Crouching back down, he could hear a stirring coming from inside. Multiple growls and barks.

Two large wolves walked wearily outside. They growled low in their throats, barking at each other as they spread out around the opening. Both had the name AGGRESSIVE GREEN FLOW FOREST WOLF floating above their heads, the names in blue. Both circled the immediate area, none coming close to Hall, who breathed a sigh of relief.

Satisfied that there was no threat, one of the wolves went back inside. The other followed but stopped, sniffing at a bone laying on the ground. That wolf grabbed the bone in its jaws and laid down. It gnawed on the bone, eating what little meat and marrow remained.

Shifting to the side, Hall pulled the javelin from the holder. He held it loosely in his right hand, waiting for the right moment. The wolf turned away from Hall, growling contentedly. Standing as quietly as he could, Hall let the javelin fly.

The small spear arced into the sky before falling back down to the ground. The wolf, its instincts telling it something was wrong, had turned and faced Hall. Blood was matted around its muzzle, a large piece of fur missing from a shoulder. A worn-out and mad animal.

It yelped as the javelin caught it in the upper shoulder. The wolf fell to the ground, whimpering softy. The green health bar above it dropped almost all the way down. Hall advanced, spear in hand with the tip down.

SNEAK ATTACK!!!
You have scored a critical hit!

The wolf tried to snap at Hall as he walked by. Looking down on the creature, pity and sadness in his eyes, Hall jabbed down with the spear. The weapon pierced the wolf's sharp eyes, blood gushing out before turning into a small stream rolling down the animal's sides. He pulled the javelin free of the wolf's shoulder causing more blood to leak out.

SLAIN: *Aggressive Wolf*
+30 Experience

Skill Gain!
Throwing Rank 2 +.1

WOLVES OUTSIDE THE HOLD
Kill Green Flow Wolf 2/8

Moving to the entrance of the cave quietly, Hall strained to listen. There was some slight stirring but nothing that indicated the other wolf, or wolves, were awake. He knew he had gotten lucky with that first wolf, the critical hit doing most of the damage. Creeping slowly, he stepped into the cave.

The opening was parallel to the rock, cutting a slice into the face before turning into a wider chamber. He paused and let his eyes adjust, getting used to the shadows upon shadows aspect of his Racial Ability. Standing against the back wall, he could see three sleeping forms. With no details evident, he had to assume there were more wolves. Quickly scanning the cave, he couldn't see anything else. No more wolves, no other openings.

Taking a step forward, javelin in hand, he aimed for the closest lump of darker shadows on the ground. The range was close, he was unable to put the full strength of his arm into the throw, but it still struck the wolf. The javelin penetrated the animal's tough hide, embedding itself in the wolf's chest.

The animal howled, waking the other two. It turned toward Hall and tried to move but failed. The wolf fell to the ground, alternating between growls and whines. Trying to crawl toward Hall, the wolf gave up and just laid on the ground, unmoving and uncaring.

The other two wolves did care.

Waking up, taking a minute to understand what was happening, the two wolves got up and turned toward Hall. They sniffed at the air, tasting it, walking toward him. There didn't seem to be any urgency to the wolves.

Hall waited until the first one was ten feet away.

He lunged at it with his spear, the six-foot length being perfectly balanced for him. The wolf sensed the attack and veered to the side. Instead of the chest below the neck, the spear struck a glancing blow as the wolf moved out of the way. The wolf growled at him, stalking. Blood dripped from the wound. Its health bar lowered a little bit.

The second one charged at him, and he swung the spear toward it, using the weapon like a staff. He smacked the wolf in the side, causing it to turn and snap at the weapon. There was barely any movement to its health bar.

Stupid, he thought as he used the spear to jab at the wolves and keep them away from him. *So stupid.* He had let himself get trapped against a wall with two wolves snapping at him and just his spear and dagger. Not the best weapons to use in this situation.

Jab at one, jab at the other, hoping to get the spear brought back again in time to push the first back. He knew it was only a matter of time before he faltered, and one got through his defenses.

It was a game, but he had no desire to die. Time to be daring.

Crouching down as much as he could, Hall activated his *Leap* ability and jumped over the heads of the wolves. The ceiling was low so he did not get that high. Coming back down, point of his spear leading, he landed on one of the wolves. He heard a sharp crack as his weight broke its spine. There was a loud yelp from the wolf before it fell to the side, taking Hall with it.

He had landed with his feet on the wolf, attempting to use it as a springboard to attack the other. It fell as he was jumping, causing him to fall to the ground. Luckily, he fell backward, away from the last wolf.

The dead wolf lay between him and the other. He could

hear it padding through the dark, working to come at him from the side. Jumping up quickly, Hall moved the opposite way. He jabbed out with his spear, using the long reach, and was rewarded with a couple of yelps. The wolf's health bar drained some more.

A couple more jabs, some more yelps and more draining of the health bar, Hall waited for his Energy bar to refill. Being so low level, he didn't have much and *Leap* took most of it. When it got high enough, he leapt into the air and stabbed down at the last wolf.

He caught it as the wolf tried to jump at him. The spear stabbed into the wolf's chest, his momentum stronger than the animals. It fell backward, taking his spear with it. The wolf landed heavily on the ground, skidding to a stop against the wall where it did not move.

Hall landed and ran to the wolf's corpse. He pulled his spear out and surveyed the dark inside of the cave, waiting for another attack. He could hear the whimpering of the wounded wolf. Stepping carefully over to it, he jabbed down with the spear, putting it out of its misery.

There was nothing, and he relaxed.

SLAIN: *Aggressive Wolf (3)*
+90 Experience

Skill Gain!
Polearms Rank 2 +.5

WOLVES OUTSIDE THE HOLD
Kill Green Flow Wolf 5/8

Leaving the corpses for now, Hall walked the perimeter of the cave. He examined every surface and nook, looking for anything special. Bones were scattered everywhere, animal excrement that caused him to cringe as he stepped in. Shifting through the bones he found nothing special in any of them. Just animal bones. No hidden pouches or coins laying around.

He glanced at the piles of animal crap and shook his head. It was bad enough stepping in the stuff, and he was not that desperate yet.

Moving over to the corpses, he wished there was some daylight leaking through the entrance. The night vision was nice but it didn't make tasks like skinning easier. He crouched down and took out his dagger.

Success!
You have skinned: Tattered Wolf Fur

Failure!
You have skinned: Useless Pieces of Wolf Fur (2)

Skill Gain!
Skinning Rank 2 +.3

One hide was better than none, he decided as he stood up and made his way out of the cave. The sun was high in the sky, a beautiful day out. The bloody remains of the wolf outside was still visible, flies gathering and buzzing in the air.

Holding his breath as the corpse was already starting to smell, he ran back into the forest trying to decide his next move. He still needed three more wolves as well as finding Scout Jacobs. That last part would be easy enough; hike back to the road and follow it to the bridge. He'd probably find three more wolves along the way.

He heard a loud growling and snarling to the side.

A wolf had found him.

CHAPTER SIX

He looked to that side, not moving too quickly, and saw the large wolf step out from the concealing shadows between the trees and the hill. It was larger than the others he had encountered so far. The fur was pitch black with streaks of gray.

With a howl, the wolf jumped.

It moved too quickly for Hall to avoid completely. He fell to the side, dropping his spear, and felt the claws of the creature slice across his back. The pain was intense, the worse thing he had ever felt. He could feel each of the tears in his flesh. The leather armor had helped but not enough; the tips had still gotten through. Hall shut his eyes, trying to will away the pain.

He had never felt pain in the game before. There had been minor jolts when hits were scored against him but never real pain.

Aggressive Wolf Attacked with Slash.

-6 Health

-2 Vitality

-1 Health every 6 seconds

Glancing at his health bar, he saw that he was down to just 75%. The new Vitality bar had dropped a little.

The wolf landed with a thud. Hall heard its feet kicking up dirt and sticks as it skidded to a stop. Slowly, confidently, the wolf turned and started padding toward Hall.

He tried to stand but could not. The pain was too intense.

Growling, the wolf came closer. It started to circle around, watching Hall warily, waiting for the man to do something besides writhe on the ground in pain.

I'm going to die, Hall thought. He had died hundreds of times in Sky Realms before but never while experiencing pain. What would it be like? Would he feel every blow, his life leaving bit by bit?

No, he growled to himself. *Not like this.*

If he was going to die, he'd go down fighting.

Moving his hand slowly, he drew the dagger from his belt. Blood leaked down his back, the wounds burning, each movement an agony.

Health didn't regenerate during combat, and he had no potions. He had to kill the wolf soon to get out of combat and get his health back. The damage over time of the wolf's *Slash* attack was going to add up quickly.

Trying to be patient, knowing he had to time it right, he waited for the creature to come closer. Each second felt like an eternity. The wolf should have just charged him. They didn't use tactics, but this one did. It stalked him, showing caution.

It must have been satisfied that he wasn't a threat because it came closer. Hall could feel the hot breath, the saliva dripping onto his neck as the wolf leaned over him. He rolled to the side, drawing the dagger and slashing upward.

The attack was weak but enough to make the wolf jump backward. He had connected, feeling the wolf blood drip onto his arm. He was on his side, the creature watching him with anger, blood dripping from the shallow wound on its throat.

Hall struggled up, dagger in his right hand. His spear was behind the wolf and he didn't think the creature would give him enough time draw the javelin and throw it. He had a greater reach than the wolf but only one weapon while the wolf had three, two paws with claws and teeth.

He realized how lucky he had been with the other encounters.

The wolf growled and charged. Hall leapt into the air, not as high. Without a spear, he wouldn't get the full benefit of the *Leap* ability, the bonus damage from the attack of opportunity upon landing given to him by the ability, but it was the only move he could make.

He went up only five feet or so, just over the reaching jaws of the wolf. Not high enough to roll and spin to face the other direction, he landed on the wolf's back facing away from the head. The impact hurt his wounds. He grunted in pain, and fought to keep from falling.

Falling to the ground with the force, Hall heard a satisfying crack of bones. He leapt off, and the wolf rolled onto its back. It snapped at him, trying to follow but unable. Hall struggled up and moved behind the wolf.

The animal's health bar was down to almost nothing. It struggled to roll over again, trying to turn to face Hall. He moved slowly, leaning at an awkward angle as his wounds continued to bleed. His health was down to half, his Vitality at 75%, dropping a little with his Health.

Bending over, biting back a scream as he felt the tears in his back ripping more, he picked up the spear. Walking slowly over to the wolf, he pointed the tip down at the creature. It was looking over its shoulder at him, growling and snapping.

Hall stabbed down, ending the wolf's life.

SLAIN: *Aggressive Wolf*

+40 Experience

Skill Gain!
Light Armor Rank 2 +.3

WOLVES OUTSIDE THE HOLD
Kill Green Flow Wolf 6/8

LEATHER CHEST
Protection +1
Durability 3/6
Weight 5 lbs.

He leaned against his spear, butt end in the dirt to hold himself up. He waited for the pain to stop, the wounds to heal. A minute. Two. The pain had lessened, the damage over time effect no longer active, but he was not regaining his health.

Turning slowly, weakly, he looked around searching for more enemies. Could he still be in combat? He didn't think so. Any other wolves would have attacked by now, sensing a weakened enemy. So why wasn't his health regenerating like it should?

Another thing that was apparently different. And not in a good way.

Ignoring the corpse, and the possible hide, Hall pushed into the surrounding bushes. He tried to remember what he knew of the options available for healing at low levels. There weren't many. Health regenerated but sometimes not quickly enough, so additional means were sometimes needed. Low levels couldn't afford health potions and wouldn't always have a Druid handy, so the only option available in the wild was Greenroot. A fairly common root, located in every zone, it had some healing properties.

At higher levels, the amount healed was negligible

compared to a character's overall health, but for low levels, it was incredibly useful.

He just had to find some.

Opening up his stat sheet to double check, there should have been a couple of health points restored by now, he saw no gain in his Health. It had actually dropped a couple more points.

Cursing, he started intently studying the ground around the trees. He was looking for exposed roots, especially those on the north face of the trees that were covered in moss.

Over the next fifteen minutes he found three of the roots. He got the same message and skill up each time.

Success!
You have harvested: Greenroot

Skill Gain!
Herbology Rank 2 +.2

The first one he found he ate quickly. He could feel the effects almost instantly. It was a sweet tasting root, crunchy, and a warmth filled his body. Looking at his stat sheet, he saw the Health start to rise. Slowly, but it was rising.

He knew the effects did not stack, and there was a cooldown between uses, so he forced himself to wait. Already he was feeling better, the pain not as great.

Using the map, he plotted a course toward the road.

As he walked, he kept looking for more Greenroot, finding a half dozen more of the root that he stored in his pouch. His body may have healed but his leather chest had not. He could feel the cool air through the rips in the armor. He was still fully benefiting from the armor, statwise, but it couldn't take too many more blows before it became useless. He'd have to be careful.

He had also apparently gotten two full points in Herbology for his efforts. A new line had been added to the Skill Gain prompt each time it happened.

Congratulations!
You have gained a Skill Point
Herbology Rank 2, 12 Skill Points

A couple hours of slow walking later, the sun was starting to set and Hall knew he would need to find shelter for the night. Shelter and food.

He started surveying the land, looking for a pile of boulders or similar to what he had the night before. Thirty minutes later, he had found nothing.

Not willing to give up yet, Hall pushed on but started to hear an odd noise through the woods. He stopped, listening, and turned in that direction.

It was crying.

———

Hall crouched down, moving through the forest as silently as he could.

The crying wasn't loud, just sobbing, but it was deep and gravelly. Hall thought he had heard the voice before but wasn't sure.

He peeked around a tree and saw a Dwarf sitting on the ground, two-handed axe next to him, head in hands. Hall recognized the Dwarf as Roxhard, from the Laughing Horse in Grayhold. His chain armor was ripped in a couple places, blood matted on his arms. He looked weak and exhausted.

Hall checked Roxhard's Character Status, the parts he could see, getting an *Identify* gain, and saw that the Dwarf

Warden was down to just 25% of his health. The Vitality was even lower.

He started to back away to leave Roxhard alone. It seemed a private moment. Hall remembered how the Dwarf had reacted in the Inn. He was overwhelmed. *So are we all*, Hall thought as he took a step away.

A loud growl came from near where Roxhard was. The sobbing stopped abruptly.

"Go away," Roxhard said. The voice was the deep, gravelly voice of a Dwarf but the tone was that of a kid. "Leave me alone."

Cursing, Hall turned back. He gripped his spear tighter and charged out of the shadows of the trees.

A wolf was ten feet from Roxhard, the Dwarf still on the ground. He had made no move to grab his axe or back away from the wolf.

Hall ran forward with his spear leading. He slammed into the wolf, the point piercing the hide and exiting the other side. The wolf yelped loudly, falling to the ground. Hall pulled up, stopping himself from falling, his spear sticking out of the wolf.

SNEAK ATTACK!!!
You have scored a critical hit!

SLAIN: *Aggressive Wolf*
+30 Experience

Skill Gain!
Polearms Rank 2 +.3

He pulled his spear out of the wolf and was about to start skinning it when he heard a low growl from behind him. Turning, Hall saw another wolf walk slowly out of the forest. He glanced at Roxhard, the Dwarf still not moving. Cursing, Hall stood up and faced the new wolf.

It advanced on him, picking up the pace. It glanced at Roxhard, licking its lips, but knew it had to deal with the threat first. Hall didn't give it a chance. He threw the javelin at close range, taking the distracted wolf in the shoulder. It was knocked down, and Hall used *Leap*, landing next to the wolf.

He stabbed with the spear, ending the wolf's life. He was glad the wolf had growled, giving him warning. If it had attacked, he'd probably be dead now, and the Dwarf would be next.

SLAIN: *Aggressive Green Flow Forest Wolf*
+30 Experience

Skill Gain!
Polearms Rank 2 +.1

Skill Gain!
Thrown Rank 2 +.1

WOLVES OUTSIDE THE HOLD
Kill Green Flow Wolf 8/8

Congratulations!
*You have completed **WOLVES OUTSIDE THE HOLD**.*
Return to Guard
Captain Henry in Grayhold for your reward.

A new prompt appeared, one he hadn't seen before.

*You have gained **LEVEL 2!***
You have gained +1 Stat Points to spend.
Your Health, Energy, and Vitality have increased.

Hall looked for additional prompts showing skill level increases or points to add, but there was none. Apparently, skill increases only came through use. At least he had gotten some points added to his Health and other attributes. One stat point would be useful. He just had to decide where to add it. *Probably Strength or Agility*, he thought. Maybe Wellness. The other three, Intelligence, Willpower, and Charisma, could wait.

Better wait until found I've found shelter, Hall thought as he bent down to skin the wolf.

"Should have let it kill me," Roxhard said. He was no longer crying but his voice showed how miserable the Dwarf was. "At least I'd respawn back in Grayhold. Spending another night in an alley is better than out here."

"Are you sure about that?" Hall asked, stuffing the wolf hide into his pouch. Another tattered hide and another skill-up.

"Which part?"

"The respawning."

"Why wouldn't we?" Roxhard asked, confusion in his voice. It was not something he had thought a possibility.

"Don't know," Hall replied. "Not something I'm personally willing to test out though."

"I don't care," Roxhard said bitterly.

Hall ignored the remark, settling down on the ground next to the Dwarf. He had thought the player to be only thirteen or so and was thinking the guess was close. Hall could understand how overwhelming this would be for a kid. It was for all of them. Hall was just a person that only let things he could control affect him. He couldn't control this so he'd play it out.

"What did you mean by sleeping in an alley?" he asked. "The Inn was right there."

"Most of us didn't have any money," Roxhard grumbled. "The innkeeper had the guards come and kick us all out. Had to huddle in an alley."

That was a little surprising, Hall thought. Inns cost money.

Even if you just logged out inside one, which most people did for the instant logout function, it still cost a couple coppers or silver that was automatically deducted. At higher levels, it was such a small amount of money that players tended to forget it happened. One kill would yield enough loot to pay for a couple nights at an Inn. But for lower levels, it could get costly.

He hadn't even considered that possibility.

"Why the crying?" he finally asked.

Roxhard looked up sharply, embarrassed. It took him a minute before he finally started talking.

"I got two quests from Guard Captain Henry, so came out looking for wolves to kill. Needed the coin. Encountered the wolves, went at them like I normally would," Roxhard started and shrugged.

Hall could picture it. He had played a Warden a couple of times. The class was the tank in the game, able to dish out punishment, but more importantly, take it. At almost any level, a Warden could take on multiple enemies of a level or so higher without breaking a sweat. But with the new rules that the world apparently had, those tactics could be deadly.

"I didn't realize I wasn't healing as quickly until an hour ago. It started getting dark. I couldn't find my way back to Grayhold and..." Roxhard stopped talking, head bowed into his hands again, and Hall was afraid he'd start crying again.

It had all finally proven too much for Roxhard, and he had broken down.

"How old are you, really?" Hall asked.

Roxhard's head shot up again. More embarrassment and shock. He was about to say something but the look from Hall stopped him. It said to not bother.

"Fourteen," he finally said.

He had guessed right. "How'd you get an account?" Hall asked.

"My older brother," Roxhard said. "It's his account. He lets me play it now and then."

What crap luck being online when the attack, or whatever it was, happened

"Why haven't you been eating Greenroot?" Hall asked, handing some of the herb over to Roxhard. The Dwarf accepted it gratefully. "Doesn't do much, but better than nothing."

"Didn't even know what to look for," Roxhard answered munching on the crunchy root. "Not bad," he added. Already, some of his visible wounds were starting to close up.

"How? Just have to look at it, and the stuff practically glows," Hall remarked.

"Not to me," Roxhard replied with a shrug.

That was strange, Hall thought, bringing up Roxhard's Character Sheet. Besides being a Dwarf, not much was different except for the class. Maybe it had something to do with the races? Hall mentally clicked on the arrow next to race, which pulled up in-game information on the Dwarven race.

Dwarves live deep in the mountains, carving tunnels and chambers out of the rock while also building halls in the valleys. They spend as much time outside the mountains, on the slopes and valleys, as they do inside. Born with a natural affinity for blacksmithing and mining, Dwarves have the Starting Skills of Mining, Smithing, and Survival. Each gains at an accelerated rate and can be used without formal training. Dwarves also receive a starting Attribute bonus of +2 to Strength and +1 to Wellness. Dwarves also receive a bonus of +7 to Health, +1 to Energy and +2 to Vitality at each level.

Interesting, Hall thought. Races had always gotten Attribute bonuses but never Skill bonuses. Another new feature, which made sense as it added some more realism to the game. He hit the Question Mark next to his race, Half-Elf, and got a similar message.

> *Half-Elves are a mix of Human and Elven parents. They can live in either culture but are never truly at home anywhere. Most Half-Elves tend to wander, never staying in one place, but can be incredibly loyal to anyplace they end up calling home. Half-Elves have the Starting Skills of Herbology Rank 2, Skinning Rank 2, and Survival Rank 2. Each gains at an accelerated rate and can be used without formal training. Half-Elves also receive a starting Attribute bonus of +2 to Agility and +1 to Wellness. Half-Elves also receive a bonus of +5 to Health, +2 to Energy and +2 to Vitality at each level.*

As a Skirmisher he got starting combat skills in Polearms, Thrown and Light Armor. Each of those started at Rank 2.

"I guess races get some starting skills now along with the Class starting skills," Hall said. Roxhard looked at him in confusion. "Lets you learn some skills without training and at a higher rank."

Roxhard got a blank stare as he looked past Hall's shoulder. *So that's what it looks like,* Hall thought, watching the Dwarf's staring eyes move as if he was reading. A minute later the eyes came back into focus.

"Yeah. That's neat. Being a Dwarf lets me learn Mining, Smithing, and Survival… whatever that is." Roxhard smiled. "Makes sense that I haven't gained in any of that. No mines or ore around." He waved his hands, indicating the forest around him.

"I wonder if your *Survival* is different from mine," Hall said. "I've gotten some gains here and there. Biggest was when I made a campfire the other night."

"Maybe because we're in a forest, yours is related to Survival aspects in this environment?"

"Yeah, maybe," Hall said, standing up. "Come on, let's go find some shelter?"

"Really?" Roxhard asked. The look was full of hope, gratitude, and lots of other emotions.

Hall shrugged. He wasn't sure why he was helping the kid. Feeling bad was part of it. He'd never had siblings, no little or big brother, so he had learned to rely on just himself. Roxhard was just a kid and way out of his depth. Hall knew he'd feel horrible if something happened to the Dwarf.

"Yeah," Hall said. "Come on."

"Lead the way," Roxhard said, sounding much better than a couple minutes ago, and stood up. He was barely taller than Hall's waist.

CHAPTER SEVEN

IT HAD BEEN ANOTHER RESTLESS AND UNCOMFORTABLE NIGHT.

But at least it had been warm.

Having learned his lesson the other night, Hall had stoked the fire up high before laying down and trying to sleep. He'd woken up a couple times and thrown more wood on the fire.

He felt more refreshed than the previous morning but had still gotten the Vitality debuff, -3 this time. The effects must have been cumulative until he did something to fix it. Being injured and fighting probably didn't help either. A good meal and night's sleep would probably do the trick and regen the Vitality.

They had managed to snare a couple rabbits and some edible berries so they had at least gotten some food. Hall had given most of it to Roxhard, doubting the kid had eaten at all. Surprisingly, sleeping on the hard ground didn't seem to bother Roxhard. Perk of being a Dwarf.

The kid was still sleeping. As there really was no schedule, and it would probably be a long day, Hall let him. He sat cross-legged next to the fire and opened his stat sheet. He had two stat points to use up. He was surprised to see he had six in total. Apparently, he got some bonus stat points at level one that he hadn't used.

Each character had six Attributes that helped determine the two, now three, attributes as well as other features like Protection, Attack Power, Attack Speed, Resistances, and carrying capacity. The stats quantified the various physical and mental aspects of the character's body. The Statuses were the characters Health points as well as their Energy levels, and now apparently their Vitality as well.

Strength helped determine how hard the character could hit and how much they could carry. While inventory was kept in the magical bags and were essentially weightless, the character could only carry so much in the way of armor and weapons. The Attribute also aided in determining how much the character could lift.

Agility was a measure of the character's speed and dexterity, their flexibility. It helped with their Attack Speed as well as their Protection. The more agile the character, the faster they could attack and the easier they could avoid attacks. It also added in climbing up walls and other such actions. A character with low agility would be clumsy.

Overall quality of a character's health was measured in Wellness. How well did they resist disease and poison? How weak was the body? A character could be physically strong but weak in body. They could hit hard but not often before tiring. Wellness was the biggest measure in determining a character's Health.

Hall wondered how, or if, it affected the new attribute of Vitality.

Willpower was similar to Wellness but helped determine the level of a character's Energy as well as their ability to resist mental attacks and debuffs. How well a character's own debuffs worked on enemies was also determined by Willpower. The higher the stat, the higher the characters pool of Energy.

The power of a character's spells was determined by Intelligence. The higher the intelligence, the stronger the damage or effect of a spell. It also affected the cooldown and casting speed of spells and abilities. Smarter meant the character could cast more and faster.

Charisma, the last stat, reflected how well the character could bluff or negotiate. How convincing would that character be?

The Attributes could also affect some skills and abilities.

Abilities were the various class-based actions that a character was granted to use in combat. These were specific to each of the seven classes; Warden, Duelist, Skirmisher, Skald, Shaman, Druid, and Witch. Skills were the various actions a player could learn to help round out the character. There had originally been four types, Combat and Magic based, Character and Professions. Now there was one more, Environment. The Character, now called Activity, were skills that helped build the story aspect of the character, part of the immersion that the developers had tried to put into the game. The Combat and Magic skills were useful for raids and leveling up, the ones that helped define the character's overall power.

Skills were divided into Ranks, five in total, with a maximum level of one hundred. Each rank had character level and stat requirements to advance to the next rank, and possibly some quest component. Abilities were gained automatically as the character leveled and the skills leveled.

It was a lot to consider every time a character leveled. While all skills would be useful, some were better than others for what the game had evolved into. There were pages and pages in the various forums and Wikis of the best builds, a combination of specific skills for each class, that worked for high-end raiding and other aspects of the game. That was the min/max gameplay style that had never suited Hall. He had followed most of the guidelines for his class, the best to help out his guildmates, but had never truly enjoyed playing that way.

That philosophy had been designed to defeat the bosses of the game, to rise up and be considered an elite guild and player.

But was it the best way now?

If this really was his new life, then that added a new dimension to leveling up. He had to think long term as well as survivability. He'd already seen the negative effects of not eating or sleeping, two things that had never been a concern before.

He had originally thought to put the point in Strength or Agility, a Skirmisher's main stats. In parties, their role was just pure offense. They were never meant to get hit or attacked by the enemy, so the prime build was laid out that way. Pure attack power for damage. In solo play, the Agility allowed the Skirmisher to avoid hits and get away from multiple enemies as they were restricted to Light Armor. They could take some hits but it was best to avoid it when possible. Most players had leveled their characters with the endgame builds in mind.

Did he have to rethink all that now?

Most skills had been considered roleplaying only but leveling skills would still grant Attribute gains, so most people had still leveled the ones that would gain the Attributes they wanted. At least, until they got high enough that there were no more gains. They never cared about the skills themselves, just the Attribute gains. Want to increase Strength fast? Try mining a lot. There was an additional bonus of being able to make some gold at early levels.

Each character could only learn one-thousand levels of skills, any combination, and three-hundred levels in professions. A Human or Half-Elf, could get another fifty points due to their original Racial Abilities. Because of the roleplay nature, there ended up being some odd builds made of the different skills. Characters would have the few beneficial ones, taken up to the rank that gave the most advantages when combined with others, and the rest of the points would be used by whichever random skill they had used to gain stats.

Hall was already learning two profession skills, *Skinning* and *Herbology*, along with three skills, *Survival, Tracking,* and *Camouflage,* which would all be useful at early levels. He had some time before had to make a final determination of what his skills would be. And it wasn't like he couldn't choose to unlearn one to learn another.

Or could he? Would that aspect still work now? Would he be stuck with the ones he chose to begin with?

Doubtful. People had the ability to learn new skills in real life, so it would make sense to do the same in the game or this new life that they had.

Am I overthinking? Hall thought with a sigh. Before he could live this new life, he had to earn some gold and level first. He put the newly gained point in Wellness, thinking of how painful the wounds from the wolf had been.

He closed the Character Sheet and stood up. His legs felt cramped. The morning was chilly, and he had sat like that for a while. Stretching out his legs and arms, he walked over to the sleeping Roxhard and nudged the Dwarf with his boot.

One blurry eye opened, staring up at Hall.

"Come on," he said. "Time to go."

———

Using the map, Hall found the road easily.

He thought about turning and heading back to Grayhold. They could use some supplies. Blankets, flint and tinder, water, and some food. Could also use some healing potions, but he knew there wasn't enough money for that yet. Probably not even for some bandages, which were useless without points in

Triage to begin with. That would require training. Which would require money.

Instead, he turned north, Roxhard following without complaint. Hall tried to remember where the bridge across the Green Flow River was. It came from the north, the water falling from Edin above to crash onto Cumberland and start flowing south. It went in a pretty southwesterly direction, almost cutting Cumberland in half.

The map was frustrating. It was clouded out, only showing the areas he had been. There had never been a need for mapmaking in the game before, no cartographers, but he could see a need for them now. It had taken about a day to get to the wolf cave, but that had been slow walking and tracking. He had heard that a person could do four MPH walking normally, so could possibly hit thirty-two miles in a day? That seemed high. Maybe twenty-five was more realistic? But without seeing where the bridge was in reference to Grayhold on the map, he couldn't estimate how far it was by using the wolf cave as a scale.

There was no way to really tell how far away it would be but he had a feeling it would be at least another night in the wild.

He looked back over his shoulder in the direction of Grayhold.

Blankets and food would be nice, but there was the lack of money issue.

Facing front again, he continued the walk down the road.

It was one wagon-width wide, hard-packed. Ruts ran down the middle made from heavy wagons being pulled through muddy roads. Horse tracks filled the ground between the ruts, going in both directions. Evidence of traffic but they didn't see any.

Trees lined both sides, the road rising up hills and down into small valleys. They could see small animals running through the forest, birds in the trails. The sun was high in the sky, shining down onto the road, part of it in shadows from the trees.

"You were a beta," Roxhard said after a while of silence.

Hall hoped the kid wasn't a talker. Not being one himself, he tended to find non-stop talking annoying. Talking was for useful things, not random chatter.

"Yeah," he replied. "Day one."

"I always wanted to play a Norn," Roxhard continued. "Such a cool looking race. Tried all the other races and classes, settled for a Dwarf Warden."

Hall nodded, thinking of Groven, his former guildmate, a Firbolg Warden and the best one he had ever played with. He shifted the thoughts away, not wanting to think about Groven or the others. Were they dead or alive? Was he alive or dead to them? Did it matter anymore?

"I remember running this road," Roxhard said after silence had fallen again. "Didn't take that long to run from Grayhold to Land's Edge Port."

"Nope. Even less once got the first horse."

He wondered how riding was going to work now. There had been horses in the stable back in Grayhold, stood to reason they were still available for the players. Did he still have to wait until level twenty and purchase the ability?

Silence fell again, and this time, Roxhard didn't try to fill it.

———

Hall figured they made about twenty miles, give or take, by the time they had to find shelter for the night. He had pushed them, stopping only to rest and for a light meal of berries and nuts, which earned him another gain in *Survival*. Because they would need to return to Grayhold to turn in the quests, he wanted this journey over with quickly, cut down on the number of days before might be able to get a comfortable bed in the Laughing Horse Inn.

Shelter was hard to find, and they had to venture off the road a quarter mile or so. Hall thought he might be getting good at judging distances but had no real way to tell. He was just making it up as he went but it seemed to comfort Roxhard.

The Dwarf wore leather leggings with steel plates attached to the upper leg, leather boots with metal plates, and a thin chainmail shirt. Starting gear for a Warden. He carried a two-handed axe with only one head and a dagger at his belt. Deep-set black eyes and large nose were surrounded by a bushy brown beard. Long hair hung past his shoulders, the beard almost down to his waist with a single braid down the middle. The ends of his moustache grew out and ran down to his chin. Roxhard looked carved from stone, the face cracked but the eyes looked young... Squat and wide, powerful. Strong.

Until he talked.

The voice was deep and gravelly, the voice of a person born from the stone under the mountains. But the tone and words were that of a fourteen-year-old boy.

Hall had to remember that when he dealt with Roxhard.

In game it wouldn't have mattered, but here and now? The kid was overwhelmed, scared, and confused. As they all were. But Hall was an adult, thirty. That made a big difference.

They eventually camped in a shallow cave set into the side of a grass-covered hill. Hall triple checked to make sure there was no sign of an animal living there, or another entrance, before claiming it for the night. Only about ten feet deep, the opening was wide with nothing to block the night wind.

Building a fire, they managed to keep warm but hungry. Neither were able to catch a rabbit, or even a squirrel, that night. There were more nuts and berries, but it was not very filling.

Hall was getting tired of seeing his Vitality bar not regenerate fully. The trek had taken a toll as well. Twenty or so miles would tire anyone out.

He built the fire at the front, but deep enough in to be fully covered. They stoked it high and settled in, each waking up a couple times with the chills. Each time they would stack more sticks and logs on the fire, getting it warm, before falling back into a restless sleep.

The morning dawned cloudy and chill, threatening rain.

The weather on Hankarth was hard to understand. Each island was by itself, floating above nothing. Some islands were lower down, and the lower they were, the colder they were with shorter days. Others were along the same level, offset a hundred feet or ten, similar weather and temperature. Then there were the ones above the others, the hottest ones with the longest days. The sun somehow rotated around all of them, starting on the east and setting on the west. Night came when the sun was blocked by other islands or somehow went below them.

Just the one sun and a single moon that followed the same pattern. There were stars, filling the night sky with areas blocked by the other islands. The ones farther down barely saw the stars because of all the other islands in the way.

Weather tended to be localized, focused on that one island at the time. It might be raining on one and snowing on another.

Some players had complained that none of the weather, or the islands themselves, were possible but they would be quickly shut down. It was a game, a world of magic. It didn't need to make sense as long as it was fun. There were in-game, lore-based reasons, and that was enough for Hall. The islands stayed floating. That was all that mattered.

Hall hoped it would not rain. With no cloaks, they'd be soaked in a matter of minutes. He was tempted to just stay in the cave longer, so they could wait out the coming storm.

He was surprised how quickly he was adapting. Things that previously would not have been a concern were now influencing every decision.

In a way this was what he had always wanted, just not how he had envisioned it. Fantasy games and novels had always been a big draw for him. He loved those worlds. The magic, dragons, swords, and dungeons. All of it. The ultimate escape.

And now he was living it.

———

The rain held off.

They were cold, tired, hungry, and miserable but at least they weren't wet.

There had been some travelers, having been passed by a couple of wagons throughout the day, heading south toward Grayhold. The drivers had not stopped, just nodded at the two as they stood off the road to let the wagons move by.

A couple hours past noon, or what Hall thought was noon, the road rose up a hill, turning as it did so. At the top, they looked down the other side and saw the bridge.

The Green Flow River was wide, about thirty feet across, and raging. It did so for the majority of its length. The force of falling a hundred feet from one island to the other pushed it downriver with great force. White waves formed as the water crashed against rocks, the banks and the supports of the bridge.

Wooden, as wide as the road, the bridge was of simple construction. Flat planks laid across wide beams set on posts stuck into the muddy bottom of the river. Thin rails lined the sides, only a couple of feet high and looking weak enough to fall over if leaned against.

The edges of the bridge facing the raging current of the

river were wet, splash spraying up and onto the surface, which was only a couple feet above the water.

They walked onto the bridge, their boots loud against the wooden planks.

Hall scanned the ground as they stepped onto the north side of the road. The quest log had said that Scout Jacobs was north of the bridge. That could be anywhere but there should be some sign or indication. He moved slowly and carefully, eyes searching everywhere. Hall moved to the west of the bridge while Roxhard went east.

"Roxhard," Hall called out as he spotted the first sign.

Footprints marked a muddy patch of ground near the water's edge. Booted feet, Human, and three-toed ones that were half the size. They stepped around each other, pointed in all directions, turned and circled.

A fight of some kind.

He recognized the three-toed feet, two long in the front with a shorter and stubbier one in the back, as belonging to Goblins. Foul creatures. Among the most vicious in the world. They stood only about three feet tall, thin but with wiry muscles. Gray-skinned with large heads and even larger bat like ears. Their noses were long with small and yellow eyes, mouths full of sharp teeth. Ugly but cunning. They were not stupid, they used tactics when attacking. Always in packs, never alone. Even though they wore no armor, just rough hides and carried wooden clubs, they were still tough opponents in numbers.

"Jacobs?" Roxhard asked, crouching down and running a metal gauntleted hand over the tracks.

Hall crouched down as well, placing his fingers onto the ground. The mud was still somewhat wet, the tracks fairly fresh. Only a couple hours old possibly.

"Dammit," Hall said, standing up and moving toward the river where it looked like some of the tracks split off from the others. "Looks to be recent. Not that long ago."

"But that means…" Roxhard started to say but let it drop.

It meant that if they had moved faster, then they might have gotten here in time to help Jacobs. He had to be dead, Hall knew. There were too many Goblin tracks. But where was the body?

He found the first drops of blood about ten feet away, a thin trail of it on the grass.

If it had rained, the blood would have washed away, and they never would have found the trail.

Motioning to Roxhard, they followed the blood trail. There were few tracks, the Goblins moving lightly through the forest. Alongside the blood and tracks there were odd marks in the ground, long and staggering. It was slow going, Hall having to keep low and stopping to find the next splatter or drop of blood or Goblin track. He wished he could have Roxhard in front. Wardens were tanks, meant to take punishment, while Skirmishers were meant to dart in and deal damage before darting out. But he was the tracker and was gaining in the skill.

He just felt defenseless, vulnerable, as he crouched low to the ground.

About forty feet away, dragged into some bushes, they found Scout Jacobs.

QUEST COMPLETE!
You have found the body of Scout Jacobs.
There is evidence of Goblin activity that led to the Scout's death.

GOBLINS AMOK I
Reward: +100 Essec Reputation, +50 Experience

CHAPTER EIGHT

HALL CLEARED THE QUEST PROMPT, NOT EVEN PAYING attention to what it said. Reputation and experience. Great. It didn't matter right now. A man was dead.

Jacobs was torn apart. A bloody mess. There was nothing recognizable, just barely could tell the body was Human. It was Jacobs, had to be, no reason for anyone else to be out here. But what had done this? The Goblins?

They were extremely vicious creatures but this was too much. Even for them.

"God," Roxhard said, stumbling back. "They tore him apart."

Blood was everywhere, splattered across the ground and the bushes. Pieces of Jacobs were scattered around. Large and small. His uniform was torn and ripped, but only the cloth. The armor and weapons were gone, scavenged by the Goblins.

"I've never seen Goblins do this," Roxhard said. The smell was overpowering, and the Dwarf took a couple steps back. He looked around warily, expecting the Goblins to return.

Hall forced himself to stay close, to study the body. He had never seen Goblins do this either but the more he thought about it, the more that was wrong. He had only seen what the developers had programmed the Goblins to do. The lore said they were vicious but within the confines of the game that viciousness had not been truly realized.

Now he was seeing an example of what the creatures were really capable of.

The body revealed nothing. More of the Goblin tracks were scattered around, along with the strange, long marks. He crouched low, studying what he saw, trying to understand it. He now knew what the odd marks were. Jacobs had been dragged, kicking and fighting.

Alive.

Why hadn't the Goblins just killed him by the bridge? To hide the body from any travelers?

That was a scary level of thinking from the Goblins. It showed they were capable of reason, to think long term. Which made them that much more dangerous.

Walking around the bloody mess, Hall found what he was looking for. Goblin tracks, light steps on the forest floor, leading deeper into the woods.

You have found the body of Scout Jacobs. You have also discovered a trail that could lead to the Goblin raiders. Guard Captain Henry will want to know about the death of his Scout but could use more information on the raiders' location or their destruction.

What will you do?

GOBLINS AMOK II
Report the death of Scout Jacobs immediately to Guard Captain Henry.

Reward: +100 Essec Reputation, +50 Experience

ACCEPT QUEST?

GOBLINS AMOK II ELITE (optional)
Follow the trail to the Goblins camp to gather more information on
the raiders or destroy them.

Reward: +300 Essec Reputation, +100 Experience

ACCEPT QUEST?

Congratulations!
You have been given your first Optional Quest.

ELITE quests have the chance for greater rewards but will be much
more dangerous and deadly. If you choose to not take the ELITE
quest, it will not be offered again.

"Are you getting this?" Hall asked, looking back at
Roxhard.

The Dwarf nodded, still avoiding looking at the bloody pile
that had been Scout Jacobs.

"What the hell is an Optional and Elite Quest?" Roxhard
asked.

Hall shrugged. "Want to go and find out?"

He knew what his choice was going to be. Everything said
they should head back to Grayhold and get some more experience and money. More supplies. Then come back and deal
with the Goblins. That was the smart and safe play.

A look of fear came across Roxhard's face, gone quickly.
He forced a smile.

"You're the boss. I go where you go."

"I'm not the boss," Hall protested but still accepted the
optional quest.

He took a couple more steps in the direction of the tracks,

studying the ground, trying to gauge the number of Goblins. It was hard. The footsteps kept crossing over each other, twisting and turning. Hard to follow a single set of footprints. The Goblins also moved lightly, almost skipping through the forest. One track and the next would not be where it was expected but farther beyond. It was like every other step didn't touch the ground.

Roxhard went wide around the body, trying not to step in any of the blood.

———

They tracked the Goblins for almost another hour. The trail somewhat paralleled the river for a time, sometimes cutting north and returning or just moving alongside the river. There was no pattern, just meandering. The Goblins were not in a hurry to get to their destination.

The farther from the road they got, the easier the trail was to follow. The Goblins stopped caring. They trampled bushes, stepped in mud, broke sticks and branches. Hall still had no idea how many of the creatures there were.

He started to worry that they would have no choice but to turn back. The sun was starting to set, and he had no desire to try and find shelter in an area of woods shared with Goblins. That would mean no fire, no hunting. A dangerous night. They could make it south of the bridge before dark, a little safer.

Hall started to tell Roxhard to turn around when he heard the noises from ahead.

Voices, talking in a rapid-fire language full of cackles. Hall could not understand the language but he knew the sound.

Goblins.

He signaled to Roxhard, and they slowed their already slow pace.

There was light ahead, flickering flames along the ground. An orange and red glow.

Motioning for Roxhard to stay, Hall crept forward. He crouched low, taking care to place each step carefully. The Goblins were making a lot of noise, celebrating it sounded like, but he didn't want to take a chance of being heard.

The creatures were in a small depression at the bottom of a hill, the land sloping down. They had a large fire burning. Sticks and logs piled together, no pattern, just stacked. Across the fire something was set in the flames. It looked like a pile of some kind of meat cooking.

Hall fought back the bile, knowing what the Goblins were cooking.

There were five of the creatures dancing around the fire, hooting and cackling. Each still held a club, dressed in rough hides and rags. There was a large pile at the base of the stony hill. Hall could not make out what it was, but it was unmoving. A sizable pile.

He watched the Goblins for a couple minutes as they danced.

A plan started to form.

Hall crept back to where Roxhard waited.

———

He crouched at the top of the steep slope that led down to the Goblins' encampment. They were still dancing, the flames casting odd shadows against the stone behind them. The mass of meat they were cooking was gone. He could see pieces held by two of the Goblins. The rest was eaten.

Outnumbered, probably outleveled, they needed surprise and luck on their side.

Hall had never been reckless, always thinking before moving, and he admitted this was probably not his smartest idea. Turn back, get help. That would have been the smart idea.

It was too late now. They were committed.

Taking a deep breath, loosely holding his spear, he used his *Leap* ability.

Up into the air he jumped, spinning the short spear in his grip. A high arc brought him over the middle of the camp. With a war cry he came down into the middle of the Goblins. He had hoped to land on one, but this worked too.

He stabbed out with his spear, catching one of the creatures in the chest. It stared at the wound gushing blood as Hall pulled his spear back. Its hands went up to the wound, staring dumbly at the blood on its hands. The Goblin fell.

Hall jabbed backward with the spear, clipping another Goblin in the shoulder with the butt end. Holding it tight, he spun the weapon around, keeping the others at bay. One Goblin was done, unsure if it was dead, but there were still four of the monsters.

This was the biggest hole in his plan. He was counting on someone he barely knew.

Roxhard was a fourteen-year-old kid that was overwhelmed. Scared. He hadn't been too thrilled with the plan. Would he do his part?

Hall was unable to connect with the creatures. The fire was behind him, protecting his blindside. Sweeping back and forth with the spear kept the Goblins at bay. For now. He could not hit them, could not go on the offensive as it would open him up to attacks from the others. He wished he had his *Flying Aim* ability. He could have thrown a javelin while in the air, possibly taking out one of the Goblins, or at least wounding it.

Roxhard should have made his move by now. Hall was starting to worry.

The Goblins were hooting, a different kind. Mean, angry, promising pain.

A new sound filled the hollow: heavy boots against the hard ground and a battle cry.

The Dwarf appeared at the top of the slope, axe in hand. He roared and charged toward the nearest Goblin. He was like a boulder rolling down the hill, gaining speed and momentum with each step.

He slammed into a Goblin, knocking the creature off-balance and launching it into the air. The Goblin landed hard a couple feet away. The axe swung at another Goblin, catching the creature in the chest. Blood spurted out as the sharp weapon almost cleaved the thin creature in half.

The other two were distracted, turning toward the roaring Dwarf. Taking advantage of the surprise of the Dwarf's appearance, just as he had planned, Hall slammed one of the Goblins in the back of the head. The creature staggered, almost falling.

Hall spun the spear in his hand and jabbed out with the pointed end. He caught the other Goblin in the shoulder. The tip pierced flesh, tearing a chunk out of the creature. It yelped in pain, twisting away from Hall. Roxhard stepped forward, bloody axe connecting with the one Hall had hit in the head. The creature fell to the ground, not getting up.

Pulling the spear back, Hall twisted toward the last Goblin. It swung toward him with the club, trying to bat the spear away. Expertly, Hall parried with the wooden shaft, feeling vibrations through the wood as the club connected. He smacked the Goblin in its good shoulder with his spear. It staggered a couple steps.

Three down. Two to go.

Roxhard advanced on the one he had sent flying. The creature was getting up from the ground, weaponless, holding its head with one hand. It wobbled. Roxhard's axe chopped down into its shoulder. It wobbled one more time before collapsing to the ground.

The Goblin facing Hall continued to bash at his spear. He continued to smack it with the wood. It watched the last of its fellow raiders fall, its expression showing sudden fear. It took a couple steps back, eyes darting around, out of the reach of the spear.

Cackling and hooting, the Goblin turned and started to run away.

It didn't get far. Hall's javelin landed in the middle of its back. The tip of the missile burst through its chest, the momentum and force carrying it forward a couple of steps where it finally fell down.

Hall looked around the hollow, the flames casting shadows against the trees and the ground. Nothing moved.

SLAIN: *Green Flow Goblin Raider x 3*
+75 Experience

Skill Gain!
Polearms Rank 2 +.3

Skill Gain!
Light Armor Rank 2 +.1

Skill Gain!
Thrown Rank 2 +.1

"You good?" he asked Roxhard.

The Dwarf was staring at the blood dripping from his axe.

"Rox, you good?" Hall repeated.

"Yeah," the Dwarf answered with a shake of his head, focusing on the area and not the axe.

Hall retrieved the javelin, returning it to the harness on his back. Nudging at the Goblin, dirty and filthy, he could see there was nothing of value on the corpse. A quick search of the others revealed the same.

He walked over to the large pile against the hill. He could see that it was made of small crates, bags, and cloaks thrown together. The Goblin raiders pile of loot. A large pile of loot.

More than these five Goblins could have gotten on their own.

———

"More of them," Roxhard almost shouted, staring around wildly as if they would attack at any time.

Which they could. There was no way of knowing how many more Goblins there were or when they would return. Or even if these five would respawn. Did such things happen anymore?

"Yeah, so we need to hurry," Hall said, looking at the pile of loot.

He pulled up a cloak that looked decent enough. A deep brown color, he thought, since it was dark and getting hard to see. Color didn't matter at this point. He held it out, trying to see if there were blood stains or anything else stuck to it.

Folding it up, he set it aside, along with another one that could be cut to fit Roxhard's shorter height. He started shifting the crates when he felt one move beneath him.

"What the hell?" he said, quickly moving them out of the way.

The largest crate, stuck on the bottom, was shaking. Something was thumping the walls, causing the thing to move. There were holes cut into the top and sides. Breathing holes. Whatever was inside was alive.

"What is that?" Roxhard asked, coming up closer.

Hall didn't answer. He started to crouch down to examine it closer when something slammed into the rocks near his head.

Stone on stone echoed through the depression, the missile bouncing onto the crates.

The Dwarf and Half-Elf turned in the direction the thrown stone had come from. At the top of the depression were four more Goblins, cackling and hooting and growling. In front of them, holding a sling, was a larger Goblin. A couple inches taller and wider, it looked much more dangerous.

A Goblin Chief.

Five against two, and they no longer had the element of surprise.

CHAPTER NINE

HALL CURSED, MOTIONING AT ROXHARD TO MOVE FARTHER away, to put space between them. The Chief roared, its deeper voice drowning out the others. It grabbed a stone from the ground and fitted it into the sling. Lifting the weapon above its head, it started spinning and released the stone.

"Ow," Roxhard muttered.

The weapon didn't do much damage, Hall hoped, but every little bit was going to be costly.

Laughing, a hideous sound, the Goblin Chief pointed at the two. The others charged down the hill, the Chief remaining at the top. Two went after Roxhard with two coming after Hall. Quickly judging speed and distance, he knew he didn't have time to throw a javelin at the Chief. The Goblins were too fast.

"Keep moving," he shouted to Roxhard. "Don't let that Chief get a bead on you."

He didn't know if Roxhard heard or said anything in response because the Goblins were on him.

Jabbing out with his spear, he kept one of the creatures at bay but the other slipped by. It swung its club. Hall not able to avoid the blow. The wooden club slammed into his side and he bit back a yell. The pain made his side go numb. He swung out with his fist, catching the Goblin in the head.

A rock impacted with his head, cutting a bloody line across his scalp. It hurt, making his head ring. He cursed at himself. Told Roxhard to move but didn't take his own advice. He stepped to the side, using the spear to drive the Goblin to turn with him.

He feinted a stab and quickly brought the spear back, jabbing it out to where the Goblin had stepped. It had moved to avoid the expected jab and gotten stabbed when it moved. The creature yelped, jumping back and yanking the spear tip out of its side. It swung its club against the shaft.

With a jerk, Hall slid the shaft down his hand, gripping it closer to the tip. He swung it around, the tip pointing to the side, grabbing it with his other hand and pulling. The tip rushed forward, catching the dazed Goblin in the throat. It dropped to the ground, clutching at the wound.

Hall felt claws ripping into his arm, almost making him drop the spear as he grabbed it with his right arm, intending to point it back at the Goblin. The fast creature had leaped at him, landing and attacking with the wicked claws on its hand. Hall jabbed at it with the butt end of the spear, pushing the creature back. Blood leaked down his arm from the wound.

The cuts weren't deep, no muscle or nerves cut.

I need a short sword, he thought as he kept jabbing at the creature. It moved fast, avoiding the attacks, not giving Hall a chance to reverse his spear and bring the sharp tip back. Hall kept moving, side to side, only a couple steps, hoping to avoid another rock from the Chief's sling.

Skirmishers abilities all revolved around the spear and javelin but they were able to train in small weapons like short swords and daggers. None of which did him any good now. He had a dagger, but the reach was not good, and he was untrained in the *Small Blades* skill so would just get the minimum weapon damage.

Another stone slammed into the ground at his feet.

He faced the Goblin. It had a club in one hand, his blood dripping from the claws of the other. With a vicious smile, the creature licked at the blood drops, it eyes locked on Halls.

The club batted at the wooden shaft of Hall's spear. Another stone hit the ground a foot to the left, ricocheting up and grazing Hall's shin.

"Enough of this crap," Hall said with one last jab at the Goblin in front of him.

The creature stepped to the side, batting the shaft with its club. The shaft fell to the ground, surprising the Goblin. Its eyes followed the weapon as it clattered against the ground. Its eyes lifted up in time to see Hall take the couple steps to close the distance.

Hall drew his dagger with his left hand, the blade pointing down. The weapon had a short blade. Only five inches, it would have to do.

He barreled into the Goblin, swinging up with his left hand. The edge of his blade cut across the Goblins arm. His weight drove them both to the ground. They landed hard, the Goblin under Hall. It tried to move the heavier Half-Elf but could not.

Hall couldn't get at it with his left arm. He yelled out as the Goblin's claws raked across his back. Once. Twice.

Pushing up with his knees, he got some space between himself and the smaller creature under him. He stabbed down with his dagger, connected with the Goblin's chest. The creature clawed at him, and Hall stabbed down again and again. Blood fountained up, the Goblin no longer clawing but batting at Hall. He ignored it, stabbing again.

The Goblin no longer moved, its arms falling limp.

Breathing heavy, Hall stood up only to catch a large rock in the shoulder. He staggered back a step, almost falling over. Looking up to the top of the depression, he saw the Goblin Chief searching the ground for another stone.

"Bastard," he yelled and *Leap*ed into the air.

He didn't have the *Flying Aim* ability yet. The ability increased his targeting while leaping and throwing, but he could still throw from the air. It was always a difficult maneuver, throwing a javelin from the air. Hall hoped he got lucky.

Grabbing the javelin, he let it fly at the Chief.

He got lucky.

The Goblin had not moved, finding a stone. It stood up fully, smiling and putting the stone in its sling. It heard the whistle of the javelin, looking up to catch the weapon in its shoulder. It staggered back, dropping the sling.

Hall landed ten feet farther from where he had jumped, that much closer to the Chief. He landed and ran the last few feet. He had grabbed his spear on the run, jabbing out with the weapon. He speared the Goblin Chief through the chest. The Goblin stepped back, taking the spear with it, but Hall grabbed it first and pulled it from the Chief's shoulder.

Screaming in pain, the Chief tried to punch out at him but Hall took the punch on his arm and batted the Chief's arm away. He stabbed into the opening with the spear, scoring another hit. The Chief fell down, off-balance, a javelin sticking out of its shoulder. It tried to get up but couldn't as Hall's boot pressed down on its stomach.

Pushing down with all his weight, Hall pulled the javelin out of the Goblins shoulder before it could attack with its arms. The Goblin yelped in pain, which became a gurgle as Hall's javelin stabbed into its throat.

He pulled the javelin out again, ready to stab down to make sure the Chief was dead. Sounds from the hollow pulled his attention. He saw Roxhard wildly swing his axe.

One of the Goblin raiders was down, not moving, but the

other was dancing out of the way of Roxhard's swings. It was toying with the Dwarf, keeping just far enough out of the reach, waiting for the Dwarf to tire. Roxhard was bleeding from multiple wounds, moving with a limp that indicated one of his legs was numb. A club must have connected with a nerve.

Reversing his grip on the javelin, Hall took aim and threw. It sailed across the short distance and buried itself in the Goblin's leg. The creature yelped and jumped up, right into Roxhard's swing. The weapon swung to the right, the axe head digging into the Goblin's side and pushing it right with the momentum. The axe stopped swinging but the Goblin continued, sailing a foot or two before falling to the ground.

"Thanks," Roxhard said, leaning on his axe.

Hall waved his hand in acknowledgment, trying to catch his breath. He grabbed his spear, holding it ready just in case.

SLAIN: *Green Flow Goblin Raider x 2*
+50 Experience

SLAIN: *Green Flow Goblin Chief*
+30 Experience

Skill Gain!
Polearms Rank 2 +.3

Skill Gain!
Light Armor Rank 2 +.1

Skill Gain!
Thrown Rank 2 +.1

Crouching down next to the Chief, who was dressed in better quality hides, he used the tip of the spear to poke at the clothing. Better quality was subjective. The hides and other bits used for clothes were poor quality by his standards, but would have been high by the Goblins. He found nothing useful on the boss.

QUEST COMPLETE!

You have found where the Goblin raiders have been hiding out.
You have eliminated the raiders and their chief.

GOBLINS AMOK II ELITE

Reward: +300 Essec Reputation, +100 Experience

He looked at his Character Sheet, seeing the bump in experience he had gotten for the quest reward as well as the Goblins he had killed. Not bad, but nothing to indicate why this quest had the ELITE tag. A new quest replaced the completed one.

You have defeated the Goblin raiders and their chief.
Now is the time to return to Guard Captain Henry and tell him of your success as well as the death of Scout Jacobs.

GOBLINS AMOK III

Report the death of Scout Jacobs and the destruction of the Goblin raiders to Guard Captain Henry.
Reward: +1000 Essec Reputation, +50 Experience

Reward: Grayhold Short Sword
Damage 2D4 (+2)
Durability 12/12
Weight 5 lbs.

ACCEPT QUEST?

A blue-colored weapon for a reward. A nice upgrade to the dagger. Hall found it odd that right after the fight where he had wished for a short sword, he was now getting one. And a blue colored one at that. The +2 bonus to damage was nice.

Magical, crafted, or enhanced items came in four tiers. White was the beginning, the basic weapons and gear that everyone started with. The next tier was blue. Those items had a couple of small magical bonuses. Above those were orange items, which had more bonuses applied. Green was the highest tier, the strongest of weapons. White was considered Common, blue was Rare, orange was Epic, and green was Artifact quality.

The short sword's bonus to damage meant that it would always do at least four points of damage with a successful hit. Still had to hit the target and get past its Protection. If the blow was just a graze, it would do less damage than if the hit was a full hit. But the bonus meant that the weapons edge was magically sharp. Even a grazing blow would do a minimum of two damage.

They still had to get back to Grayhold so he could get it.

The wound on his arm had stopped bleeding as had the new ones on his back. He grunted in pain as the walk down the hill aggravated the tears in his skin. Pulling some *Greenroot* from his pouch, he started chewing on the root.

At the bottom, he saw Roxhard already chewing on his own root. The Dwarf was kicking at the Goblin's body, muttering to himself.

"There's always at least some copper, but this guy is empty."

Hall nodded, surprised at the lack of loot from the monsters. He looked at the large pile of stolen goods, wondering what would be there.

Hall stopped in front of the shaking box, returning to his examination as if the attack had not happened. The box was about two feet long, wide, and high. The air holes were only in the top and along the edge. It moved a little, something thudding against the sides.

He didn't know why or how, but something was telling him that it was safe to open the box. He had no idea what was inside, it could be dangerous, but instinct was telling him to open it.

So, he did.

Using his dagger, he pried at the nails and managed to take the top off. He set it aside and bent to look in when something flew out at him. He felt wings touch his face as he fell back, the thing a blur. He could hear the flapping as whatever the creature from the box was flew into the air. He expected it to continue flying but it didn't. He heard a screech as it circled and the sound of the wings as it landed nearby.

In the dark he could barely make it out as the creature perched on a crate against the stone. It was lost in the shadows but he knew that shape.

A dragonhawk.

A foot long, standing a foot tall, it had a wingspan of almost three feet when flying. It had the head of an eagle, sharp beak and piercing eyes. Feathers ran down its back with scales down the front. While it had a head shaped like an eagle, the eyes were more like a reptile. It also had a long, thin tail that widened at the end curled around the sharp talons that gripped the wooden crate. The wings were spread, settling back against its body, shaped like a bat's with a single claw at the end.

The dragonhawk stared at Hall, the eyes locking on his.

Congratulations!
You have freed the dragonhawk. As thanks, the dragonhawk will bond with you and be your creature companion for life.

Do You Accept?

Hall didn't hesitate. He accepted quickly.
The dragonhawk screeched, a friendly sound.
A new prompt appeared.

Rename "a dragonhawk"?

He thought about calling it Screech, the name of the one he had before. Skirmishers, Druids, and Witches were the only classes that could receive creature companions. Witches were able to get familiars that added in the casting distance and power of their hexes. A Druid was able to get an animal that served as additional offensive support as the Druid was primarily a healing class. Skirmishers didn't have a choice in their creature allies. They always got a dragonhawk.

From the lore, the Skirmisher was a class developed by the High Elves. They were meant to be border guards, trained to hold back the enemy. As a gift, the ancient Elven leaders had granted the Skirmishers the dragonhawk to serve as a companion as Skirmishers were meant to be solitary guardians. The dragonhawks serving as the Skirmishers eyes over long distances.

The more he thought about it, the less a name like Screech fit. He had never given much thought to it before, the creature companion just being additional damage. But now he felt he had to treat it differently. Already, this dragonhawk felt like a real animal. The dragonhawk looked at him, head tilting.

"Pike," Hall said. The bird screeched, an acceptance.

The name was in reference to the long spears used by infantry soldiers. They gave the soldier a longer reach, and that was what a dragonhawk could do for a Skirmisher.

Pike stretched out its wings, screeched, and rose into the air. He settled in the trees overhead, Hall hearing the rustling.

Congratulations!
You have Learned a new Class Ability. **Shared Vision**.
This allows you to view the world through the eyes of your Companion.

"Nice," Roxhard said, looking up into the trees.

Hall smiled, feeling somewhat complete. He couldn't explain it. A part of himself had been missing but was now whole.

"What else is there?" Roxhard asked, breaking Hall from his contemplations.

Together, they quickly searched the contents of the crates and bags. There was a lot of cloth, silk, and cotton. A couple crates of ore and some miscellaneous leather. They found some packed food, dried jerky, and bread. Both grabbed some, eating as they searched. Hall had forgotten how hungry he was. There was flint and tinder, rope and climbing gear. They even found a couple of bedrolls to go with the cloaks he had set aside earlier.

Enough equipment for both of them, along with some extra packs to use, and a good amount to sell. They found no coin or jewels but they would make a decent profit with what they had found. The equipment they gathered would save them having to buy it.

"Damn, we got lucky," Roxhard said, taking the ore. They had divided the crafting material up. Roxhard got the ore, and Hall the leather. They'd split the money from the sale of the cloth.

"We got lucky with the fight," Hall said, motioning back to the Goblin corpses. *"ELITE quests have the chance for greater rewards but will be much more dangerous and deadly,"* he continued, reciting the quest text.

"True," the Dwarf said from where he sat on the ground, arranging the various goods. His magical pouch was now full, and he was dividing the rest up into the extra bags for transport.

Hall stood up, looking at the last bag. The pile of crates was off to the side, not worth breaking apart or bringing with them. He had already divided up the goods he would carry and was just left with this last bag he had set aside.

Unlike the others, which were backpacks or sacks, this one was long and skinny. It was tube shaped, about a foot in length, three inches in diameter. The bottom was stitched with hard leather, the tube sides a lighter and thinner leather. The top was the same as the bottom but able to be removed. The hard ends would prevent the tube from being crushed. A long strap was attached to the top and bottom edges.

"What's that?" Roxhard asked, standing up.

Hall shrugged and pulled the top off. He couldn't see much in the dark and firelight, but inside looked to be a paper rolled up.

Capping it, saving it for daylight, Hall stuffed it into his magical pouch.

"Let's go," he said. "Need to find some shelter for the night."

"At least we'll be warm this time," Roxhard said cheerfully, patting his new bedroll and blanket.

Together, they walked out of the hollow in the ground, leaving the Goblins behind. They had kicked the fire apart, spreading it out so it wouldn't catch the forest on fire. Hall looked up and saw the dark shadow of Pike flying through the air above them.

Roxhard had been right.

They were warm the rest of the night. They had found a cluster of boulders, three sides protecting them from the night's wind, and more importantly, far enough away from the carnage of the dead Goblins that nighttime scavengers would not be a problem. A real fire made with the flint and tinder, real and enough food, and the bedrolls and cloaks had made for a fairly comfortable night.

With no Vitality negatives when they woke, it was a good night.

Hall was happy. The ELITE quest had been a risk. Both had gotten wounded and were still recovering. The fight could have gone either way, but the rewards seemed worth it. They had recovered enough items to at least get some silver and wouldn't need to spend money on supplies.

He looked over at Pike, the dragonhawk perched on a low branch just outside the rock shelter. As far as Hall knew, the bird had been there all night. Having the dragonhawk was far better than anything they would get in return for selling the goods. A month of cold and hungry nights wouldn't equal out.

He still didn't understand why he felt that way. He'd played ninety levels with one in the game, not normally getting the Creature Companion until level ten, and it had been nothing but an additional attack that never really amounted to much damage. But Pike was different. More independent, not confined to a preset command structure of actions. The dragonhawk was smarter. What else was different? Hall was excited to find out.

With the sun out, he could now see the coloring of Pike. A dark forest green color to the feathers, the scales a lighter orange. The bird was beautiful.

As excited as he was to find out what Pike was capable of; he was also excited, more curious, to find out what was in the tube case.

The sun was up high enough that he could see the details in the case. Golden runes ringed the top and bottom edges, a line of runes down the center of the case. He didn't recognize the writing, but it appeared to be non-magical. He tapped it a couple times, trying to activate the runes. Nothing.

He'd already opened it in the night with no trap so he assumed it was safe.

Holding the end, he tipped it upside down, and the rolled parchment fell out. He opened it up, holding the opposite ends and saw a rough map of what he thought was the island of Cumberland. He could see the Gray Dragon Peaks, the Green Flow River, and what he thought was Grayhold at one end and Land's Edge Port at the other. It was heavily stylized, with some features exaggerated, especially at the northern edge. In that area, there was a roughly drawn line, snaking through the Far Edge Peaks to what looked to be a cave. There were numerous notations, handwritten notes explaining landmarks and other directions.

Congratulations!
You have uncovered a Treasure Map Level I.

X MARKS THE SPOT
Reward: +50 Experience

ACCEPT QUEST?

Success!
You have deciphered: Treasure Map Level I
Cartography Rank 2 +10

Hall stared into space, focused on the prompts floating across his vision. He read them multiple times, trying to make sense of it all. A treasure map? Cartography? He accepted the quest, watching it show up in his quest journal and log.

Both the map and skill were things he had never encountered in the game before. Had never even heard of them existing in the game before. Another new skill and a new kind of quest?

Opening up the skills tab, he saw that Cartography was now listed under Professions. It would be one of the three Profession skills he could learn. It wasn't a gathering skill, as he already had two of those in *Skinning* and *Herbology*, and theoretically should not have been able to learn another. That made it a crafting Profession. With this, he wouldn't be able to learn Blacksmithing, Leatherworking, or any of the others.

Clicking on the *Cartography* skill, he was curious to learn more.

Cartography is the art of making and reading maps. You will learn to make accurate and scaled maps of cities, dungeons and the land. You will be able to note your personal map with markers, using that to generate maps that can be sold to Players and shopkeepers.

These maps can be used by Players to add those locations to their personal maps. You will also be able to decipher Treasure Maps. Only with Cartography will Treasure Maps be usable.

Interesting, he thought, closing out the prompts. He stared at the map in his hand. The skill could be extremely useful, but it depended on how often these Treasure Maps dropped and what was available at the end of them. The other aspects would be more useful. It sounded like he could make his personal map more detailed and basically copy that for others to use. Essentially, he would be able to do what the various game Wikis had done: take game maps and plug in important NPCs, quests, and other locations. Since there was no access to the Wikis or forums, that would be very useful.

But at the cost of Leatherworking or Smithing? That remained to be seen.

Either way, he now wanted to see what was at the other end of the path shown in the map.

"What is it?" Roxhard asked, sitting up in his bedroll and pointing at the parchment.

"Our next task after selling the goods in Grayhold," Hall answered, already planning the journey.

PART TWO
THE TREASURE MAP

CHAPTER TEN

AFTER TWO MORE NIGHTS IN THE WILD, ENCOUNTERS WITH A couple of wolves and an aggressive bear, they returned to Grayhold. Both had managed to get multiple skill gains from the Goblin fight as well as the random encounters and ones that happened while traveling. Hall was getting pretty good at finding herbs in the wild. They both had a good supply of *Greenroot*.

Walking unchallenged through the gates, Hall noticed the guards on duty were all different. He tried to remember. Guards in the game had been background, and he had never really paid attention, if they had changed before. He didn't think they had, being static NPCs. These guards were definitely different, none he recognized from when he had left.

Guard Captain Henry was still there but not in the small guard house. He was up on the wall, and they had to search for him.

"You're back," he said to both of them. "It's been almost a week. I thought you had perished," he continued, walking by and signaling for them to follow. He led them to the guard-shack, remaining outside before he talked again. "Tell me, did you thin out the wolf populations? Find Scout Jacobs?"

"We killed the wolves," Hall said.

"Excellent," Henry replied, reaching over and shaking both their hands and handing each a small stack of copper coins.

QUEST COMPLETE!
You have slain the wolves that had been threatening Grayhold.

WOLVES OUTSIDE THE HOLD
Reward: 50 copper, +100 Essec Reputation

Hall noticed that they did not get the Experience reward, as that had come when the quest conditions had been met.

"But what about Jacobs and the Goblins?" Henry asked, all serious with an undertone of worry. He was concerned about his soldier.

"Jacobs is dead," Hall replied.

Henry sagged against the side of the small shack. He shook his head.

"Jacobs was a good man," Henry said, looking up. "A good soldier."

"We're sorry for his loss," Hall said, not understanding why he had said it. Henry nodded, seeming to appreciate the sentiment.

"Are there still Goblins to deal with?"

"No," Hall replied. "We dealt with them along with their chief."

QUEST COMPLETE!
You have informed Guard Captain Henry about the death of Scout Jacobs and the destruction of the Goblin raiders.

GOBLINS AMOK III
Reward: +1000 Essec Reputation, +50 Experience

Your reputation with Essec has changed.
You are now "KNOWN" and "FRIENDLY" in the kingdom of Essec and all areas it controls.

"That's good to know," Henry said, moving into the guard shack. He started digging around in a chest in the back, looking over his shoulder as he did. "How many were there?"

"Nine plus the chief," Hall answered.

Henry paused, looking back at the two.

"Damn, I'm impressed," Henry said and turned back to the chest.

You have earned +1000 Alliance points with Guard Captain Henry.
You are now "FRIENDLY" by Guard Captain Henry.

He was impressed by your willingness to go into the unknown and face the Goblins, avenging Scout Jacobs.

Something else new, Hall thought, wondering what exactly it meant. Quest givers had never had that response before. He didn't have time to think on it further as Henry stepped out of the shack carrying two items, a sword and a set of chainmail armor. He handed the sheathed sword to Hall and the armor to Roxhard.

"We can't thank you enough for your help," Henry said. "Those Goblins were a nuisance. They hadn't killed anyone yet, except for Jacobs," he paused, a sad look passing across his face, before continuing, "but had wounded many and stolen a lot."

Hall drew the sword from the scabbard, which was plain and unadorned. The weapon didn't look like much but the edge was sharp. A short, single-handed handle with heavy cross piece that was curved up. The blade was double edged, thick and a little under two feet in length.

"Were any of the stolen goods recoverable?" Henry asked.

Hall glanced at Roxhard, who had a slightly panicked look. With a sigh, Hall answered. Thoughts of the coins they would get drifted away. He was worried about having to return Pike and the Treasure Map.

"Yes, we have what could be salvaged."

Henry looked at them, a hard look in his eye that quickly faded. He smiled.

"I wouldn't sell them in town," he said with a wink. "The merchants might still be here."

Hall nodded, surprised. *It was a good point*, he thought, thanking Henry.

"You did the hard work," the guard captain said. "Those merchants should have hired more mercenaries to protect their shipments." There was a little bitterness in his voice, like he didn't respect the merchants. "I'll pass word to the other guard posts about you. They'll be more receptive if you pass by. Might even be willing to give you some work."

"We appreciate it," Hall said, shaking the captain's hand.

With a final wave, the two walked away and deeper into Grayhold.

"No selling?" Roxhard asked, a little disappointed.

"Let's not risk it," Hall said, assuming Henry had given the warning for specific reasons. He glanced up at the sky, glad that Pike had stayed outside the fort. "At least, not all of it."

The dragonhawk would be very recognizable to the merchant that had been transporting him.

"Doesn't give us much inventory space," Roxhard grumbled.

Which was true. Their magical pouches had quickly filled up, and they had discovered that bags did not slot like before.

Now they had to physically carry anything that did not fit into the pouch. Each had a backpack slung over a shoulder as well as pouches hanging across their bodies. Hall had returned the Treasure Map and its case into his magical pouch.

It was awkward as each also now carried their new gear as well.

"All that talk about not selling here felt like a quest prompt," Roxhard commented, looking back over his shoulder toward the gate and Guard Captain Henry.

"Yeah," Hall replied. "But with all the weird new reputation and alliance things that are popping up, not sure I want to risk a negative one."

"Good point."

There had not been any negative reputation quests before but nothing prevented them from being implemented.

"Can we stop at the bank?" Roxhard asked. "Want to drop off this ore."

Hall nodded. He remembered Roxhard mentioning how the PCs had slept the first nights as he looked between the buildings into the small alleys. There were people there, not in all but in some. Only a handful.

Not all were PCs.

The difference was easy enough to see now. The PCs were dressed in starting gear, not dirty, but still recognizable. There were only a couple of them huddled in the corners of buildings. The NPCs were in a mixture of clothes. Rags, some decent. They were thinner, weaker looking. Had no life in their eyes. The PCs looked lost, but newly so, and confused. The NPCs were just lost and resigned to their lot in life.

"Were there always beggars?" Hall asked.

"Not sure," Roxhard answered. "I don't remember ever seeing any but not something I would have been looking for either."

Hall understood what he meant. Even a game that had

been as immersive as Sky Realms Online, there were elements of that immersion that got ignored as the players rushed to play the game.

It was odd seeing the homeless beggars. Why were they there? Grayhold was not a town, but a fort. Everyone there should have been working as a guard or in support of the guard functions. Being at the very south of Cumberland, there was not much trade coming out of the fort but a lot coming in. There were a few farms around so work should have been available.

They walked up the steps to the bank, passing by the guards and stepping inside. The building was solidly built, even more so than the town hall. The only building in Grayhold to be made completely of stone. Great square blocks fitted together. The inside was a wide-open space, with a large vault at the far end, six guards standing at attention in front of it. Along the sides were the Vaultkeepers, three to a side, each behind a counter and barred window.

None were occupied so they picked two at random.

Setting the packs down, Hall dug through them, trying to determine what to set in the vault. Did he need to hold onto the hides he had gathered? The herbs? He wasn't sure what he was going to choose as his professions yet. Cartography sounded interesting but that would mean sacrificing a craft that could produce armor or weapons.

He wanted to see what the map led to before making any major decisions. Handing the hides over to the Vaultkeeper, a woman named Mara, he rearranged the contents of the packs. Did it make sense to keep everything on hand if they weren't going to sell in Grayhold?

Some of it they did need to sell. So far there was only the fifty copper from killing the wolves. That wouldn't go far. There would need to be repairs to the weapons and armor, lodging, and food at the Inn. He wanted to train in *Small*

Blades and *Triage,* which would mean a supply of bandages. What would be the safest things to sell?

The cloth goods would be too noticeable, and he could use the wool for bandages, just leaving the silk to sell. The extras of the adventuring equipment wouldn't fetch as good a price, but it would be easier to get rid of.

He could feel eyes on him and glanced over to see Roxhard studying what he was doing. The Dwarf was organizing the same as Hall was. Giving the silk goods to the Vaultkeeper, he managed to clear out one of the packs that he handed over as well.

Hall undid his belt and attached the scabbard of his new sword. He drew the sword and gave it a few practice swings. Excellent quality.

"Help me with this?" Roxhard asked, pulling at his starting chain shirt.

Sheathing the sword, Hall stepped over to the Dwarf and helped him out of the shirt. There were a couple links missing, tears in the armor. Hall knew his leather armor didn't look much better. Roxhard picked up the new chain armor he had gotten as a reward. Much better quality, there were plates of iron attached to the shirt. He managed to pull it on.

"Not going to sell it?" Hall asked as Roxhard handed his old shirt to the Vaultkeeper.

"I like to keep some extra just in case."

"Smart."

Exiting the bank, they headed toward the General Goods store. The shelves of the store were fairly empty, random items stacked here and there. No dust. Behind the counter, in front of the door to the backroom, was the shopkeep. A portly man, bald headed with a ring of graying brown hair. His name was Jerrod.

"Good afternoon," he said as they entered. "What can I help you with?"

"We have some items to sell," Hall said and set the pack on the counter.

He pulled out the random extra gear they had gathered. Roxhard emptied his pack as well. A couple bedrolls, some rope and climbing equipment, flint and tinder, and a lantern.

The shopkeep looked the various items over, picking up some, examining them more closely. He turned a shrewd eye to Hall.

"There was a merchant here the day before last, said his wagon was raided by Goblins. Lost a good load of supplies. His list looked something like this," Jerrod said, waving his hands over the items.

Hall waited, expressionless. He could see Roxhard's features betraying them. The Dwarf looked worried, guilty.

Jerrod laughed.

"His loss, your gain," the shopkeep said. "My gain as well. Now I don't have to pay his fees for these items. Been a lot of interest in adventuring gear the last couple days," he said and pointed toward his empty shelves. "This will sell right quick."

They walked out with ten silver each. Not a fortune but enough to get them through the next couple days.

Next stop was the inn. The day was getting late, and they were hungry. Hall's plan was to set out first thing in the morning for North Cumberland. A week or more of hard walking. They'd buy whatever additional supplies they would need, as well as some training. A good night's rest and hearty meal were necessities before starting the journey.

The Laughing Horse was fairly empty. Almost the same dozen NPCs, workers getting a meal before heading home, as well as off duty soldiers. There were a couple of PCs, some he recognized from the first night. He searched their faces. No Sabine.

He wondered if she was okay. She had not returned his

mail, and he had been too busy the last couple days to even think of her.

A single room for the night and two meals cost them about three silver. *Worth it*, Hall thought, as they ate large slabs of steak with bread, cheese, and ale. The food was good, the ale surprisingly so. Cumberland Dark. He'd never bothered with food or drink in the game before and was surprised how well it tasted and that it even had a taste at all. Had it always tasted this way? Not something he thought would have been programmed in. Why bother wasting bandwidth on the taste of food?

He was glad they had.

The last couple days, he hadn't even noticed there had been a taste to the meat from the animals he had hunted. He'd just instinctively known he had to cook it. Raw food should not have made him sick in a game, but somehow, he knew it would. He had thought it a carryover from real life. Raw food was bad, everyone knew that. Now here, he had not even considered trying to eat anything raw.

He was happy knowing that food had a taste. It added another element to the game, this new life of his. And it was something he knew he would have missed eventually.

Conversations filled the inn's common room. The NPCs were talking about crops, the strangely aggressive wolves and other mundane concerns. Hall found the PCs conversations much more interesting.

"Of course, I'm pissed. Wouldn't you be? I chose Bodin because the racial bonuses and stats were perfect for the Shaman class. I never thought I'd be stuck like this or I would have chosen Elf or Human. I don't want to be stuck this size."

The speaker was a male Bodin. About four feet high, thin, with skin the color of dirt. He had large and pointed ears, green eyes with yellow irises, and long black hair. Bodin were plains dwellers, attuned to the magic of the world, basically looking like small crosses between Elves and Humans. This Bodin picked up his fork and buried his head in his food, eating away his misery. His companion, a Human Warden, laughed.

Hall shifted his focus to the next table over. A female Elf was talking with a female Human.

"I picked a female avatar 'cause I always played one. Figured if I was going to be staring at the backside of a character for hours, might as well be one I liked to look at. Right? But now I'm stuck as a woman?"

"I'm sure there are some lesbian players around that won't care that you're really a man. Or could just go with one of those new Ally NPCs. The new AI for them is off the charts."

Hall wondered what they meant about new Ally NPCs. There were such in the game but they had fallen out of player's favor a long time ago. Good for lower levels, but too much work to maintain at the higher levels.

There were two types of NPCs, Interactive and Stationary. The Stationary were the simple AI ones. Shopkeepers, innkeepers, the random people walking the streets. They had simple tasks, not much required in the way of interaction. They sold and bought items or just walked the streets. The same routines all the time. The other kind were more advanced. There were some that had simple interactions like quest givers. Then there were the ones that players could advance in relationships with. Performing tasks for these NPCs, through quests and other means, raised your level of alliance, and at higher levels there were rewards associated with the NPCs. There had been romance options, similar to some older single player RPGs, but most people avoided those aspects. These were the Ally NPCs.

Over time, most of the Interactive NPCs were ignored as the rewards weren't that useful. They had been intended for more immersive roleplaying but the focus of the game had shifted. Hall had still found them to be fun and a break from the grind, but there was a lot of work involved in raising Alliance levels to unlock the really good benefits. He wondered if the Alliance Reputation he had gotten from Guard Captain Henry was connected.

Some of the Interactive Ally NPCs could become adventuring companions and fight alongside the players as extra party members. They, too, came with their own quests. They didn't level with the player though so it became almost leveling up two characters at the same time. More annoying than useful.

Hall wondered what this new AI they were talking about was and where the Ally NPCs had been encountered. He hadn't seen any in Grayhold yet.

He studied the other Players in the Inn. They were eating and had drinks but nothing extravagant. They were all trying hard to save money. There wasn't much in the way of new equipment, most of it the starting gear. They had probably done the wolf quest and sold all the hides and herbs they had found. Some had probably gone into the Gray Dragon Peaks.

The mountains south of Grayhold were more dangerous than the forests with higher level monsters, but the rewards would be greater. There were Caobolds in the foothills, which would drop some coin and possibly ore. Rarely, they'd drop some jewels.

He thought of the Players outside in the streets. The ones in here, like Roxhard and himself, had somehow recovered quickly. They had accepted, somewhat, the new reality and were making the most of it. How many Players were currently lost in the wilds, or dead in the wilds, like Roxhard would have been?

Hall didn't know how he was managing to cope. By rights he should have been like Roxhard had been when found. Just ready to give up. In the outside world, he had never been that adventurous or risk taking. He hated trying new things, a person of routine. He liked what he liked, did what he did. Being thrown into a new reality should have shut him down.

Some of the Players probably still thought of all this as temporary. They'd be able to log out soon and wake up as themselves again. A funny story to tell later in life. Hall didn't believe it. No real evidence except his gut feeling. This was real. He knew it.

CHAPTER ELEVEN

HE WOKE WITH THE SUN THAT STREAMED THROUGH THE window.

The bed was the most comfortable thing he had ever slept on. It wasn't really, but after days on the hard ground, it was amazing. He'd slept well, even with Roxhard snoring in the room's other bed.

Standing up, he pulled on his leather armor, poking his fingers through some of the gaps. He needed to repair it or buy new armor fast. The shirt was the worst, the wolf's claws had done major damage. The rest could last a while longer.

Belting on his sword, he kicked at Roxhard's bed.

"Get up."

The Dwarf grumbled, pulling the blanket tighter around himself.

"Going to be a long day, need a good breakfast."

———

Learning the first ten points in *Small Blades Triage* was costly, two silver, but needed. The *Triage* skill gave Players the ability to self-heal by the use of bandages. Health had always regenerated over time, but not that quickly and not during combat. Bandages allowed for some healing during combat and accelerated healing outside of combat.

At least that was how they used to work.

Hall had noticed that the regen rate of health was much lower now. Almost non-existent. Both still bore aches and pains from wounds received during the fights with the wolves and Goblins. Neither was at full health and had not been since the first day. Or at least they didn't feel at full Health. The status bar was full but they had lingering effects of their wounds. This was reflected in their Vitality rating. The night's sleep had restored most of it.

His back hurt, the scabs over the wolf claw marks stretching with each movement he made. There was a large bruise just starting to fade on his temple from the Goblin boss' sling stone.

The bandages might not do any good, but he wasn't going to take any chances. A benefit of *Triage* was making *Greenroot* and other healing properties more useful.

The armorer was open early, and Hall was able to replace his leather chest armor. It was too badly damaged to repair, but he got a decent price for it, and the new chest didn't cost that much. It was a dent in his money supply he didn't want, but another necessary cost.

LEATHER CHEST
Protection +2
Durability 8/8
Weight 5 lbs.

After the armorer was a return to the General Goods shop

for some provisions, and then they set out toward the gate. Guard Captain Henry was walking toward the gate just as they got there.

"Good morning," Henry said. "Heading out? You wouldn't happen to be heading north to Land's Edge Port, would you?"

"Eventually," Hall answered.

"Excellent," Henry said with a smile. "You'll pass by River's Side. It's a small outpost not quite halfway between the bridge over the Green Flow River and Land's Edge."

"How can we help?" Hall asked. The conversation had the feel of a quest prompt, and he wanted to explore what the increase in Alliance with Henry had gotten him. Henry seemed to be one of these new AI Ally NPCs he had heard about in the Inn the night before.

"I can't spare any guards," Henry said. "But need some Letters delivered to Watchman Kelly at River's Side."

"We can do that."

SPECIAL DELIVERY

Guard Captain Henry has asked you to deliver some Letters to Watchman Kelly at the outpost of River's Side.

Reward: +100 Essec Reputation, +100 Alliance with Guard Captain Henry, +25 Experience

ACCEPT QUEST?

Hall accepted the quest and looked down at Roxhard, who nodded. He had accepted it as well. There was something a little odd about Henry's request. There were other, and more official ways, to get Letters delivered to another town. Faster ways as well.

Was this a result of the new Alliance points with Henry

and being Trusted? Was this something Henry didn't want done through official channels or any way that could come back to haunt him? Hall had suspected that Henry wasn't as law abiding as he seemed.

Only one way to find out: deliver the Letters and see what happened.

"Let me mark River's Side on your map," Henry said, holding out his hand.

Hall glanced at Roxhard, who looked just as confused. Previously, anytime something was 'marked' on the map, it just appeared. Henry looked like he wanted a physical object. Hall paused, not sure what to do. A nagging feeling started in the back of his head, an impulse that he wasn't sure where it came from.

Reaching into his pouch, thinking of a map, he pulled one out. Rolled up, made of a light parchment with slightly frayed and worn edges. Unrolling it, he saw the island of Cumberland laid out, the places he had been and explored marked. The rest was not shown, just the boundaries of the island seen. It matched the map that opened up before his eyes when he called for it.

Wanting to check something, he thought about his map, and it appeared before him. Hovering and translucent, a duplicate to the physical one that he was holding.

"River's Side is here," Henry said and pointed at the map.

An icon of a tower appeared about a quarter of the way between the bridge and the farthest north boundary of Cumberland, more to the east where it was most likely along-side the river.

Staring at the map in surprise, Hall folded it up and replaced it in his pouch.

"Thanks," Henry said, shaking their hands. "Appreciate it."

Hall took the Letters, placing them in his bag. They were

thick envelopes, three of them bound together with twine. Henry looked happy, like a weight had been removed. He turned to start his duties for the day.

With a shrug, Hall and Roxhard left Grayhold.

———

The rain that had been threatening for days no longer held off.

It came in a downpour.

Visibility was cut down to almost nothing. Dark clouds blocked out the sun, thick drops of rain formed an almost solid screen. Hall was glad they had found the cloaks, but only two hours out of Grayhold they were getting soaked.

Hoods were pulled up tight, water dripping from the edge and splashing into the large puddles on the ground. It was like an obstacle course, having to avoid the puddles that were filling up the many ruts and holes in the hard-packed road. There was no drainage, the water just pooling.

Both were miserable, wet, and cold.

Pike flew high above them most of the time, flying ahead and taking shelter beneath some branches.

Hall thought about stopping and finding some shelter as well. A look into the dark clouded sky showed the rain would not be letting up anytime soon. Nothing but a mass of dark gray filled the sky. *Push on*, he thought, bending over a bit to keep the wind from driving the rain into his face, pulling his cloak tighter. *Need to get some miles in.*

They trudged on, seeing nothing and no one.

Another hour and the rain let up. It didn't stop but it wasn't as bad, going from torture to bearable.

Now that he could see, Hall was able to make out his surroundings. Using the map with the new markers he had been able to set up thanks to the *Cartography* skill, they were able to find the shelter of boulders they had used before but late in the evening.

Cold and hungry, they quickly built a fire and ate from their supplies. There had been no sign of any animals all day, so hunting was not an option. Using the cloaks, they were able to form a somewhat decent cover, which allowed for the small fire. Hall also got a couple *Survival* skill gains.

The next day dawned with no rain. The clouds were lighter, not as thick a gray. The sun was trying to peek out around them. The wind still carried a chill but they made better time without the rain. After a couple hours, the bridge was in sight.

———

Hall walked around the area where they had seen the tracks and blood. Nothing remained. No evidence, no respawn. The rain had washed the tracks and blood away, clearing the mud and making it all fresh. He looked off into the woods the way they had gone.

Would the Goblins still be there, just bones picked clean by scavengers? Or would the camp have respawned? That was an interesting question, one he hadn't seen an answer for yet. In the game, the camp would have respawned and so would the quest starting point. Now there was nothing. Did that mean it was a one-time quest? Only he and Roxhard had gotten it?

"The Goblin quest," he began, looking toward Roxhard, who was leaning against the bridge railings and staring down into the raging waters. "Did you have that before we met?"

Roxhard's eyes stared off into space, the pupils moving as he searched through his menus.

Hall turned away, not wanting to see it. The vacant look was disconcerting.

The Dwarf's gaze snapped back into focus.

"That's odd," he said. "I didn't. The only quest I have for that is the one we picked up from here."

"How'd you get the quest without the first part?" Hall asked, moving his foot along the ground where he remembered there being blood.

"From you, I guess," Roxhard answered with a shrug. "Not sure how but glad I did," he said, pulling at his new chain shirt.

Hall laughed. "Come on, let's go."

Thinking of the map and opening it before his eyes, Hall reviewed where the outpost they were looking for was. The icon was where Henry had placed it. Hall knew the distance from Grayhold to the bridge and was able to get a measurement from the bridge to River's Side now that he had a scale. Three more days on the road. He closed the map and reached into his pouch, thinking of the map again. It came out in his hand, neatly rolled up.

"Weird," Roxhard said.

He reached into his own pouch and pulled out a smaller rolled up parchment. Opening it, they saw Cumberland, but in less detail and with less areas revealed.

"That *Cartography* skill looks useful," Roxhard stated, rolling the map up again.

Hall played around with it as they walked, noting locations and measuring distances. The game map, which before had just shown major areas, was not much more useful.

They sheltered in what looked to be an old and abandoned building the first night past the bridge. Hall had found it, just off the road and hidden by some trees. They had searched it, finding nothing of interest, just evidence that it had been used as a camping spot before. Three walls, stones standing with a timber roof. The supports were intact, with no thatch of shingles. The front wall was half-collapsed, stones in small piles. Not much to look at, but it was shelter.

The morning brought the sun and a clear blue sky as well as an early start.

Instead of returning to the road, they decided to cut overland.

While they were in no true hurry, a straight shot through the woods might cut the distance down some. It could also provide a chance for some random encounters.

It was past noon when they heard the first sounds.

Ahead of them, through the thick woods came a bright flash, a roaring from something large and an odd growl of something else.

Pike flew down, settling on Hall's shoulder. The dragonhawk gave a small screech.

"What's there?" Hall asked, not expecting an answer.

To his surprise, he got one.

The dragonhawk reared up, talons hooked into Hall's shoulder, and spread his bat like wings. The bird squawked and Hall saw what Pike had seen.

The view was from high overhead, looking down at a small clearing. A break in the thick forest, a small pool of water fed by a stream coming down a hill at the clearings edge. Covered in grass, both the hill and the clearing. Against the side of the hill was a woman and a small, shaggy cow. She was dressed in leathers and carrying a staff. The cow was next to her, standing as high as her waist. Across from the cow and the woman, facing them, were two ogres. The creatures were tall, ten feet each and six feet across. Large bellies, long arms, small heads. Colored a dull green, dressed in hides. Each of the ogres held tree trunk clubs.

Ogres were higher level creatures, not normally found in this part of Cumberland. Their territory was more east toward the island's edge. Strong, not that smart but not as dumb as they looked. A single one was a tough fight for an equal level player. There were two of them.

But they were attacking a lone woman. A Druid, judging by the animal companion. She would be no match for them. Even if they were higher level, Hall couldn't ignore the sounds and the woman needing help.

"Come on," Hall said to Roxhard, taking off running toward the clearing. Pike screeched and leapt into the air.

CHAPTER TWELVE

THE CLEARING WAS A HUNDRED YARDS AWAY. HALL MADE THAT distance quickly, a sprint that would have made any football kick returner proud. He jumped fallen logs, skirted around trees, all while using the noises to guide him through the thick forest.

His Vitality dropped as he ran. He could feel his heart racing, his legs aching.

He could see the clearing ahead, a thinning of the trees.

Bursting through the tree line, he used *Leap* and jumped into the air. The clearing was only about a hundred feet long and half that wide with a large pool near the far end. He didn't jump high, using the ability to cover the distance in a single bound.

Leading with the spear, Hall slammed into the back of an ogre. The creature weighed over three hundred pounds but was staggered by Hall's weight and momentum. The tip of the spear pierced the creature's shoulder, cutting through the thick and leathery like skin.

The ogre roared and turned, swinging it's arm around

Hall felt like he hit a wall. He let go of the spear that was still embedded in the ogre and dropped to the ground. His training let him land on his feet, and he quickly jumped backward. His body hurt, small pains and bruises everywhere. The ogre was hard, like a mountain.

He looked up into the ogre's face. The head was small, a bony and pronounced forehead hanging over two small eyes. Large tusks pointed up from the wide mouth.

It roared at him, swinging a club that was the size of a small tree.

Hall ducked, feeling the air move as the weapon passed above him. It would have done a lot of damage if it had struck him.

Pike's cry split the air as the dragonhawk dived. Sharp talons dug lines across the ogre's head as the bird passed. The ogre swatted at Pike, the dragonhawk moving too quickly out of range.

The other ogre ignored the small fight, stepping closer to the woman and the cow.

Facing only the one ogre, she now had time to cast a spell and waved her free hand in the air, making gestures and sweeps, fingers moving deftly. Holding the staff, a long piece of gnarled and thick wood, she pointed her hand at the ogre. The creature looked down at its feet dumbly as the grass grew and grew, wrapping around the thick legs. It roared as it tried to lift its legs, one after the other, unable to move.

The roar turned into a bellow of rage and pain as the barreling form of Roxhard slammed into the back of its legs. The ogre bent forward, twisting the wrong direction.

Roxhard stood up, staring into space, shaking his head to get his focus back.

The ogre backhanded the Dwarf, who went flying across the field, landing hard and skipping another ten feet or so. Showing its great strength, the ogre lifted its legs up. The grass tore, pulling out in clumps. It stalked toward the Dwarf, ignoring the woman and the small cow.

Hall jumped again, avoiding the great club as it slammed into the ground making a dent. Dirt and small rocks exploded at the impact. He had drawn his short sword and slashed at the ogre's side, cutting a line across the wide belly. The ogre roared, green blood falling to the ground. The answering swipe by the ogre's free hand just barely caught Hall in his shoulder. His smooth sidestep was pushed into an awkward fall. He landed hard and managed to roll away, putting more distance between himself and the ogre.

He could see the other ogre advancing on a still shaken Roxhard. The Druid was looking from one to the other, trying to figure out the best way to help.

Or to run.

She didn't run.

Raising her hands, she pointed the staff at Hall's ogre. Shards of sharp wooden splinters flew from the staff, striking the ogre in the back. It roared, reaching back to dig at the splinters.

Hall jumped up, sheathing his sword and drawing the javelin with the now free hand, grabbing his spear with the other. Taking aim, he threw the javelin and used his momentum and weight to pull the spear from the ogre's shoulder. A large chunk of shoulder, flesh and muscle, tore out with it.

The javelin flew straight and struck the second ogre. A glancing blow, cutting a thin line across its arm. Just enough to draw its attention away from Roxhard.

Hall landed between them, back to one, but spear in hand. Grabbing the shaft in both hands, he turned the tip and jabbed backward. The ogre grunted in pain, reaching down to grab the weapon but Hall pulled it away quickly. He flipped the spear, using his body as a pivot, and stabbed out at the other ogre. It had been stepping toward him, reaching down with its large hands, when the spear slammed into its stomach.

The ogre stepped back, roaring.

Using *Leap*, Hall sprung into the air just ahead of the falling club from the ogre behind him. He jumped over that ogre, landing behind it and slamming his spear into the creature's lower back. The point dug in deep, and Hall twisted, causing the ogre to roar the loudest yet. The cry echoed through the forest.

With a screech, Pike attacked. The dragonhawk dove down out of the sky, a whistling missile. The ogre's head was back, roaring in pain, and Pike slashed across the face. The creature lost an eye, the dragonhawk's talon gouging deeply into the ogre's face.

It stumbled forward, arms batting uselessly in the sky. Pike circled, flapping his wings to hover in place. He let out a screech, and a bolt of lightning shot out of the dragonhawk's mouth, striking the ogre in the chest. Smoke curled up from the burn mark against the dull green skin.

Grass and vines grew around its feet, climbing its legs and across its body. The ogre roared, thrashing about as Pike dove for its face again. The second ogre took a step to the side to try to get around its companion to come at Hall. It roared in pain as Roxhard swung his axe hard into its back.

The closest ogre leaned low, reaching down to tear at the grass and vines. Hall slid to the ground, rolling onto his back and stabbed up with his spear. The tip caught the ogre in the throat, and Hall pushed with all his might. The ogre tried to rear up, to get away from the spear, but the tip was in too deep.

Green blood splashed across the ground as Hall rolled out of the way. The ogre fell forward, its body leaning as the legs were trapped, the spear wedged between the creature's head and the ground.

Standing up, Hall turned to face the last ogre, which had

turned to confront Roxhard. The club swung and hit the Dwarf's axe, the head embedding in the wood. The ogre pulled, and the axe was ripped from Roxhard's hands. Dumbly, the creature shook its club, trying to dislodge the weapon. Drawing his short sword, Hall ran the couple feet and slid to his knees. He drew the blade across the back of the ogre's heels, severing the tendons.

The beast roared in pain, turning to swipe at Hall, who dove out of the way.

It slumped to its knees, trying to stand but could not. The club dropped to the ground, and Roxhard pulled his axe from the wood. He got a grip on the axe and swung, taking the ogre in the neck. The creature gave one final roar and fell silent.

SLAIN: Green Flow Deep Ogre
+40 Experience

SLAIN: Green Flow Deep Ogre
+20 Experience

Skill Gain!
Small Blades Rank 2 +.5

Skill Gain!
Polearm Rank 2 +.3

Skill Gain!
Thrown Rank 2 +.1

Hall walked over to the ogre he had slain, trying to pull his spear out. It was wedged tight. He pushed at the ogre, trying to roll it onto its side but it did not budge.

"How did we kill two ogres?" Roxhard asked, breathing heavy. He was leaning against his axe, the head on the ground, staring at the nearly severed ogre's head. Green blood leaked out of the wound, dripping down the body and onto the ground. "The lowest level is at least ten."

Shrugging, Hall walked around the creatures toward the Druid. He had no idea why they had managed to kill creatures that were so much higher level. But were these ogres really? Higher level, yes, but that much? They had been tough, a lot of health, but not that difficult. And the experience was only that of creatures a few levels above.

Another mystery. Another thing different.

The Druid was a young woman, about his age. Human. Gael from the look. She had very fair skin, bright red hair with green streaks that matched her bright green eyes. The hair was long, wild and curly with two braids hanging down over her shoulders. Freckles covered her face, multiple piercings in her ears. A small ring up high in the lobe and short dangling chains that ended in small green jewels. The avatar was one of the prettier ones, Hall thought. Not stunning or striking, a girl next door kind of look. She wore leathers. A halter top left her midriff bare. Bracers on her wrists covered some of the light blue swirling tattoos that curled up her arms. Calf-high boots of a darker leather and a short leather skirt cut on an angle with laces on the sides leaving a gap between front and back of the skirt. A thin belt held a pouch and dagger. She carried a staff that was a foot taller than her five-foot five height. Made of gnarled wood, the staff was knotted with rough bark patches. A branch taken from an Ashwood tree with minimum work done to it.

She stayed near the wall, staff in both hands, looking from Hall to Roxhard. Behind her, the cow, a large calf, gave a menacing moo. It was shaggy and black with a white patch on its chest. It was about three or four feet tall and wide, heavy looking, with long horns that curled toward the front. The fur was thick, hanging down, but soft looking.

"Who are you?" she asked.

"You're welcome," Hall said, instead of answering. He wiped his sword on the ogre's dirty hide clothing and sheathed the weapon. Spreading his arms, he took a step forward. "I'm called Hall. That's Roxhard," he added, nodding toward the Dwarf who was still leaning against his axe.

The Druid relaxed, pushing loose strands of hair out of her face.

"Leigh," she said with a nod. "Thank you," she added as an afterthought.

You have earned +500 Alliance points with Leigh.
Saving her life has made the Druid, Leigh, think highly of you.

That caught him by surprise. He had been thinking that she was a PC, not an NPC. He studied her. Was she one of those new Ally NPCs with the advanced AI he had heard about? She gave him an odd look, taking a step back, not liking his scrutiny.

He smiled, trying to show he meant no harm. *Probably thinks I'm a creeper*, he thought, looking at the calf instead of Leigh.

"Where did the ogres come from?" Roxhard asked, saving Hall from his embarrassment, probably not realizing that he had done it.

"The foothills to the east," Leigh answered. "This is outside their normal territory. I don't know why they were here. My bad luck to run into them."

"Why were you here?" Hall asked.

Leigh studied him now, her head slightly cocked at an angle. She was appraising him, wondering what to say or if she should just leave now. Whatever she saw seemed to satisfy her.

"I am a Druid of the Tree," she said. "My Circle is to the southeast. I was on my way to Land's Edge Port to catch an airship to Edin. There is a Grove there that we lost contact with."

Hall nodded. Made some sense. Druids were followers of nature, using the energy of the world around them to power their spells and abilities. They believed that the world was connected by a large tree called Yggdrasil, the World Tree. When Hankarth exploded into the islands, each was supported by Branches of the World Tree. This is what allowed them to stay afloat in the air, what kept them from being destroyed completely. Two demons, Surtr and Ymir, fought for control of the world. They were always in balance until another demon, The Feardagh, upset that balance and caused Hankarth to shatter. The power of Yggdrasil kept them all alive. The Druids of the Tree tended the Groves where offspring of Yggdrasil, called Branches, were living. They feared that if these offspring were to be destroyed, the islands would lose their anchors and fall to the nothingness below.

Because of their solitary nature, Druids of the Tree were often seen wandering alone or with their animal companions. Judging by the size of the calf, Hall reasoned that Leigh was low level. Possibly still first or just barely second. The calf was an odd choice for an animal companion.

"The Elder of the Grove thought it a simple journey, safe enough, so sent me and Angus to scout the Grove. Apparently, it was not that safe," Leigh finished, pointing toward the corpses of the ogres. She shrugged. "Caught me by surprise."

"The cow's name is Angus?" Hall asked, trying not to chuckle. He glanced at Roxhard, who was also trying not to laugh.

"Yes," Leigh answered. "Why?"

"No reason," Hall said, realizing she would not understand why Angus was an odd name for a cow kept as a companion. "Long way to Edin."

Leigh shrugged.

"I'm originally from there, sent to the Grove here on Cumberland for training," Leigh said. "It's why I was sent to investigate."

"We're heading toward River's Side," Hall told her. "You could come with us."

"I could," she said with a smile. "Could use some company. Angus here isn't that much of a talker." The cow gave a low moo, Leigh chuckling. "Don't be getting any ideas now," she added.

Hall laughed. Was she flirting with him?

THE LOST GROVE

Leigh, Druid of the Tree, is journeying to a Grove on the island of Edin. She is looking for companions to help her on the dangerous road.

Reward: +500 Druids of the Tree Reputation, +500 Alliance with Leigh, +50 Experience

ACCEPT QUEST?

Hall saw the quest dialog box open up in front of his eyes. He went to quickly accept it when something caught his eye. The quest name was in blue, indicating it was a quest only a couple levels above his current one. Edin was a higher-level zone, twenty and higher, his favorite realm in the whole game. The quest should have been in green, the color of a much higher-level quest.

He was still only level two. This should not have been a quest he could do, let alone accept.

With a thought, he accepted the quest.

You have earned +100 Alliance points with Leigh.
Agreeing to accompany her to the Grove has pleased her.

"What's in River's Side?" she asked, finally walking away from the side of the hill. The cow trotted alongside her.

Angus looked up at Hall with annoyance, not happy for some reason. At least, Hall thought it was annoyance. It was hard to tell as the cow's hair covered most of its large eyes and made them hard to see. Pike settled on his shoulder, watching the pair walk by. Hall turned and followed, once again stopping at the ogre to try to push it off his spear.

"Just a stop on the way north," Hall answered. "From there we're heading into the Far Edge Peaks. Hope you don't mind, but we have something to do there before can head to Edin."

Leigh shrugged.

"The Grove hasn't been heard from in months," she said, standing next to him and examining the ogre. "What's another couple of weeks?"

Hall expected to see a decrease in Alliance points because of the delay but there was none. Leigh really did not appear to mind the sidequest.

"He's stuck good," she said, poking at the ogre.

"Yeah. I'd leave it but can't afford a new one," Hall said, leaning his shoulder into the ogre. He pushed, his feet sliding on the ground. "Bastard is heavy."

"Let me," Roxhard said.

The Dwarf moved alongside Hall and put his weight against the ogre. He started pushing, his thick legs and feet digging into the ground. Slowly, inch by inch, the ogre started to move. Leigh grabbed the spear, pulling at it as Hall and Roxhard nudged the ogre.

"Got it," she said, holding the spear aloft.

The ogre had a lean to it now, the grasses and vines holding the body upright. Roxhard and Hall stepped away, breathing heavy.

"Thanks," Hall said, taking the spear back.

He held it by the end, sighting down the long shaft. It looked straight, the yew wood strong but somewhat pliable. Moving his hands along the shaft he felt for cracks, not finding any.

SPEAR
Attack +1
Damage 1d6
Durability 3/6
Weight 5 lbs.

The durability had taken a hit but it would last for a while longer. He hoped.

Roxhard crawled under the ogre, searching it, finding nothing of value. He made a disgusted face as his hand landed in a puddle of blood.

"No loot," he said with a sad shake of his head. "And this thing smells."

He staggered a bit as he stood up fast, cringing as he moved his shoulder.

"Hold still," Leigh told the Dwarf.

She walked over, laying her left hand on his shoulder. Holding her staff in the other, planting it firmly on the ground, she closed her eyes. Light flared along the tattoos on her arms, a dull blue that followed the lines. Her palm started glowing, matching the color of the tattoos. Roxhard stood straighter, smiling.

"Thanks," he said as she stepped away. He swung his arms, moving his shoulders.

Hall looked up into the sky. It was later than he had thought.

"We need shelter and then food," he said. "I don't think any of us want to stay here for the night."

"I don't know," Leigh said, looking around the clearing and

leaning against one of the ogre corpses. "It's got a certain charm."

Hall laughed.

———

The first night they spent in a shallow cave. A small fire and decent meal.

Hall was surprised that Leigh ate meat with them, a couple of small rabbits. He had assumed because of their connection with nature that Druids were strict vegetarians. Leigh had laughed. Some were, some aren't, she had said and took another bite of the greasy meat.

He found that he agreed with the statements made back in the Laughing Horse. Leigh was an NPC but acted like a PC. She thought for herself, acted how she wanted and when she wanted. There was no preset sequence of conversations to have with her. He started to think of her as a real person.

Which she was, he finally decided on the second night. If they, the Players, were now just digital copies of themselves, what made them different from the NPCs? Not a thing.

After that decision he found her company much more enjoyable.

Roxhard acted like a typical fourteen-year-old boy did when in the company of a beautiful and lively woman. He was nervous, stuttered a lot. Completely infatuated.

At night, Leigh curled up next to her cow, a breed she said was native to the Edin island. Angus, when they sat down at night around the fire, would purposefully place himself between Hall and Leigh. The cow did not like him, Hall decided. Pike made quick friends with Leigh, spending as much time on her shoulder as he did on Halls.

It was mid-afternoon on the third day when they came upon River's Side.

The Green Flow was wide and raging, coming down from the north before turning east for a couple miles before heading south and would finally turn west for good and bisect the island. The water bounced over rocks, forming small waterfalls as it stepped down the sloping ground. The land rose up to form a small, grass-covered plateau. A road could be seen coming down and heading west, stone walls framing it. A wide wooden bridge spanned the river giving access to the eastern forest.

River's Side was surrounded by a low wooden wall made of thick logs stuck into the ground. The tips were pointed with a single arched gate set into the wall. A tall six-sided tower, the upper level under a green plank roof open with a railing, rose above the wall. Armed guards could be seen walking the wall and the tower and standing at attention beside the open gate.

CHAPTER THIRTEEN

They were able to enter without incident. The guards watched them, warily, but did not stop or hinder their progress. Even the sight of Pike riding Hall's shoulder or Angus the cow did not cause a stir.

River's Side was a busy place. Inside the wall was a wide and open area, a steep-sided hill rising up in the middle. The tower was built on the hill, a set of railing-less stairs leading to the tower's single door. An arch of stone with a wide wooden door could be seen set into the hillside. Walkways, with stairs leading to them, ringed the inside edge of the wall. Buildings filled the rest of the space, laid out in an organized manner. All were set back from the wall, leaving a space of about twenty feet. All the one-and-two-story buildings faced the middle, away from the wall.

Hall could see a long barracks building, a blacksmith, healers, General Goods shop and other tradesmen. At the far end, only seen after walking around the tower and hill, was a large three-story building. A wide covered porch was on the front, a stable to the side.

An Inn.

"Let's get a room, and then we can find Watchman Kelly," Hall said, the others agreeing.

They went left, randomly, passing the smithy and General Goods store. Guards roamed the wide street that ringed the hill, some obviously off duty and some on patrol. There was a large number of visitors, merchants, and their guards. Hall hoped there would be rooms at the Inn still. They could spend the night in the forest, but a good night's sleep in beds with full meals would do them all good, restoring their Vitality. There was no telling how long they'd be roughing it while looking for the treasure.

Hall looked at the people as he walked, passing a couple other shops. None were noticeably Players, all had the look of Non-Player Characters. He noticed that he could no longer see their names or occupations floating above their heads.

When had that changed? he thought, trying to remember if the information had been there when they were still in Grayhold. He glanced at Leigh, realizing that he had not been able to see anything about her, either.

"What?" she asked, smiling at him, her eyes sharing the smile. It was a look that said she did not mind him looking at her.

"Nothing," Hall replied, returning the smile.

Angus mooed and pushed himself tighter between Hall and Leigh. She laughed, reaching down and scratching behind the cow's ear.

Hall didn't notice the jealous look that crossed Roxhard's face, fading quickly.

Digging his talons into Hall's shoulder, drawing a wince, Pike spread his wings and lifted off. He spiraled into the air before turning to the east and flying over the wall. Guards turned and watched the dragonhawk disappear over the trees.

The Inn was well maintained, the sounds of a large crowd already coming from within. The covered porch ran the full length of the Inn's front face. It was a deep porch, chairs and tables spaced around it. A railing sat at the edge with stairs leading up. The wooden doors were carved with fanciful designs, the top half panes of glass.

A sign hanging from the porch's roof named the Inn as the River's Fall.

Opening the doors, they walked inside into the common room. Like many in the realms of Essec, the common room was a large and open space. Long bar running down the left wall, a large stone fireplace on the right. Tables – round, square, large and small – filled the space in disorganized order. Barmaids moved from table to table, taking drinks and dropping off food. Two bartenders, Humans, male and female, worked behind the granite counter. A set of stairs on the left would lead to the Inn's Portal Room. Opposite, on the right side, the stairs would lead to the rooms above.

The common room was crowded, and the noise was loud, so many talking at once. Guards, merchants, mercenaries, tradesmen, and farmers from the outlying fields.

They had taken a couple steps into the room when a deep voice barked at them from behind. Turning, they saw a large man sitting on a stool to the side of the door where he had a view of the entire Inn. Large was an understatement. Over six foot and over two hundred fifty pounds. He was dressed plainly, no armor, but a short sword was strapped to his waist. Leaning against the wall was a large club.

The Inn's bouncer.

"The cow has to go in the stable," he said. There was no inflection to his voice. He was neither caring or annoyed. He just was. "2 copper a night."

Leigh glanced at Hall, and he nodded.

"I'll be right back," the Druid said.

"We'll get rooms," Hall told her and pointed to the bar.

He threaded his way through the crowded space, avoiding

chairs that were unexpectedly pushed back, barmaids that expertly danced around him, and patrons that just stood up. One of them, a woodsman by the look, stood up and bumped into Hall. Facing away from them, the woodsman hadn't noticed the pair making their slow and careful way to the bar. The woodsman turned an angry glare at them. The glare faded and he sat back down, without saying a word, when he noticed the javelin strapped across Hall's back, the sword belted at his waist as well as the short spear he carried.

They found a clear spot at the bar and caught the attention of one of bartenders. The Human female approached with a smile, a rag in her hand busy cleaning a pewter mug.

"Afternoon," she said, her accent Essec. "What'll it be?"

"Two rooms," Hall answered. "Meals for three."

"We're pretty busy today," she replied, nodding toward the crowded room. "Only got one room but it's got four beds. 1 silver a night, food is 5 copper."

"That'll work," Hall said and pulled the coins out of his pouch, placing them on the counter. "Just for the night, meal now and again at dinner."

The coins swiftly disappeared into the bartender's apron. She walked to the far end, reaching down below the counter, and returned with a small brass key.

"Room Two, first door on the right. There's no tables so I'll have the food brought here. Three?"

"Yes, thank you. Two ales as well." Hall thought about ordering a third for Leigh but wasn't sure what her drink of choice was. He looked down at Roxhard, who had pulled a stool over and was working to get on it. The kid was only a teen but Hall didn't feel weird getting the Dwarf a drink. Most likely, he had drunk the game's drinks as often as possible, and the rules and laws were different here anyway. Probably no law about a couple-hundred-year-old Dwarf that was really only fourteen not allowed to have a drink.

"Thanks," Roxhard said when the bartender set two pewter pints down in front of them. Foam spilled over the edge and down the sides. He took a deep swig of the ale. "Good stuff."

Hall agreed as he drank his. He'd never bothered with the alcoholic drinks in the game. He enjoyed his beers, a fan of small brew craft, but it had seemed silly while playing the game to drink in the game. But now? Why not.

And the ale was good. Patterned after a German style, which were his favorites.

A few minutes later, Leigh pushed up against the bar, nudging Hall to the side to make room. Once he shifted, she didn't move away. He could feel her against his side.

"They only had one room," Hall told her. "Four beds."

"That's fine," she said, still not moving away from touching him.

She ordered an ale.

———

The meal for lunch consisted of chunks of cheese, a thin slice of meat and some bread. They all ate it quickly, each having another drink.

Hall had asked for directions to find Watchman Kelly. The bartender had told him that Kelly would be found in the barracks at this time of day, working in the office. It was a short walk from the Inn to the guard barracks. Leigh had stayed behind to check in on Angus. She said she'd meet them for dinner later or see them in the room.

The barracks door was open, leading to a small lobby. An open door on the right led to the office, a closed door on the left to a storeroom. A stair next to the office led to the second floor. Ahead of them was an open arch that led to a long room with rows of beds spaced apart evenly. Stone fireplaces lined the wall at intervals, and large trunks were at the end of each bed.

Stepping inside, Hall and Roxhard turned to the office. Inside the small space – just large enough for a desk and two chairs in front of it, a cast iron stove in the corner – sat a guard. She was bent over, using a quill to write on a piece of parchment. Long black hair held in a ponytail. Leather armor with a tabard bearing Essec's symbol.

"Excuse me," Hall said, and she looked up. A face that could have been pretty if it hadn't been scowling with jet black eyes. She looked annoyed at being interrupted. "We're looking for Watchman Kelly?"

"You're looking at her. Who are you and why are you here?"

Not what he had been expecting, Hall quickly recovered.

"Guard Captain Henry in Grayhold asked us to deliver some Letters."

He reached into his pouch, pulling the Letters out and handing them over to Kelly's outstretched hand. She took the letters and set them on the desk, still looking at Hall.

"Anything else?"

QUEST COMPLETE!
You have delivered Guard Captain Henry's letters to Watchman Kelly.

SPECIAL DELIVERY
Reward: +100 Essec Reputation, +100 Alliance with Guard Captain Henry, +25 Experience

"No," Hall said and turned to go.

"Wait," Kelly said as she untied the string that held the letters together. She quickly read through them, a couple of times. Setting the letters down, she leaned back and looked at

Hall and Roxhard. She studied them for a long time. Hall started to feel uncomfortable with the scrutiny.

"You didn't read them," she asked, finally pointing at the letters.

By her tone of voice and intense stare, Hall knew there was only one acceptable answer. He hadn't read them, hadn't even thought to, so he was comfortable answering.

"Of course not," he replied with just a trace of annoyance that she would bother asking.

Kelly studied the two of them again, fingers of one hand tapping on the desk. She sat forward quickly, finally coming to a decision.

"Henry apparently trusts you," she said. "Not sure why, but you'll need to prove yourself to me if you want in on this," she added, tapping the letters.

In on what? Hall wondered but didn't ask. He had suspected there was more to the letters from Henry than everyday guard notices. Now, Hall knew his suspicions were correct. He just wasn't sure what was going on. There was only one way to find out.

"Prove ourselves how?"

Kelly sighed, looking like she wasn't that thrilled with the idea and had been hoping they'd leave.

"Give me your map," she said, holding out her hand. This was a woman not used to being kept waiting, used to people anticipating what she would want.

Hall did so, pulling it out of his pouch and handing it over. Kelly spread it out on the desk. She pointed to an area an hour or so east of River's Side.

"There's a small gang of smugglers camped just past the river," she explained. "They need to be," she paused and looked up at Hall with her intense stare, "removed. The gang's leader has a ledger book. I want that."

HELPING KELLY

Watchman Kelly at River's Side wants a gang of smugglers removed.
The leader has a ledger book that she requires.
Smugglers 0/8
Smuggler Chief 0/1
Recovered Ledger 0/1
Reward: +200 Alliance with Guard Captain Henry, +500 Alliance with
Watchman Kelly,
+50 Experience

ACCEPT QUEST?

Hall quickly accepted the quest under Kelly's intent and impatient stare. She looked down at Roxhard, back at Hall, and nodded. He was surprised that the quest reward was Alliance points with her as well as Henry. That was not how the old system had worked. Were all of his actions now giving or removing Alliance with the various people he met? Did each have their own reputation and how would that ultimately affect him and their interactions?

Kelly was still staring at them, waiting.

Without a word they left the barracks.

"Eight plus the leader is not a small gang," Roxhard muttered once out of Kelly's hearing.

"I'm wondering why she needed us to eliminate them and not the guards," Hall said, looking at the guards patrolling the walls.

They had seen a large number at River's Side. It was an outpost in the middle of a wild forest with the ogre territories to the east. Having a lot of guards was a necessity but surely some of them could have been spared to take out the smugglers.

'Get in on this,' she had said.

Hall was beginning to have an idea of what Henry and

Kelly were involved in. He wasn't sure it was something they should get mixed up in, but it was too late it seemed. They were already committed.

"Let's get Leigh," he said. "We'll need her help."

————

"Why did I let you talk me into this?" Leigh asked as they crossed the bridge over the raging Green Flow. "I could be at the bar with ale in hand, or even better, taking a nap in a nice comfy bed."

Hall laughed.

"You don't sound much like a Druid," he chuckled. "Aren't you supposed to like being outside?"

She shrugged.

"I do," she admitted. "But what's wrong with wanting a nice bed and cold ale now and then?"

"Not a thing," he said with another chuckle.

No one had questioned why they were heading across the bridge, no shouts from the watchtower above. The path was overgrown, not well maintained, indicating that it was not well used. As long as the ogres and other creatures in this part of the forest kept to themselves, there was no need for the Essec guards to cross the river. No villages or anything else in this section of the Green Flow Forest, so no reason for anyone to cross the river.

But they were.

Pike soared through the trees above, and Angus trotted along behind them. His hooves made a clopping noise on the wood of the bridge. Roxhard walked next to the cow, Hall and Leigh in the front, side by side.

The trees were cleared for twenty feet or so past the edge of the river. Grass and flowers, signs of stumps now overgrown. At one time the trees had been cleared to provide clear space between the tree line and river. Well within bow shot, Hall figured looking over his shoulder at the watchtower. But now, they were letting it start to grow back.

Once they entered the forest, they slowed and went on guard. Instead of side by side, they went single file and some space between. The area Kelly had indicated was an hour's walk from the bridge, but they had to assume the smugglers would post watch.

Hall took the lead with Roxhard behind. Leigh and Angus were in the rear. A standard party alignment. The scout or puller, tank next, and healing in the rear.

Classes in Sky Realms were set up to fill roles in the party. Each could adventure, and more importantly, survive solo, but they excelled as part of a team. The three main classes – Warden, Shaman, and Druid – were the tank, magical and ranged damage, and healing parts of a party. After that was the support classes – Skirmisher, Duelist, Skald, and Witch, the same name for both male and female characters. Each support class would bring additional damage, or buffing and debuffing, into the mix. Together, any mix of the main three and two support classes, one damage and one buffing, would create a well-rounded party that could handle any of the dungeons or castle raids in the game. Of course, there were the min/maxers that had the 'perfect' builds and party mixes, which there was some truth to, but overall, any combination would work.

Hall wondered if the same rules applied. Currently they without a true tank, magic damage, and a buffer/debuffing class.

Each class had a set of abilities that defined that class. From there, the player could tailor the skills to build their character as they wanted. A Warden could be a thief or swashbuckler, knight or assassin, even an archer; but they would still always be somewhat of a tank, designed to take hits and give them.

The forest was made up of oaks, maples, and birches with a scattering of pines. This part of the forest was less dense, more space between the trees and gaps in the leafy canopy that let in the sun. It was a pleasant stretch of woods, but Hall knew how dangerous it really was.

As they got deeper into the woods, closer to the smuggler's camp, Hall's *Tracking* ability started giving him gains. He saw animal tracks, but now noticed boot prints. Not recent, heading the way they were going. Checking his map periodically to make sure they were still on course was giving him *Cartography* gains as well.

He glanced up at the sun, trying to see how far through the sky it had progressed since the start of the quest. He couldn't tell, and without it, there was no way to keep time. Hall started to check the map more often, using that as a guide for their progress.

The boot tracks started to multiple, a couple different sets, moving back and forth. Fresher.

They were getting close.

Hall stopped and glanced into the sky, looking for Pike. The dragonhawk circled over them a couple of times and then headed north, the direction they had been heading. He flew low, eyes scanning the trees. The sharp eyes found the camp. Erected alongside a small brook, a couple of tents could barely be seen through the treetops.

Moving slower, even Angus the cow being mindful to not step on any loose branches, they closed the last couple hundred feet. Hall brought them more to the east, wanting to approach the camp from that side, which he hoped would be the most unexpected side for the smugglers. They would think anyone coming from River's Side would come from the south or west.

Hall debated scouting ahead, getting an idea of how the camp was arranged and where the smugglers were. The tactic had worked good against the Goblins. He really wanted to have Pike do a fly over but the trees were too dense. The dragonhawk was on a low branch nearby, waiting to fly into the camp. Instead, Hall opted for a straight-ahead approach.

Through a gap in the trees, Hall could see the camp. The brook was behind the tents, five of them scattered in a small clearing surrounded by trees. Made from hides, the tents were held up by wooden poles, openings in the front and back. The remains of a fire sat in the middle of the rough circle of tents. A pile of crates and bags were between two of the tents.

Three smugglers sat on logs around the ashes, talking and polishing weapons. Each wore leather armor and carried various weapons, swords and an axe. A fourth smuggler was down by the brook. All four were Human and male. Of the leader and the other four, there was no sign.

They had not seen any sign of the other smugglers, which would mean they were not in the camp and would return at any time. They had gotten lucky that all nine were not there. But they had to deal with the four quickly.

Hall glanced up at where Pike was nestled in the trees. With a thought, he gave the dragonhawk the command. Pike screeched and chirped, a sequence that was loud through the quiet woods.

The signal.

CHAPTER FOURTEEN

THE SMUGGLERS LOOKED INTO THE WOODS AND THEN BACK TO what they were doing. Bird calls, even one like Pike had done, were common in the forest.

They weren't ready for what came next.

Roxhard charged out of the woods. Short and compact, strong as stone, the Dwarf was a speeding battering ram. He had chosen his path well, coming in from the north and into the back of the startled smugglers. Axe leading, Roxhard slammed into one of the seated smugglers. The man yelled out, twisting awkwardly and falling with the Dwarf on top of him.

The others jumped up, weapons in hand. The one down by the river stood, looking on in confusion. A javelin caught a smuggler in the shoulder, a glancing blow, the shaft sliding by and cutting into a tent. The man staggered, twisting in pain. The last of the smugglers around the ashes tried to move but could not. Grass and roots twisted around his ankles

Caught, unable to move, the smuggler sliced down with his sword trying to cut the vines. He shifted his feet, trying to dislodge them. He never heard the strange noise coming his way. Angus crashed through the trees, the small cow's hooves churning up dirt. Mooing, the shaggy cow slammed into the smuggler. One horn pierced the smuggler's armor, the cow's weight pushing the man off-balance. He fell.

Hall burst from the trees, his target the one he had missed with the javelin. Bleeding from his shoulder, holding that arm awkwardly, the smuggler turned to face the running Skirmisher. Hall leveled his spear, knowing it gave him the reach over the smuggler. Only feet away, he stumbled, staggered as something pushed back against him.

He felt the pain in his shoulder, looking to see an arrow shaft sticking out, blood leaking out of the hole in his armor. He stopped, his momentum gone. The smuggler smiled, moving forward and stepping to the side. Beyond, Hall saw the last smuggler down by the brook armed with a bow. The man was reaching for another arrow.

Pike screeched down, darting past the smuggler, distracting him.

With a grunt of pain, Hall jumped into the air. He leaped over the head of the nearest smuggler, landing ten feet from where he started. Still too far from the archer. He leaped again, watching his Energy bar all but disappear. He landed about five feet in front of the startled archer and jabbed out with his spear.

The weapon's tip slammed into the archer's stomach, not enough force to pierce the armor but it made the smuggler drop the bow. Hall pressed his advantage, stepping forward. He pulled the spear back, reversing his grip with his left hand. Swinging the butt end of the spear in an arc, he caught the smuggler in the shoulder.

Dropping the spear, he drew his short sword. As it pulled from the scabbard, he sliced it across the smuggler's chest. The sharp edge sliced through the leather, drawing blood. The smuggler punched forward trying to hit Hall's bleeding shoulder. Hall twisted to the side, rotating around the surprised smuggler.

Skirmishers counted on their high agility for their leaps and jumps, but it also aided them in close quarter fighting along with the Evade Ability, making them hard to hit. They were deadly with their spears, but almost equally so with swords in close. Where Wardens most often relied on brute strength or technical skill with their weapons, and Duelists used their dual-wielding and speed to block and attack constantly, Skirmishers were all about speed on offense, darting in and out to attack.

Hall's boots splashed in the water's edge as he turned. His back was to the smuggler's back, and then he completed the turn, facing the smuggler but on the man's other side. Hall stabbed out with his sword, using the twists momentum and positioning. The weapon, in Hall's right hand, was now flying straight into the smuggler's chest. The man grunted in pain, body arching as the weapon pierced armor and flesh. Hall kicked out, and the smuggler fell back into the water with a splash, red blood flowing down the brook. He didn't get up.

Hearing boots against the ground, Hall turned, raising his sword. He barely got it up in time, deflecting the blow that would have cut him in half. The blade sliced along his arm, drawing blood and making him growl in pain. The smuggler he had grazed with the javelin pulled his sword back to swing again.

Stuck at an awkward angle, Hall could do nothing but block the smugglers attacks. He needed breathing room.

———

Roxhard slammed the butt end of his axe into the smugglers side, loosening the man's grip. Taller, not as strong, the smuggler had done the only thing he could have when the charging Dwarf had slammed into him. He had wrapped his arms and legs around Roxhard and held on tight.

The Dwarf couldn't bring the axe head to bear and couldn't get up. Together they struggled, thrashing around on the ground, rolling. Roxhard's weight was the advantage. Armor plus the Dwarf's natural, stone-like density kept him on top.

Grunting, gasping, the smuggler tried twisting away from the butt end of the axe. Not able to apply his full strength because of the angle, Roxhard kept hitting the smuggler anyway. He could feel the man's fists hitting his back, a pounding that didn't amount to much. Lifting himself up with one arm, Roxhard slammed his bulk onto the smuggler. The man coughed, gasping for breath.

Again, Roxhard lifted up and slammed down. The smuggler stopping twisting, his struggles lessening. Pushing himself up, Roxhard looked down at the man. Human, mid-twenties. Blond hair, no beard. Scarred, rough looking from a rough life. Coughing, the smuggler tried to roll out of the way.

Roxhard grabbed the handle of his axe with both hands, lifting it up and ready to swing. He paused.

He'd been playing Sky Realms Online for only a year or so. At only fourteen, he shouldn't have been, but he wasn't the only one in his school using an older siblings name and account to play. His entire guild had been made up of kids from his school. He'd never before hesitated in slaying an enemy. Most of them were nonhumans, monsters, but there had been plenty of Humans.

Why was he hesitating now?

The smuggler coughed, gasping for air, holding a hand up to try and stop Roxhard. His other grasped his side where the axe's handle had been hitting him in the kidneys or some other painful body part. This man was like the monsters, would kill Roxhard without a care.

So why was he caring?

The smuggler could be an innocent, only doing this because he had no choice. They had attacked the camp without cause. There was no good or right reason for this. Smuggling was wrong, but so was attacking the camp and killing in cold blood. Who was more wrong?

Wasn't what Roxhard and his friends doing murder? And for what? Experience and some coin? He was starting to feel overwhelmed again. He was just a kid, a teenager, not a battle-scarred Dwarf. A scrawny kid.

Hall was accepting of it all. None of this seemed to bother him. He just went on. He accepted this new life, if that was what it was.

Roxhard very much wanted to impress Hall. He would have died if not for the Skirmisher, been lost with no direction. He might have respawned, he might not have. For whatever reason, Hall kept him around. Roxhard didn't think it was pity. He hoped not. Hall felt like what an older brother should be. Roxhard's real brother, the only nice thing he had ever done was allow his younger and annoying sibling to use his account to play the game.

Hall was what he had wished his real brother had been like.

Roxhard felt a sharp pain in his leg. Yelling out, he looked down to see a knife sticking out of his thigh. The smuggler, while he was distracted, had grabbed a knife from his boot and struck. Angry at himself as well as the smuggler, Roxhard swung his axe.

The hand holding the knife fell slack, blood splashing into the air.

Roxhard staggered back, gasping as he placed weight on his injured leg. The blade still stuck out, a slow trickle of blood leaking down his leg.

"Idiot," he muttered to himself staring down at the wound.

He cursed his stupidity. He could feel pain. This wasn't a game, not any more, he had to keep reminding himself.

He wasn't the scrawny kid pretending to be a Dwarf. He was the Dwarf. Roxhard of Clan Stonefire, born of the Hard-edge Mountains.

He was strong. He was iron. He was stone.

He looked down at the body, the human body. Blood dripped from the edge of his axe onto the ground. A great gash torn in the smuggler's lifeless body, blood streaming out, organs exposed.

Roxhard fought the urge to collapse and cry.

———

The smuggler's blade got through his defenses. Hall stepped back, splashing in the water, trying to avoid the cutting edge. He twisted to the side. The smuggler was now off-balance, leaning too far forward but Hall was not in position to take advantage.

He took a couple more steps back, farther away and onto dry land. Glancing into the camp he saw Roxhard's axe swing down and taking out the smuggler laying at his feet. The last smuggler was trying to swing at Angus but missing, having to avoid the spray of wood splinters that Leigh was shooting at him. They had their battles under control.

The smuggler turned to him, swinging, and Hall ducked under the sword. He twisted and rolled to the side, slashing out with his sword. He scored a hit, slicing along the side of the smuggler. The man yelled in pain, making a wild swing down that Hall easily avoided.

Springing up Hall stabbed straight out, forcing the smuggler back. The man stumbled again. Stepping forward, Hall swung. The smuggler raised his sword to block, catching Hall's blade. Which was what Hall wanted. Metal clanged on metal, and Hall reversed his swing, out and back down through the smuggler's side. The man dropped, bleeding out into the water.

Hall grimaced, his own wounds hurting.

He turned back to the others, watching the last smuggler fall with dozens of wooden shards sticking out of his chest.

SLAIN: *Green Flow Smuggler Archer*
+25 Experience

SLAIN: *Green Flow Smuggler Warrior*
+25 Experience

HELPING KELLY
Smugglers 4/8
Smuggler Chief 0/1
Recovered Ledger 0/1

Skill Gain!
Polearms Rank 2 +.1

Skill Gain!
Small Blades Rank 2 +.2

Skill Gain!
Light Armor Rank 2 +.1

Skill Gain!
Thrown Rank 2 +.1

Glancing up into the sky, he watched Pike circling, keeping an eye out for the other smugglers.

"You okay?" he asked Roxhard.

"Yeah," came the distracted response.

The Dwarf was staring down at a smuggler's body. It had been cut almost in half by the axe. There was a strange look on Roxhard's face. Too many emotions to decipher. Hall had to keep reminding himself that the Dwarf was really just a kid.

He reached down and grasped Roxhard's shoulder, squeezing, not sure what else to do or say.

"That was fun," Leigh said as she picked her way around the bodies. She swiftly looked away from the corpse Roxhard was still looking down at.

She reached out and touched Hall's bare arm, her fingers light. Chanting, the tattoos on her arm glowing, Hall felt a warmth coming from her touch. It spread throughout his body. Flexing his arms, he felt the muscles knit and the cuts flow back together.

"Thanks," he said.

"No problem," she responded, her hand remaining on his arm after the healing spell had faded. She smiled up at him and turned her attention to Roxhard. "Let me help," she said.

Bending down, laying her hand just above where the knife blade stuck out of his leg, she took hold of the hilt with her other hand.

"Hold still," she said.

"Why..." he started to ask and gasped as she yanked the knife out.

Quickly, she chanted and the blue glow once again crawled up her arms. Roxhard smiled, watching her. *That could be trouble*, Hall thought, recognizing how Roxhard was watching Leigh. The kid had a crush. Had it bad.

"Thanks," he stammered, the words sounding odd in his rough and gravelly voice.

Hall looked around the camp. Tents, remains of a fire, and the small collection of crates and bags. He could see a bag or two in the tents. Each of the smugglers was wearing pieces of leather armor. Decent shape, not bad quality and their weapons had been well maintained. A decent amount of loot.

But no time to collect it. Not yet.

Pike screeched from above.

The other smugglers were returning.

CHAPTER FIFTEEN

They made a lot of noise. Branches being pushed aside, talking. Not trying to hide their return. The other four were similar to the first. All Human, all male. Dressed in leather armor and carrying swords. Two also had bows. Each of the bowmen also carried a collection of rabbits and other small animals. The leader was different. Taller, bulkier but not overly so, looking more experienced. He moved with an easy step, eyes searching everywhere, constantly moving. Dressed in a chainmail shirt and leather leggings, longsword strapped to his waist.

Two Smuggler Archers, two Smuggler Warriors and the Smuggler Chief. Using the *Identify* skill, the Archers and Warriors showed white, which meant equal level. The Chief was blue, higher level.

The four Smugglers spread out as they entered the camp, not paying attention.

The Chief did. He stopped at the edge, scanning what he saw. Or, more importantly, what he didn't see.

He didn't see the others. The camp was empty.

No sounds. No snoring. Nothing at all. Silence.

He drew his sword, the sound drawing the attention of the other four.

Before they could draw their weapons, a screech tore through the air. They all looked up, watching a streak dive toward the camp. It was fast, a orange blur. It came in over the brook and into the camp. They watched it and then jumped back as a fork of lightning shot from the blur. One of the Smuggler Warriors jumped back, yelling, as the bolt slammed into his chest. He fell down, smoke curling up.

All eyes turned to the fallen man, the Chief quickly turning back to the what had been the streak of orange. A dragonhawk hovered in the air, its scaled wings flapping. The bird screeched once more, another bolt of lightning shooting out. The Chief stepped to the side, avoiding the blast.

"Kill it," he shouted.

Before the Archers could -nock arrows, the dragonhawk was gone.

"What the-" one of the Warriors started to say. He never finished his thought, a javelin catching him in the chest. He stared stupidly down at the weapon, reaching for it, before falling to the ground.

Noise came from across the camp drawing the smugglers attention. First a small cow, shaggy but with sharp looking horns, came barreling out of the woods. It was followed by a charging Dwarf. Above them all leaped a man armed with a spear.

———

Hall felt the branches push aside as he leapt.

The spear pointed down as his arc brought him toward the Smuggler Chief. The man stepped to the side, and Hall swung the spear. The tipped smacked the Chief as Hall landed. He pulled the weapon back and jabbed quickly at the Chief. A sword smacked the tip out of the way.

Next to him, Angus slammed into the Archer that had been blasted by Pike's lightning. He was starting to get up, saw the cow, and raised his hands to cover his head. The Archer dropped his bow, falling to the ground and screaming as the cow's hooves ran over him. Roxhard slammed into the Warrior farthest on the right edge. He stopped his run, and the Smuggler Warrior fell backward, hitting the ground hard.

The Warrior on the left drew his sword, taking a couple steps forward and stumbling. Somehow, he maintained his balance, looking down to see grass and roots snaking around his ankles. He heard a chanting and saw a woman at the far end of the camp, standing in the bushes. She held a gnarled staff, and her free hand was making strange patterns in the air. He leaned down, slashing at the grass and vines.

Hall twirled the spear, trained to use the weapon as a spear and like a quarterstaff. He jabbed with the tip, smacking with the butt end. The Chief blocked most of the strikes. He would stop the bladed tip, allowing a hit from the non-edged end. Hall had to keep the shaft moving quickly to avoid the Chief's longsword. They had to end this quickly, he knew. They were tired while the smugglers were fresh.

He heard the piercing sound of Leigh's splinters as they flew through the air. The Smuggler Archer on the left screamed, yelling out in pain as dozens of small splinters pierced his skin. Hall couldn't spare a glance as the Chief pressed his attack, working to get the sword past Hall's defenses.

Angus snorted, stomping down on the Smuggler Archer. The man struggled to get up, rolling and trying to avoid the small cow's hooves.

Roxhard took a step forward, axe swinging. The Smuggler Warrior on the ground barely got his hand up in time. The weight of the axe forced the Warrior's arm back, bending awkwardly at the elbow. He grunted, trying to keep the axe from descending. Roxhard leaned into it, pushing down.

The Smuggler Chief pushed Hall backward. He had gotten inside the reach of the spear, and it was all Hall could do to keep twisting out of the way of the man's longsword. The leader was good. Had to be a couple levels higher, maybe even as much as three. Pike was flying back and forth behind the leader, looking for an opportunity to attack.

Somehow sensing the dragonhawk behind him, the Chief forced Hall to twist. The dragonhawk squawked in frustration as Hall was now between him and the leader. Hall leaned back, avoiding a slash, twisting to the side to avoid the back swing of the longsword. He cursed, frustrated. The Chief was just too good, not giving him a second to adjust and regain the initiative.

Hall had hoped the speed and intensity of their attack would have given them the advantage. It hadn't. The numbers had been trimmed down, eliminating the smugglers' advantage, but now the two sides were evened out. It was down to who would make a mistake first.

It appeared that Hall did.

The Smuggler Chief grabbed the shaft of the spear, Hall slow on pulling it out of reach, catching it between the arm and body. He yanked, trying to get Hall off-balance, a wicked grin on his face as he thought he had the fight won.

Hall dropped the spear, the Chief reacting as he wanted. Hall jumped into the air, drawing his short sword. With none of the expected resistance, the Chief was now the one off-balance, stepping backward and trying to stop himself from falling. With sword drawn, Hall landed in front of the Chief and kicked out.

Falling down, the Chief landed hard, the longsword falling from his grasp. Pike swooped in, darting around Hall and shooting a bolt of lightning at the Chief. Smoke curled up from the burn mark on the smuggler's chest, eyes filled with pain. The Chief gasped, spitting up blood, as Hall drove his sword into the man's chest. Pulling the blade out, the Chief coughed up more blood. He tried to stand, gasping, but Hall kicked him hard in the face.

The Smuggler Chief fell down, head smacking hard against the ground, and did not get back up.

Hall turned to survey the battlefield. The cow was moving from the Smuggler Archer he had trampled to death to the one Leigh was holding immobile. That one had ducked down, preventing Leigh from shooting him with more splinters, feeling along the ground for the bow he had dropped. He had a dozen or more splinters sticking out of his body, each bleeding. Roxhard was standing up, his axe dripping blood, the Smuggler Warrior below him unmoving.

Angus ran at the Archer, the man having to stand up and jump out of the cow's way. He moved to the side, bow in hand, reaching for an arrow, tracking Angus who was skidding to a stop and trying to turn around for another charge. The Smuggler Archer screamed as splinters tore his arm to shreds. He stared at the bloody mess of his arm, the ruined and broken bow. Another *Leap* by Hall, sword slicing through the air as he landed, and the last smuggler fell to the ground dead.

SLAIN: *Green Flow Smuggler Warrior*
+10 Experience

SLAIN: *Green Flow Smuggler Chief*
+30 Experience

HELPING KELLY

Smugglers 8/8

Smuggler Chief 1/1

Recovered Ledger 0/1

Skill Gain!

Polearms Rank 2 +.2

Skill Gain!

Light Armor Rank 2 +.2

Leigh stepped out of the woods, Angus rushing to her side. The cow snorted as he passed Hall. Stepping back from the dead body, Hall looked the group over. No injuries that he could see, nothing significant. Roxhard had a haunted look in his eyes as he looked down at the body below him. The Dwarf was breathing hard, more than he should have.

"Come on," Hall said, catching Roxhard's attention. "Let's gather the loot and find that ledger. We could be back in River's Side before dark."

Roxhard shook his head, bringing his focus back. He nodded and bent down to the corpse at his feet, carefully searching.

"Your kill, your loot," Hall told him as he bent down over the body of his shared kill.

The body was a mess. Wooden splinters, three or four inches long, stuck out everywhere. The leather armor was ruined, ripped and torn, not worth salvaging. He stared at the bloody arm. Muscle and flesh wrapped around bone, torn and bloody. Holes cut through it, bones fractured, ligaments and nerves torn. The game mechanics should have hidden most of damage done, turning it into raw numbers and not bloody wounds.

The mechanics had also previously saved them the trouble of searching the bodies themselves.

Trying to avoid the pieces of the Archer, Hall quickly searched the remains. The quiver full of arrows was still good, the bow ruined. He removed the man's boots, searching for hidden compartments. In a hollow heel he found three silver coins. The wrong size, but boots with a hollow heel could still be worth something, he thought, stuffing them into his pouch. Grabbing the Archer's sword, he added it to the pile he was starting with the quiver.

The smugglers had been out hunting. They would have been traveling light so Hall was not surprised there was nothing else to find. He moved onto the Chief.

Struggling to get it off the dead weight of the Chief, he threw the chainmail shirt onto the pile. At the very least it might be worth something to a smith to smelt down. The longsword was decent quality, nothing special. He had no training in the weapon, *Small Blades* versus *Large Blades*, but it would fetch a decent price from a weaponsmith. It went into the growing pile as Leigh and Roxhard added armor pieces and weapons. Daggers, some leather, swords, an axe, a bow, and three quivers of arrows.

Hall removed the Chief's belt. He could feel bulges along its length indicating coins stitched into the leather. A small pouch was attached, feeling heavy. Opening it, he saw a collection of coins, some silver, and the glint of a gold coin or two. Both went into his pouch. The only other thing the Chief had was a ring on his right hand. A simple silver band, no runes or inscriptions. No way to tell if it was magic, not without a Witch's *Scry* spell.

Putting the ring in the pouch with the coins, Hall stood up and moved to the tents. Five total. One for the Chief, the others shared by the eight smugglers. Lifting up the flap, he looked inside. Two bedrolls with blankets, a couple packs, and nothing else. A quick search through the packs found nothing of value. Spare clothes and boots. They got added to the pile along with the bedrolls. Two other tents were the same. The fourth ended up being the Chiefs.

Alongside the single bedroll were two packs and a wooden strongbox. The first pack was extra clothes and a pair of boots, along with various survival gear. Inside the second pack was a map that Hall set aside for the moment and a small leather case. Inside the case were half a dozen small vials made of thick glass with wooden stoppers. Each was filled near to the top with thick liquid. Two were gold, two were light green, and the last two were a light blue color. He recognized them as Minor Potions. Gold would be Health, green had to be Vitality, and blue was Energy. He carefully set the potion case into his pouch, noticing there were straps stitched to the back of the case so it could be threaded through a belt. The leather was thick and stiff, offering good protection for the potions.

He shifted position and brought the strong box closer. A foot long, six inches wide and six inches tall. It was made of oak or some other hard wood, with thin metal straps at the corners and along the top and bottom. The top was hinged with no lock.

No visible lock at any rate.

Picking it up, he took it outside and placed it on the ground in the middle of the camp. Leigh and Roxhard walked over, looking down at it. They had gone through the other tents, and there was a sizable pile of gear. Nothing out of the ordinary, but would still get a decent return when sold back at River's Side.

The real prize was the strong box.

If they could get it open.

"I suppose neither of you has the *Detect Traps* skill?" he asked.

There was no true thief or burglar class in Sky Realms

Online, but a character could, and sometimes needed to be, built for that role using any of the other classes and select skills. Doors, chests, and other items were locked both magically and physically. There was a need for those that could get them open.

"Let me try something," Leigh said.

She motioned everyone away from the chest, leaving it where Hall had placed it. Pike settled on Hall's shoulder, the dragonhawk's weight comforting. He reached up and scratched Pike under the bird's chin where feathers met scales.

Holding out her staff and moving her free hand in a quick gesture, Leigh cast the *Grasping Roots* spell. Hall watched the grass around the box start to grow. It snaked around the box and over the top, roots sliding out of the ground to join them. Ends pushed their way into the thin seam between top and sides, more and more sliding into the space. The grass and roots kept coming, covering the box and pushing the top up. Hall watched as space started to form between the sides and the top, more and more.

The explosion was quick and loud. Flames erupted out of the now open lid, shooting out of the thin crack and curling up five or more feet into the air. From where they stood, they could feel the heat and pressure wave. If he had been standing in front, the explosion would have done a lot of damage, Hall knew, maybe even killing him. He had yet to learn if they could respawn, and had no desire to find out the hard and painful way.

Leigh laid her hand flat and sliced it through the air, ending the spell. The roots and grasses slid back down into the ground, shrinking back to original side. The top of the strongbox was open a crack, smoke curling out.

Stepping forward, Hall reached down and used the tip of his sword to lift the box's lid all the way open. A thick cloud of smoke billowed into the air, borne away by the wind. The inside of the lid was unmarked, clear and unstained wood. No burn marks or evidence of the magical explosion.

Waiting a couple seconds, Hall stepped forward and looked down into the box.

Crouching down, he pulled out a large bag of coins. He shook it, hearing the clink of metal on metal. Opening it up, he poured a dozen gold coins into his hand.

"Nice," he said with a smile.

He handed four coins each to Roxhard and Leigh. Roxhard smiled, putting them in his pouch. Leigh stared at them in surprise.

"Why are you giving them to me?" she asked, reaching down to pat Angus, still looking at the coins.

"You helped get them, you get equal share."

"Thank you," she said, smiling at him.

You have earned +300 Alliance points with Leigh. You are now "FRIENDLY" with Leigh. You could have kept the gold, and she would not have cared, but your willingness to share with her has increased your standing with her.

The only other thing in the box was a small book. Leather-bound, only three inches wide and four inches tall, there was nothing remarkable about it. Opening it up, Hall just saw columns of numbers and random letters. Some kind of accounting and in code.

You have found: Smuggler Chief's Ledger

HELPING KELLY
Smugglers 8/8
Smuggler Chief 1/1
Recovered Ledger 1/1

Putting the ledger into his pouch, Hall stood up. He stretched, working out the muscles that were starting to stiffen. He might not have received any wounds in the last fight, but his body was still sore and tired. He noticed that his Vitality bar was lowered and not regenerating.

Apparently, prolonged fighting would take its toll no matter what. Getting rest was vital.

"Wonder what they were smuggling," he said and stepped over to the pile of bags and crates.

There were only two crates, both small, and a half dozen packs. No wagons or pack animals, the smugglers walked and carried. The crates had leather straps to aid in carrying.

"These tents could come in handy," Roxhard said and moved to start taking them down.

He was right. That was one thing they had not gotten yet. Tents were expensive and neither minded sleeping under the stars, but there was no reason to not use the ones left by the smugglers.

Leigh walked over next to Hall. She knelt down and opened one of the bags.

"I can't think of anything that is illegal in Essec that would be worth smuggling," she said, working to untie the knot.

"Most likely trying to avoid the taxes," Hall replied and grabbed another bag.

The crates were nailed shut, and they could not open them here. It would have to wait or get left behind.

"You're right," Leigh said and pulled out a pile of thick hides. There was fur attached, rough and long, white in color.

"Crag Cat," Hall said, recognizing the material.

Large animals that roamed the foothills and mountains in the lower down and colder realms. The hides were prized for their ability to retain heat. They made excellent winter cloaks and boots. But being from Storvgarde, they were heavily taxed when brought into Essec.

His bag contained more furs, small pieces like Leighs. Crag Cat and what looked like Dire Wolf.

Shaking a crate, he could hear the sound of glass clinking.

"I bet this is Highborn Vale wine."

Like the hides from Storvgarde, any goods brought in from the Highborn Confederacy were heavily taxed. This made the goods rarer and commanded a higher price. If a merchant could get goods in without paying the taxes, they'd make a substantial profit instead of just a good one. More than enough to offset paying the smugglers and any bribes that might be needed.

Highborn were a branch of the Elven race. Paler of skin and hair color compared to their cousins the Woodborn, or Wood Elf, they were also far more cultured than their cousins. At least, as they saw it. Player Elves were Woodborn. Sophisticated in their tastes and culture, the Highborn thought of themselves as just that, higher than the other races. Their art, as well as their wine, were highly sought after and prized.

"How much do you think is here?" Roxhard asked.

"A lot," Hall said. He did some quick math in his head. Not knowing the current prices or the style of wine, he thought a bottle was twenty gold easily. The hides were five or so gold. There was a good size amount of money sitting in front of them.

And they couldn't take any of it with them.

"We can't bring any of this into River's Side," he said with a sigh.

"Why not?" Roxhard asked, pausing as he went to put a bag into his pouch.

"They'll arrest us for being smugglers," Leigh replied. She closed up the bag, redoing the knot.

"But it was Watchmen Kelly that sent us here," Roxhard protested.

"To eliminate the competition," Hall said, standing up. He

looked around, trying to see past the trees, examining the surrounding land.

He unrolled the map he had found. It was the island of Cumberland with key points marked and notations. A thin line started in the mountains to the southeast of Grayhold and continued up to locations slightly east of Land's Edge Port, avoiding the roads, towns, and any patrolled areas. The smugglers route. It made sense to start near Grayhold. Too many guards and watchers at Land's Edge Port, and Cumberland was the closest island to Edin, and Edin was closest to the Highborn's main island of Arundel. Shorter routes and distances made it easier to avoid the Essec and Highborn patrols.

"What?" Roxhard asked. "She's a smuggler? But she's an Essec Guard."

"I don't know for sure," Hall told him, picking up one of the bags. "But it makes sense. Come on, let's see if we can find a place to hide this stuff. Might be able to come back for it later."

CHAPTER SIXTEEN

They found a small hollow below a large oak alongside some boulders. No evidence of an animal using it and with decent protection from the weather. Marking the location on his map, they filled it with the bags and crates. Hall had expected Leigh to protest but she didn't.

She was like no other Druid he had met.

Followers of the World Tree, believers in the natural order of things, they were strict on non-interference in the goings-on between the kingdoms unless it impacted the natural world. Leigh should have been rushing to go to the Grove on Edin and not as interested in the smugglers or Hall's sidequest, which was delaying her journey to the Grove. Druids were also known to be aloof and otherworldly, not quite in this existence. While nature itself was considered chaotic, Druids, as guardians of that chaos, were very orderly and structured. Druids were not the storms, they were the trees that stood tall in the storms. Unbending, roots deep in the ground, protecting the rest of the forest from the storm's rage.

"You're not like other Druids," he said again as they made

their way back through the forest after hiding the smuggler's loot.

Leigh laughed. Hall was discovering that he liked her laugh. There was a freedom to it.

"And why is that?" she asked. "Not as stuffy or rigid?"

"That," Hall answered with a laugh of his own. "And there's Angus," he finished with a nod to the small cow that trotted along between them.

For his part, Angus looked up at the mention of his name, eyes lost behind the fur, and snorted.

Leigh looked off into the forest, studying the trees and the small animals moving through them.

"Most Druids hear the calling," she started, hand moving down to scratch behind Angus' ears. "I didn't," she said, regret in her voice. "I come from a small village, Cliff Fields. It's a couple days northeast of Auld. We were very poor. My parents had a lot of kids, of which I was the youngest. Papa was a Cooper, and there wasn't much call for that in our area. My older brothers worked in the shop, my older sisters worked with mother. Small village, not much in the way of marriage prospects. My sisters were already engaged, and there wasn't much hope for me. One day, a Druid came through the village. Old and frail, needing help. I helped, and it was discovered I had an affinity for Nature Magic."

She held up her hand, moving her fingers, as if remembering the first time she had used magic. Angus snorted that he was no longer getting scratched. She smiled and returned to the scratching and her story. Hall was fascinated. It sounded like the backstory a Player would have come up with, not an NPC.

"The Druid needed an apprentice. My parents needed a place for me. So, I was sent with the Druid. Problem solved." She shrugged. There was no bitterness or weary acceptance. It seemed she was at peace with what had happened. "I did end up having the calling. I love nature and want to protect it, preserve the Branches, the aspects of the World Tree that grow in the Groves, and I'm skilled at Nature Magic. But the rest of it, I just never felt like I belonged. The Elders sent me to the Grove on Edin hoping it would help me find the way, as they put it."

She loved being a Druid, just not necessarily the way it happened or how she was supposed to behave. Hall understood. Some organizations and followings had no room or acceptance for free thinkers. Follow the routine, the rules. Leigh was obviously not like that. In the short time he had known her, Hall knew Leigh to be more like the storm and not the tree. Like him, she went with the flow of what was happening around her.

"So that's why I'm not in a real hurry," she continued. "I feel kind of forced to go to the Grove, like it's supposed to change me. I'll go and see what is happening but…," she trailed off with a shrug.

Hall nodded, understanding. In a way, she was rebelling, using the delay to hold off on what the Druids were trying to push her into. Her sense of responsibility would make her go but she would do it on her own time and her own way. Delaying what was being forced on her.

Again, Hall was struck by how more Player like she was. The Players back in the Laughing Horse had been right. The new AI was amazing.

"And Angus," Hall prompted a minute or so later. "Not what I'm used to seeing for a companion."

"He's not, is he," she said, smiling down at the cow, giving a hard scratch under his chin. The cow actually smiled, large tongue hanging out. "He comes from a herd kept at Cliff Fields. Always been friendly with me, and when I left, he escaped the herd and followed. Instead of turning around and returning him, I decided he could come." Angus mooed, a happy sound. Leigh laughed. "Not like the wolves or bears a Druid normally has but he does all right."

Hall thought about the smugglers the cow had attacked, the one that had gotten a horn in the chest and the other that had been trampled. Not a wolf or a bear, but Angus definitely did all right.

He looked back over his shoulder where Roxhard was following behind. He carried two packs filled with the looted gear of the smugglers while Hall and Leigh each carried one. The Dwarf was lagging a bit, staring down at the ground. Something was bothering him. Hall had caught Roxhard looking at Leigh a couple times and knew a crush when he saw one. Was that bothering him now, or was it the killing of the smugglers? A combination of both?

Hall was an only child. He had no idea how to deal with a younger brother.

———

They crossed the bridge an hour or so later, the sun setting before them. A red sky, a beautiful sunset. They weren't challenged at the gates, which remained open. Hall was glad they had made it in time before the gates were closed for the night. He hadn't wanted to try to talk their way in. He had a feeling that Watchman Kelly probably wouldn't like it, especially if his suspicions were true.

Kelly was walking out of the barracks as they approached. She caught sight of them and motioned to follow. Walking around the corner of the building, she stopped in the space between the barracks and the wall.

"Well?" she asked.

Reaching into his pouch, Hall pulled out the ledger and handed it over.

QUEST COMPLETE!

You have removed the smuggler gang and given the Ledger to
Watchman Kelly.

SPECIAL DELIVERY

Reward: +200 Alliance with Guard Captain Henry, +500 Alliance with
Watchman Kelly,
+50 Experience

You have gained **LEVEL 3**!
You have gained +1 Attribute Point to spend.
You have accessed a new Class Ability: Leaping Stab Rank 1
See a Class Trainer to learn your new Ability.

THE FIRST TRAINER I

You have accessed a new Class Ability. Visit a Skirmisher Trainer to
unlock the Leaping
Stab Ability.
Reward: +50 Experience

ACCEPT QUEST?

Hall smiled. A new Class Ability was always good and
Leaping Stab was one of his favorites. It allowed him to stab out
with his spear as he was leaping into the air. The first rank
allowed one thrust. Higher ranks would grant more attacks
during a single leap. Abilities, like Skills, came in Ranks. Each
Rank would grant new bonuses to the abilities. With Skills, the
Ranks would grant titles as well as access to new recipes and
patterns. Ability Rank increases came at set character levels
while Skill Ranks increased with Skill use and gains.

The part about having to see a Trainer was new. Or, more
accurately, old. When Sky Realms Online had first launched, all
Class Abilities had to be learned from a Trainer. Years later, in

one of the patches, they had removed that requirement in a move to make the game more casual. It seemed like it was back. Not a big deal, Hall thought, just would mean having to find a Trainer.

Hall glanced at Roxhard to see if the Dwarf had leveled. Nothing seemed to show that he had. The Smuggler Chief had been worth a lot of experience compared to other kills, that was probably the difference. It didn't appear that Leigh had leveled either.

Kelly was quickly flipping through the Ledger, trying to read it in the dark. The high walls of River's Side completely blocked out the last rays of the setting sun, making the space dark with shadows. The guard couldn't really see anything.

"Yeah," she said finally, smiling. "This is it."

She slipped the Ledger into a small pouch on her belt. She looked up at Hall, waiting.

"Was there anything else there?" she asked after a bit.

"No," Hall answered with a shrug.

She glanced at the packs they were all carrying, raising an eyebrow in question. Hall just shrugged again.

"Whatever," Kelly said with a smile. "Helps us out more if the stuff never turns up," she added with a glance.

Hall nodded, understanding. She was saying to not sell the smuggler's goods anywhere in Essec. With the loss of that shipment, it meant whatever she and Guard Captain Henry were able to smuggle into Grayhold would be in that much greater demand.

"Yeah, you get it," Kelly said with a nod.

You have earned +300 Alliance points with Watchman Kelly. She appreciates your silent understanding of the situation. It would be easy to reveal her operation, and she respects you for not doing that.

"Thanks again," Kelly said. "Henry said I should take a

chance on you and looks like he was right. Don't have any additional work right now, but once you get settled, seek out a merchant in Land's Edge Port named Marken or one in Auld on Edin named Dyson. I'll send word to them to keep an eye out for you."

Hall thanked her, and Kelly walked away back toward the front of the barracks. They turned the other way, back toward the River's Fall. He didn't understand what she meant by settled, but having the contacts would come in handy. He wasn't sure he wanted to get involved in a smuggling operation. Not that deeply, anyway. More options for the future was good, though.

Stepping back onto the streets, they saw the shops closing for the night. Any attempt at selling the loot would have to wait until tomorrow. That was fine with Hall. He was tired and looking forward to a good meal and comfortable bed.

"Long time, no see," a voice said from behind and to the side. One he recognized.

Turning he saw the Witch, Sabine, walking toward them. She was smiling and dressed differently. The robe she wore was tight, form fitting, but one piece. There were long slits up the sides, exposing upper thighs, and long flared sleeves covered her arms. The neckline was still plunging, a necklace with a large jewel visible, but the material looked thicker and sturdier than what he had last seen her in. Knee-high leather boots finished her new look. She carried a smooth wooden staff topped in a jewel. It was hard to make out colors and details in the dark.

She turned a full circle, arms out.

"Like the new look?" she asked. "Turns out that a Witch's starting outfit really isn't that useful for adventuring in the forest."

Hall laughed. Most of the armor in the game had not been

designed with environment or weather in mind. It was designed for aesthetics only, not practicality.

"How have you been?" he asked. "Where have you been?"

"Around. After that first day I went out into the wilds. Got a quest to kill some wolves and found a lot of herbs. Made some skill gains, but more importantly, I was able to get some money. Upgraded my gear and headed out to see what I could discover about our new world. You?"

"The same pretty much," Hall answered. Even though they had only interacted for a brief conversation, he was glad to see her. "Working on a couple quests. Heading out tomorrow."

Sabine nodded and glanced at Roxhard and Leigh, who she studied longer. She looked down at Angus with a frown. Hall wished Pike was on his shoulder and not in the trees outside of town. He wanted to show off his Companion, which he found odd. He was not a bragger, but for some reason he wanted to impress Sabine. He immediately thought of Leigh. He wanted to impress her as well, but didn't feel the need to brag. Hall wondered what was different between the two women.

"Roxhard," he said, introducing the Dwarf. He saw recognition flash through her eyes. Hall hoped she wouldn't say anything about Roxhard's behavior the first day in the Laughing Horse. She didn't. "And this is Leigh, a Druid of the Tree. We were heading to the Inn for dinner. Want to join us?"

Roxhard nodded, and Hall worried the Dwarf might develop another crush. Or maybe he was happy Sabine was around, which could take Hall's attention away from Leigh? For her part, Leigh did not look eager to have Sabine join them. But she didn't protest.

"Sounds good," Sabine replied, moving to walk next to Hall with Leigh on the other side.

———

"I sent you a mail," Hall said after the meal and first round of drinks had appeared. "Never heard back, was wondering how you were."

"Didn't get it until I checked the post office here in River's Side," Sabine replied. "I was going to write you back before I left tomorrow." She took a drink of her wine, a red. "Weird that we have to actually physically receive the mail, right?"

Hall shrugged. He hadn't really thought about it as Sabine was the only one he had sent anything to and couldn't think of a reason anyone would send a letter to him.

"How else would the post work?" Leigh asked. Sabine ignored her.

"That's not the only thing," she said, leaning in closer, excited. "When out adventuring with Roxhard, were you partied up?"

"No," Hall replied. "Didn't even think of it." *Which was odd*, he thought. That was a normal thing, almost automatic, to do when heading out with someone else.

"I tried the morning after we met when we went looking for the Goblins," Roxhard said. "But there was no tab or command that I could find. Gave up and it just slipped my mind. Had forgotten all about that until now."

"But you were able to share the quest?" Sabine asked.

"Yeah," Roxhard said. "I got the later part when we got to that spot, not the first part that Hall had which started the chain."

"Hold on," Hall said, his mug stopping midway as the thought occurred to him. "How did the post even know you'd be here?"

Sabine sat back, surprised.

"I don't know," she replied. "That is very strange. It's like some aspects of the game mechanics are kept and the rest are as if the world was real. Haven't you noticed how this world feels so," she paused, thinking of the right word, looking up at the ceiling and then the hearth before returning her gaze to Hall, "more real?"

He thought about it and realized she was right. When playing Sky Realms Online, he had known it was a game, everything computer generated. But now? It had never looked completely real, obviously a computer program. Ever since the glitch, or the patch, or whatever it really was, he had noticed that everything had more life. More definition, like the bloody wounds he had seen and left on monsters and enemies. He thought of the Smuggler Archer's arm torn to shreds. He thought of the actions of NPCs he had encountered, less confined to parameters set by programming and more free thinking.

"The mail from Electronic Storm said it's been two years," Roxhard pointed out. "Better tech."

"No way," Sabine said. "Trust me, I work-" She paused. Sadness and confusion passed through her eyes before she started speaking again. "I *used* to work, I guess, in the industry. There is no way the tech advanced that fast in two years."

"I agree. It seems real. It seems true," Hall said. "But if it's not tech, then what is it?"

"I don't know."

Hall thought back to their first, and previously only, conversation. The Duelist, Cuthard, had said they were stuck in the game, nothing really different. Sabine had asked if he agreed, and he had said that he wasn't sure. Something was telling him that this was real. Even if they were just bits of data saved on a server, it felt and seemed real. It looked and smelled and felt real.

"The Inn looks pretty full," Sabine said after a while.

They had finished the meal and started in on their second round of drinks. Leigh was still drinking ale where Sabine had started her second glass of wine.

"We managed to get a room earlier," Roxhard said quickly. "It's got four beds, and there's only three of us."

"Are you inviting me to spend the night with you?" Sabine said with a smile directly toward Roxhard.

The Dwarf coughed and sputtered, spitting out his drink. Both Sabine and Leigh laughed. Roxhard just looked embarrassed.

"You can have the last bed," Hall told her.

"Thank you."

———

The moon shone through the room's glass filled window. The shutters were pulled to block out most of the light but some still crept in through the cracks in the boards. The beds were comfortable, four of them with two to a side and a small hearth at the far end of the room. There had been no need to stoke the fire, the blankets provided were enough.

Hall stared up at the rough beam ceiling. The two women were silent while Roxhard was snoring. He had his Character Sheet open, looking through his Attributes and Skills. He was doing pretty well, he thought. A strong mix of Skills that gave him some versatility and damage along with the means of making some money. He wasn't sure about *Cartography* yet, but had until after they discovered the treasure to decide. Would Sabine be interested in going with them? He allocated his new Attribute point to Willpower. He would need an increase in Energy once he had *Leaping Stab* trained.

With a thought, he closed the sheet.

He was approaching leveling with a new mindset, he realized. Before it had been all about what skills and stats would best aid him in combat. Now there were other concerns. Even if they were just bits of data, the world was vastly different. It wasn't about just combat anymore. All the roleplaying skills and abilities would now have a purpose.

It meant a new way of thinking and playing, or more accurately living, the game.

He rolled over on his side. Leigh had the bed next to his. She was on her side, sleeping and facing him. He studied the lines of her face in the moonlight. He realized that he had been wrong before. Leigh's features were unique, not similar to any other NPCs he had seen. He had thought her pretty but he was discovering she was far more beautiful than he had first thought.

To save server space, the developers had used repeated looks for the non-essential NPCs, the ones that weren't unique or vital to the various storylines. He had thought some of her appearance to be shared among other NPCs, but that was wrong. She was uniquely Leigh. The more he thought about it, the more he realized he had not seen a single repeated look since arriving in the Portal Room at the Laughing Horse. Just like in reality, here everyone was different.

More evidence that this new world, new version of the game, was different. Was real.

Leigh's eyes opened, and she looked at him. She smiled.

He smiled back.

CHAPTER SEVENTEEN

Morning came, sunlight replacing the moonlight through the cracks in the shutters.

Hall woke at first light. His movements, not quiet enough, soon woke the two women. Leigh was up first, stretching and yawning. Her curly red hair was a mess, sticking up in all directions. It took her a couple minutes to somewhat smooth it down. Sabine was more graceful, her hair already presentable. Roxhard kept snoring until Hall kicked his bed.

The four made their way down to the common room where breakfast was ordered. Roxhard tried to get an ale but a stern look from Hall had him switching to juice like the others.

"You said you were heading out this morning," Sabine asked as she finished up her plate and pushed it out of the way. "Where are you going?"

"Have a couple quests," Hall answered. "After finishing one up in the mountains to the North, we're heading to Edin to help Leigh."

Sabine stared down at the table, quiet and not as confident as she normally appeared to be. She sighed and looked up, not focusing on any of them.

"The last few weeks have been rough," she admitted. "When I first set out from Grayhold I went out with a couple of other Players. I wish I had managed to find you," she said to Hall. "I feel like I can trust you. Those others I couldn't. They weren't…" she paused and shook her head sadly. "They weren't good people."

Hall waited for her to say more but she didn't, lost in her private thoughts. He wondered what exactly had happened. Players of the game ran the full length and breadth of humanity. There were some that lived out fantasies, good and bad, and there were some that were angels while others were more devils. Luckily, that was the smaller percentage of players, but they were the loudest. Hall had discovered that was common on the internet, the loudest people were often the worst.

"Long story short," Sabine continued, once again focusing on Hall. "If I could, I'd like to tag along with you guys. I really don't want to be alone out there anymore."

It didn't take long for Hall to make his decision. He had liked Sabine from the start, and he didn't think it was just because of her good-looking avatar. No one judged anyone on looks alone in the Sky Realms game as all Players were near-perfect physical specimens. In a world where everyone, the Players at least, were all handsome and beautiful, it took more to judge a person.

"I'm good with that," Hall answered. "But not up to just me."

He had noticed that everyone, now even Sabine, was deferring to his judgement. He had hated being the Raid Leader the couple times he had done it. He was good at it, had received lots of compliments, but being the leader was not something he desired.

"Yeah, I'm good," Roxhard said quickly. Too quickly. He hadn't really thought it through, just followed Hall's lead.

Hall looked at Leigh. She had been watching the conversation, not joining in. Now she was surprised to be included.

"You're asking me?" she asked, looking at Hall.

"You're part of the group," he answered.

He saw the quick look of surprise and confusion that passed across Sabine's face. She knew that Leigh was not a Player, so must have not been expecting Hall to treat her like she was one. He wondered how many NPCs Sabine had interacted with and if she knew how less restricted by programming they were now. Or was there now going to be Player prejudice against NPCs? It would be something he'd have to keep an eye on if Sabine was going to journey with them. As far as he was concerned, Leigh was an equal.

You have earned +500 Alliance points with Leigh. She is surprised to be included as a full member of the group. She knows she is along because you agreed to help her with her quest. By including her as part of the group, she feels closer to you.

That caught him by surprise. So far, there had been no mention or discussion between Player and NPC about their statuses. He had wondered if the NPCs even realized there was a difference. Was there even a difference? They were people, and if he was really trapped in this world with them, he was going to have to start thinking of them that way. He already thought of Leigh as a person, he would have to add all the other NPCs to that thinking as well. He was as computer generated as they were now.

"Yeah," Leigh said, still shocked. "I'm fine with that. A Witch is always handy to have around."

"Thank you," Sabine said smiling, relieved.

Hall wondered what had really happened to her since he had last seen her that first day.

———

"Have you noticed how few Players there are?" Sabine asked as they exited the gate, following the road toward the west and the main road that led to Land's Edge Port. "Besides you two, I haven't seen any others here, and River's Side used to be busy."

"Last time I saw any were down in Grayhold a week or more ago," Hall said as he looked over the people in River's Side. They were all NPCs, people he amended. Merchants, shop keeps and guards. "And there was only a dozen or so that first day in the Laughing Horse."

"Doesn't seem like many," Sabine added. "Twenty million or so players, right? So, say a couple million playing at a single time. How many were caught in the glitch like we were? I don't know. A dozen just seems a small amount."

He hadn't thought about it but she had a point. There should have been hundreds appearing in the Laughing Horse like they had. The low number didn't fit with the ratios. There were a lot of people playing. Even something random like that glitch should have affected more, and it didn't make sense for Electronic Storm to upload just some of them at a time.

"Grayhold isn't the only starting zone," Roxhard pointed out.

Which was true. Each of the five races, eight if you included the three Human races, had their own starting zone. But Hall had noticed Dwarves, Elves, Firbolgs, and Bodin in The Laughing Horse, were at level one. They should have been in their own zones. He pointed that out.

"That's what makes it even weirder," Sabine said. "Did anyone even appear in those other starting zones, and if so, why did Roxhard appear at Grayhold? I saw a Firbolg, and there was that Elf, Cut-something or other."

A single wagon pulled by two horses came down the road

toward them. They stepped off the road and let the wagon pass. As busy as the sideroad to River's Side usually was, it was still only one wagon wide. Hall took the time to pull out the treasure map. He compared the landmarks on that map to his own and made some marks on his.

Skill Gain!
Cartography Rank 2 +.2

It looked like they could follow the road north for two days before heading through the forest toward the mountains. It would be about four days of hard traveling to reach the base of the mountains. They could go overland right away but it would be slower going, adding at least a day. Hall decided that sticking to the road made sense for now.

The wagon passed, they had started back on their way, when Pike appeared through the trees. With a screech, the dragonhawk darted down. Hall felt wind against his face, moving his hair and his cloak, as Pike hovered and settled down on his shoulder. He felt the weight of the dragonhawk and the sharp edge of the talons as Pike shifted and sat.

"You've got your Companion already," Sabine exclaimed. "We aren't supposed to get those until level ten." As a Witch she would get a familiar as her Companion. It could come as a cat, raven, lizard, or frog.

"I know," Hall said. "I was surprised. Found him in a box buried in a bunch of stuff some Goblins had stolen from merchants." He reached up and scratched under Pikes chin. "No quest or training either. Found him and he bonded."

"I hope that means I get mine soon," Sabine said, a little jealous. Familiars were different for Witches than other Companions were for the other classes. For a Witch, the familiar acted like a buff for her spells.

"I'm going to be the only one without a Companion," Roxhard grumbled.

"You can help me take care of Angus," Leigh said, leaning down and putting her arm around the Dwarf. She gave him a squeeze. Roxhard turned bright red, the part of his face that was not covered in hair anyway. She pointed over at the cow.

Angus was standing in the middle of the road, a large patty dropping onto the dirt.

They all laughed.

———

The two nights were spent just off the road, sheltered by trees or rocks. Both passed uneventfully. They had managed to sell some of the common items they had been collecting and had taken from the smugglers, getting a decent profit, which had gone into repairing their weapons and armor as well as restocking their supplies. Hall had sold off a small bit of the items they had gotten from the Goblins, keeping Guard Captain Henry's warning in mind.

That morning, he directed the small group off the road. He set a northeast course, hoping to arrive where the treasure map showed the trail entering the mountains. This part of Cumberland was still heavily forested but had more hills. They rose and fell, the smaller still covered in trees and some that probably should have really been mountains with exposed tops. They heard wolves in the night, other animals throughout the day. Small rivers and brooks flowed through the area, some wide that required finding a place to cross, but most small enough to jump over.

It was peaceful enough, pleasant hiking, but Hall still kept a guard. These woods were wild, unpatrolled, and home to things besides just Goblins.

They found the ruins midway through their second day in the woods.

A single tower was built on the top of a lone hill. Steep sides of exposed rock rose up fifty or more feet above the forest floor, putting it a good distance above the tops of the trees. Only their low angle and the thick leafy canopy had prevented them from seeing the tower. From below, they could just make out a crumbling ring wall around the stones of the building. They never would have noticed it at all if not for Pike, who had spotted it from the air.

Hall used his bond with the dragonhawk and the *Shared Vision* ability to examine the tower. He didn't allow Pike to fly too close, not wanting any harm to come to the dragonhawk.

The ring wall surrounded the tower, about ten feet or higher, crumbling in many places that had once been a thick and formidable defense. There was one opening in the wall, wide enough for a wagon, the wood of the gate long rotted away. The wall and the tower were both made of large blocks of a white stone. The tower was fifty feet tall, thick at the base and tapering slightly to the flat and open top. There appeared to be posts along the top of the wall that would have once held up a wooden roof and shingles. While the wall was crumbling, most of it was still in place, and the tower was sturdy-looking with only a couple gaps in the round walls.

Looking down from above, Hall could see what appeared to be a trail cut into the side of the hill, which wrapped around the sides.

Telling the others about the trail, they started walking around the base of the hill looking for it. None of them thought about moving past the tower. They, except for possibly Leigh, knew what a lone tower in the middle of a forest meant. Loot, or at least a quest.

It didn't take long to find the trail, a few brambles and bushes hiding the starting point. Once cleared, the trail was only about six feet wide, a gentle slope cut into the hill and spiraling around. Not wide enough for a wagon, but no problem for a mount or mounts in single file.

Being so low level, Hall hadn't even been thinking about a mount yet. Typically, they were available at level 25, for the first one. Expensive, though, in the cost of the mount as well as the training. Mounts were useful, and besides the basic starting one – typically a horse for Humans – there were a lot of special mounts that were available.

As they made their way up the trail, he wondered if mounts had changed at all.

They were shown a spectacular view as they walked past the treetops. Even from this height, not the top, they could see for miles. Cumberland was relatively flat, allowing an unobstructed view. The green canopy of the trees looked like an ocean, spreading out in all directions. The road a couple days away was visible as a thin dark line through the canopy, like a small brook. The tower of River's Side was barely visible once they reached the top of the trail, coming onto the flat top of the hill.

That was when the Boarin attacked.

CHAPTER EIGHTEEN

THE PARTY HAD CRESTED THE TOP, THE TRAIL ENDING WITH A slight turn onto the hill. There was ten feet or so of space between the cliff and the base of the wall, the open gate directly before them. Seeing nothing immediate, they had all turned to look out over the forest and the view.

Only the screech of Pike circling in the air saved them.

Hall turned and instinctively leapt into the air. He twisted to face the wall and saw three Boarin rushing from the opening. Large creatures, eight feet tall and heavily muscled, they resembled humanoid boars. Short legs ending in hooves, long bodies and long arms with thick fingers. The head was massive, seemingly out of proportion with the rest of the body. Small and dark eyes, small ears growing off the top of the skull, which was long and thick, ending in a snout and mouth with two tusks. Covered in thick and bristly fur, each Boarin had a ring through the nose and wore leather kilts. Straps crisscrossed their chests, each carrying a large sword and shield.

For such large creatures, they moved silently.

They were too close for Roxhard to use his *Battle Rush* ability but he managed to get in position in front of the two women. He caught the swing of the closest Boarin's sword on his axe, grunting as the taller and heavier creature pushed down with all of its considerable weight and strength.

Hall landed behind the rushing creatures and turned, stabbing with his spear. He wished he had managed to train the *Leaping Stab* ability. He hated knowing he should have been able to attack while in mid-leap and not being able to do it yet.

His thrust caught the trailing Boarin in the side. It had seen Hall leaping, stopped its run, and started to turn. Just in time to catch the point of the spear. Boarin wore no armor but their hide was naturally tough. The tip punched through the hide, doing some damage. The large creature grunted, reaching for the spear shaft, hoping to snap it, but Hall pulled it back out of range quickly.

Leigh moved her free hand quickly, chanting. Beside her, Sabine held her staff in both hands, her mouth moving in a silent chant. Lines of purple energy were climbing up the staff from where her hands gripped it. They reached the stone at the top of her staff, causing it to glow the same purple color.

Roxhard stepped to the side, using his axe to push the Boarin's sword wide. He shifted his grip and swung the axe to the other side, catching the second Boarin's sword strike. He stepped away from the edge and the two women, giving them some more space. He had no inner conflict about this fight. Boarin were evil creatures, caring nothing for innocents, just caring about gaining strength.

Done her casting, Leigh willed the scrub grass at the feet of the left Boarin to start to grow. She could feel the roots of some long ago cleared trees beneath the surface of the hill. At her prodding, they grew, forcing their way toward the surface. The roots pushed through the hard ground at the feet of the Boarin, spiraling tightly around its feet. The monster roared, trying to shift its fighting stance but could not.

Three thin and straight lines of energy shot out from

Sabine's staff. Crackling like lightning, flickering shades of purple, each bolt slammed into a Boarin. The creatures roared in pain, the *Hexbolt* dealing damage and dealing a curse to each. Smoke curled up from the creatures' chests where the bolt hit. The curse took effect, causing a debuff to the Boarin's attack in the form of a loss in Agility. Pain shot through their bodies, spiraling out from their chests where the bolt had struck. As each tried to move, pain would lance down the leg or arm, causing short spasms.

Hall stabbed with the spear, catching the Boarin in the stomach, drawing blood. He swiped the tip, cutting a line across the creature's chest and stepped back. He swung the spear around, using his body as a pivot and stabbed out again. The Boarin had reached to its right, following the spear and did not get it's shield up in time to block the second attack. Hall pulled the spear back, planted the butt end in the ground and used it like a pole. He jumped above a thrust from the Boarin's sword and kicked out. The large creature barely stumbled with the impact. Hall felt it through his body.

He wouldn't be doing that again.

Landing, he jumped backward, putting more space between him and the Boarin. A purple bolt of lightning slammed into the creature's chest. It roared in pain and swung again but streaks of purple energy crackled around its body causing it to grunt in pain. Its attack was weaker, missing easily. It tried to avoid Hall's next attack and couldn't. The spear pierced its hide, cutting deep.

The Boarin to Roxhard's left stumbled, stuck by the roots. He stepped away, putting more space between him and it, not wanting to have to pay attention to the things attacks while dealing with the one in front of him. He blocked a sword swing with the handle of his double-bladed axe, swinging at the Boarin's side and getting blocked by the shield.

With Roxhard out of the way, Leigh cast her *Splinter Storm* attack. Inch-long splinters shot out from her staff, catching the trapped Boarin in the chest. It growled and tried to run toward her, still trapped. Sabine pointed a finger at the Boarin and cast *Shadowbolt*. A thin line of solid black energy shot out from the finger and at the Boarin striking it in the chest. Where the energy impacted looked like a wet mark, a spill, but expanding and spreading along the creature's chest. It clutched at its chest with the shield arm, growling in pain as the spell drained it of lifeforce. It swung its sword at the Witch, too far away to do any harm, its arm twitching as the purple energy encircled it.

Roxhard ducked, using his smaller size to his advantage. He got under the Boarin's shield and swung up with all his strength. He was small but built like a rock, his Dwarven heritage of centuries of mining granting him great strength. The axe pierced the Boarin's hide, cutting deep. The creature stumbled backward and Roxhard reversed his swing. The axe swung to the side and into the Boarin's sword arm. Not a strong attack because of the angle it was still enough to cut nerves and making the Boarin drop its sword.

He set his feet and pushed the Boarin off-balance. It stumbled back a couple of feet. Roxhard used his *Battle Rush* and slammed into the Boarin. A short distance, not far enough to build up full momentum, it was still enough to knock the already off-balance Boarin to the ground. On its back, unable to attack, Roxhard swung down with his axe striking a critical blow. The Boarin lay unmoving.

Hall thrust again and caught the Boarin in the shoulder. It dropped its sword, its arm going numb. He slammed the butt end of the spear into the creature's throat. It reached up to clutch at the wound, and the spear stabbed through its chest and out the back. It stumbled forward, lurching more as Hall pulled the spear out. He stabbed up and caught it underneath the chin. The spear pierced hide, bone, and into the brain. It fell backward, the spear pulling out, and landed on the ground.

Sabine and Leigh backed up a couple steps, the roots around the Boarin's legs falling back to the ground. The spell's duration had run out. It reached toward them, both backing off, the near constant swing of the sword keeping Angus at bay. They turned their heads as bits of Boarin flew through the air as the spear tip burst out from its throat. The creature reached up, running its hands along the shaft before realizing it was dead. It sagged down to the ground, and Hall yanked the spear out.

"Yuck," Sabine said, wiping a bit of Boarin blood off her face.

SLAIN: *Crush Hold Boarin Warrior*
+30 Experience

SLAIN: *Crush Hold Boarin Warrior*
+10 Experience

Skill Gain!
Polearms Rank 2 +.5

"Aren't the Crush Hold Boarin level ten?" Roxhard asked, giving his axe a flick to get the last of the blood off the heads. "These should have crushed us, not us them."

"It's like the Ogres," Hall said as he looked up into the sky and the circling Pike. The dragonhawk was seeing no more monsters, these three having been hidden in the shadows of the wall before. If there had been more, then they would have attacked by now. "What should have been higher level creatures were lower level."

"What are you talking about?" Leigh asked.

Hall looked at Roxhard and Sabine, wondering how to explain it to Leigh when he didn't fully understand himself. *You're a computer program in a game that we've been playing for years, only now we've been reset to low level again and are apparently computer programs ourselves.* That sounded nice and sane, he thought. Surprisingly, she saved him the trouble.

"The Crush Hold Boarin have always been around level four, some getting up to eight or nine, and only the chief's at level ten. Those ogres were only level three."

The three players exchanged shocked expressions.

"You know about levels," Sabine asked.

"Of course," Leigh answered, her tone wondering just what kind of idiots she had attached herself to. "Everyone does. Everyone has levels, including monsters. Most just end up around three or four, but there are some that get up to the maximum of twenty."

Hall was shocked. Even though NPCs had levels, it was always for game mechanics only. Their levels only meant how strong they were and remained unchanged.

"You mean, everyone can level up?" Roxhard asked.

Leigh rolled her eyes. "That's what I said."

"The only NPC that I've heard could level was Bastian," Sabine said.

"Don't say that name," Leigh shouted, surprising them all.

"Why not?" Sabine asked, exchanging confused glances with Roxhard.

"Because," Leigh started to say before Hall interrupted.

"Wait, you said maximum level of twenty?"

He had been level one hundred in the game, with NPCs in the zones relatively the same level as the Players. One hundred was the maximum level a player could get at that time. Not twenty. That was so low, and most players could get that in a week or two easily. Even casual players could reach twenty in a month.

"Yes," Leigh said slowly and patiently, like explaining to a child. "I have heard of some getting to level twenty-five but that is extremely rare. I've never met anyone higher than twenty and that was only the Great Elder, the leader of the Druid Order."

Hall tried to digest what he had just learned. The maximum level was twenty, or twenty-five for a select few, and only a few people ever got that high. That part made sense. Most people lived somewhat unadventurous lives. They didn't quest or fight monsters for experience so they would naturally level slowly. Even guards and others that engaged in combat didn't do it often enough to really level fast. Only adventurers would do that, and that didn't seem to be an occupation that many chose in this new world.

"The zones were always set up in level ranges," Sabine protested. "How does that work?"

"What's a zone?" Leigh asked, looking at Sabine like she was speaking a foreign language.

"This," the Witch answered, spreading her arms to indicate everything around them. "Cumberland."

"This is a realm, not a zone," Leigh clarified. "Realms don't control levels."

Hall saw that Roxhard and Sabine were having a hard time dealing with this new information. Each looked like they wanted to protest, to argue. He wasn't sure why he didn't. He'd always been pretty easy going, not letting surprises disrupt his life. There were so few things he could control so he tried not to worry about the things he couldn't. This was something he couldn't. It was what it was.

He glanced up at the sun, seeing where it was in the sky. They still had a couple hours of sunlight left before they would need to call it a day. He wanted to explore the tower. There was always a reason a lone tower existed in a forest, and he doubted that aspect had changed. The levels and associated changes were a mystery for another day. It had no bearing on what they were doing or would be doing in the near future.

"Let's finish what we came up here for," he said, pointing at the tower behind them.

Sabine looked like she wanted to say something else but just shook her head, motioning for him to lead the way. Hall could tell that she wasn't satisfied and not done with the questions, but she'd put it off for now. He worried that Roxhard would start to get overwhelmed again, but a glance at the fourteen-year-old in a Dwarf's body showed acceptance. It didn't appear to be bothering him.

They quickly searched the three Boarin bodies, finding nothing, not even any coins. Hall was tempted to try to get the leather kilts from the three. A skilled leatherworker would be able to use the material, but the Boarin were too heavy to easily move, and it most likely wouldn't end up being worth the effort. He did grab the swords and shields, splitting them between his and Roxhard's pouches, both of which were starting to get full. They redistributed all the extra packs so each carried one, adjusting the weight each had and distributing the loot that would be sold.

He was getting tired of having to drop the travel packs when they got into combat.

Instructing Pike to keep circling above to keep an eye on things, they walked through the opening and into the courtyard. The stone of the tower was well worked, showing good craftsmanship and construction. The style was similar to other buildings in Essec so they assumed it was human made.

There was about twenty feet between the wall and the tower, overgrown grass with small trees and bushes. It didn't look like anyone had been there in decades. Cobblestones, no longer smooth or flat and some missing, led from the opening to the ramp that led up into the tower.

Leigh had Angus stand at the bottom of the ramp, watching the tower. The cow was to alert them if anything came out while they split up. Leaving the packs, Roxhard and

Sabine went left, Hall and Leigh to the right, exploring the courtyard between tower and wall.

"Sorry about the questions," Hall said as they walked. He spoke quietly, not sure why, but not wanting Roxhard, and especially Sabine, to hear. The tower wasn't that large, it wouldn't take long to meet in the back. "This is just kind of new to us."

"How is that?" she asked. "You guys were sounding a little crazy back there. Where are you from?"

"I wish I knew," he answered truthfully. "But I assure you, we're not crazy."

She looked up at him, studying him carefully. She smiled after a minute. "I trust you."

"I'm glad."

And he was. For some reason, he wanted Leigh to like him, to accept him. He liked her. A lot, if he had to be honest with himself. She was extremely attractive, fun to be around. He stopped his thoughts and forced them back to the task at hand.

They found nothing hidden in the grass or along the walls. No chests or hidden trap doors. Nothing of interest. Roxhard and Sabine had found nothing on their side, either.

Angus was laying in the grass, happily munching away when they returned to the front. At least he's facing the right direction, Hall thought with a sigh. Angus jumped up, pretending he had been on guard when they returned. Leigh laughed and scratched behind his ear. He gave a low moo.

The Boarin's camp was inside the tower on the first level. A great round space with a set of stairs along the far wall and a hearth against the near wall, there was nothing of note. The ceiling was made of wood planks over beams and looked to be in decent shape. There were some rotted planks but the struc-ture looked sound. A firepit was built in the middle of the room, three rough blankets laying around it with three packs.

A quick search of the packs found some cheese and dried

meat, a loaf of near-moldy bread, and a couple ingots of iron, which Roxhard claimed. Buried deep in one, they found four silver coins.

Hall led the way to the steps, glad they were stone. He still went slow, tapping steps two or three higher with the end of his staff. None of them had *Detect/Remove Traps* so they had to proceed with caution. He slowed as his head got high enough to look onto the second floor.

The stone steps continued along the outer wall of the tower, bringing it to the second level which was another wooden floor on wood beams. This floor was also wide open, a single room, with a stone hearth above where the first was on the lower level. Seeing nothing, he continued up to the second level, stopping on the stone landing before the next run of stairs up. The others gathered around, Angus pushing them to make room.

None of them had any skills or spells to reveal hidden objects, so if there was something hidden on the level, they couldn't see it with their eyes. Hall led them up to the third level. It was more of the same, the size just smaller. The stone stairs curved along the inner wall, the floor wooden and beams supporting the next floor up.

The stairs continued past the fourth floor, ending in a rotted trap door that led to the exposed roof. The ceiling was stone, small blocks fitted tightly together. The mortar was still solid, no light visible through any cracks. In the middle of the wooden floor of this level was a single small chest. It was low to the ground, wide, with nothing else in the room.

They all stood on the stone landing, not stepping across onto the wooden floor, staring at the single chest. Light shone in through openings that would have been windows and through cracks in the wall where stones had fallen or the mortar faded. The chest was roughly two feet long and only a foot high, if that. Made of a metal, they could not identify from where they were standing.

"That's obviously a trap," Hall muttered.

Hall tapped his spear on the wooden floor in front of him. First directly in front, then moving it out a little bit at a time in a straight line. The others stepped back, giving him some space. Tapping with the wooden end and then reversing the spear, Hall repeated the process with the metal tip.

Nothing happened.

Taking a deep breath, Hall lifted one foot and placed it down on the wooden floor.

Nothing happened.

He took another couple of steps, slowly and carefully. He was leery of traps but also didn't trust the aged, wooden floor. It looked solid but he wasn't taking any chances. He had seen too many party members rush into a room and be attacked by traps. And this, with the chest just sitting there in the open, was too good a bait. There was going to be a trap in this room somewhere. The trick was to find it without triggering it and blowing himself up.

They could have just moved on from the chest. Go up to the next level, look around, and leave the tower. But it would nag at him, at all of them. They were adventurers. They had not chosen a safe life. And it was a lone tower in the middle of nowhere. Everything pointed at the chest containing something of value.

He paused, realizing what he had been thinking. He wasn't an adventurer. He just played one in a game. But now, he was considering himself a true and real adventurer. Not a person playing a role, but the role itself. He was an adventurer.

Pushing his thoughts back and focusing on the task at hand, he started tapping the floor again, reaching as far as the spear would go. He hit with the wooden butt end and then the metal tip, repeating this process as he made his slow walk toward the chest.

He stopped when he was a spear length from the chest itself. The chest wasn't that deep. Long, thin, and only a foot or so wide. The metal looked to be dark iron, a dull black. The edges were banded in a grayer metal, steel or normal iron. There was no lock on the lid. No runes or glyphs to indicate wardings. Which didn't mean much. They could be invisible or the trap could have been mechanical.

The floor was not that thick, Hall knew from the walk up. Just the wooden floorboards and the support structure. He had examined the ceiling while on the floor below and hadn't noticed anything unusual, nothing that would indicate a mechanical trap under the chest.

Leaning forward, he tapped the chest with the spear, ready to fall backward and out of the way of any blast or spray. He just hoped that Leigh's healing spell, *Touch of Life*, would be enough to take care of any damage he got from the trap.

Nothing happened.

He tried the metal tip of the spear. Still nothing.

The spear tapped the chest harder, moving it a bit.

He looked back at the others. Roxhard and Leigh looked worried, anxious. Sabine just shrugged.

Holding the spear tighter with both hands, he pushed at the chest harder, trying to move it. The chest slid along the floor, an inch then two and more.

Nothing happened.

There was nothing hidden under the chest. No pressure plate. Just the wooden floor.

With a last look back at the others, Hall took the final couple steps to stand in front of the chest. He wanted to be farther back, use the spear to open it, but there was not enough space to get the tip of the spear under the lid of the chest.

Crouching down in front of it, leaning slightly back, he reached out and touched the chest.

He held still, expecting an explosion or a shock to go through his body, or even gas to start seeping out from the chest. Nothing happened.

With one hand, he lifted the lid.

CHAPTER NINETEEN

HALL DIDN'T REALIZE HE HAD BEEN HOLDING HIS BREATH, BODY tensed in expectation. Letting out the breath, he relaxed and looked into the chest.

It was mostly empty.

An open space with a small pouch, a long tube, and two sets of bracers. He pulled out the pouch, feeling the weight and the sound of coins jingling. A decent amount. Opening it, he dumped them out in his hand.

Four gold coins, twenty silver, and twenty copper.

Not a large amount but still more than they had currently.

Replacing them in the pouch, he set it aside and examined the bracers. One pair was iron, a dark color. They were unadorned, plain, but Hall could feel the magic around them. When he used *Identify* on them, they read a blue color, indicating their relative strength.

DARK IRON BRACERS
OF LESSER ELEMENTAL RESISTANCE
Protection +4
Fire Resistance +25%
Water Resistance +25%
Air Resistance +25%
Earth Resistance +25%

Not bad, Hall thought, setting them aside.

Magic on Hankath was based on the four elements: Earth, Air, Fire, and Water. Shamans were able to cast spells that used all four and were able to specialize in a specific element making those spells stronger. Speaking the words of a spell broke through the barrier between Hankath and the elemental plains, bringing that magical energy into the world. It then shaped it to fit what the Shaman wanted. As such, each spell was strong against an element and weak against another. Druids used the power of the planet itself while Witches manipulated the darkness of the planet. Skalds used their music to influence and manipulate the mind, pulling from the body's own energy.

The bracers, being resistant to all four elements, were excellent. Typically, an item only granted resistance to one element. The resistance translated to Protection against spells or damage of that element.

He picked up the second set of bracers. These were made of leather, a white color and a type of hide that he did not recognize. There were symbols traced into the leather, knots, and runes. Like the iron bracers, these designs were a blue color.

HUNTER'S BRACERS
OF QUICK STRIKE
Protection +2
Parry +2
Agility +2

The *Parry* skill bonus and being made of leather meant the bracers were meant for a Duelist. A dual wielding class with a Class Ability that allowed the Duelist to use a weapon like a shield, the *Parry* skill increased the Protection given by that Ability. Hall could learn the skill if he wanted, but doubted he would. He wasn't supposed to get hit. Still, the other bonuses were useful to him.

Setting the bracers down, Hall removed the ones he currently wore. They were his class starting gear and were starting to show signs of heavy use and wear. Dirty, worn, the edges ripping and the stitching coming undone. Stowing them in his pouch, he picked up one of the white leather ones. It was larger than his wrist but when he slid the bracer over his arm, it shrunk to fit. He put the second on his other arm.

When both bracers were on, he felt a tingle through his body. He felt lighter, quicker.

Last was the leather tube. He knew what it was without opening it. The container was the same as the map he had found days ago in the Goblins loot. A treasure map. Where the other one was in a plain leather tube, this one was fancier. The leather was dyed a deep red color with gold thread stitching. The entire tube was made better, showing care and attention to detail.

He carried all the loot back to the others, handing the iron bracers to Roxhard.

"Thanks," the Dwarf said, looking at the bracers. "Dark iron? Very nice."

The map tube was held under Hall's arm as he handed out

the coins, an equal share to each. He had to shake the coins in front of Leigh's face to get her attention, her eyes riveted on the tube.

"What?" Hall asked.

"Do you know what that is?" she exclaimed, reaching out to touch the tube, fingers hovering over it as if afraid to touch it.

"A map," he answered with a shrug, figuring he'd examine it once they camped for the night.

"Not just any map," Leigh said, her voice filled with excitement and surprise. "That's a Masterwork map."

Hall took the tube in hand and examined it more closely. Masterwork was the highest quality a crafted item could achieve. Some items made by a highly skilled crafter had a quality mark which indicated their greater than normal strength. The higher the mark, the more enchantments an item could have as well as more durability. Most items had no mark, being just average quality. Once a crafter reached seventy-five in skill, they could start getting markers added to their items, giving bonuses. Fair, Quality, Exceptional, and Masterwork.

Only a crafter of over one hundred skill had a small chance of creating a Masterwork quality item. Skills only got to one hundred so items would need to be employed to get higher and items that granted skill bonuses were very rare.

That was what the game had started out with when the maximum class level was fifty. As the developers had added class levels, they hadn't added crafting levels. Instead, they had added realm crafting, where each new realm introduced had its own crafting levels and recipes associated with it so a player essentially started off at zero and worked their way back up again.

No matter what the new crafting rules were now, the value of the item that Hall was holding was immense.

Slowly, carefully, almost reverently, Hall pulled off the top of the leather tube. It was attached by a thin cord to the rest, and he let it hang. Turning the tube over, he held his hand under it and felt the parchment hit his palm as it slid out. Handing the tube to Sabine, he unrolled the map.

Congratulations!
You have uncovered a Treasure Map Level V.

TO THE FINDER GOES THE REWARD
Reward: +500 Experience

You cannot Accept this quest at this time.
Earn Minimum Skill of 40 in Cartography and Minimum Level of 20 to become eligible for this quest.

Failure!
You have failed to decipher: Treasure Map Level V

Skill Gain!
Cartography Rank 1 +.2

The map was old, parts of it faded, the edges of the parchment frayed. It felt weak in his hands, light, like the slightest movement would tear the map apart. With the other map, he had been able to read the notations marked in the borders and on the map itself. He was unable to with this one. There were notes, lots of them, but they appeared as nothing but random lines and dots. Nothing that made sense. No language that he knew.

There was one island featured, the edges of two others on the south and east part of the map. Only part of those neighboring islands were visible. With no scale it was impossible to tell the distances between them or the size of the one island shown.

"Can you read it?" Leigh asked excitedly.

"I can't even tell what realm it is," Hall answered. He showed them all the map and none could recognize the landmass.

He rolled it up, as carefully as he had unrolled it, and returned it to the tube. Capping it, he placed it in his pouch.

———

They spent the night on the first level of the tower, using the Boarin's already created fire pit. The meal was taken from their supplies, no one wanting to go back down the hill to hunt for fresh meat at that point.

Except for Pike and Angus.

The dragonhawk had found a mouse or squirrel and was off to the side, happily eating it. The cow had gone outside and happily munched away on the abundant and tall grass surrounding the tower.

After eating Hall had pulled out the new treasure map, examining it, trying to make heads or tails of any of the writing. It was all still a mystery. He gave up trying to identify the small island that was in the middle of the map, concentrating on the two shown in pieces, trying to figure out which ones they were. He couldn't remember a formation like it was showing. Two larger islands close to a much smaller one.

It was frustrating. Without a reference for scale he couldn't tell how big the islands were. The small one could only be a couple miles across and the others so blown up that he wouldn't recognize them. Or the small one could be the size of Cumberland. There was no way to tell.

And he wasn't getting any skill gains from studying the map.

He gave up, replacing it and the tube back in his pouch, instead choosing to watch the flames of the fire and the smoke curl up into the sky. Roxhard was already asleep, bedroll off to the side and snoring loudly. Sabine was sitting cross legged on the ground, the ends of her robe slipping to show a lot of bare leg. Leigh was once again using Angus as a pile, laying down with her head on the cow's chest.

"Tell me more about these people that can get to level twenty-five," Sabine asked, turning to look at Leigh.

"Not much to tell," Leigh replied. "Very rare, very special. The kind of people that naturally draw others to them. The ones that become famous and do great or terrible things."

"So, kings and generals? Nobles?"

"No," Leigh said, shaking her head. "None of them were royalty or anything like that. Not at first. The ones I've heard about appeared out of nowhere. No real history or background. No one could remember them as children, or growing up. That kind of thing."

Hall perked up at that, exchanging a quick glance with Sabine. That sounded kind of how a new Player entered the game. They just appeared as adventuring adults. No Player ever wanted to spend the time as a child and growing up, so that part was skipped.

"Some became kings or nobles, or just famous because of their deeds."

"Where are they now?" Sabine asked.

"None alive anymore," Leigh answered. "Not for a long time. Legends now."

Hall looked out toward the entrance of the tower, across the courtyard and where the bodies of the Boarin were just dark shadows against the ground. He thought he could see something moving out there. Angus lifted his head, looking the same way, and Pike stopped eating. Two spots of yellow returned Hall's stare. They watched each other, Half-Elf and scavenger. Eventually realizing that Hall was not going to move, the yellow eyes disappeared.

A wolf's howl broke the silence of the night.

"Let's make sure we keep the fire going all night," Hall said, still looking that way.

Sabine and Leigh both turned and looked out into the night. Two more sets of yellow stared back.

"Yeah," Sabine said, forcing herself to look away. "Sounds like a good idea."

Roxhard just continued to snore.

———

The next morning dawned sunny and bright, a red sky across the horizon.

Hall had stayed up long after the others, watching the wolves feed. He wasn't worried the creatures would attack. If they were going to, they would have done so long before. He was lost in thought, and they provided a distraction.

Something was bothering him, and he wasn't sure what. He had never been one given to introspection. Life was what it was. You did your best to go through it and make it the best you could. It wasn't fair. There were distractions. It was a struggle. He'd found his release in gaming.

And now he seemed to be living a game.

The moon was at its peak when he realized what was wrong.

It wasn't that something was bothering him, it was that something should have been and wasn't.

Roxhard was always on the verge of losing it. Walking a thin line. Everything was overwhelming. No surprise. Just barely a teenager and confronted with whatever it was they were facing. The game turning real. Killing things in a game was one thing, killing things for real was another. The kid would either come to accept it, or snap. There was no middle ground.

On the other hand, Sabine was working her way through it from another angle. She was questioning everything, trying to find the answers she desperately needed. Sabine needed the structure that the rules had given her. She didn't have that, and it was pushing at her.

And then there was him.

The experience should have been too much for him. Like Roxhard, he should be overwhelmed close to the breaking point or questioning everything like Sabine. Instead, he was going with the flow.

If he was honest with himself, he was enjoying it.

Why level twenty instead of level one hundred? NPCs that could level and think for themselves? A computer-generated world that felt more real than reality?

He had finally lain down, smiling, and slept easy with no Vitality penalty when he awoke.

———

They walked out under the arch of the wall, moving to the side to avoid the mess that was the Boarin bodies. Torn and shredded, ripped apart, there wasn't much that was recognizable. Flies were already in the carcasses, carrion birds circling overhead as they waited for the group to leave.

Once on the ground, Hall pulled out the lower level treasure map and got his bearings.

Skill Gain!
Cartography Rank I +.1

Hall opened his internal map interface and tried to adjust the size so that it scaled with the treasure map. He held the physical treasure map up in front of himself and aligned it with the translucent internal map. Because his internal map only showed areas he had been, most of that part of Cumberland was still unrevealed but there was enough on the two maps that he was able to get them aligned somewhat. They were off a little bit but close enough for him to get his bearings. A northeasterly direction, the trail they would be looking for was almost midway between Land's Edge Port and where the Green Flow River started. A large amount of area. As they got closer and more of northeast Cumberland was revealed, he hoped to be able to coordinate the two maps better.

Aligning himself in the direction that was the straightest line to the start of the path into the mountains, he put away both maps and got them walking again.

He could hear Pike flying overhead, Angus trotting alongside Leigh and the others as they made their way through the forest. There weren't as many smaller animals as he was used to seeing. There always seemed to be rabbits and squirrels wandering the forests in the game, but this felt more like when he had hiked in the forests back home in New Hampshire. The animals all hid when the intruders walked through their homes. It was quiet as they walked, the only sounds were those they made.

The trees thinned out, giving way to grasslands and hills. They could see the mountains in the distance as well as the shadow of Edin floating overhead. At the edge of the forest they all paused to take in the sight.

Fields of grass dotted with small forests ran for miles, rolling up and down small hills, small streams and brooks sparkling in the daylight. The land rose the closer it got to the mountains, the Far Edge Peaks. Those towered high into the air, up into the clouds that floated between the islands. Tips of some could be seen above the lower lying clouds, snow on the highest peaks. Sheer cliffs, steep slopes of exposed rock. To the east, the grass ran to the edge where there were no mountains, just disappearing along the horizon with the blue of the sky beyond.

High above, casting shadows upon the ground, was the large mass of Edin. From their angle they could see the underside of the realm. Dark brown and gray rock, sloping inwards as it fell below Edin's ground level for fifty feet or more. The bottom of the realm was jagged, broken rock, but no pieces fell. It hung suspended in air, floating and not moving.

The waterfall that formed the Green Flow River, fell from Edin and through the clouds to crash down upon Cumberland. They were too far away to hear the roar, and from this distance, it appeared to be just a thin line of darker blue against the light blue sky. Dark dots filled the blue sky, the other realms in the distance. They were at varying elevations, and Hall knew if he could see to the east, west and south, he would see many more.

At the time of the glitch, or the patch or whatever it was, there were only forty explored realm islands, or zones, as they were called in game. When the game had started, there had been twenty-five including the seven starting zones. The rest had ranged from level ten to the original ending level of fifty. The other zones had been added in over the years with an unlimited number that could still be created as needed with future expansions.

The latest expansion had recently been announced and was going to add in a new kingdom, the Desmarik Republic. There had been no word on if there would be a new race, if the kingdom was Human or other, or even where in relation to the other Realms it was located. All they had was the name. It had been scheduled for two years after the announcement, which Hall realized would have put it when they awoke in the game world. Electronic Storm had said it was two years after the glitch. Did that mean the Desmarik Republic was somewhere out there, just waiting to be discovered?

"I've never seen Edin from below before," Leigh said, taking a couple steps farther out, her head craned to look at the realm above her. "When I came here from home, we went to Land's Edge Port and took the road south. Too far away to see this," she finished, gesturing up at the island floating above and to the side.

Hall looked out across the sea of grass with the rising hills. It looked relatively peaceful but he knew it was anything but. The plains were home to Centaurs and the Boarin, along with other creatures. Wide open spaces, not much cover.

The alternative was to go all the way west to Land's Edge Port and follow the mountains east. It would take much longer and wouldn't be that much safer. The mountains ran from the eastern edge of Cumberland, the crumbled and jagged line of cracked rock, all the way to the western edge where the city was built. Cutting across the grasslands was the quickest route.

"Shall we?" he asked and started walking.

CHAPTER TWENTY

THE CENTAUR REARED UP, ITS FRONT LEGS FALLING WITH FORCE as it tried to crush Hall underneath them. He rolled to the side, the hooves slamming into the ground and churning up dirt. Stabbing out with its spear, the centaur tried to skewer Hall. He blocked the stab with his sword, managing to push it aside. Still rolling, he came up near the rear of the Centaur and swung low with his sword.

The blade sliced through the Centaurs rear legs. It roared, stumbling but managing to stay upright. The Centaur tried to kick out with that leg, failing, giving Hall time to get clear.

He looked over the grasslands for his spear but was unable to find it. The Centaur turned, keeping its distance, slowly moving with the hobbled leg. It still had its spear and was pointing the end toward Hall, waiting for him to move. Hall's spear was six feet long, the Centaur's was eight. It had the size, height, and length advantage.

Hall hated fighting the half-man, half-horse Centaurs with their combination of speed, power and reach. Besides their crafted weapons, they had natural weapons with their hooves.

A Centaur was a tough opponent. He had hoped to avoid them on the journey across the plains.

It hadn't happened.

They had been on their third day out from the forest, not even halfway to the foothills, when the Centaur patrol had found them. As large as they were, the horse bodies even with Hall's shoulder and the human parts another three to four feet higher, the Centaurs had somehow managed to avoid detection until it was too late.

The grass was tall, about a foot to two in some spots, Hall and his companions leaving a trail as they pushed through. It was hot on the plains with a constant wind blowing the grass. There were plenty of small streams to rest at and get water. It all made for slow going.

Hall had sent Pike ahead to scout out, as he had every morning. He had never thought to keep a watch behind them.

The Centaur patrol had caught sight of them from a mile or so away. It had circled behind and come up from the rear, charging before the party could react. They heard the noise of hooves thundering across the plain, their only warning.

Turning back, they saw the three Centaurs seeming to tower above the tall grass. Each had spears lowered. There was no intent to talk, they saw intruders in their domain, and they intended to destroy those intruders. They cared nothing for intent, or to try and reason. There were two males and a female. The horse bodies tall and heavily muscled, as were the human bodies. Each wore leather armor, intricately carved vests that left the arms bare except for the bracers. The ears were large and pointed, the noses and faces flat. Long hair that was braided fell down their shoulders and back. The female was blond, both males had black hair. Each wore a pointed leather helm. The armor was painted in greens and reds. Strapped across their backs were large, two-handed swords.

Moving at a gallop, the Centaurs were upon the party almost as soon as they had seen the charging creatures.

Roxhard was in the rear and took the brunt. He avoided the spear but not the Centaur. The force of the impact slammed Roxhard and sent him tumbling. The leg of the Centaur buckled from hitting the stone that was the Dwarf. He fell hard, the force and speed sending the Centaur into a roll.

The second Centaur, the female, pulled up short, stabbing her spear down toward Leigh who was able to move out of the way. The Centaur hadn't been expecting Angus, who slammed into her legs from the side. She stumbled but stayed up right, looking around for the cow who was running to the side.

Hall moved aside barely as the last Centaur stopped in front of him and stabbed out with the spear. He got clipped as he tried to turn, his own spear knocked from his hand. Hall cursed and rolled as the Centaur reared up to attack with its front hooves.

Moving to the side, out of the reach of the Centaurs, Sabine started casting *Hexbolt*. The casting finished, a bolt of purple energy streaking from her outstretched hand. It shot across the grasslands and struck the Centaur facing off against Leigh. *Hexbolt* was a curse, causing the target to lose dexterity, attack speed, and attack power by sending waves of energy through the body as the target tried to move. It could be cast on multiple targets, but sharing the power of the curse across the targets. At Sabine's low level, the bolt wasn't that strong but it was enough.

The female Centaur cried out in pain, purple bolts of energy cascading around her body, spiraling out from where the bolt had hit her in the chest. She reared up, trying to move, but the bolts constricted. She shook, unable to do anything. Angus slammed into her again, and the Centaur stumbled, falling to the ground hard.

Leigh pointed her staff at the prone Centaur and chanted.

Her *Splinter Storm* sent dozens of small splinters of wood shooting out from the end of the staff, slamming into the Centaur who screamed as each little bit of wood cut into her skin. Each splinter was small, alone not that painful, but dozens together was very painful. Blood started leaking down from all the small wounds.

Slicing across the Centaur's legs with his sword, Hall managed to get clear as the Centaur tried to kick out with the wounded leg. It hobbled around, putting distance between itself and Hall, awkward on just three legs. The hurt leg, dropping blood, was curled up and held off the ground. The long spear still gave the Centaur reach, and it tried to stab at Hall, quickly jabbing back and forth to keep Hall moving and off-balance.

With a screech, Pike darted out of the sky, leading with his razor-sharp talons. The Centaur saw the dragonhawk coming in, raising his arm to ward off the bird, to keep the claws away from his eyes. Talons cut into the flesh of the arm, blood dripping to the ground. The Centaur growled in pain, trying to bat at Pike with the spear.

Hall rolled to the ground, coming up under the Centaur. He stabbed up with his sword, pulling it as he jumped out to the side. The Centaur cried out in pain, dropping its spear and falling hard to the ground. Hall just managed to get out of the way as the heavy body landed. Standing up quickly, he turned around and flipped his sword so it was point down. He drove the sword into the Centaur's back, below the neck.

The Centaur gave one final groan and lay still.

Roxhard struggled up. His head hurt, the world spinning. The force of the Centaur had sent him flying, landing on his back and rolling another ten feet or so before landing on his head. He didn't think anything was broken but his whole body hurt. He saw his axe five feet away where he had dropped it and tried to walk toward it.

A shadow about ten feet away stood up from the grass of the plains. The Centaur was unsteady on its four feet. It took a step toward Roxhard, dropping the spear. A hand reached over the shoulder and drew the huge blade. The hilt was easily three of Roxhard's hands long, just barely enough for the Centaur's two. It was plain, no ornamentation. The blade was easily six feet long, thin at the bottom and thicker at the top, the back edge curved inward. It looked sharp and dangerous.

His axe lay between them, almost midway. It would be a race to see who got to it first, Roxhard or the Centaur. Only one of them was armed so Roxhard knew he had to get to it first but he also knew the Centaur was faster.

It would be no contest. He was not getting his axe. He wasn't even going to try.

But the Centaur didn't know that.

He feinted like he was going to go for the weapon. The Centaur took the bait and charged, sword ready to swing. Roxhard did not move.

Already swinging, the Centaur's blade cut through air. It went off-balance, the expected resistance to the strength of the swing not there.

Activating *Battle Rush*, Roxhard charged at the off-balance Centaur. He slammed into the horse body, knocking the front legs out. The Centaur grunted, falling to the ground again. Roxhard heard the snap of bones breaking. The legs were up in the air, the Dwarf getting tangled in them. He fell on top of the Centaur, sliding off and rolling on the ground. He had a leg trapped between his body and arm, and he pulled, twisting so it rolled under him.

He heard a satisfying crack and cry from the Centaur.

Trying to stand, he felt a slam in his back, knocking him back down. The Centaur kicked out with its rear legs, catching Roxhard hard.

The female Centaur tried to stand up, the line of purple

energy striking her in the shoulder. She fell again, the black wetness spreading. She tried to stand, struggling as the purple crackling energy shocked her limbs. Twisting her head out of the way, she screamed as more splinters embedded themselves in her side, more of her blood falling to the ground. A strange noise, like the beating of wings, made her look up to see a feathered and scaled bird with a long tail hovering in front of her face. The bird's mouth opened, it screeched and a bolt of lightning slammed into her face.

Smoke rose up from the blackened ruin of the Centaur's face, the lifeless body falling to the ground and not rising.

Feeling each of the legs kicking against him, Roxhard crawled away from the Centaur. It tried to twist, to rise but the front legs were broken, the angle awkward. Roxhard was glad of the bad angle as it kept the rear legs from hitting him with full force, but he was still bruised and battered.

Out of kicking range, he stood up, looking around for his axe.

"Here," Hall said from the side.

Turning he saw the Half-Elf Skirmisher holding his axe, a bloody sword in his other hand. He tossed the axe, and Roxhard caught it.

He gripped the handle with two hands, walking around to the rear of the Centaur. The eyes followed him, filled with anger and hate, lips curled back in a growl. Standing behind the head where the Centaur could not see him, Roxhard raised the axe. The body of the horse thrashed as the Centaur tried to lift himself up with his legs. The axe came down, and the body moved no more.

SLAIN: *Blood Cry Patroller*
+30 Experience

SLAIN: *Blood Cry Patroller*
+10 Experience

Skill Gain!
Small Blades Rank 2 +.3

Skill Gain!
Light Armor Rank 2 +.1

Hall glanced at the prompt, surprised at the extra ten experience. From Pike's assist to the women? With a shrug, not really caring just happy that he got the extra experience, he mentally closed the prompts. He had always kept the combat prompts hidden. The constant stream of damage taken and dealt along with the skill gain and experience notifications, were distracting during the game. It was no different now. Even pulling the monsters stat bars was distracting. He didn't need to see their health going down, he was too busy making it go down.

He knew he had to do a better job of tracking his gains in stats, skills, and experience. There had always been a little downtime after a fight to do that but now there didn't seem to be that kind of extra time. Now they were constantly moving. Even when stopping at night, there didn't seem to be time to do all the character maintenance that he needed to do. And there was a lot he needed to do.

"Everyone okay?" he asked.

The whole fight had only taken a minute, maybe two.

Roxhard was holding his head, looking a little unsteady. The women indicated they were fine. Leigh walked over to Roxhard, the only one wounded, and cast *Nature's Touch*. The spell healed the Health he was down but could do nothing for the Vitality loss or the shaky head.

"Got a *Concussion* debuff," he muttered. "Five minutes."

Hall nodded. A kick in the head by a Centaur would do that. The *Concussion* debuff caused a loss of Vitality, Agility, and Intelligence for a time.

Leaning down, Hall ran his fingers over the blade of a Centaur's sword. The weapon was well crafted, expertly made. Plain steel, unadorned hilt. A functional but well cared for weapon. It was also huge. Much bigger than Hall could easily handle. Roxhard could lift it, but it was just too big physically for the Dwarf. Checking his inventory to see if he could bring one of the swords back to sell, he found that he was getting pretty close to full.

They had the extra travel packs, but something like the sword would have to go into the magical pouch so the weight wouldn't encumber his movements. Each character could only carry so much weight.

The coins took up one slot for all of them, and the bag automatically sorted for him. Each type of herb and skin he had been collecting was a slot as well, and those took up most of the space. He had put the potion holder on his belt, which freed up some space in the inventory but not enough. There were still some items left from the smugglers stash. They had sold as much as they could at River's Side but still had more to sell. It all amounted to not enough space.

He looked down at the heavy sword, trying to remember how much a shopkeep would buy the weapon for. He didn't think it was much, not enough to make it worth carrying all the way to Land's Edge Port. He wanted to make sure there was plenty of space for whatever this treasure map led to, and they were weeks away from the city, and there were no towns or villages along the way that he knew of.

The sword would have to stay.

Same with the spears. He badly wanted to replace his but the Centaurs' were too long. They were pike length for a Human. Not worth taking.

He started the gruesome job of searching the bodies for anything worth taking. *The game mechanic of doing it for the player was so much easier*, he thought as he tried to move one of the heavy bodies to get at what looked like a belt pouch. He tried not to get any of the dried blood on him and just managed to get the body moved enough to grab the pouch.

Inside he found some herbs, *Greenroot* and *Purple Thistle*, along with some jerky. There was nothing else of value. The other Centaurs were the same. Nothing of value.

"I miss humanoid mobs always dropping coin," he said, adding the few items to his bag and tossing the Centaurs pouch. "Let's get out of here."

———

The next five days passed relatively uneventfully.

Hall had Pike fly a circular pattern, keeping watch in all directions. They encountered no more patrols, the dragonhawk spotting two villages in the distance that they were able to avoid. He thought one to be a Centaur village based on the style of the tents, round with sides and a canvas cap held up in the middle by a pole. The other could have been Boarin but he wasn't sure. There were Goblins and others living in the plains.

It may have been uneventful, but it was cold. They didn't risk a fire any of the days they were in the open plains. The chance of any of the inhabitants seeing it was too great. They sheltered in groves of trees when possible, at rock outcroppings, and for two miserable nights they had to camp in the open with no break from the constant wind. Each of those nights their Vitality took a small hit.

The land started rising as they reached the foothills. The mountains had been coming closer, getting larger and larger with each hour. Now the mountains were immense walls of stone rising as high as they could see, touching the cloud layer that hovered over Cumberland. Gray and black stone, sheer cliffs. Not inviting.

Throughout the trek, Hall checked the two maps, getting *Cartography* gains each time. He kept them on course, approaching the mountains at what he thought was the right place. As more of the land was revealed, he had been able to finetune the alignment and got them to what he thought was the start of the map's path through the mountains.

"We're looking for two round boulders with a flat slab of rock over the top. The trail starts on the other side," he said, taking the map out of his pouch. He unrolled it and held it up, pulling up the internal map to align the two. They were in line with where the trail started, which meant it could be a mile or two in either direction.

"That narrows it down," Sabine said with a sigh, looking at the imposing walls of stone before them. "Hope this treasure is worth it."

Hall shrugged. He had no idea and had told her that a couple times before. This was a risk in a way he knew. It could prove worthwhile or it could prove to be a colossal waste of time. There had never been treasure maps in the game before. But what else did they have to do? Leigh was in no hurry to get to her Grove and the Branch that was there. She was trying to put it off as long as she could.

During one of the nights, she had given a reason on her hesitation. She had said that once a Druid claimed a Grove, they were bound to it and the Grove to them. They were the caretakers and had the responsibility to keep the Branch alive and healthy. Harm to the Grove was harm to the Druid and the opposite, harm to the Druid was harm to the Grove. She was not sure she wanted or was ready for that responsibility.

"Treasure Maps usually are," Leigh said, responding to Sabine's comment.

"What exactly is a Treasure Map?" Sabine asked. "I mean I get the idea but…" she paused and just shrugged.

"They're magical," Leigh answered. "It's also kind of a general title," she added. "They don't necessarily have to go to a physical treasure, but because of the cost involved in making one, they always lead to something valuable." She paused collecting her thoughts. "Think of them as a key. Someone has a map made and makes copies. Only someone with that map and a way to break the code can use it to find and open the treasure."

"That sounds complicated," Sabine said after a couple minutes of digesting the information. "Why not just use a safe?"

"No physical lock is truly safe," Hall replied. "Not with the *Lock Pick* and *Disarm Traps* skills."

"Still sounds complicated," Sabine said with a sigh.

She was right, but to Hall, it made some sense. They lived in a world of magic, so maps that were keys didn't seem that odd.

"That's why whatever they hide is almost always valuable," Leigh said.

"Have you ever gotten a treasure?" Roxhard asked, looking up at Leigh. "You know an awful lot about them."

If Sabine had asked the question, Hall would have suspected her of trying to discredit Leigh, to show that the Druid wasn't to be fully trusted and did not know everything. A lot of their revised knowledge was coming from Leigh, and Sabine didn't seem to like that. Hall didn't think that Sabine was intentionally doing it because of disliking Leigh; he thought it was more that Sabine was starting to feel out of her element. Sabine needed some solid foundation to stand on, and Leigh represented the object that was putting cracks in the foundation of what Sabine thought she knew. For her part, Leigh didn't seem to care or notice.

But Roxhard had asked, which meant he was trying to flirt with Leigh. He was trying to stroke her ego.

"Thanks," she said, smiling down at him. "But I never have. Always wanted to. Everyone knows about Treasure Maps but they are very rare. It's one of those fantasies that village kids always play out."

They were walking deeper into the foothills, the going steeper.

"How is Hall able to read that one but we can't?" Sabine asked after a while.

He had given each of them the map to try to read, to help narrow down the spot and make some sense of it. None of the others had been able to decipher any of the notations. It had been a surprise. He had opened it and gotten the *Cartography* skill. They did not.

"No idea," Leigh answered, stepping around a large rock outcropping, Angus trotting along happily at her side. "He shouldn't have been able to. Not without training. Cartographers are very rare and jealously guard the secret to map making and decoding. Anyone can make a rough map but only Cartographers can make true maps."

They spent the night in the foothills, nestled in a small valley downslope of one. Another cold night with no fire or warm food. Hall, during his time on watch, heard the thunder of hooves in the middle of the night, down on the flat plains but nothing disturbed them. Which was the way he preferred it. Nice and quiet.

Each had a minor Vitality loss from the restless sleep and cold food. Only a point or two, but it was starting to add up. Each night like this added another point and lowered their overall effectiveness. Each was able to get an increase in *Survival* skill though. Even Leigh.

It was mid-afternoon when they came to the mountains. The land rose to the sheer cliff of granite. Gray and white stone rose high into the sky, impassable and imposing. Checking the maps, Hall estimated they were a mile or two off in either direction. He studied the mountain, leading the group a half mile back to get a better look. All he could see was cliffs in both directions, no breaks. Almost straight up, unclimbable.

Birds could be seen flying around the cliffs, large ones. Pike sat on Hall's shoulder, eyes watching the birds, a low growling sound coming from his throat. Hall reached up and petted the dragonhawk, trying to calm him.

"Pick a direction?" Sabine asked.

Hall shook his head. He wasn't ready to leave it to chance. Not yet.

He studied the mountains, studied the map. There had to be something to help narrow it down. Whoever drew the map would want to make it somewhat easy to find the right spot if you knew what to look for. The mountains on the map were not detailed, roughly drawn triangles next to each other. The common indication for mountains. The trailhead, the two boulders with the flat slab, were drawn bigger; exaggerated and enlarged. There had to be something he was missing. He looked closer at the mountains around the trailhead. There was something a little different about them.

Skill Gain!
Cartography Rank 2 +.2

Smiling, Hall looked up at the mountains. Off to the east, he saw it. The map indicated a mountain with a cliff that jutted out over the plain. The real thing was a half mile to the side, maybe a mile, and about halfway up the sheer face there was an outcropping that leaned out over the foothills.

"There," he said and started them in that direction.

An hour later, they saw the boulders. There was a crack in the cliff, hidden from view except from the east direction. The boulders were about five feet high, almost that in width. Decent sized, rough cut, made of a white stone. The slab was a large piece of the cliff that had fallen from the crack, landing by chance on the two boulders that were somewhat side by side. The crack itself was about eight feet wide, almost smooth on the sides. It was like an earthquake had split the mountain in two. It began behind the boulders, having to move around them to see it. Few pieces of rock or boulders littered the path through the crack.

The passage was in shadow, dark.

"Looks inviting," Sabine said. "How far do we have to go?"

Hall shrugged. "The mountains are thin here, not that deep until get to the island's edge. Shouldn't be more than a couple hours walk."

The map showed the 'X' they were looking for to be on the side of the mountains overlooking the sky and the nothingness below the island.

They started walking, Hall in the lead. The temperature dropped considerably once they were out of direct sunlight. There was some ambient light, enough to see by. Hall led, wishing there they had some thief skills among them or the Perception skill. With the lessened light, he was afraid he would miss something, a marker, or at worse, a trip wire.

There was no true thief class in the game. A Duelist was close, having some stealth and hiding abilities but did not have the *Detect/Remove Trap* or *Lock Pick* skills as part of the class. The Duelist class concentrated on the sneaking aspects of a standard thief class from almost any game and not the actual thieving skills. Any Class could train in those skills if they wanted to. Not many did as they were not truly necessary.

For the most part, the passage led straight and true, slowly sloping up. They came upon only one intersection with the path splitting. Hall consulted the map and saw a notation that only read 'continue in the direction of the cliff.' Taking that to mean the cliff overlooking the plains, he took the path that led east.

It continued straight, rising steeper, the going becoming harder. More and more rocks and boulders appeared in the path, forcing them to climb over some. Angus somehow managed to keep up, working his way with a little pushing from Roxhard over the rocks. The cow didn't seem to even complain, just mooing contentedly, apparently enjoying himself. Pike rode on Hall's shoulder, constantly shifting position which made it hard for Hall to keep his balance.

The wind blew through the passage, the rock walls funneling and channeling it, blowing it into their faces. The temperature was already cold from the lack of sun, the wind adding to the chill. They all pulled their cloaks tighter, the ends flapping.

The sun started to appear farther up, a light at the end of the passage. They had gotten used to the darker shadow of the continuing passage, the tight turns, but each picked up their pace with the light now visible. The passage got steeper, light visible on the sides and not just the end. The mountain angled back toward them, the passage appearing to turn to the east.

They emerged onto a flat shelf, the passage coming out on the western edge. The mountain on that side angled back steeper, creating a cliff overlooking the nothingness below. On the eastern side the mountain curved around to create the walls of the shelf. Only about twenty feet deep and that long, the shelf was worn smooth from constant exposure to the wind and elements.

Holding themselves to the eastern side, away from the edge, practically hugging the wall, they stepped out of the passage and onto the shelf. The wind was harder, physically pushing against them. Hall grimaced as Pike's talons dug deeper into his shoulder, the wind pushing the dragonhawk and trying to lift him up. He extended to his full height, wings flapping to try to hold steady.

Hall saw the cave right away. On the far side of the shelf, close to the edge, was a dark opening into the side of the mountain. Laying outside the opening was a pile of white.

Bones.

CHAPTER TWENTY-ONE

THEY APPROACHED THE CAVE CAUTIOUSLY, STAYING NEAR THE mountainside. The wind blew every which way, pushing and pulling. It came in off the sky around the island, slamming into the sloped sides of the mountain.

The bones were half in and half out of the cave, pushed against the side by the wind, a jumbled mess. Judging by the bones Hall could identify, it had not been Human or Elf. Definitely not a Firbolg. Dwarf, or Bodin then. Stepping away from the edge, he looked into the cave, not able to see far inside. It appeared to only be about ten feet deep, a dark shadow possibly indicating a tunnel.

Stepping into the cave, Hall let his eyes adjust. His Racial Ability let him see more definition of the shadows within the dark cave. It wasn't large, the ceiling only a couple feet above his head. The insides were smooth as if the wind had scoured it clean. More bones were scattered in the corners, pushed by the wind.

He saw the skull and bent down to pick it up. It was small, relatively, in size but larger than it should have been. A Dwarf skull with a large crack down the center. The Dwarf had most likely been caught by the wind and slammed against the side of the mountain. He tossed it back against the wall and stepped over to the darker opening that was a tunnel.

Only about five feet wide, eight feet tall, it led deeper into the depths of the mountain.

"Come on," Hall called back watching as the others carefully made their way around the bones and into the cave.

The small space seemed crowded. Angus walked over to the side out of the wind and curled up on the ground. In seconds, the cow was asleep. Pike jumped off Hall's shoulder and landed on a boulder near the cow. The dragonhawk's eyes watched the party.

"I think they want to stay here," Leigh said with a chuckle.

"Don't blame them," Sabine complained.

Hall leaned his spear against the wall. It was too long to use in the cramped tunnel.

"Whoa," Roxhard exclaimed, drawing their attention from where he stood a couple steps into the side tunnel. "That's so cool."

He felt their stares, looking back over his shoulder at them, taking a couple steps out of the tunnel.

"I can see in the dark," he said happily. "Got a prompt that I uncovered a Dwarf Racial Ability. *Dark Vision*."

"You weren't able to see in the dark at night?" Hall asked. "I discovered that I have *Limited Night Vision* the first night out."

"What's yours like?"

"I see shadow upon shadow, different shades that let me make out the details. Yours?"

"Similar but I also see bright spots, different colors like veins in the rock. I think it's different types of ore, some are brighter than others," he said, stepping back to the tunnel and running his hand along the wall tracing one of the lights that he saw.

"You two are weird," Leigh said with a laugh. "Of course, Elves and Dwarves can see in the dark."

"Do we have torches for us lowly Humans?" Sabine asked with a trace of annoyance.

Hall reached into his pouch and brought out two torches, getting flint and tinder. He struck the flint against the tinder and produced sparks, letting them fall on the end of the torch. The wooden stick soon caught fire. Cupping his hand around the small flame, he blew on it and soon the entire head of the torch was on fire. He lit a second off the first and handed them to the women.

Taking point and walking about ten feet ahead of the others, wondering if the next time in town he should invest in *Detect/Disarm Traps*, Hall stepped into the tunnel. The sun barely reached this part of the cave but there was still some ambient light. The passage did curve and as he followed the curve, the light disappeared. He took a couple more steps and was plunged into complete darkness.

He stumbled, falling against the wall and catching himself, surprised that he could not see.

"What the hell?"

"What's the matter?" Roxhard asked from behind him.

"I can't see at all. It's pitch black," Hall stated, holding his hand in front of his face. He could barely see the outline as he moved his fingers.

He started to see again as the torches came closer. Each only gave off a small cone of light, the flames flickering and casting odd shadows against the rock. As Sabine stepped closer, he started to see again, the shadows upon darker shadows.

"Now I can see again."

"Must need a little light," she said. "It is night vision, after all. There's always some light at night from the stars and the moon."

Hall looked around the passage, debating. He could see

well enough now with the torch so near but that would require Sabine or Leigh walking pretty close behind him. If there was a trap, they'd be caught in it as well. He had wanted to keep the distance so only he would be caught. He could send Roxhard ahead as the Dwarf could see in the dark but that put the risk on the fourteen-year-old kid and not the adult.

Hall just felt wrong doing that. He refused to put anyone else at risk. This quest was his idea.

"Can I have a torch?" he asked, holding out a hand to Sabine.

She looked like she was going to refuse, not understanding the dilemma he was facing. With a final shrug, she handed it to him and stepped back closer to Leigh.

Holding the torch out in front of him, Hall started back down the tunnel.

————

The passage ran for about two hundred feet give or take. Straight with no side tunnels. Roughly carved but clear without obstructions. The floor sloped down, steep in spots and almost flat in others.

Only their footsteps could be heard, echoing down the tunnel.

Hall held the torch out, providing just enough light. The flickering flame along with his *Limited Night Vision* made the progress easier. The others were farther back, Roxhard about ten feet and the women another five or so. Their torch was a small point of light, the radius just enough for them to walk.

Ahead, Hall could see where the tunnel ended into a wider room, the light from the torch spilling out of the opening. He stepped out of the tunnel and into a roughly circular and domed room. The ceiling was high up, the walls curving, beyond the light of the torch. The shadows were so dark and deep he could see nothing.

About twenty feet in diameter, the room was as roughly carved as the tunnel, just not as smooth. Parts of the wall bumped out, boulders and smaller rocks littering the floor. But it was the object in the middle that caught Hall's attention.

Barely illuminated by the torch was a large square block of stone. It stood about two-feet tall, three wide. He couldn't see how deep it was. The square of stone looked solid.

Shining the light on the ground, he examined the path to the block. It appeared smooth, no obstructions and nothing odd. No cracks, no joints or seams in the floor. There was just the right amount of roughness and unevenness. Nothing to indicate a trap. No obvious tripwire or pressure plate.

Holding the torch out as far as he could in either direction, he tried to examine the walls but was unable to see anything.

Looking back at Roxhard, he motioned for the Dwarf to pause.

Taking a deep breath, Hall took the first steps toward the block. He wished he had his spear so he could repeat what he had done in the abandoned tower. Tap the floor, take a step. The dark made it that much more difficult. He moved slower, carefully stepping down and slowly placing his weight on the foot.

Each step, he expected to feel an explosion, flames, the burning of acid, the crackle of lightning or the fumes from a toxic cloud. Anything. But nothing happened.

Finally, he was in front of the block.

Skill Gain!
Cartography Rank 2 + 2.0

He was surprised at the two-point gain for finding the treasure chest. Most skill gains were in a tenth of a point at a time, sometimes two tenths. Never a point at once, let alone two. The full ten points when he had gained the skill made sense. Training a skill, or gaining a skill to start, granted ten or more points because it was assumed training had been given. Normal skill usage gained in small amounts, the one tenth at a time rate.

QUEST COMPLETE!
You have successfully found the location marked on Treasure Map Level I.

X MARKS THE SPOT
Reward: +50 Experience

The sides of the stone chest were perfectly smoothed, the block actually part of the floor. There was no joint. Someone had carved the block out of the mountain. He could see a line along the top, about an inch down, creating a cap. Slowly, he walked around the chest, looking for anything obvious. He tried to look into the joint itself but there wasn't enough light.

"Rox," he called, waving the Dwarf toward him.

Roxhard's steps were the loudest. The Dwarf, naturally heavy, could not step lightly. His leather boots with iron greaves attached clanked with each step. Sabine and Leigh stopped at the tunnel opening.

Hall stood facing them on the other side of the stone chest, watching Roxhard approach. He couldn't hear anything but the Dwarf's footsteps until it was too late. Something scratched across the mountain floor behind him, and Hall turned.

He grunted in pain as something sliced across his side, cutting through the leather jerkin. He felt the sharp edge cut skin, tearing as it slid across his body, blood flowing. He fell to the side, the torch falling to the ground but not going out. Something chattered and growled in the shadows.

DAMAGE!

Sneak Attack Failed. Half Damage Taken.
-20 Health
-5 Vitality

You have been afflicted with: Bleeding Out
-2 Health every 5 Seconds

The attacker stepped into the light. Standing about three feet tall, the creature was stooped and bent. It had stick-like legs, the feet wide and long with thick and long toes. Barefoot, it wore rough leather armor over its chest and waist. Long arms ended in oversized hands. The head was humanoid, a little larger than normal, with great bat-like ears that extended past the crown and below the neck. Long black hair hung down its back and on either side of the ears. An angular face, almost to a point, with large round eyes. In one hand it held a short sword made of stone, the edge jagged. A mouth full of sharp pointed teeth caught the light.

A Caobold.

Creatures of the mountains, Caobolds looked thin but were immensely strong, almost as strong as a Dwarf. They lived in the high cliffs and in the depths, equally at home in either. Vicious and mean, they were territorial of what they thought was theirs.

The Caobold hissed and spat at Hall, pulling the stone sword back to deliver another attack.

It never got the chance.

Roxhard ran and jumped onto the stone chest. Using it as a springboard, he jumped again and slammed into the Caobold, tackling the creature to the ground. Both landed hard on the stone floor, the stone sword clattering to the ground. Hall struggled to draw his sword, the jagged edge of the Caobold's sword had opened a larger wound. He could hear the two,

Dwarf and Caobold, struggling in the shadows, rolling farther away, exchanging blows.

Managing to stand up, one hand clutching at the wound, the other reaching into his pouch for a bandage, Hall heard more scratching. Turning to the sound, away from the fighting, Hall saw two more Caobolds step into the ring of light from the torch.

Cursing, hand still clutching the wound, the other drew his sword.

"Hall," Leigh yelled out as the light from Sabine's torch came closer.

Added to the light of the dropped torch, they could see the two Caobolds, the block of stone, and Hall standing with one hand holding his sword. Leigh moved to the side opposite the Caobolds, closer to the wounded Hall. Sabine was stuck holding the torch and her staff, neither hand free, as one of the Caobolds turned toward her.

Hall swung his sword, the metal weapon clanking dully against the Caobold's stone sword. The creature tried to use its surprising strength to push Hall's blade out of the way. It was at a disadvantage as Hall was that much taller and swinging down. He managed to push the Caobold's weapon out and away, quickly bringing his lighter and faster weapon back in to attack. He sliced a line across the creature's chest, cutting leather and drawing blood.

The Caobold hissed and stepped back out of Hall's greater reach.

He followed it, taking a lunging step forward, stabbing out with the sword. He caught the Caobold in the chest, his weight and length pushing the weapon through the thin creature's bony body. Its sword dropped to the ground as it fell backward off Hall's sword.

Hearing wood smacking against stone, he turned to see

Sabine stepping backward. She was awkwardly swinging her staff, using it to block the attacks from the other Caobold.

She wanted to drop the torch, to grip the staff with both hands, to try to force the Caobold back to give her time to cast a spell, but the creature kept pushing, and she knew she needed the light.

The creature advanced, using its strength to push her staff out of the way. Seeing an opening, it took a step forward, sword pulled back and ready to swing. Sabine set her feet, ready to move out of the way when the Caobold stumbled forward, carried by the impact of a javelin slamming into its back and out through its chest.

Hall stood over the stone chest, leaning forward with arms extended. He held the javelin out as far as he could get it, Leigh to the side, helping to keep him from falling over.

The Caobold struggled, its sword dropping to the ground and looking down at the point protruding from its chest. It grasped as the javelin's shaft, trying to push or pull the weapon out of its body. Hall pulled back, the creature stumbling off-balance.

There was another clatter as Sabine dropped her staff. She pointed a finger at the Caobold's face and cast *Shadowbolt*. The defenseless Caobold took the spell full blast, black energy splashing around its face, and fell motionless. Hall let the javelin go, and the dead Caobold fell to the ground, Sabine stepping aside out of the way. Smoke rose from the ruins of the creature's face.

SLAIN: *Dark Hole Ambusher*
+30 Experience

SLAIN: *Dark Hole Ambusher*
+10 Experience

Skill Gain!
Small Blades Rank 2 +.1

Skill Gain!
Polearms Rank 2 +.1

Stumbling, still bleeding out, Hall turned toward where he had last heard Roxhard and the Caobold struggling. There were no sounds of fighting, just heavy breathing.

"Rox?" he asked.

"I'm okay," Roxhard answered with a cough, stepping out of the shadows.

In the weak light, they could see that his face was bruised and bloody. There was a gash in his arm, blood running down and dripping onto the ground.

"Damn things are strong."

Hall stood up, wobbling, clutching at his side. He felt Leigh's hands lightly touching him on either side of the wound. The blue tattoos on her arm started to glow, the blue light mixing weirdly with the light from the torches. Hall felt a warmth growing outward from the touch, spreading through his body, but concentrating on the wound.

The skin pulled together, melding and healing, the blood drying. In moments, it was done, the gash gone. He still felt stiff, would feel stiff for a while. Checking his status, he saw that his Health had risen a lot but the Vitality was still down. He stretched, trying to work out the stiffness. He had been feeling all the wounds for days, each one a little worse than before.

An accumulation of restless and uncomfortable nights, healed and unhealed wounds, pushing his body each day. Even magical healing could not take care of that. He needed a couple good nights of sleep and hearty meals.

Or a good Vitality Potion.

While he had two Minor ones, Hall didn't want to use them yet.

"Thank you," he said, smiling.

She smiled back.

Leigh moved over to Roxhard, touching him on the forehead and the arm below the gash. Again, her tattoos glowed blue. Hall watched as the gash on Roxhard's arm slowly disappeared. The skin fused back together, the blood drying. The bruises on his face shrunk, changing from black and blue to the normal dark complexion.

She stepped back, and he shifted his arm, testing the movement.

Sabine picked up the torch, moving to the far end of the cave. She waved the torch around, examining the walls. In the back, between two boulders, she found a small tunnel. Barely three feet high and that round, it must have been where the Caobold's came from. Footsteps behind her signaled Hall's approach.

He crouched down and looked down the tunnel, unable to see far.

"Dammit," he muttered, standing up. "I feel like an idiot. Should have checked for crap like this," he said, waving his hand at the tunnel.

"Live and learn," she replied. "Check out the chest. I'll keep an eye on this."

She couldn't see if he nodded, but assumed he had. She had noticed that he did that a lot, nodding as a way to communicate. A man of few words and decisive action. She liked that. It was one of the reasons she had stayed with him and the Dwarf.

Hall moved back to the chest, motioning to Roxhard to stand on the other side. Across from each other, they both grabbed corners of the stone chest's top. At the same time, they lifted the heavy slab, grunting with effort, and managed to get it up just enough to slide it to the side. They revealed an opening in the chest, just enough to see inside. Pouches lay on top of what looked to be books on top of weapons and armor.

Holding the torch closer, Hall started pulling objects out.

One bag felt like coins, the other had sharper edges. Jewels. Each felt heavy. The two books were large, heavy and thick. Bound in leather with metal at the corners. The light wasn't good enough to read what was written so he set those aside for now.

The weapons were piled casually on top of each other, the edges still sharp as they caught the light. The first was a hand axe, the head smooth with no markings and the metal handle wrapped in leather. Holding it, Hall felt the familiar tingle of magic. He handed the axe to Roxhard, who glanced at Sabine.

"I can't *Scry* until level six," she replied to his unspoken question.

Quest reward items came identified, their stats and abilities known. When an item was found in the wild, during a raid or a dungeon, or as loot from a random creature killed, the item was sometimes unknown, especially if the item level was higher than the characters. It took a Witch casting *Scry* to discover what the item's properties were. Items that were dropped by quest mobs or bosses were immediately identifiable.

The next item was a piece of gnarled and knotted wood. Two feet long, an inch in diameter, the wood thickened to a wide and thick end. A cudgel. Light, Hall gave it a couple practice swings. It could be swung quickly but he felt the end was thick enough that it would land a heavy blow. It also tingled in his hand.

Leigh was surprised when he handed it to her. She ran her hands along the length of wood, holding it and taking a couple swings.

"Thank you," she said happily, sliding it into her belt.

Hall pulled a short sword out of the chest. It had barely fit, put in at an angle and on its side. The blade was thin, the edges sharp, straight and tapering to a point. The crosspiece was a square bar extending only an inch beyond the blade. The hilt was wrapped in leather, the pommel a metal diamond shape set in a square. There was a symbol etched into it, but in the darkness, Hall could not make it out.

He ran his finger over the etching, feeling a triangle with a horizontal line through it, a half circle connected to the ends of the line. He felt like he should know what the symbol meant but could not think of it.

Setting the short sword down, he reached for the first piece of armor. There were four pieces of armor, each with the tingle of magic, strong enough to feel without touching. A thin cloth belt went to Sabine. The leather with metal plate attached shoulder pad was given to Roxhard.

The third item was a single leather bracer. The color was hard to tell but it was plain with little to no scroll work. Two small throwing knives were set into sheaths on the top and bottom of the bracer. The blades were only about two or three inches long, weighted at the end. Hall put the bracer in his pouch.

The last piece of armor, the last item in the chest, was a leather helm. Plain, nothing more than a skull cap. It was odd shaped. Smaller than a human head, but wide. Made for a Dwarf and so Hall gave it to Roxhard.

"That's it," he said, standing up. The short sword, books, and pouches went into his bag. "Let's get back outside."

While Hall had been going through the stone chest, Roxhard had searched the Caobolds. There had been nothing worthwhile. Not even the weapons were worth salvaging.

They quickly retraced their steps, moving faster as they knew there were no traps and had already walked the path. It was harder going as the passage now sloped up, and the steeper angles were tough. They all grew tired but none wanted to stop.

Each wanted to see the sun.

Pike squawked and Angus mooed as they entered the cave. The dragonhawk fluttered up and landed on Hall's shoulder, the cow moving over to Leigh and nuzzling at her hand. She quickly scratched behind his ear. Retrieving his spear, Hall led them outside.

The sun was higher but still a couple hours before dark. Plenty of time to head back down to the foothills. He started that direction, hugging the wall when Roxhard spoke up, calling for their attention.

He had stopped to get a better look at the leather cap, holding it in his hands now that they were in the sun. The cap was plain. No ornamentation, not well crafted. Functional and that was it. Hall had felt the tingle of magic so the item had some hidden value.

Roxhard held it in his hand, arm extended so all could see.

At first there was nothing standing out, but then Hall saw the color. The leather was dyed, patchy and streaky, like it had been dunked in a vat and hung out to dry.

It was a dark red, the color of dried blood.

"Redcaps," he cursed.

CHAPTER TWENTY-TWO

DISTANT COUSINS TO THE DWARVES, RELATED MORE TO Gnomes, Redcaps were considered the finest airship builders in the entire world. Their ships were strong, armored, and heavily armed. Not the fastest ships, but they made up for it in power. Elven ships, especially those of the Highborn, were for more graceful, but the ships of the Redcaps were more feared.

Because of this, the Redcaps were pirates. They raided villages and cities on the edges of all the islands, roaming the entire world, as well as attacking any other airships they came across. More often than not, those ships would choose to run away instead of trying to defend themselves against the Redcaps. They would count on their speed over the bulkier Capships to escape.

As vicious as Goblins, as strong as Dwarves, the Redcaps were feared fighters.

Duntin, as the race was truly known, earned the name Redcap because of the tradition of dunking their leather skull caps in the blood of their enemies.

"This was a Redcap treasure chest," Sabine exclaimed, also cursing.

All eyes went to the sky, scanning the clouds and the blue beyond. Were those dark spots in the distance islands or ships? Both? Hall fought the temptation to walk to the island's edge and look below. He'd done it before, everyone had, but the way the wind blew around the shelf he didn't feel safe enough to satisfy idle curiosity. The chances of the Redcaps returning at that moment were slim.

But then he remembered this was a game, or supposed to be. Opening the chest would have been a triggering event and prompt the return of the Redcaps.

Nothing seemed to be happening. No ship shockingly appeared from below. No shadow in the distance came quickly closer.

"Let's get out of here," he said, not wanting to tempt fate.

There was no way they could handle an airship's worth of Redcaps.

Hall led the party back into the crack in the mountain. He was cautious, not wanting to rush, listening hard. The crack was just wide enough for one but if someone or something came up from below there would be no way to turn around. It would be too easy to become trapped in the tight space. He held his spear, ready to use the length to keep anything at bay.

They made it safely through the crack and onto the foothills. The journey was slower because of caution, along with it always taking longer going down. It was close to night-fall when they stepped out of the crack and next to the two boulders with the slab. Hall glanced up into the sky, seeing the moon on one side and the setting sun on the other. The sun made the clouds red, a beautiful sunset.

Not enough time to find a suitable campsite.

Hall looked back into the crack. It was wider at this part, and the boulders did provide some cover from the foothills. It would have to do.

They didn't light a fire, the night cold. The crack did

provide some shelter from the wind across the foothills but the stone was hard and sloped. None of them got a truly restful sleep, and Hall had more watches taken throughout the night, each taken two shifts, with himself pulling the last.

The morning sun woke them, all with another loss of Vitality. They were tired, aching, and irritable. Until they were able to get the items identified, or able to afford it, it would be hard to tell if the trek was worth it.

Leaning against the stone wall of the crack as the others woke up and stretched, Hall had pulled out the treasure map. Now that it had been decoded and used, the magical map was just parchment. All the lines were there, the text and markers readable by the others. The case was still a nice piece of work, worth a decent amount if he wanted to sell it. By itself, the map was worthless. He didn't think he'd sell either of them. Not a truly sentimental person, Hall still thought they would be good to keep.

Returning them to his pouch, he pulled out the short sword, wanting to examine the etched symbol. He remembered the feel of it in the dark, and he had guessed pretty good. Now in the light he saw that there was a triangle with the point up. Midway through the triangle was a line connected to an arc. A pyramid with a crescent moon? It appeared like the point of the pyramid was breaking through the crescent which loomed behind it.

Something about it was definitely familiar but he still couldn't place it.

Replacing the short sword in the pouch he pulled out the bags of coins and jewels. The bags were simple canvas with hide strings threaded through the top. Undoing the tie, he opened the bag and dumped the contents out in his hand. Eight gold coins, twenty silver and eight copper. Not a huge amount but decent. Replacing the coins in the bag, he dumped out the jewels.

"Is that what I think it is?" Sabine asked.

Hall nodded. It was.

Five jewels lay in his hand, all rough cut, all small. Each was about a half inch long and that high, sharp edges. Three of them were rubies, another an emerald, but it was the last that had them excited. Smallest of the five, it was green with an orange tint. It seemed to glow with an inner light, accenting the green aspects.

A Sun Emerald.

A very rare jewel.

Hall had no idea what the small one he held was worth but knew it was counted in hundreds of gold. Holding it between fingers, he held it up to the light. The orange color was not lines or a stain but more spread out, part of the jewel.

This single jewel alone made the trek worthwhile.

"We need to do more treasure maps," Roxhard said, looking at the small jewel in Hall's hand.

Hall placed the jewels back in the bag, tying it tight, and returned it to his pouch. Standing up, he grabbed his spear from where it lay against the wall. His bedroll had already been packed, and the others were rolling theirs up.

"None of it is worth anything until we can get to town and sell it," he said, stepping out of the crack.

He looked out over the foothills and the plains. Birds circled in the morning sky, but otherwise all was silent and empty. For now.

Pulling up his internal map, he scaled the distance from where they were to Land's Edge Port. At least four days, most likely five. The Far Edge Peaks were home to many creatures living in the valleys between mountains and on the peaks themselves. While the Boarin and Centaur tribes lived in the plains themselves, Goblins and other nasties lived in the foothills at the base of the mountains. It would not be an easy trek across the mountains, and Hall contemplated taking the time to go into the plains themselves instead of the foothills.

Which would be safer?

There were risks involved in both. No way would they avoid all the various dangers. Would the added travel through the plains be any safer? He glanced at his Vitality bar, how low it was and not rising. That made his choice.

The sooner they got to Land's Edge Port, the sooner they could get a good rest and regain their much-needed Vitality.

———

Pike soared overhead, keeping out over the plains and not close to Far Edge Peaks. Cliff Shrikes had been seen, the aggressive and larger birds would be too much for the smaller dragonhawk. Shrikes were dangerous birds, fast with long and sharp talons and serrated beaks. Their screech could produce a stunning debuff.

Hall had hated the few quests out of Land's Edge Port that involved the Shrikes. Any quests involving Shrikes on any of the islands he hated. They always attacked in pairs and were almost impossible to target. It took forever to wait for one to swoop low enough to be able to attack and that one's call would bring another into the fight. Some Players were known to avoid quests involved Shrikes just because of how annoying the fights were.

He had chosen a path that was midway between the plains and the mountains, staying in the foothills but not directly mountainside. The walking was easier, the land not as steep or rocky, and the dangers from creatures like Cliff Shrikes was lessened. Staying in the foothills kept them away from Centaurs and Boarin.

Not that the foothills were without dangers of their own.

Because of their numbers, the mountain cats and other

predators stayed away. They kept small fires at night hoping any visible smoke would be mistaken for Centaur or Boarin campfires, using the fires to keep the night predators away. They could see plenty of fires out on the plains in the time after the sun set and full dark appeared. The plains were busy at night. They fell asleep to the sounds of wolves howling, the great cats prowling, and other nocturnal hunters.

In a way, Hall found it peaceful. He'd spend his watch hours, typically first and last, sitting and staring out across the grassy plains, just listening to the sounds. He'd grown up in the woods and had moved to the city, gotten used to the city noises, but had always remain a lover of the woods. He missed these sounds. It was different, he knew. This wasn't the woods of his home, this was the wild. The noises belonged to dangerous creatures.

But he found it peaceful, felt like he belonged.

The second night from the passage, he was on first watch. He had just put some more sticks and small logs on the fire, building it back up for the cold night. The wind had died down and they were fairly well sheltered in a hollow formed by a fallen tree and some boulders. Standing at the edge, he watched the land around him, listening to the sounds of the others sleeping. Around midnight, he heard Leigh get up from camp and approach.

Her turn on watch.

He didn't immediately turn and head to his bedroll but stood there as she came alongside, standing close and almost touching. Together, they watched the plains.

"We should be in Land's Edge Port in two days," Hall said, finally breaking the silence. He hadn't wanted to, enjoying her silent company, but felt he should. "I figure a day to recover and then can take the airship to Edin and head for your Grove."

Leigh stiffened at the mention of the Grove. From their

conversations he knew she was not truly looking forward to it, had been trying to delay. But it was time.

They were silent for a little longer, Hall thinking he should head to bed but Leigh started to speak.

"These foothills remind me a little of Edin," she said. "It's one hill after another, large ones covered in grass and rocks. Cold and windy. Foggy. But beautiful."

"I know," Hall replied. "Edin is probably my favorite of all the realms."

"You've been?"

"Yes," he replied before he could stop himself. He had been in the previous game, not this new one. Now he had not been to Edin before. He could picture it though, knew what it was like. And Leigh was right. It was rugged but beautiful.

Like she was.

"Ever been to Cliff Fields?"

"Nope, never heard of it before you mentioned it was where you were from."

And he hadn't, which was odd. He had explored every inch of Edin before, and there had never been a village called Cliff Fields. He wondered how many other new villages there were.

He caught her smile in the moonlight.

You have earned +200 Alliance points with Leigh. She is pleased that you remembered the name of her small village on Edin.

"There's a lot about you and the others that doesn't make much sense," Leigh said.

Hall glanced down at her. The Druid was looking out at the plains and not at him. That statement worried him. He had been afraid that Sabine's questioning was going to make her nervous about them, question their sanity even.

It shouldn't have even been an issue. They were Players, she was an NPC. Her AI programming should have basically prevented her from understanding what they were saying or even caring. But she did somewhat understand and did seem to care.

"Sometimes you all sound a little crazy."

There was nothing accusatory in her tone, or fear, or nervousness. It was just a simple statement of an observation. Hall still expected her to say she was leaving them at first light. He wouldn't blame her but he knew that he'd miss her.

"Sorry about that," he started. "It's just…" he paused, unsure of what to say.

"Don't worry about it," Leigh told him, looking up at him with a smile. "For whatever reason, I trust you. That might make me the crazy one."

She laughed lightly.

Hall liked the sound of it.

"That means a lot," he said and meant it.

They fell silent again, Hall wondered if he should say or do more.

"Shouldn't you be getting some sleep?" Leigh finally said after a couple minutes.

He knew she wasn't trying to get rid of him, there was a hint of disappointment in her voice. She was just stating a fact, something he should have thought of himself.

"You're right," he replied, making sure a similar note of disappointment was in his voice.

With reluctance, he bid her goodnight and walked back to the fire. Adding another log, he spread out his bedroll and curled up under the blanket. He stared at the stars for a couple minutes and fell into a relatively restful sleep.

———

Two days later they left the foothills and crossed the last bit of the plains. They could see forest just to the south, a gap between the trees that marked where the Grayhold Road was. As they got closer, they could see some traffic on that road, wagons pulled by horses and people walking on foot. Coming in from the east there was no farmland or surrounding villages.

Hall had been surprised to learn from Leigh that there were a handful of small villages surrounding the city. Places where the local farmers could meet and organize along with the tradespeople that supported them. Most were only a day at most from the walls of the city. He remembered there being a handful of farms around Land's Edge Port, there had been some quests involving them. But those had just been small collections of buildings, the homestead and a barn or two. There had been a logging camp in the woods to the southwest, a half dozen buildings. Beyond that, nothing but the city itself.

From what Leigh had said, Edin didn't seem that much of a different place then he had known. Grayhold and even River's Side were similar, just farther apart because of the scale and distance differences. He was expecting Land's Edge Port to be similar to what he had remembered.

He was wrong.

They joined up with the hard-packed road, alone on it for now. Wide enough for two wagons side by side, it was well maintained. No ruts or potholes. It ran north where it met the plains and then west to where the city was nestled in a small valley at the edge of the island. Hall stopped at the top of the rise, the road descending into the valley and the city.

Which was not what he had expected.

Like all cities and villages in Sky Realms Online, Land's Edge Port had not been true size. There had been a handful of random homes but the majority had been functional buildings. Shops, tradespeople, guilds, the bank, and so on. Only about three dozen buildings surrounded by a wall with the docks built out from the edge of Cumberland.

What he saw now was a true city. There were hundreds of

homes; wooden and stone, two or three stories. A wall of gray stone still surrounded the city, a large half circle with towers at the island's edge, surrounding the two gates, and spaced evenly between. The road led to the east gate of the city, another road coming out of the west gate and heading toward the farms and villages.

Fields filled most of the space between the slopes of the valley and the walls of the city. Hall saw a large pond to one side and clumps of trees scattered around, a larger forest nestled against the eastern slope of the valley.

Hall estimated the city to be about four miles long, maybe three miles deep. There had to be thousands of people living within its walls. Smoke rose from countless chimneys, evening supper fires starting.

Laid out in five or six pie shaped sections, all roads in the wall led to an open space in the middle of the city. The market. Halfway between the market and the docks was the largest building in the city. Four stories tall, made of wood and stone, Leigh said it was the Duke's palace. The docks were built out from the edge of the land, over the air and nothingness below. There were numerous small airships docked, and others could be seen coming and going, their large propellers and steam engines keeping them afloat.

Hall glanced at Roxhard and Sabine, seeing them equally surprised and confused.

Even scared.

As immersive as Sky Realms Online had been, it had still been limited by the game mechanics and processing ability of the servers as well as the programming ability of the developers.

What they were looking at should have been impossible. No game, not even non-VRMMORPGS, had a city that looked this true. No game had a city of this scope and size. How much processing power would a city of thousands take?

"You three act like you've never seen a city before," Leigh said with a chuckle. "Come on, we need to hustle if we hope to find an Inn with enough vacancy." She started down the road leading to the city.

With a shrug to the other two, Hall followed.

PART THREE
THE GROVE

CHAPTER TWENTY-THREE

THEY PASSED THROUGH THE GATES UNQUESTIONED. GUARDS stood on the outside and on the inside, armed with sword and spear, dressed in the standard Essec tunic. Hall wondered what level they were, figuring they had to be higher than the ones at Grayhold but were they maximum level? Which now appeared to be twenty.

Using Identify, getting a gain, he saw that they were level twelve.

Their small group were the only ones walking through the East Gate, the Grayhold Road empty for now.

Once through the wall, the noise of the city erupted. It came from almost nowhere. There had been no warning, the walls of stone blocking out most of it. Merchants, horses, people yelling and arguing. The noises of a city. There were mostly Gaels in the city, but some of the other races were spread throughout the crowds. Elves, Wild and Highborn. Nords and Arashi. Firbolgs and Bodin. Dwarves and even their rare forest dwelling cousins, Gnomes.

Land's Edge Port had never been a huge city, or a diverse city, just serving as the Port where lower level players could get airships to the other islands. It had shops and trainers, everything a low-level character would need. But this? Hall was amazed. This was a true city.

And a bustling port.

Which made some sense, he thought picturing Cumberland's location in the world of floating islands. It was pretty central to the rest of the world, a buffer between parts of Essec and the unclaimed islands like Edin. Land's Edge Port would be a way stop for ships traveling from the islands to the east on the way to the west or the islands above and below.

They pushed their way through the crowded streets, heading toward the central square where most of the inns and taverns were located. Pike sat on Hall's shoulder, squawking at anyone that came too close, screeching each time Hall got bumped. Sharp talons would dig into Hall's shoulder with each collision, and there were a lot of them.

Leigh seemed to be having less problems. Angus walked ahead of her, the cow pushing people out of the way. Roxhard used his bulk to push a path while Sabine followed close behind in his wake.

Hall kept a watch for other players but saw none. Just NPCs, or what he assumed were NPCs. There were plenty of people dressed in arms and armor, mercenaries and guards most likely, but none that he could identify as another Player.

Was Sabine right that the number was low? There had been a dozen or so at the Laughing Horse. They should have been seeing some others. But in a city of thousands, other Players would be easy to miss.

They passed shops that catered to people with real lives, not adventurers or Players. Book shops, dress makers, bakeries. A true city filled with people that had their own lives.

He was finding it hard to believe that all these random people were computer generated.

It took over an hour to push through the streets and get to

the market, which was even more crowded. The market was in a large open area, cobblestone pavers with a large fountain in the middle. Round, fronted by many buildings on the perimeter and all the roads leading into it, the market was filled with organized rings of stalls and tents. The outer ring faced the buildings, back to back with a second ring that had a wide space between it and the third ring, which was back to back with a fourth. It continued like that until the last ring that faced the fountain. There were gaps between every ten or so stalls that formed lanes to pass from ring to ring.

All the stalls and tents were full, people yelling and hawking their wares. All the shouting turned into one massive noise, no way to pick out individual sellers. The stalls they could see sold a collection of everything imaginable. Carpets, books, cloaks, belts, and even food. It was if every shop in the city was represented here in the central hub. And somehow it was even more crowded.

"This way," Hall said, turning the group to the left.

The Land's Edge Port, he remembered, had two inns: one near the market, which was not even a quarter the size of the one they were walking through, and the other near the docks. He pulled up his map to check to see if they were going in the right direction.

City maps had always been stylized but what he was looking at now was not. It seemed as if every building in the city was represented, most unlabeled. There were no labels at all, no streets, no special features. Just blocks for buildings and lines representing streets.

So much for the Cartography skill, he thought as he scanned the wooden signs hanging over the doors of the buildings. On a whim, an instinct telling him to do it, he opened up his internal map again and saw that the buildings along the market ring were starting to get identifiers.

Skill Gain!
Cartography Rank 2 +.2

He glanced up at a sign, reading it as the Carl's Family Butchery. The words were along the top and bottom of the wooden sign, faded letters that were barely readable. They encircled an image of a meat cleaver stuck inside a rack of ribs.

On his map a small dot appeared on the same building. Concentrating on the dot, it brought up the name of the business. He checked some of the other buildings with dots, seeing the names of the business he had passed pop up.

Apparently, the skill did come in useful.

Halfway around the ring, almost directly opposite of where they had entered the market, they finally found an Inn. The Market View had a set of double doors facing the market, glass filled windows on either side. It was a three-story building, an alley to the side leading to what Hall assumed would be the stables. A couple of teenage boys leaned against the wall near the alley. They were well dressed and attentive. As the group approached the doors one of them stepped forward to meet them.

"Begging your pardon, sirs and madams," he said, well-spoken along with dressed. Had to work for the Inn, Hall figured. "But your, uhm... cow and bird can't go inside," he finished and pointed toward the doors. "We can lead them out back to the stable."

The boy looked down at Angus with a worried expression, not sure if he could actually do what he said he could. He would try, no way would he risk his job. He looked up at Pike, the dragonhawk returning the glance with a glare of his own. Pike opened his beak, showing off how sharp it was.

Now the boy was visibly nervous.

"How much?" Hall asked.

It took a moment for the boy to register what Hall had said, still staring at Pike.

"3 silver a day," he managed to get out.

The price shocked Hall. It was expensive. That kind of coin would have bought almost a week at Grayhold or even River's Side. There had been plenty of horses when they first entered the city but he had noticed less and less the deeper into the city they walked.

"The nearest public stable is almost at the wall in the Trades Quarter," the boy said helpfully, most likely hoping they would take the animals there. He pointed toward the southeast.

Hall had no desire to walk through those crowds again only to turn around and come back. They were only there for the one night, hoping to fly out in the morning. Fishing the money out of his pouch, he handed it to the boy.

Stepping up to Angus he looked for the lead rope. Leigh chuckled.

"Follow him," she told the cow, who looked up at her and mooed with annoyance.

Reaching his hand up, Pike stepped from shoulder to wrist, and Hall transferred the bird onto Angus' back. The cow grunted as Pike's talons dug in as the bird secured himself.

"Stay with Angus," Hall told Pike. The bird just squawked.

The boy laid his hand on Angus' side and nudged the cow forward toward the alley.

"And no biting," Hall told Pike.

The boy looked back, really scared now as he moved his hand away from Pike.

"I was talking to the cow," Hall said with a laugh.

The boy didn't look amused.

———

Hall woke up refreshed.

First thing he did as he lay on his back looking up at the post and beam ceiling with wood decking was to check his stats. His Vitality was fully restored. A good night's sleep in a comfortable bed, a full meal, and a lot of the small accumulated aches and pains were gone.

He got out of bed, stretching and feeling completely healthy for the first time in weeks.

Roxhard was still snoring away in the other bed. They had rented two rooms, the women in one and them in the other. The Inn's common room had been full but they still had a couple vacancies.

Even with magical healing, the various wounds he had picked up had still hurt and hampered. His side, where the Caobold had cut him, had been stiff and tight, preventing full movement. Even without the wounds, just the wear and tear on the body from spending weeks in the wilds had started to take its toll. After just one night he felt renewed.

Congratulations!
You have achieved a Full Night's Rest. All Vitality has been restored.

Leigh had said the airship from Edin to Cumberland had been a three-day trip. If the trip from Cumberland to there was the same, that would be three more days of decent sleep and meals. As long as they had no random encounters while in the air.

"Get up," Hall said, nudging Roxhard as he pulled on his armor and cloak.

The Dwarf grumbled, one jet black eye opening up and staring at Hall with annoyance. He closed his eye, but another nudge from Hall, this one a little harder, and Roxhard finally sat up. Yawning, stretching, he climbed out of the bed.

"Look at that," he said.

"Full *Vitality*?" Hall asked, and Roxhard nodded. "Meet you downstairs."

Grabbing all his gear, Hall walked out into the corridor, closing the door behind him. He could hear Roxhard stumbling about the room, grumbling as he struggled into his boots. Turning toward the stairs, Hall headed down into the common room.

Mostly empty, the room was filled with round tables and a long bar on the right wall, a door leading into the kitchen. A large fireplace was directly opposite the stairs, the doors to enter on the left. A bartender, different from last night, was behind the bar wiping it down. The lone barmaid was moving around the tables making adjustments to the placement and seating. Only three tables were occupied.

He found one with four seats leaning his spear against the table, noticing that one of the men at a table of three was watching. The man was older, gray hair and beard with a few streaks of black. Functional but well-made clothing. Thin. He was seated with his back to the bar. Hall figured him to be a merchant of some kind. The other two were obviously bodyguards. They wore leather pants with chainmail shirts, swords strapped to waist and shields leaning against the table.

Taking the harness that held his javelin off, setting it down besides the chair, Hall sat down in a seat where he could see the door as well as the man that was studying him. The merchant didn't try to hide his interest. Hall tried to pull the man's name and class, hoping for a level reading at least but there was nothing. His *Identify* must not have been high enough, something else new to worry about. Hall stared at the merchant, wondering what he wanted. The man smiled and turned back to talking to one of the two guards.

Shaking his head, Hall motioned to the barmaid.

She had just set down the drink he had ordered when Sabine walked down the stairs. She was fully dressed and carrying her staff. Asking the barmaid for a drink, she sat down opposite Hall.

"Leigh was up early," she told him. "Said something about checking on Angus and Pike."

He nodded. Using his bond, he had checked on Pike already this morning. The dragonhawk had spent a restful night in the rafters of the stable, a building behind the Inn. There were a half dozen fewer mice now as well.

"What's the agenda for today?" she asked.

"Sell some stuff," he answered. "Empty the packs, and then see if can find a Witch to *Scry* the items for us. I need to get some level three training. After that, hitch a ride on an airship to Edin."

Sabine was quiet for a moment, staring out the window at the activity on the awakening street. People could be seen walking past, getting an early start on setting up for the day's market. During the brief time, more patrons had come into the Inn seeking breakfast.

"What's the plan once on Edin?" she asked, looking over at him.

He shrugged.

"Go to Leigh's Grove and see what's going on," he answered. "After that, don't know."

"No long-term plan?"

"Not really. Not at this point."

"Roxhard going to tag along?"

"Probably," Hall answered. "Hadn't asked him but don't see why not. Someone needs to look out for him."

Hall studied the Witch. She was nervous about something, hesitant.

"You're more than welcome to come along as well," he said, taking a guess at what was bothering her.

She smiled.

"Sure," Sabine replied with some of her usual confidence

back. "Didn't have plans of my own, and the more the merrier."

At that moment, Roxhard finally came downstairs, lugging his gear, and Leigh walked in through a back door.

"Let's get some breakfast and then head out," Hall said, signaling the barmaid.

———

They didn't have to go far to find everything they were looking for. Hall decided to hold off on selling the jewels, especially the Sun Emerald. The others agreed. They didn't end up needing the money from the jewels as they were able to sell the excess gear they had acquired and repair their own without hitting their coin funds.

Hall knew that wouldn't last. Their next stop was a Witch.

Out early enough in the morning, there wasn't as many people, and they didn't have to fight the crowds. Which also allowed them time for a bit of haggling.

Sabine turned out to be a natural. Equal parts flirtatious, knowledgeable, demanding, and begging. It was masterful to behold. They left the merchants thinking they had gotten the better of the party but Hall was satisfied with the deals they had gotten. He wondered if she was raising the *Negotiation* skill.

Following directions from the leatherworker that had done his best to repair Hall's tunic, they left the market ring and turned down one of the main roads that cut the city into segments. Taking a side street, they soon found the shop they were looking for. The first floor of a three-story building with two large windows covered by black curtains and a single door, The Crystal Seer had a very small sign over the door. The only thing that indicated a shop there at all.

Entering, they found a small room; shelves filled with books, scrolls and wands along one wall and a curtained door in the back. A single table sat in the middle of the room on a circular carpet made of elaborate shapes in gold on a red background. The table itself was plain, stained oak, with nothing on top. Two chairs sat across from each other. The space was dark, lit by oil lamps set in the corners. Just enough light to see by.

"Hello?" Hall called out.

A woman walked out. Dark of skin showing her to be from Arashi. Older, with long, wavy gray hair. She wore a blue robe, cinched at the waist and cut up high on the sides. She wore large hoop earrings and a smaller hoop through her nose. Dark blue eyes surveyed the group, appraising them. They made an interesting group. Three Gaels; a Druid, Witch, and Skirmisher. A Dwarf Warden. A cow and a dragonhawk.

"Adventurers," she stated more than asked, no hint of an accent. "I am Idita. What can I do for you this fine morning?"

"We'd like a couple Scryings done," Hall answered.

"Your Witch not high enough yet?" she asked, sitting down at the table and motioning for Hall to sit across from her. She didn't wait for an answer. "I charge 10 silver for the spell regardless if it succeeds or not. Another 5 silver for each attempt after the first."

"We have five items," Hall said, taking the bracer out of his pouch and placing it on the table. He thought about including the Redcap's leather helmet that Roxhard had, but that could lead to questions. There was nothing wrong with having it, but it was not a typical item one would carry. For some reason, he thought it best to not advertise they'd found a Redcap's stash.

From what Leigh had said, the ability to read a treasure map was rare and he didn't want to be bombarded with questions that he couldn't provide answers to.

Following the bracer, he pulled out fifty silver and set it on the table, wincing as he did so. It was a good amount of coin. But he had known it would be costly. Scryings always were.

Even once a Witch learned the spell, they sometimes still had to visit higher level Witches. The spell rose in power with the character's level. Lower levels, it could only identify the quality of an item. Higher levels could reveal more information. Only a max-level Witch could fully identify Artifact quality items.

Sliding the silver across the table, counting it with her eyes, Idita picked the pile up and quickly made it disappear in the folds of her robe. She laid a hand over the single bracer. Her smooth skin took on a golden shine, brighter at the fingertips and flowing up her arm. After a couple seconds, she lifted her arm up and smiled.

"Orange," she said in surprise, glancing at Hall who had to fight back a smile.

He acted like it wasn't a shock to have a Rare item. He picked up the item, studying it.

QUICKDRAW BRACER
OF SHARP TEETH
Protection +2
Attack Power +2
Agility +4
Durability: 20/20
Weight: 1 lb.

Contains two Throwing Knives (1d2 +2 DMG, +4 Lightning DMG, 25% chance of Critical Strike bonus of +6 DMG).
Once thrown, a knife will reappear in the bracer after ten minutes.
Cooldown of twenty seconds between throwing knives.

Hall stared at the item, really surprised there wasn't some kind of restriction. There should have at least been a level restriction or a minimum required Agility. Instead, he could use this at his low level. The stats were really good but the throwing knives were a true bonus, giving him additional ranged capabilities. Especially good now that his javelin did not return. Each knife did a maximum of two damage, with the two additional bonus points and lightning damage and with the critical strike chance that could add another four damage. A maximum of fourteen damage for a throwing knife was crazy.

Pulling off his current left bracer, Hall fit the new Epic one around his wrist. It was larger but shrink for a snug fit. He held his arm up, flexing, to make sure it was not too tight. Pulling up his stats, he was a little disappointed to see that he had lost the bonuses given by the old set of bracers. He still got the Protection bonus so kept the one on.

"Next," Idita said with a hint of excitement. The first item was Epic. What else would this odd group have?

Sabine handed her the cloth belt, laying it across the table.

It was made of a thin material, shinier than silk. Hall wasn't sure what it was, but the weaving was of excellent quality. Only an inch thick, it was a dark blue with a lighter blue edging along the entire length. The buckle was a single large smooth red jewel, a ruby, as wide as the belt set in an iron clasp.

"Satin," Idita said running her fingers along the belt.

She held her hand over it, palm down, and repeated the spell. They all looked down to see the belt was identified. A blue item, Rare quality.

BELT OF SHINING STARS
Protection +2
Spell DMG +4
Durability: 15/15
Weight: .5 lbs.

Sabine took the belt back, fitting it around her slim waist. Idita's eyes followed, no doubt wondering if it would be for sale. Sabine shook her head, and Idita smiled, shrugging.

Pulling the shoulder pad out of his pouch, Roxhard set it down on the table. Idita repeated the procedure over the single pad. The leather was a dark color, stained, with the iron plate attached by studs. She lifted her hand, and Roxhard smiled. Another blue, Rare item.

ARMORED SHOULDER OF STRENGTH
Protection +2
Strength +2
Durability: 15/15
Weight: 1 lb.

"Too bad it wasn't part of a set," he said as he set the shoulder pad over his left shoulder. Leigh reached over and helped him set the buckles and attach it to his chain shirt.

Once the pad was in place, he pulled out the hand axe. It turned out to be another Rare item.

AXE OF QUICK STRIKES
DMG: 2d4 +1
Agility: +1
Durability: 15/15
Weight: 3 lbs.

"That will come in handy," he said, slipping the axe through his belt.

Roxhard stepped back and motioned Leigh forward.

Nervously, almost afraid, she laid the cudgel down on the table. Hall wondered if she had ever owned a magical item before. Her gnarled staff had no magical properties of its own, just serving as a conduit for her *Splinter Storm* spell.

Once Idita was done, Leigh looked nervously at Hall as if she expected him to take it back. The cudgel was orange, an Epic quality item.

"Congratulations," he said.

IRONWOOD SHILLELAGH
OF THUNDER
DMG: 4d6 +2
Strength: +1
Durability: 20/20
Weight: 3 lbs.

A successful hit has 25% chance of casting Thunderclap. Effect of dealing additional +10 physical damage and stunning opponent for 15 seconds.

Leigh held the weapon carefully, tenderly, running her fingers down the two-foot length.

Hall pulled the last item out, the short sword. He placed it on the table, making sure the etched symbol was hidden. There was a chance that Idita could recognize it, and that could lead to questions they couldn't answer. The Redcaps had stolen it from somewhere. Like the Redcaps leather helmet, he felt the symbol was something he should keep quiet about. At least until he learned what it meant.

The sword turned out to be another blue Rare item.

Exceptional Short Sword Of Fighting
Attack Power +1
Damage 2d4 +3
Agility: +2
Strength: +1
Durability 20/20
Weight: 5 lbs.

Hall pulled up his Inventory Screen and the stats for his currently equipped short sword.

Grayhold Short Sword
Damage 2D4 (+2)
Durability 12/12
Weight 5 lbs.

Both were short swords so they had the same basic damage. That stat never changed for a weapon type as it was based on weapon size, weight and standard material. Craftmanship, which created a stronger or sharper edge, or different materials would add additional damage along with any magical additions. The bonuses to the Exceptional Short Sword of Fighting would grant it higher damage on a successful hit. In Sky Realms Online, damage from a hit was based on a relatively simple formula. Weapon damage versus the Target's Protection value. A short sword did 2D4 damage, a minimum of 2 points and a maximum of 8 points. That value was adjusted based on Attack Power and any damage bonus, which was +3 in the case of the new short sword versus +2 for the old. The new short sword would do a minimum damage of 6 without factoring Hall's own Attack Power value into the equation or any buffs. The Exceptional marker meant the weapon had been forged by a high-level blacksmith before being enchanted. Any crafter could make an item that could be enchanted, turned magical, but items made by a max level crafter could gain a quality marker. This gave them additional slots for enchanting and increased the durability.

The new sword was a big upgrade on his current weapon. *Hopefully there will be a spear upgrade soon,* he thought sliding the sword into the sheath at his waist, replacing the one he had gotten as a quest reward at Grayhold, which went into the pouch to be sold later.

Idita leaned back in her chair, eyeing Hall.

"Interesting collection of equipment," she said. "Where did you find them all?"

Hall shrugged and stood up.

"I only ask for professional interest," Idita hastily added.

"Thank you for your time," Hall told her as the group headed for the door.

He thought she might say more, try to buy some of the items, but instead she stayed sitting. Hall felt like she was studying him. It made him feel uncomfortable. Magic items were very common. Or at least they used to be. How common were they now? Aside from the Epic bracer, he didn't think their haul to be anything that special. The equipment was a boon for them at such a low level, but still nothing that game-breaking.

So why the interest from Idita?

Were magical items really that rare that this many at once was odd?

He thought to ask Leigh but couldn't think of a way without coming across as stupid. How common magical items were in this world would be common knowledge.

No matter what, he thought, *we need to find some more treasure maps.*

CHAPTER TWENTY-FOUR

UNLIKE THE REST OF LAND'S EDGE PORT, THE GUILDHALL WAS just as Hall had remembered it. A different location, but it looked the same. In the original game, it had been located just off the market ring along with the Vault and Auction House. Now it was on the city's edge near the western wall. A large three-story building, the first built of stone with wood above, it was surrounded by a high wooden fence running from the edge of the city wall to a hundred feet past the building and back toward the island's edge, the front wall breaking the fence.

Large gray square stones, stacked tightly together, framed a wide wooden door. Made of a dark wood and banded with metal, the large doors were open but not inviting. Two armed guards stood on either side at the top of the steps that led up.

The developers had changed Sky Realms Online so that training Class Abilities was no longer needed. Now it appeared that aspect was back and after leaving the Witch, they had headed to the Guildhall so Hall could train.

They walked up the steps, and the guards let them through.

Inside the first floor was one large open space. Stairs ran up to the upper levels on both sides, the floor sunken with wooden steps that served as seats. At the bottom was a dirt floor, stained with blood. Weapons racks lined the walls of the room. There was barely enough space to walk around the edges, the sparring pit being the main feature of the floor. Large doors were against the far wall. Along with the racks were numerous suits of armor and trophies of war. Tattered banners hung from the ceiling over the pit, mounted heads of dragons were set in the four corners. Old weapons hung in places of honor.

There was no one about, the place empty.

Hall led them to the righthand staircase. They walked up into a long room, coming up on the outside wall. The room spanned the whole length with benches filing the entire space. Across, the far wall was lined with doors. At the far end was another set of stairs leading up. It was empty.

"Barracks," Hall said as he led them toward the far stairs.

He looked into the rooms as they passed, some doors opened, and saw the rows of beds. Before, there had always been NPCs roaming the halls. Not trainers but filler, there for immersion. Now there was no one.

They emerged onto the third level and into a long hallway, farther down they could see another stair that led back down. Hall led them through the halls, following a path he had not walked in years.

"Need to talk to the Guildmaster," he said, wondering why he was bothering to say anything.

The others, maybe even Leigh, should have known how it had worked. When it came time to train the first Class Ability, a quest would be given to seek out the Class Guildmaster in that Class' Guildhall. Wardens, Duelists, and Skirmishers shared the same Guildhall, the other Classes having their own. The Guildmaster would determine if the character was worthy, they always were, and then send the character to a trainer. After that first time, the character could go straight to the trainer.

Many players had complained about the extra step. To Hall, it had just added another level of immersion, of realism.

He led them to the office of the Skirmisher Guildmaster, but it was also empty.

Confused, Hall led them back down the other way, coming into the fighting pit from the other set of stairs. The other barracks, identical to the first, was also empty. They headed for the doors at the end of the pit, opening them and stepping outside.

Wooden stairs led down to a grassy area, about two hundred feet between the building and the edge of the island. They could see the blue sky, clouds, and the black dots of the other islands. Dozens of dirt circles ringed with wood were scattered about, extending to both sides around the building. They could finally hear the sounds of activity to the right side.

Walking around the Guildhall, they came to another series of fighting circles and saw a half dozen men standing around one circle. Two people, both Human, could be seen sparring with wooden practice swords. One of the spectators saw them and headed their way.

A large man, bald with long gray beard, a scar cut across his left eye, the orb milky white. He wore leather pants with metal plates on the legs, leather boots, and a sleeveless leather vest. He had a broadsword strapped to his waist and a two-handed bastard sword in a scabbard over his shoulder. Two daggers were sheathed at his waist opposite the sword.

There was a saying that no true Warden was ever without a weapon.

"Ho, visitors," he said. "Don't get many nowadays. Garick is the name. What can I do for you?"

"Where is everyone?" Hall asked, waving his hands to indicate the emptiness.

Garick looked down at him strangely, the man having eight

inches in height and easily a hundred pounds on Hall, all hard muscle.

"New to Land's Edge, I take it," Garick rumbled, the man's voice as strong as he was physically.

Hall nodded.

"Ain't much call for adventurers anymore," Garick said with a sad shake of his head. "All the able-bodied folks rather get regular jobs with the Guards and the Watch, or guarding a merchant's caravan. Some become mercenaries," he finished, spitting on the ground. "Ain't much call for our specialized Abilities anymore."

That makes some sense, Hall thought. If there weren't that many players anymore, then there wouldn't be that many people needing training. There had been very few NPCs with Class skills, like Leigh. Most had just been more common professions such as Guard or Soldier. Even the Smugglers they had fought had the same skills as guards. Those could receive combat training anywhere and had no need for the specialized Class ability training. And no need of the Guildhalls.

"I have need of Training," Hall told him.

"Can see you're a Skirmisher," Garick said, motioning to the spear and javelin on Hall's back as well as Pike sitting on his shoulder. "Your dragonhawk is a young one, freshly bonded, I'd say. Reckon you're level three?"

Hall nodded.

Garick turned and looked among the spectators, finding the man he sought.

"Brandiff," he yelled.

A man turned and stepped away from the others, annoyance clearly visible on his face. He was as tall as Hall, athletic build, and finely muscled. Fiery red hair and beard, streaks of gray. He had the fair skin of the Gael, green tattoos snaked up the exposed skin of his arms. He was dressed similarly to Garick in leather, armed with short sword and dirk.

"What is it?" he said, walking toward them. "Corbin is going to finish off Harlan in three moves."

"No way," Garick said, looking past Brandiff and at the fighters. "Harlan has this match."

"Use your eyes man," Brandiff growled, stopping alongside Garick.

From the sparring pit they heard the clap of wood on wood and something hitting the sand, one of the men yelping in pain. The spectators all gasped.

"Match to Corbin," someone yelled out.

Brandiff looked up at Garick with a smile. The other rolled his eyes.

"This here Skirmisher is in need of some Training," Garick said and pointed at Hall.

Hall felt naked as Brandiff looked him up and down, side to side, and every other way. Sizing him up, looking at the wear and tear on his weapons and armor. Even studying Pike.

"What's your name?" he finally said.

"Hall."

"Level three and *Leaping Stab*," Brandiff stated.

"Yes, sir."

Garick laughed. Brandiff glared.

"Don't call me *sir*. I fight things for a living," Brandiff growled and walked off toward one of the fighting circles, a rack of spears and javelins near it. "Come on," he muttered.

QUEST COMPLETE!

Brandiff has agreed to train you in your new Class Ability.

THE FIRST TRAINER I

Reward: +20 Experience

THE FIRST TRAINER II

Learn the Ability, Leaping Stab, from the Skirmisher Trainer.
Reward: +20 Experience

ACCEPT QUEST?

Hall hurried after the trainer, accepting the next stage of the quest, the others along with Garick following. Brandiff noticed.

"Don't you have anything better to be doing?" he muttered.

"Nope," Garick replied with a laugh.

Brandiff muttered something under his breath. Hall was surprised to hear a couple Arashi swear words, along with a mix of Gael and Nord with some Firbolg mixed in. He had never heard an NPC swear before.

They got to the pit, and Brandiff pulled a spear from the rack.

"Come on then," he said and stepped into the circle. "Show me what you got."

———

Hall landed in the compacted dirt hard. He had only fallen ten feet this time, not fifteen like before. The five feet made a lot of difference in how much it hurt when he crashed.

"You're leaning forward when you stab," Brandiff said from the edge of the pit. "You keep pushing yourself off-balance."

Brandiff came across as hard, muttering and glowering at first, but was proving himself to be an able teacher. They had been at it for an hour now, Hall sweating and aching. They had also drawn a large crowd. The spectators from the earlier sparring match, the fighters themselves, and another half dozen men and women that had wandered in earlier. All stood around the small circle, some sitting down and lounging. All enjoying the entertainment.

Level Twelve, Brandiff had shown Hall to do the *Leaping Stab* a couple of times. The Ability was at the heart of what the Skirmisher could do. Using *Leap*, they would jump over an enemy and land on the other side or jump closer. Landing gave them an attack of opportunity, one that lowered the target's Protection which meant the Skirmisher did more damage. Adding an attack to the *Leap* was difficult but gave the Skirmisher a big advantage in battle. They got an extra attack while in mid leap that the enemy could not defend against. The problem, Hall was discovering, was that using the Ability caused the leaping Skirmisher to push forward with their arms and muscles, which changed the trajectory of the flight. The trick, Brandiff had said and shown, was in not doing just that. Put all the force and strength behind the attack but not change the leaping motion so the Skirmisher would land exactly where they wanted to.

Brandiff made it look easy. His leaps and stabs were almost elegant. Hall felt clumsy.

And embarrassed.

The number of people watching didn't make it any easier. He had expected a couple quick words from Brandiff and to receive the Ability. He had not expected to actually have to train to learn it.

"Wasn't as bad that last one," Brandiff said in way of encouragement. "Hold your back more rigid. Now try it again."

Grunting, trying to ignore the audience, Hall set his feet and activated the *Leap* ability. He jumped into the air, aiming to land equal distance on the opposite side of the hay dummy that had been set up in the center of the ring. At the height of his arc, holding his back rigid, he stabbed down with his spear, catching the dummy in the shoulder. He pulled the spear back, keeping his body in the same position, and landed on the other side. He did a quick side step and rotated to face the dummy stabbing out with the spear again. The second blow landed.

QUEST COMPLETE!
You have learned your new class Ability, Leaping Stab Rank I

Leaping Stab Rank 1
Grants the Skirmisher an attack while in mid-leap. This attack has a bonus of 1D4 to adjusted weapon damage. Target's Protection is lowered by -2 for Damage calculation from the attack. The Skirmisher still gets the attack of opportunity from the Leap.

THE FIRST TRAINER II
Reward: +20 Experience

Hall smiled.

"Good job," Brandiff said, walking over and clapping him hard on the shoulder. "Excellent form. Now do it again."

Hall groaned.

———

"You've got the makings of a pretty good Skirmisher," Brandiff said an hour later as they made their way out of the sparring ring.

The spectators had all dispersed once Hall had gotten the forms down. The fun part, watching Hall fail over and over, was done, and they had other things to do. That had left Roxhard, Sabine, Leigh, and Garick behind. Angus had found a patch of green grass and settled down to eat. Pike had flown off long before looking for a few mice.

"Thank you," Hall said and meant it.

In just the few hours they had been training, Hall had come to realize how skilled Brandiff really was. The man was gruff, blunt, but knew his stuff.

"You come back in a couple levels and see me again," Brandiff said with a chuckle. "But I have a feeling it won't be long before you outlevel me."

At the steps leading to the door back into the Guildhall, the two men clasped hands in the warrior's way, forearm to forearm.

"Good luck in your adventures," Brandiff said as they walked up the steps.

"Roxhard, when you need training, come and find me," Garick said.

The Dwarf turned and waved, a movement that Garick returned a tad confused. It had not been the wave of a battle-hardened, decades-old Dwarven Warden, but the wave of the fourteen-year-old boy.

They walked through the still empty indoor sparring ring. Hall wondered where the other spectators had disappeared to. He thought he could hear footsteps in the floor above. It seemed the Guildhall still provided cheap lodging to member. They walked out the main doors, the same two guards on duty, and down onto the cobblestone street.

"The docks are this way," Hall said, pointing to his left.

"Think we'll still be able to catch a flight," Sabine asked, looking up into the sky. The sun was setting. "It's late."

"If not, we can book an early passage," Hall said leading the way. "I hope we can catch one, I'd rather not pay for another night's lodging."

CHAPTER TWENTY-FIVE

THE LAND'S EDGE PORT DOCKS WERE A CHAOTIC PLACE. LOTS of people, all the races. Lots of noise and motion, people moving all over the place with no pattern, horse drawn wagons moving all over the place with no pattern. A long and open strip, the buildings stopping at the ends and the side, the edge of the island forming the other border. Wooden docks stood off from the edge, extending out into the air with nothing below them. Supports ran down to the rock of the island below, the planks of the docks flexing in the wind and with the weight.

There were half a dozen docks, each as wide as two wagons and as long as two airships. Not all berths were filled. The port could handle up to two dozen airships. Most of the buildings along the port's edge were large warehouses with taverns spaced between. There were a couple of Inns that catered to sailors exclusively and one building that Hall thought looked like a brothel.

They made their way through the crowd, pushing and excusing themselves. Angus received many odd looks, people cursing the cow who didn't bother being polite as he pushed his way through, stomping on feet as he passed. The Portmaster's building was a one-story structure set in between the two middle docks. Not large. It didn't need to be. It still was a dominant structure. Vertical wood plank walls, a couple of windows, and a sloped roof with green shingles. Smoke drifted up from the stone chimney. The door was open as they approached.

An office made up the front room, two other doors leading to other offices. A single desk sat in the middle, chairs on either side wall, a set of stairs leading to a second-floor loft, which was set over the two back offices. A railing ran along the edge of the loft, and they could see two men standing on a balcony that overlooked the docks. They had telescopes mounted to the railing. Two guards in Essec colors stood on either side of the door, a single man at the desk. He had a large ledger book open in front of him, piles of paper on either side and a small stack of coins he was currently counting.

Hall was not sure what to expect. Previously the Player had needed permission from the Portmaster before being able to board an airship for the first time. There had been several docked at Land's Edge Port, each with a set destination.

Looking up from the ledger, the man behind the desk motioned them to step closer.

"Coming or going?" he asked. A thin man, the top of his head bald with a ring of gray hair. Clean shaven, he had a sharp nose that held up a pair of glasses.

"Going," Hall answered.

"Just passengers or with cargo?"

"Passengers."

"With livestock," the Portmaster corrected, pointing at Angus.

"Just the one," Hall clarified.

The Portmaster grunted, not caring. "Destination?"

"Edin."

The man looked down at the ledger, running his finger over some lines, turning a page.

"All the Passenger Ships are currently out but you're in luck. A light cargo ship, The *Twisted Gale* is leaving for Auld on Edin in an hour from Berth Three."

"Thank you," Hall said and turned to leave.

The Portmaster cleared his throat. Hall turned back, and the man tapped the small pile of coins in front of him.

"3 silver each plus 1 for the cow."

"Is that for passage?" Hall asked, genuinely confused. The fee had usually been paid to a sailor stationed at the bottom of each ship's gangplank and would need to be paid before the Player could board and wait for the ship to leave.

"Customs," the Portmaster replied, annoyed. Again, he tapped the desk. "Passage will need to be negotiated with the ship's captain."

"And if we can't negotiate a price?" Hall asked as he set down the requested coin.

"Guess you'll have to come back tomorrow and try again," the Portmaster replied, taking the money and adding it to the pile.

"And pay the customs fee again," Hall muttered.

The Portmaster shrugged and returned to his book.

Grumbling, Hall led the others back outside and turned toward the last dock at the far end, which contained the first four berths. They could see that only one ship was there currently.

─────

The *Twisted Gale* was a Gael vessel, designed and built in Spirehold.

Four large propellers set off from the hull, mounted horizontally to provide uplift, at the four corners. The ship itself was long and lean, built more for speed and less for cargo. It had a raised forecastle and two raised decks in the aft where the two steam engines were mounted. It looked well maintained and cared for. A wide gangplank, twenty feet long, hung from where the ship floated and connected to the dock. Lines went from the ship to cleats on the dock, the propellers adjusted to provide just enough lift to keep the ship in position. It drifted five feet higher than the dock.

"Hello the ship," Hall called from the dock.

There had been no one stationed there, the dock itself empty of anyone. Four large wooden cranes set aside each airship berth.

A sailor appeared at the top of the gangplank, looking down at them.

"What?" he called down, his accent hard to place.

"We seek passage."

The sailor studied them, measuring, eyes lingering on Sabine and Leigh before raising in surprise at Angus. Pike had returned as they had walked out onto the dock, landing and settling on Hall's shoulder, getting another raised eyebrow.

"Wait here," the man said finally. He turned and disappeared.

It was another minute or two before a second man appeared. He studied the group from the deck without saying anything before making a decision. He walked down the gangplank, and Hall stepped aside so the man could step onto the dock. Wearing black pants and boots polished to a shine, a sleeveless leather vest over white shirt and red sash belt with a scimitar through it, the man had to be the ship's Captain. He had long black hair tied in a tail, neatly trimmed beard, dark eyes and the pale Gael skin. Dark blue tattoos could be seen on the exposed skin of his arms. His eyes focused on Sabine and stayed there until he was in front of Hall, identifying him as the leader.

"Captain Hart," he said by way of greeting. "The *Gale* is my ship. I fly with an experienced crew. They are all level four to six, and I, myself, am a level eight Sailor. I hear you are looking for passage?"

"To Edin," Hall answered. "The four of us, the drag-onhawk, and the cow."

Hart looked down at Angus and smiled.

"10 silver each plus 5 for the cow. A cabin you all can share and two meals a day," he said quickly without thinking. The price seemed fair to Hall, who nodded. "You feed the animals from your own meals, and you clean up after them."

"Agreed," Hall said and held out his hand.

The Captain clasped it, giving a firm up and down shake. The deal was sealed.

"Come on and get yourself settled in then," Hart said and motioned toward the gangplank. "We set off in thirty. Welcome aboard the *Twisted Gale*."

———

Hall stood at the starboard rail, watching the buildings of Land's Edge Port shrink as the airship lifted off. The deck vibrated with the spinning of the four propellers, shaking as the engines in the rear ignited. Smoke could be seen drifting up from the aft, a great rumble building and sliding through the ship's hull. He could feel it beneath his feet and where his hands gripped the rail.

The wind picked up, the ship pushing against it. Sailors moved about the deck, stowing lines and tying things down. Hart stood at the highest point in the rear, next to the helmsman.

The *Gale* was facing north and turned to the east as it rose higher. The engine room kept the engines low, barely any forward thrust, just enough to keep the ship turning. It banked and came about, sailing over Land's Edge Port and the Far Edge Peaks where a couple days earlier Hall and friends had been treasure hunting.

He looked down at the mountains, trying to see if he could find the ledge and the cave, but they were too high and cutting an angle that didn't bring them over that part of the range. The rumbling of the engines grew as they increased in power, and the wind started to buffet Hall even harder as the ship picked up speed.

Captain Hart had said the trip from Land's Edge Port to Auld on Edin was four days because the winds were against them. It could be more if they encountered trouble.

In the previous version of the game, Hall had to start thinking of this as a new version, encounters on airships had been random. Most trips only took a couple minutes but sometimes there would be a pirate or roc attack or some other kind of winged monster. Some players did nothing but sail on airships all day waiting for the random encounters as the loot, which was rare and random, could be excellent. With no interruptions the longest airship ride had been twenty minutes, not four days. The distance from Cumberland to Edin was not great. Hall wondered how many days it could take to get to the Realms that were farther away.

It was a slow trip, the Captain had told them as he gave them a brief tour of the ship, or at least the parts he was allowing them access to, because of going against the wind and upward to the higher island. Even though they were technically farther away, the other islands that made up Essec were on relatively the same level so they were able to get there a little quicker.

Hart had been loud, grandiose as he bragged about his ship. Smiling the whole time, wide arm gestures, it was obvious he was showboating. And flirting. With both Leigh and Sabine, but especially Sabine. It seemed he had taken a liking to the blond-haired Witch.

She appeared flattered at first but kept her distance, putting up a cold wall the more Hart pressed, which kept him pressing harder. There was no response, nothing to show that his flirtations were accepted, but nothing to show they were unwelcomed either. Sabine just didn't respond. Hall remembered her comments about the time from when they had met the first day in the Laughing Horse Inn until meeting again at River's Side. She had not said much at all, just that it was not a good experience, and she had been with some not so nice people. He had some suspicions of what could have happened, but felt it was not his place to bring it up. Her behavior with Hart strengthened his suspicions. When she offered, then he would be there for support but not before.

Hall just hoped that Hart would stop before he pushed her too far. Attacking the ship's captain was not a good option, especially with a crew that outnumbered and outleveled them.

The *Gale* settled at altitude, midway between Cumberland and Edin. The winds calmed somewhat, still enough to cause his eyes to water if he faced them head on. The crew all wore goggles for just that reason. He watched some large birds, their wingspan in the dozens of feet. Rocs, the only birds capable of flying in the deep sky between the islands. They soared and swooped, taking off and landing from their high mountain homes or perches underneath the islands. Luckily, none had an interest in the *Gale*. Fighting Rocs from a ship's deck was not easy.

"A lovely view, is it not?" Captain Hart said, coming down to the deck and standing next to Hall. "I do not know how anyone can live on the land. The sky is so beautiful."

And it was, Hall agreed. He had always enjoyed flying, and if he was being honest with himself, he was looking forward to the trip taking days instead of minutes. More time to enjoy the sky and the vista.

Blue sky all around, clouds floating above the islands as they floated at different elevations. Pitch black smudges of rock against the blue landscape. And far below, just the black of nothing. The sun was high in the sky off to the east where they were heading, casting its light across the sky and spreading out amongst the clouds.

"I have not been entirely honest with you," Hart said after a minute of silence. He turned to Hall, leaning against the railing. He was smiling, the one he thought so charming.

Hall looked at him quizzically, raising an eyebrow.

"Normally we do not take on passengers," Hart answered with a shrug. "At least not so close to launch."

"Then why did you?"

"I captain and own the *Twisted Gale* but I work for another," Hart said. "It was at his direction that we took you aboard."

"And who is this person?" Hall asked, curious. They knew no one from Edin. Leigh did, but no one that would control an airship.

"That is why I am here," Hart replied, stepping back from the rail and gesturing toward the door and stairs that led to the rooms below. "He asked me to bring you to him when the *Gale* was at altitude, and now we are and so…" He gestured again.

With a shrug, Hall pushed off from the railing, part of him wishing he still wore his sword. He doubted he would need it, but he was a warrior and never felt comfortable going into an unknown situation without a weapon. But it was considered bad form to walk a ship armed, or so Leigh had informed them. He still had his new bracer and the two throwing knives along with his dagger, so he wasn't completely defenseless.

Hall followed the Captain through the door, down the stairs and into the hall below the rear of the ship. Doors lined both sides with an observation balcony at the end. Hart led him toward it.

"Ninety percent of the time the *Gale* is free to do what she wants," Hart said, feeling like he should explain himself to Hall. He had spent so much time when the party had first come aboard talking himself up that now admitting he worked for someone, he feared it would change their opinion of him. Hart was a man that very much cared what others thought. "It is costly running an airship," he continued. "So, having someone to help with the bills and only beholden ten percent of the time, that's not a bad deal."

He stopped talking, and Hall continued not to care.

Pulling open the glass door, Hart indicated for Hall to step outside.

It was loud and windy outside, the deck under the engines and open to the sky. A solid half-height wall railing ran in a half circle, just enough space for a couple of people to stand. One person was there, off to the side where he could not be seen from the hallway. Hart closed the door and walked away, leaving Hall alone with the man.

Hall studied the other and realized he knew the man. It took a minute to place him. He was from this morning, the stranger inside the Inn that had kept staring at him.

"Who are you?" Hall asked.

Up close there was more gray in his hair and beard than Hall had first thought. Not as thin, but not overly muscular, he appeared to be fit and agile. The clothes were well made, expensive, but functional.

"Dyson," he answered, holding out his hand.

"Watchman Kelly's friend," Hall said, shaking the offered hand.

"The same," the merchant answered with a chuckle.

You have become Known to Merchant Dyson. He has been told about you and is eager to learn more as he gets to know you.

"I suppose I should thank you for the ride," Hall said, watching the man.

Dyson's behavior in the Inn now made sense. He had thought he recognized Hall from whatever description he had been provided, but had not been sure.

The merchant shrugged in response.

"You helped out Kelly with a little problem so I felt it fair to return the favor. I asked Hart to give you a discount on passage but it is his ship," Dyson said with a smirk. "What takes you to Edin?"

"Helping a friend," Hall said after thinking about his response. He saw no reason to not tell the truth. "The Druid has been sent to investigate a Grove that has gone silent."

"Noble endeavor," Dyson said, smiling. "Guard Captain Henry and Watchman Kelly are good judges of character. It's why I brought them into the operation."

Hall nodded, knowing a sales pitch was coming.

"Most of my work is legal," Dyson continued. "I only recently started the…" he paused and winked. "Side business when import taxes on certain goods got too high. Finding Kelly and Henry was the hardest part."

"I would have thought finding a place to moor a ship of this size in the Gray Dragon Peaks would have been the hardest part," Hall said, catching Dyson off guard with his observation.

The merchant smiled.

"Henry was right about you," he said, chuckling. "That was actually pretty easy. There are lots of spots on the south face, and no one ever goes there. Even Essec patrol ships pass in front of the mountains."

"Probably because of the dragons."

The Gray Dragon Peaks earned their name from the creatures that made them home, nesting in caves mostly on the southern face. Gray Dragons were the largest of dragonkind. Fiercest, too.

"We're on the eastern edge," Dyson explained. "Away from their range." He stopped and shrugged. "For the most part."

The ship tilted as a wild gust of wind slammed into it. Only a couple inches, but enough to make everyone slide a bit.

"Let's continue this inside," Dyson said and opened the door.

Hall stepped into the corridor and moved aside so Dyson could walk in. The merchant led him down the short corridor and into a room on the left. An office, a large maple desk bolted to the floor covered in loose papers some of which had dropped to the floor during the ship's motions. Shelves lined one wall, a couch against the other next to a small bar cabinet. Two leather backed chairs faced the desk with another behind. Dyson, stopping to pick up the papers first, walked behind the desk and motioned Hall to take one of the seats.

"So, you funnel the goods through Grayhold and River's Side up to Land's Edge Port?" Hall asked.

Dyson nodded. He leaned back, staring at Hall, smiling, waiting.

"Why are you telling me this?" Hall asked, figuring that was what Dyson wanted him to ask.

"You helped out my operation," the merchant replied, still leaning back and smiling.

Here comes that sales pitch, Hall thought, wondering what quest he was about to receive.

"I've been on the lookout for some adventurers to bring on board for a while," Dyson said after a minute or so of studying Hall, who had returned his gaze without moving. "I don't know if you've noticed but you seem to be a dying breed. The riches aren't there like they used to be. Most of the Great Dungeons have been tapped out, many of the threats put down."

Hall had not noticed. He was used to dungeons, great or small, respawning, and no threat ever truly put him down for good. There was always pockets of resistance, even after a storyline was over. If what Dyson said was true, it worried Hall and what the future would bring.

"And you have need for services only adventurers can provide," Hall guessed.

"I do," Dyson said and fell quiet, saying no more.

Hall waited what he thought a comfortable amount of time. Enough to show that he wasn't going to get pushed around by Dyson, led to where the merchant wanted him to go.

"What do you need?"

"Nothing yet," Dyson replied leaning forward. "But you helped me out once and I figured you could do so again. At some point. When you're ready. No real rush."

"You need us to level some more, don't you," Hall said, a statement, not a question.

Dyson smiled and gave a slight nod.

"I'll have to check with the others," Hall said. "They may not want to get too caught up in a smuggling operation."

"I am so much more than just a smuggler," Dyson said, a little offended. "But your people will follow you. You are the leader, after all."

Now it was Hall's turn to be surprised. The leader? No. He wasn't. He didn't want to be. They all made the decisions. He thought back over the last couple weeks and realized that Dyson was right. He had been leading them, without realizing.

Dammit, he cursed silently.

Not a responsibility he wanted but it seemed he was stuck with it.

For now.

DYSON'S OFFER I

Merchant Dyson has made you an offer for future work. Impressed and thankful for how you helped out his operation, he has a job that he would like you to do when you are ready.

Requirement: Level Six

Reward: +20 Experience

ACCEPT QUEST?

Hall thought about it. There was most likely an illegal element to the job that Dyson was proposing, a reason why he had not gone to the Guildhall to get adventurers. Hall had no true loyalty to Essec, it had just been the race and zone he had chosen to start in. He wouldn't feel particularly bad about smuggling goods illegally into the kingdom. So why would doing something else bother him?

And having something lined up for the future could be handy. As well as building up reputation with Dyson and his operation. There were numerous small factions in the game, and it seemed he had just found a new one.

Hall accepted the quest.

Dyson nodded, smiling. He stood up and moved over to the bar cabinet. Reaching inside, he brought out two glasses and a bottle of a dark liquid. He poured a small amount in each glass and handed one to Hall.

Raising the glasses, clinking them together, they both downed the liquid in one swallow. It was hot going down Hall's throat. A whiskey of some kind.

You have earned +500 Alliance points with Merchant Dyson.
He thinks he can trust you but won't be sure until you have helped him out more.

"I think we're going to do some excellent business together," Dyson said, pouring himself another shot. He offered one to Hall, who declined, setting the glass down.

Hall started to say something but paused. Dyson raised an eyebrow, a question. With a sigh, Hall held out his hand.

"Let me see your map."

Confused, Dyson pulled it out of his pouch. He laid it on the table, moving some papers out of the way. Hall mentally opened his map, shifting it to Cumberland as it now showed where the airship was between islands. He zoomed in on River's Side and the camp across the river. Looking down at Dyson's map, he made a couple quick map on a piece of paper he grabbed off the desk. He handed the map to Dyson.

"There's a cache of Highborn Wine along with Crag Cat and Dire Wolf furs," he said, pointing at the map. "Don't know how well the furs will be by the time you get there but the wine should still be good."

He described where and how they had hidden the cache and what the features of the land were to find it. Without meaning to, he had created his first Treasure Map.

Congratulations!
You have Created: Treasure Map Level I

Skill Gain!
Cartography, Rank 2 +2.0

Congratulations!
Your Cartography is now 15.6.
Reward: +1 Intelligence, +100 Experience

You have gained +200 Alliance Points with Merchant Dyson.
He is thankful for the information leading to the hidden cache of contraband.

Hall read through all the prompts. He had gained an Intelligence point for getting Cartography to 15? Plus experience? It seemed that aspect of the game remained the same. He wasn't surprised that Cartography was associated with Intelligence. All Skills had an Attribute associated with them. Every five levels in the Skill gained an Attribute Point.

Learning that he could make Treasure Maps, really magical keys according to Leigh, was exciting. It made the Cartography skill much more useful. He could envision lots of uses for this new ability. "Thank you," Dyson said, examining the map.

Hall shrugged. Not like they would have been returning there any time soon, if at all. Better the goods be sold before they were ruined. And maybe Dyson would share some of the profits.

Probably not, Hall thought, walking out of the office and shutting the door behind him.

CHAPTER TWENTY-SIX

THE REST OF THE FLIGHT WAS UNEVENTFUL. DYSON INSISTED they join him for dinner and breakfast each day. Captain Hart joined them as well and kept up his never-ending flirtation with Sabine. The Witch still ignored him, which made Hart try all the harder.

It was late afternoon as the ship approached Auld on the island of Edin. Hall stood at the front with Dyson, watching the large landmass getting bigger. They could see the underneath of the island as the ship rose, jagged cliffs of rock hanging upside down. Dark brown and gray. Far to the south the waterfall could be seen falling the hundreds of feet onto Cumberland.

The *Gale* floated up, coming level with the edge of the island and then rising above. They got a good view of the island itself. Edin was called the highlands, steep and gently sloping hills of grass dotted with forests and exposed stones. A range of mountains divided the island which was three or four times as large as Cumberland. Beautiful but harsh country.

Auld was set at a low point. A small lake lay to the city's west, homes and keeps built on the hill to the east. Not a large city, there were still hundreds of small one-and-two-story wood houses. They were spread out, small gardens between them, making the city look bigger than it was. Docks jutted out from the edge of the island, smaller than those at Land's Edge Port. Auld was a free city, as was the majority of Edin.

No kingdom claimed the island, and none wanted to try. The natives were as tough as their land and would fight beyond death to keep the island free.

Hall had always thought Auld to be an odd name for a town until he had learned of its origins. All the fractured realms in Hankarth were modeled after locations in the real world. Some more closely than others, some just names. The culture of Essec was based around that of medieval Britain while Storvgarde was based on Norway and the Vikings. The Kingdom of Arash had a more ancient Middle Eastern origin. Cumberland took its name from a county in Great Britain, the shape of the island realm even resembling that of the British land. Edin was modeled on Scotland. The island itself was similar in shape. The land of Edin resembled what was found in Scotland, a land that Hall had always wanted to visit but never made it. Auld was part of a nickname for Scotland's capital city, Edinburgh. Auld Reekie, which had just been shortened to Auld.

"My keep is there," Dyson said, pointing to the island's east where the homes and larger buildings ran up the side of a gently sloping hill. There was a wall at the far end, well past the homes, that circled down to the edge and back toward the center of town.

Auld did not have a surrounding wall, just parts of ones that did not connect. Some were visible in the middle parts of the city, showing that it had grown past them. Others, like that around the keep, just stopped. There were towers spaced along the segments, some manned and some empty.

Like Land's Edge Port, Auld was far larger than he remembered. Which was fine. The city was one of his favorite places, as was the entire island.

"Neither Henry or Kelly said you were a Cartographer," Dyson said after some silence.

Hall shrugged.

"They didn't know," he said. There was no need to point out that he didn't know at that time or still didn't fully understand what it meant.

"Makes me even more glad to have met you," the merchant said, clapping Hall on the shoulder. "Cartographers are rare, especially unguilded ones." He glanced sideways at Hall. "You are unguilded right?"

Hall nodded. It seemed like the correct answer. He had no idea what guilded versus unguilded even meant.

Dyson smiled. "Good, good."

The *Gale* aligned with a set of docks, the Essec flag flying from a pole in the middle. The ship was registered out of Essec and had to land at the docks assigned to that kingdom. As wide as two wagons, there were four berths with two to a side. Only one berth was occupied, a Passenger Airship out of Spirehold judging by the flag flying from its mast. Settling into the berth opposite, the *Gale* floated as sailors and dockworkers attached mooring lines.

Hall felt the vibrations through the hull cease as the engines shifted to low power. The propellers still spun, slowly, to keep the ship level. The ship bobbed up and down with the motion of the propellers and the wind blowing across the docks.

He could see the others gathered at the gangplank which was being lowered. Leigh was scratching behind Angus' ears, Pike perched in what was now becoming his customary spot on the cow's back.

"Don't forget," Dyson said as Hall started to walk away. "I look forward to seeing you again soon."

Hall nodded.

Captain Hart walked up as Hall took his packs from Roxhard.

"My dear," he said to Sabine, reaching out to take her hand. She fought at first but relented and let him take it. He pulled it up, leaned over and kissed the top. "I will miss you and regret we did not get a chance to learn more about each other."

"Maybe next time, Captain," she said, taking her hand back. She smiled at him but turned quickly to follow Hall down the gangplank.

———

"What do you mean my reputation isn't high enough? Since when has any airship been rep controlled?"

Hall stepped from the *Twisted Gale*'s gangplank onto the wooden dock built out from the edge of the island, out over the nothingness below. He looked toward the speaker, across the dock. Two guards in Essec armor and uniform stood at the bottom of a gangplank that led up onto the Passenger Airship, a vessel with *Wales Beauty* written across the bow, more guards roamed the deck while some guards at the end of the dock in the colors of Auld showed interest.

The speaker was a Duelist, level one or two probably, judging by the armor and weapons. Bodin. A Player, most likely. Three feet or so tall, brown hair with green streaks wore long and loose, skin the color of bark with no tattoos on the parts of the arms that were exposed. The Duelist was starting to get angry, facing off with an armed guard that controlled access to the ship.

"You have not proven yourself to be a friend of Essec. You're Unknown to us. We cannot allow you to board the airship to any island in the kingdom."

"But I took that same airship from Cumberland to here," the Bodin Duelist complained in an angry whine.

"You chose to leave Essec. That was your choice."

"I need to get off this island," the Bodin said. "Now."

Hall watched other guards approaching, moving to surround the Duelist.

"You can try to book passage with any of the merchant ships," the guard said, pointing at the *Gale* across from him.

"I don't have the money," the Bodin grumbled.

"That is not my concern."

The Duelist tensed up, hands straying toward the rapiers sheathed at his waist, but then noticed the other guards stepping closer. Gritting his teeth, angry, he muttered a curse and turned and left, walking toward the end of the dock and the city's crowd.

Hall turned to look back at Roxhard and Sabine, who had not stepped off the gangplank yet. He did not want to get stuck on Edin.

"What's your Essec rep at?"

"Friendly and Known," Roxhard replied. Sabine, and even Leigh, nodded.

"Good," Hall said and led them away from the airship.

Once off the docks, the crowd was thick, passengers coming and going, merchants leading wagons to their warehouses or stacking goods to wait for ships. They pushed their way through the crowd, emerging out the other side in front of a broad road that cut straight through the town. The road was hard-packed dirt, most of the buildings set off the ground by a step or two. They rested on stone foundations or wooden piles set deep into the ground.

Glancing at the sun, it was late afternoon, Hall thought they could get a couple hours of walking in before settling down for the night. No need to pay for an Inn. Leigh had told him there were two or three small villages between Auld and the Grove along the road. There should be plenty of places to rest for a night to regain any lost Vitality before finding out what awaited them at the Grove.

Heading down the street, Hall noticed the Bodin from the dock was leaning against one of the buildings. The Duelist's head was down, his posture appeared bored, resting. Completely different from how he had acted on the dock only minutes before. Hall could see the small flickers of movement as the eyes darted back and forth, searching and studying. The Duelist was anything but bored and resting. It was an act. He was looking for something.

A mark, most likely, thought Hall. Someone to pickpocket to get the coin needed to get back to Cumberland. He wondered how many other Players, after waking up in Hankarth, had made the same mistake. Just headed out at random and now found themselves unable to return because they hadn't done the starting Reputation quests.

The Bodin stood up straight, heading into the crowd. He had found his mark. Hall kept the group moving, not really caring who the Bodin was targeting until he realized the Duelist was heading right for them.

"Well, aren't you a sight for sore eyes?" the Bodin said with relief, falling into step alongside Hall, glancing back at the others. He paid more attention to Roxhard and Sabine than he did Leigh. "I haven't seen any other Players in days. Was starting to think I was the only one."

Hall took a longer look at the Bodin, trying to remember if he had seen him in the Laughing Horse Inn on that first day. There had been about a dozen Players of different races and classes, he had not paid as much attention as he should have to who was there.

"Name's Jerry," the Bodin said. "Well, I guess it's Davit now."

"Hall."

"Good to meet you," Davit said. He was talking fast but confidently.

There was something off about him, Hall thought but couldn't figure out what exactly. Overly friendly with a bit of desperation behind it. He remembered how Davit had reacted back on the docks. Hall didn't think he could trust Davit, or even believe anything he said.

"Quite a shock that was," Davit continued. "I'd only been playing for about six months. Girlfriend, ex-girlfriend I should say, got me into the game. She'd been playing for a year or so and wanted me to start when we started dating. Convinced me to play this," he said, spreading his arms to indicate his body. "I wanted to play a Warden, Firbolg, but she wanted this. She was a Bodin Shaman, and well..." he shrugged. "Got to keep them happy, know what I mean?" Davit finished with a laugh.

Hall had a feeling that Davit didn't care about keeping anyone happy but himself.

"We broke up a couple weeks ago," he started up again without prompting. He hadn't realized that the others were basically ignoring him. Or he didn't care. "I called it off but kept playing and then," he spread his hands in a gesture mimicking an explosion. "Now we're here."

"Can we help you with something?" Hall asked before Davit could continue talking. He knew he was being a little rude but he was starting to get annoyed.

"Since you're the first Players that I've seen, and judging by your gear you've been doing really well for yourselves, I figured I could come with you," Davit said, showing no reaction to Hall's tone of the question. "We Players should stick together."

The desperation was back in Davit's voice, and now his eyes were moving back and forth, darting from shadow to shadow, door to door.

"You've been on your own since the Laughing Horse," Hall pointed out. "Why the need to stick together now?"

"Been lonely," Davit replied, a little too quickly. "Would like some company."

Hall looked around at all the places Davit's eyes were touching and quickly moving on from. He saw nothing that called out to him. There could be some truth to what Davit was saying. He could be lonely and wanting the company of others like him, but Hall's instincts told him that was not the truth. Or not the full truth.

"What did you do?" he asked, stopping the group and looking down at the smaller Bodin.

"Do?" Davit said with a nervous chuckle. "What do you mean? I didn't do anything."

Hall glared. Davit sighed and his manner completely changed.

"Fine, whatever," he said with a shrug, taking a step back. "Not that it's any of your business but I'm in a little trouble with the authorities." The friendliness was gone, the desperation as well. It had been replaced with arrogance and annoyance. Davit was acting like he was explaining himself to his lessers.

"What kind of trouble?" Leigh asked.

Davit shrugged.

"Not your business," he told her with a sneer.

"It is if you think you're coming with us," Hall said, an edge to his voice.

Davit's eyes flashed to Hall, anger and annoyance

"Whatever," he said. "I killed a man," he finished with a shrug. "Just an NPC, no big deal. A shopkeeper that caught me trying to steal some coin."

Leigh gasped, shocked at the casual admission. Davit ignored her.

"The guards are looking for you," Roxhard asked.

"No, but not a good idea to stay here," Davit replied. His eyes widened as he looked at Roxhard. "Aren't you that Dwarf that cried the first day?"

Roxhard mumbled something quiet, looking down at the ground.

Davit laughed.

"You better hurry then," Hall said, the edge in his voice sharper.

"What?" Davit asked, confused.

"You better hurry out of here before the guards catch you," Hall told him, no hint of friendliness in his voice.

Davit studied Hall, looking at the others. Leigh looked like she was tempted to call the guards herself.

"I can't come with you?" he asked, surprised.

Hall didn't bother to answer, just stared at the Bodin, who took a couple steps back.

"What about sticking together?" he asked, his manner changing once again. He was back to being overly friendly, more desperate. "You can't just leave me. They'll probably kill me if they catch me."

"Should have thought about that before killing an innocent," Roxhard said.

"But," Davit started to say but Pike let out a screech, standing up on Hall's shoulder and spreading his wings.

With a last desperate look, almost pleading, Davit turned and stepped into the shadows of an alley. His eyes searched everywhere, marking everyone and everything. Hall watched as the shadows enveloped the Duelist, and he was lost to sight.

"I can't believe how casually he admitted to murder," Leigh said a minute later.

They were all still staring at the alley where Davit had disappeared.

Hall didn't know if he should feel guilty but he could partly understand Davit. The shopkeeper was an NPC, and if this was still a game, it wouldn't necessarily be a big deal to kill an NPC. Or would it? That was the part Hall was having a problem with. This was supposedly their life now, and as such, killing a shopkeeper should and would have consequences. He was already making some strange and possibly illegal alliances with Dyson and his smugglers. Having a murderer in their group would be stepping over a line he did not want to cross.

Killing was a part of life in Hankarth but murder was still wrong.

———

They walked out past the last of the houses, a segment of wall to their left. There was no gate, no guards to watch the roads. The houses just got fewer and fewer, more space between them. Fields started to appear, then barns and other buildings in the distance.

A mile from the last section of wall, the road forked.

"Cliff Fields is that way," Leigh said, pointing to the east fork.

She took a step that direction, looking down the road with longing. Hall wondered how long it had been since she had last been home, how long since that wandering Druid had taken her to Cumberland's Grove to start a life she barely wanted.

Hall wondered how he would do in that situation. Pushed into a life and unsure it was the direction he wanted. How would he have rebelled because he knew he would have, somehow. He admired Leigh. She was stalling in her mission, putting it off as long as she could, but she was still going to do it.

With a sigh, Leigh turned and started down the west road. The others followed.

She didn't look back.

CHAPTER TWENTY-SEVEN

HALL AWOKE, A NEW SOUND DIFFERENT FROM THAT OF THE night. He had fallen asleep with the fire high, Leigh taking the first watch and he taking the last. The usual noises had followed him to sleep. The howling of the wolves, the small animals running through the forest, the hooting of the owls, and the bats darting through the air. All peaceful and expected sounds.

The new sound was not natural. It was a sniffling sound. The sound of someone crying.

Roxhard was on watch, and judging from the moon's position in the sky, not due to wake Hall for his turn for another hour or so.

Sitting up, pushing his blanket aside, Hall looked around the site they had chosen for the night's camp. The small dell was surrounded by a thick ring of pines at the top, a hollow carved out of the ground of the highlands. The noise came from the top, where a darker shadow sat on the shadows that were a rock.

Quietly, Hall stood up, stepping lightly over Angus, who raised his head and gave a soft moo before falling back to sleep.

Pike opened one eye, saw there was no danger, and settled back down on top of the cow. Hall made his way to the top, the sniffling quickly stopping.

Roxhard was wiping his sleeve across his eyes as Hall settled down on the rock next to him.

"Couldn't sleep," Hall lied. "Figured I'd start my turn early."

"That's okay," Roxhard replied, his voice a little hoarse. "I don't mind finishing up."

"I'm awake," Hall said. "So, I'll stay up with you."

"Sure."

They sat in silence, Hall wondering what he could say that would get the Dwarf to talk about why he had been crying. Hall was sure Roxhard had been. But how to prod in a way that wouldn't embarrass him?

Hall didn't have to worry about it. Roxhard started talking on his own.

"Davit," Roxhard began, searching for the words. He stared out into the dark forest, eyes not focused on anything, just looking. "What he did, how he didn't care. He acted like this was a game but it's not, not anymore. Right?" He turned and looked at Hall.

"No," Hall replied, deciding that being honest with Roxhard was the best. "It's not. For better or worse, this is our life now." Hall paused, looking up into the night sky. The stars were out, constellations that he had never bothered to study. There had always been stars during the night in the game, but he had never looked up. Now he did. He had half expected to see the familiar shapes from the real world. But they weren't. Everything was different. "Even if it really is a game still and some day we can log out, we have to treat it like it's truly our life from now on. Actions have consequences."

Hall decided not to tell Roxhard that he didn't think the Bodin thought of it as a game, and that was why Davit thought he could get away with murder. No, Hall thought. Davit just enjoyed killing and thought NPCs were nothing, not worth a care. Just digital code.

What Davit didn't realize was that was all they were now as well. Digital code.

"It just…" Roxhard started and paused. He shrugged. "I guess I really hadn't believed, you know, not until then. I kept thinking of it as a game, wanting it to be a game. Every morning I'd wake up and check my Options, seeing if the Log Out button was working again. Every morning it wasn't. And I'd force myself through the day by thinking that the next morning the button would work."

"And it didn't," Hall said. He had not bothered to look since the first day. He had also thought Roxhard had accepted the new reality as readily as he had.

"No," Roxhard said, looking down at the ground. "I think about my brother sometimes. Is he here with me? Was he one of the ones that Electronic Storm said was killed by the feedback? I don't remember if he had been playing when the glitch hit. But mostly, I think about my mom. A lot. What is she thinking? Does she think I'm dead? Does she know about this?" he said and raised his hands to indicate the world around them. "Does she know I'm here?"

He fell silent. Hall tried to think of something to say, anything. It was so easy to forget that Roxhard was only a kid.

"Does she miss me?" Roxhard said, quietly, barely a whisper.

"Of course, she does," Hall replied. "As much as you miss her."

––––––

Roxhard went to bed soon after leaving Hall alone on the rock.

He looked out into the forest, getting accustomed to the

noises and movements. His thoughts turned to his own family. His parents. He felt guilty. Not once since the glitch had he thought about them. They were close enough. He talked to his parents once a week, saw them on holidays and a couple times during the year.

But not once had he thought about them. Where they were, what they were doing. Did they know he had somewhat survived the glitch? Did they understand what it meant? Or did they think he had died? Had buried him in his hometown?

Hall had been so caught up in this new reality that he had not given himself time to miss them.

He did so now. Looking up at the unfamiliar stars, constellations he did not know the names of, Hall thought of his family. He wished them well. Hoped they would manage to move on, would not mourn him forever. He hoped to always be in their hearts but not to let grief ruin their lives.

Looking back out into the forest, Hall thought about the task at hand. The Grove was a week's hard travel, at the far edge of the island. No formal roads, the one they had followed out of Auld heading almost due west while their destination was more north. They would be going overland through dangerous country. There were Centaur tribes living in the highlands, Goblins, and other creatures. Leigh had said there were a couple of Firbolg villages as well.

Thinking about it, he opened his map. The slightly translucent window opened before his eyes, the entire landmass of Edin shown but the features not revealed. He zoomed in on the southwest corner, where they were now. Auld appeared as well as the immediate area around it. The rest uncovered, grayed out, nothing to see. They had not been there yet so nothing had been revealed. Leigh had marked the general location on the map so he had a reference point to direct them too.

A week of travel if there were no surprises.

He knew there would be.

———

The fog rolled across the hills, down into the valleys. Visibility was poor, in some spots almost non-existent. Hall had forgotten about the fog in Edin but it had never been anything like this. In the game, the fog had kept to the far edges of the field of vision, there to show the effect was happening, but never truly affecting vision. Now it was thick, leaving moisture on everything as they pushed through it.

They were cold and miserable, having to slow their pace.

Pike rode on Hall's shoulder, shaking the water off his feathers often. Flying above would have done nothing. The fog blanketed everything for miles. Leigh insisted it would burn off soon, and Hall took her at her word. This was her home. While he was familiar with Edin, the fog showed that this was not the Edin he knew.

Sounds were distorted through the fog. It was hard to tell what was close or far away, or where it came from. The trail cut across a grass-covered hill, barely two feet wide and beaten down to exposed dirt. An animal path.

When the attack came, they never saw it coming.

Six Trow stalked out of the fog, appearing as if from nowhere. They were silent, no war cries or even the sound of foot on ground. Medium height, standing up to Hall's shoulder, the Trow were thin but muscular. They had light gray skin, the color of the fog, and wore mismatched, roughly-crafted leather armor that left parts of the body exposed. Long and lanky black hair hung from roughly human-shaped heads, their ears overly large and pointed, eyes wide and gray with jet black irises. Flat noses that were just two slits and wide mouths with sharp teeth gave them a reptilian appearance. Dark gray streaks were painted across all their exposed flesh, including their faces, highlighting their already monstrous appearance. Each carried a rough sword and wooden buckler.

The monstrous humanoids struck first. They came three to a side, the ones on the right coming downhill while the ones on the left were striking uphill. Hall was in the lead, turning as the first Trow stepped out of the fog. The creature swung its sword, and Hall barely managed to turn to avoid the blow that would cut across his side, instead cutting along his right arm.

DAMAGE!
Sneak Attack Successful. 2x Damage Taken.
Evade Successful. Damage 50% Less.
-10 Health
-1 Vitality

Hall cursed as he ducked to avoid the Trow's backswing, glad that he had managed to avoid the full Sneak Attack. Pike screeched in the air, having leapt up as Hall had turned. The dragonhawk streaked down and slashed across the Trow's face, leaving bloody trails. The Trow fell back.

Angus, behind Hall, cried out in pain as a Trow sword slashed across the cow's body. He managed to stay upright, turning and using his bulk to push the Trow off to the side, away from Leigh

"No," Leigh cried out as the cow was attacked. She raised her staff, turning to defend the cow, when she felt a sharp blow against her wrist.

She dropped her staff, reaching out to clutch at her wrist. A Trow looked up at her, wicked grin, as he raised his sword. He twisted the weapon so it was blade down, not the flat of the sword like his first attack. The creature was no fool; it recognized a spell caster. Without the staff to focus her energy, Leigh could not attack with her primary spells.

Roxhard got his battle axe up in time to catch the swing of the Trow on his right, metal sword clanging against metal axe handle. He grunted, his strength more than enough to keep the

Trow from pushing him down, even with the Trow having the advantage of the higher elevation. He didn't realize there was another behind him.

The sword slammed into his armored back, metal sliding across the rings of his mail. He cursed and was pushed forward with the force and the pain, his stance adjusting and the other Trow pushing down on him. Roxhard stumbled, one leg dropping to the ground.

Sabine, between Leigh and Roxhard, was the most protected from the sneak attack. She heard Roxhard get attacked from both sides, stopping the first and grunting in pain at the second. She saw the Trow attack Leigh and managed to step back as another came up the hill toward her. She had an extra second to plan.

Quickly she held up her arms, the stone on her staff glowing, as she chanted two quick words. She felt herself shift to the side, pushed by some unseen force, just left of where she was. Next to her, someone else occupied part of where she had been. She saw an exact duplicate of herself. Same body, hair, clothes. Same glowing jewel on a staff in the same hand.

The attacking Trow hesitated, coming to a complete stop, unsure which to attack. Where there had been one Human woman, there was now two. With a fierce cry, an odd howl that echoed through the fog, the Trow swung its sword toward the Human on the right.

Striking true, so it thought, the Trow smiled wickedly only to watch as its sword thrust wavered. Instead of hitting the woman in the chest, the sword struck somewhere in the middle of the two. It heard a cry of pain but saw its sword strike nothing.

The Trow yelped in pain as blasts of energy shot out from the two staffs, striking it in the chest. Pitch black liquid fire slammed against it, smoke rising from the impact.

Sabine smiled to herself, the image repeating the action.

Raising her hands, she cast *Hexbolt*. Five shafts of solid dark light flew out of the raised hand, straight to the chests of five of the Trow. The shafts struck each of the creatures in a different spot, crackling purple bolts of energy spreading out from the areas. Across shoulders, chests, backs and thighs.

Hall saw the shafts out of the corner of his eye. None hit the Trow in front of him. It had stepped back, wiping at the blood across its eyes from Pike's attack, giving Hall time to draw his short sword. He kicked out, foot connecting with the Trow's stomach, pushing the humanoid back another couple steps. Following up with a lunge, Hall slashed his sword across the Trow's chest, drawing a thick line of blood.

Pike streaked out of the sky, a bolt of lightning leading. The bolt slammed into the Trow's shoulder, smoke rising from the wound. The humanoid yelped out in pain, distracted, which allowed Hall's next attack to stab through its throat. The Trow fell to the ground.

Hall turned to look over the battle.

Leigh had her cudgel out, slamming it against a Trow's raised buckler. Angus, bleeding hard from a wound in the cow's chest, was grunting and slamming his horns into a Trow that was striking the cow's back with its sword. Bright red slashes marred the cow's thick hide.

Hall was momentarily surprised to see two Sabines facing off with another Trow before Hall remembered the Witch's *Second Self* ability. Casting it gave the Witch a magical doppelganger. This image had no physical or magical capabilities but it drew half the damage of any attack until its Health, equal to half of the casters, was depleted.

Roxhard was the hardest pressed, facing off against two Trow. He had managed to get one of them turned so he faced both, but he was at a disadvantage. One of the Trow had his weapon engaged, which allowed the other the freedom to attack the Dwarf's side. Only his armor was saving him but that wouldn't last long. Each blow depleted Roxhard's Health. Checking the status bars, Hall saw that Roxhard was already at 50% Health.

Sheathing his sword, mentally telling Pike to circle up for another attack, Hall pulled one of the throwing knives from the bracer. He threw it as he used *Leap*, pulling his spear from the sheath on his harness.

Straining against the force of one Trow pushing down against his weapon, seeing the sharp edge of the blade coming closer, trying not to let the pain of the other Trow's attacks push him aside, Roxhard saw a small streak of lightning slam into one of the Trow. A flash of light, followed by a crackling bolt of lightning, slammed into the Trow's shoulder. It yelped in surprise and pain, stepping back and taking the pressure off Roxhard's battle axe. Reaching down to his belt with his right hand, Roxhard pulled his hand axe free and swept it back toward the second Trow.

That creature had its sword raised for another swipe at Roxhard's unprotected side but had to step back as the axe head sliced through where it had been. Reversing the swing, holding the battle axe with one hand, Roxhard pushed the two-handed axe up. He swung with the hand axe, catching the Trow in the side. He pulled the hand axe back to swing again.

Hall landed behind the Trow, spear slamming into the humanoids shoulder. It staggered under the blow, collapsing to the ground.

Roxhard dropped the hand axe, taking the battle axe in both hands and pushed against the Trow in front of him. Smoke still rising from the knife wound, the Trow staggered back and took a blast of lightning in the face as Pike swooped by. It cried out in pain, the echo dying as Roxhard's battle axe slammed into its chest, the strong blow ending the Trow's life.

Pulling his spear out of the slumping Trow, Hall reversed his grip and stabbed it forward. The Trow in front of Sabine cried as the tip caught it in the side, pushing the creature a couple steps. Sabine struck with a *Shadow Bolt*, staggering the Trow, both images raising their hands in casting. Hall pulled back his spear, stepped forward and thrust again. The Trow dropped dead to the ground.

Roxhard adjusted his grip on his battle axe, flipping the weapon so the head was on the right. He turned, pivoting on his feet, and swung the weapon into the Trow behind him. He struck the creature in the shoulder, hard, causing its arms to fly up, giving Angus the ability to slam his horns into the Trow's stomach, thrashing his head back and forth, ripping the Trow's belly apart.

Leigh slammed her cudgel against the Trow's buckler, the attack aided by the weapon's magic. The Trow was forced back a step, unable to bring its sword in to attack. Leigh knew she couldn't keep it up, the wound on her arm throbbing and each swing getting weaker. She needed space but couldn't let up the attack to get it. The effects of the *Hexbolt*, already weak because of the five targets, were wearing off as well. The Trow only needed a second to go back on the offensive.

Her next strike was the weakest yet, a shaking and unsteady swing that barely landed on the Trow's small buckler. It grinned at her, sensing its opportunity, and raised its sword to attack. Sabine's *Shadowbolt* slammed into its shoulder, pushing it back. Hall landed next to it, coming from above, his spear piercing it from behind. The Trow's sword fell from its lifeless hands, the body propped up by the spear.

"Everyone good?" Hall asked, using his boot to push the Trow off his spear as he lifted the weapon out.

"Yes," Leigh said as she turned to Angus. She lay her hands on the cow's bloody hide, light coming from her palms and spreading around the cow.

"Are there anymore?" Sabine asked, a note of fear in her voice as they all turned to gaze out into the fog.

Above them Pike circled, sharp eyes trying to pierce the thick gray fog.

"I don't think so," Leigh replied a couple seconds later as they all warily watched the fog, back to back. "Those are Trow. They hunt in thick fog like this."

"Nice of you to warn us," Sabine snapped. "This is supposed to be your home."

"I'm sorry," Leigh said weakly, miserably. "There are no Trow villages in this area. Not that I knew of."

"Seems to be one now," Sabine muttered.

"Enough," Hall told them all. "Eyes front."

He took a moment to look at his Notifications.

SLAIN: *Stonesky Fog Hunter*
+30 Experience

SLAIN: *Stonesky Fog Hunter*
+10 Experience

SLAIN: *Stonesky Fog Hunter*
+10 Experience

Skill Gain!
Small Blades Rank +.3

Skill Gain!
Polearms Rank 2 +.1

Skill Gain!
Light Armor Rank 2 +.2

Skill Gain!
Thrown Rank 2 +.1

He dismissed the Notifications, clearing the log. Some good skill gains and experience.

"I leveled up," Roxhard said happily.

"Congrats," Hall said, relaxing slightly. "I think we're safe. If there had been more, they would have attacked by now. We're on guard, they wouldn't want that."

"I hope so," Sabine grumbled as her *Second Self* image faded.

Hall had Roxhard stand at the back, eyes scanning around as he did the same at the front. The two women quickly looted the bodies. There was nothing of value, a handful of silver and that was it. The Trow weapons and armor were not worth taking. They pushed and pulled the bodies off the thin edge, letting them roll down the hill into the deeper fog.

Moving much slower, Hall led them on.

CHAPTER TWENTY-EIGHT

THEY RAN INTO THE FOG THREE MORE TIMES DURING THE TREK, extending their journey by a couple more days. Not wanting to take chances, Hall had called a halt when the fog had grown so thick that visibility was lost. On one of the clear days, with Pike high up in the sky, they had found the Trow village. Nestled in a valley between hills, a couple miles north, and easy enough to avoid but still adding more time.

Hall was frustrated with the added time, wanting to get to their destination before any more random encounters came their way. He didn't know what they would encounter at the Grove and wanted to be at full strength with all the potions they had come with and gear at full, or near full, durability. Random encounters were great when grinding out experience but not when on a mission.

The closer they got, the more withdrawn Leigh got. No longer her normally cheerful self, the Druid was quiet and distracted. Everyone understood why, and even Sabine didn't bother her about it. Each step moved her farther down the path of a Druid of the Grove. Which may not be what she wanted.

She had been sent to find out why the Grove was not communicating with the rest of the Circle. A simple exploratory mission. But none of them were fooled. It was obvious what the Elders wanted. For a Grove to go silent, it meant some malevolent force had taken over the land and killed the caretakers. Leigh would discover this and be prompted to act. And by doing so, she would tie herself to the fate of the Grove.

For someone like her, that had been rebelling against such a thing, the Elders had neatly forced her into doing what they wanted and she did not. Her own sense of duty would compel her to act. To discover what was happening and turn back, take all that time to return to Cumberland or another Grove, to find aid? No Druid would do that. She would act, and her path would solidify.

Hall felt somewhat guilty for agreeing to help. He could have stalled longer, found some other excuse to delay their going. But that could only last so long. He could have also said no, not helped, but then Leigh would be confronting whatever was ahead on her own. After traveling with her for weeks, that was not something he would allow.

He wasn't sure how he felt about Leigh. He liked her company, she was beautiful and made him laugh and smile. Roxhard had a crush on her, that was obvious. But she was still an NPC. Was there anything more that could develop? And what about Sabine? Gorgeous but a little cold and arrogant. Was there anything there? He hadn't been trying to develop something with her, had she been with him?

There had been hundreds of Players that had developed in-game relationships, some even meeting In Real Life and getting married. He had never been one of those. It was a game. There had been some flirting over the years but he had not let anything become more.

Now he was? He tried to focus on the path ahead, eyes

scanning for any dangers, but his thoughts kept wandering to Leigh. Was it the change in mindset, he thought, where this was no longer a game but life? Life was different. Life was about the relationships formed; romantic, business and friendship. That was how one got through life, with those relationships. If the game was now his life, he was building toward those.

Dyson was a step toward a long-term business relationship. The group he was with – Sabine, Roxhard and Leigh – were building friendships and allies to adventure with. *Never adventure alone* was one of the mottos of Sky Realms Online. Was Leigh going to become the romantic relationship?

He sighed, forcing himself to focus on the task at hand. Time enough for those thoughts later.

Pulling open his map once again, Hall scouted out the path toward their destination, still a couple days away.

———

"There," Hall said, pointing toward a high ridge a couple of miles away. "It's on the other side."

The edge of Edin was near, mountains running north and south. He was pointing at a low point between two great peaks, a ridge of grass and stone that ran between the two. A path was carved into the side of the steep slope, crisscrossing as it ran toward the top, ending in the middle between two tall stone pillars. Not natural, carved and placed, the pillars were easily a dozen feet tall and almost half as wide.

Standing on top of a hill, the land sloped down and rose back up again toward the ridge, a brook running down the bottom. Grassy sides, exposed rock, with few trees.

"Not a very inviting looking place," Sabine said, looking toward the ridge.

"Steep climb with nowhere to find cover," Hall remarked,

studying the path up toward the top. "Very defensible position without having to build a wall."

"Let's hope no one is on the other side with similar ideas," she muttered and started walking down the hill, loose stones slipping under her feet.

Hall laughed but hoped for the same.

He sent Pike high overhead, circling over the ridge. The dragonhawk saw no movement. From the high vantage point, Pike saw the ridge drop away on the other side, not as steeply, and opening onto a wide flower covered meadow that extended all the way to the edge of the island. In the middle of the meadow was an odd construction of grass covered peaks and deep trenches in the ground. A brook cascaded down from the mountains on the north, falling down from plateau to plateau in steps and pools before flowing across the open plain and disappearing into the ground beneath the ridge in a larger pond.

On one of the plateaus Pike could see a series of standing stones.

Mentally telling the dragonhawk to stay circling, Hall opened his eyes and focused. The world blurred a bit as the images Pike had sent faded, and the world he was seeing came back into full clarity. He looked up at the high ridge, and the path carved into the side. Wide enough for a thin wagon, the hard-packed path switched backed running the full length of the ridge to cut down on the steepness.

It was going to be a long and exposed hike up to the top.

———

"What was this village called?" Hall asked.

He stood at the top of the ridge, wide and relatively flat, between the two standing stones. He looked down into the valley on the other side.

"Skara Brae," Leigh answered.

Hall glanced at her in surprise. He had never heard of Edin having an area with that name, and in the original game he had explored every inch of the island. He would have known if such a place existed. But he had never seen a branch of the World Tree or a Druid's Grove in this area of the island either. In a way, he was glad. He had been afraid there would be nothing new to explore in this game life.

The village was set nearer the island's edge than it had appeared from Pike's view. The road switchbacked down the less steep side of the hill, across the meadow and down into the village square. The buildings were built into the ground, the grass of the meadow running up onto the roofs and down the sloping sides to the road and square. About a dozen buildings faced the square, most just hollow shells in the mounds of earth. The ones along the island's edge were built fully into the ground. Some looked like they would have descended down, very low roofs that were small mounds of grass. Others, opposite the edge, looked like they had been normal shaped homes with the sides and roofs covered in the grass. There were openings on either side, the roofs sharply angled.

Midway down one curved side was a larger mound, the walls built of stone. The roof, what was left and had not collapsed, was covered in grass. Moss grew up the sides of the exposed stone. A three-story structure, two above ground.

Hall counted about twenty individual buildings in all. A ring with some homes in the middle, all covered in grass and earth. The middle rows of homes had mounds of earth that connected to the rings, tunnels boring through to allow passage. It was possible to run along the tops of all the buildings.

"Wooden walls once covered the faces of the homes," Leigh said pointing down at the village.

With the cliff's edge behind, the mountains and hill on the

sides, the village was isolated. Alone and practically hidden. The wind tore down the mountains, pushing the stalks of grass and the few trees. It had a rugged beauty, Hall thought.

"The Grove is there," Leigh said, pointing toward the northern mountain and the lowest of the two plateaus.

Hall looked toward the tall peak, the top covered in snow, the sides bare rock. There were two plateaus that he saw, both covered in grass and a few trees. The highest was about a couple hundred feet up, the larger one only fifty or so feet above the village. Paths led up the mountain side to each. On the larger one he could see a circle of standing stones. Slabs of smoothed rock standing in a pattern, some with horizontal slabs across them. Beyond the stones was a thick growth of trees. A stream came from the top plateau, falling down the mountain to land in a pool on the second plateau. From there it flowed across the flat surface and fell down the side into a small pool on the meadow before flowing southeast and into a larger pond at the base of the ridge they stood upon.

"The tree is in the middle of a small pond surrounded by those stones."

Even from here Hall could tell something was wrong. Unlike the green and healthy grass and trees of the meadow and the other plateau, the middle one was dark. The trees drooped, the limbs lifeless. There was brown along the ground instead of green, a dark purple moss growing along the rock faces of the cliff and the standing stones.

He couldn't see the Grove, the tree itself, just the standing stones with the waterfall behind them and another in front. Beyond the look of death there was a chilly feeling coming from the plateau, a wrongness that he could feel even this far away.

Glancing up at the sky, he saw the sun was starting to set. The hike up the ridge had taken longer than he had thought it would. They could have gone faster but he had been cautious, not sure what to expect. At each switchback, the road had widened into a flat place to stop, where wagons and horses could wait while another went down or up the single width path. There had been remains of low rock walls and carvings that had been beaten down by time and rain.

When he had explained what Pike had seen, Leigh had told him that there had once been a village in the meadow. Hall had to wonder who would have thought to build there. The meadow was so isolated, hard to get to.

Now it seemed like the ruined village was going to be the only sensible place to camp for the night. He just hoped they could get to it before whatever was in the Grove could see them. He felt exposed on top of the ridge and hustled the small group down the other side quickly.

Something was in the Grove. He knew it.

CHAPTER TWENTY-NINE

HALL PUSHED THEM, ALMOST RUNNING DOWN THE MEADOW SIDE of the ridge. He was tempted to go straight down it, not follow the path, but with the sun setting and the uneven and rocky ground, it was safer to follow the road. Not quicker, but safer. Once on the meadow itself, they sprinted across the open ground to the sunken village. He kept Pike circling high above, eyes alert for any kind of movement anywhere else in the meadow.

At the bottom they found the remains of a wide road heading straight from the ridge to the village, leading right to a ramp that led down into the village proper, a full story below the ground. The trench was in shadows, the higher peaks and walls blocking the sun. The temperature dropped but they were protected from the wind.

They moved cautiously down into the village, passing through one of the tunnels formed by the grass meadow above. Most of the wood that had formed the fronts was rotted away, the stone that made up the side walls remaining. The roofs of the buildings were intact, not much debris or collapse. It was too dark in the buildings' interiors for Hall to see what the roofs were made of. If it was wood, then the roots of the grass that covered the roofs had grown together to form a mesh that held it all up.

He had never seen, or even heard, of a village built like this. It was an interesting design. The hard-packed road, evidence of cobblestones grown over, was wider than a wagon, fully circular so horses and wagon would have to make a complete circuit to exit. There was only one way for a wagon or horse to get down, the ramp on the eastern side. Between some of the buildings there appeared to be old staircases made of granite blocks, small roots and plants growing out of the cracks.

It had been a long time since anyone had lived here. There was no evidence of the inhabitants fleeing because of disease or raiding. Everything that remained was organized, looking as it should after years of abandonment and no maintenance. It looked like whoever had lived here had just decided to move on.

They followed the ring road about halfway around, stopping in front of the largest structure, the three-story building. It had to have been an Inn or a town hall, maybe both. But what was out front had Hall's attention.

It stood about four to five feet tall. A gray square stone obelisk tapered toward the top. About nine inches wide at the base and five or six at the top where the four sides came together in a point about six inches higher. It sat on a wide pedestal, about three inches off the ground. There were runes carved into one face of the obelisk. It appeared to have been carved all from one piece of granite, smoothed and shaped. There was no sign of erosion or cracking.

"What is that?" Sabine asked from where she stood a couple feet away. She kept her voice quiet, all of them did, afraid the sounds would carry on the wind.

"It's a Settlement Stone," Leigh answered, surprised the

others didn't recognize it. "All towns, villages, cities, and outposts have one."

"What does it do?" Hall asked, intrigued as he stepped closer.

He could almost feel a power coming off the stone, like it was vibrating with energy.

"The town leader governs from it," Leigh said with a shrug. "I don't know the particulars but basically the leader, or leaders, can see all the settlements stats from the stone and control various town functions."

"So, it basically lets someone create a town," Roxhard asked, awed.

"I guess," Leigh replied, again shrugging. "The higher the population, the more the stone can do. The more productive a town, the more bonuses it bestows.

"And all towns have this Stone?" Hall asked, fingers hovering an inch or so over the rocky surface.

"Anywhere that has people permanently settled there has a stone."

"Why is the Stone here?" Sabine asked, spreading her arms to indicate the village around them. "No one has been settled her for a long time."

"No idea," Leigh replied. "I just lived in a village. I didn't govern one."

Hall couldn't resist any longer. Not sure why, he reached out and touched the stone. Instantly a large prompt filled his vision. It was translucent like all the others, the village and the stone visible beyond, like looking through a stained window. Unlike the other Notifications and prompts, this one was square and bordered on what looked like stone.

Skara Brae

This settlement is dormant. Do you wish to reactivate it?
Yes or No?

As he removed his hand from the stone, the prompt did not disappear.

"Do you guys see this?" he asked.

"See what?" Roxhard replied, the others shaking their heads.

"When I touched the Stone, I got a prompt asking me if I want to reactivate this settlement."

The other three exchanges surprised glances, especially Leigh. Roxhard smiled, fighting back the impulse to cheer loudly. Sabine had an odd expression, almost jealousy but not quite.

"You get a town," Roxhard exclaimed. "That is so awesome."

Hall stared at the prompt but there was no other information available. No timer, no help button. Nothing.

"I'm not sure I want it," he said taking a step back. The prompt did not disappear.

"Why not?" Sabine asked and reached out to touch the stone. "Isn't that the dream of every Player?"

A new prompt appeared over the first, that one fading so the new was readable.

*This settlement has already been claimed by **Hall**. No other Player can attempt to claim Skara Brae until Hall chooses not to reactivate the settlement or ten days have passed.*

"Well, it was worth a try," Sabine said, stepping back with a shrug. She had gotten a similar prompt.

The new prompt faded and Hall was left with the first.

"Do it," Sabine told him.

She had been right. Owing a town had been the dream for MMORPG Players since the genre had started. One of the first, Ultima Online, had allowed Players to own homes, and some had banded together to make Player-Towns, but had had no true town interface. Other games had tried but none had come close. Sky Realms Online had just Player housing but now it appeared to have taken things a step, or twenty, further.

He wished there was more information available. This could be a game-altering, life-altering, decision. Was there a way to get more information?

Mentally clicking on *Yes*, assuming he could always cancel at a later prompt, Hall saw a new screen appear. There was some more information now available. And a chance to back out.

Congratulations!

You have chosen to reactivate the settlement of Skara Brae.

Note that ownership of one settlement does not prevent ownership of other settlements but there are restrictions. Skara Brae is a Rank II Settlement with a maximum population of 100 permanent settlers. Some Buildings will not be available to a Rank II Settlement.

You may concurrently own a Rank II and a Rank I Settlement. Rank II Settlements cannot grow without owing Fealty to a Rank IV or above Settlement.

Reactivation of Skara Brae will not alert neighboring Settlements of its reactivation. All previous Alliances have been dissolved.

There are currently:
Allies: 0
Enemies: 0
Trade Alliances: 0

Skara Brae Town Stats:
Population: 1
Production: 0% (+0% bonus)
Status: Ruins
Faction: None

Do you wish to continue with Skara Brae reactivation?
Yes or No?

Hall read through the mass of information quickly, trying to process it. There was a lot to take in. Settlements had Ranks, and it sounded like it was difficult for them to raise in Rank, if not impossible. It also sounded like there were some safeguards in place to prevent empire building. He assumed that only a Rank IV or higher Settlement could become the capitals of a kingdom or empire and that the smaller ranked Settlements owed Fealty to the bigger Settlements, which meant the larger had to keep them happy. There were ways around it, the system sounded much like any kingdom or empire.

Looking around at the buildings, doing a quick estimate, he realized that the Settlements maximum population was greater than the buildings alone would support. That meant more could be built. Farms in the meadow, a blacksmith near the mountains? Already his mind was working through the logistics.

He scanned the text again, stopping at the Stat for Population. There was a number where there should have been nothing. The town was abandoned, why was it showing a population of one?

Unless the Grove was considered part of the Settlement?

That meant there was someone at the Grove. A single person, or at least what the Stone thought of as a settler. A permanent settler. Someone living in the Settlement's area.

The person they needed to talk to, the one they had come to find.

But first Hall knew he had a decision to make.

The prompt was giving him his final chance to back out. He knew what he was going to do. Once had had started reading the information, starting thinking about population and structures and empires and kingdoms, he knew what his choice was going to be.

He had never wanted a kingdom. Empire building, ruling thousands, was not something he wanted to deal with. A simple man. He wanted simple things. A place to call home was one of those. Hall had assumed he would build a home in the new Sky Realms, just like he had in the original. The idea of having a town had never crossed his mind.

But why not? Why not take the leap? He could build a safe haven for his friends and himself, a place to come back to after adventuring. A place where they could repair and sell gear. A place to train and to just live.

Hall mentally clicked on *Yes*.

He didn't know what to expect and was surprised, and a little disappointed, at the lack of anything happening. There was no sound, no flash of light, nothing to indicate he had just become the owner of a Settlement. The prompt disappeared, and he was left staring at the Settlement Stone.

Hall looked at the others, his eyes asking if they had seen anything.

"Did you do it?" Roxhard asked.

Hall nodded, looking at the ruins of the town, his town, in the setting light of the sun. The shadows deepened, details being lost, but nothing looked different.

He reached out to the Stone, and a new prompt filled his vision.

Skara Brae
Lord: Hall
Status: Ruins
Morale: Not Available

Government: Not Chosen
Appointed Officials: None

Population: 2
Production: Zero

Faction: None
Allies: None
Trade Partners: None
Enemies: None

Next to each line was a Question Mark, indicating more information could be learned. A couple had a large Arrow, which meant there were submenus to review. There was a lot to take in.

Hall dismissed the prompt. There was too much to get into now.

"We need to find a safe place to rest," he said to the others. "We head to the Grove tomorrow."

———

One look into the large building and Hall had decided it would not do. The first level was sunk down into the ground, a stone stair looked to be in decent shape but there was only the one way in or out. He confirmed the structure as the town's Inn.

He could picture how it would look when reconstructed.

A large and open space, there would be a great round stone lined fire pit in the middle of the room set down a couple of steps onto the hard-packed dirt floor. Tables and chairs would fill the space around the pit, a bar along the back wall and double doors that led out into the kitchen area. The walls would be stone blocks with wood paneling, and the front half would be open to the high roof with four large posts, that still existed and would need reinforcing, those would hold up the sloping roof above. Even in the dark, thanks to his *Limited Night Vision*, Hall could see steps in the roof that indicated hidden smoke holes. A set of stairs on the side wall would lead upstairs to the sleeping rooms in the back half of the building, the upper two stories.

Functional, a gathering place. Homey. The smoke would drift out but still fill the room with its scent.

He had to shake his head, clear away the thoughts. Already he was planning for the future and there was still much to do. The future was a long way away, and in the present, the Inn would not do for the night.

One way in, sunk down a floor, it would be too easy to be trapped in the space.

Instead they choose one of the inner ring buildings. A two-story structure, a shop with living quarters above and store room in the back half. Most of the upper floor had fallen in, but they could clear enough space for them all to spread out their bedrolls.

It would be a cold night. No fire and watches throughout. Like usual, Hall took the last watch.

Sabine had first watch and stood near the front wall, looking out into the village. Hall could tell she was disappointed in how the Settlement had ended up. She had obviously wanted it while he had been unsure. He hoped it wouldn't be a problem.

Roxhard was snoring, and Leigh was curled up next to Angus, Pike asleep on the cow as well. Hall lay on his back, staring at the wooden ceiling above. Planks laid over thick beams. He was tempted to start exploring the Settlement menus. He had mentally opened the prompt, curious if he had to be touching the Stone. Now that he knew he didn't need to be touching it, curiosity was eating away at him.

But there was going to be a fight tomorrow. A big one. He just knew it. Whatever was living in the Grove was not going to be friendly. That wasn't the way these quests worked. It would be a Boss fight, a higher level and higher difficulty enemy.

They were still only level threes and twos. Not strong. And not even a full party. Only four and not the typical five. They had the basics, though. A Tank, DPS, Debuffing, and Healing. The fifth slot was for more Debuffs or more DPS.

He needed his rest. They needed to be at full strength, which they weren't. The trip, as well as the Trow fight, had sapped some of their Vitality. None of them would be full up.

Learning more of what it would mean to be the Lord of Skara Brae would have to wait.

Closing his eyes, turning onto his side, and tucking the blanket up closer, Hall tried to sleep.

CHAPTER THIRTY

They ate a cold breakfast.

Which did not help their Vitality to raise.

The morning was chill, the newly risen sun not getting down into the shadows where they were camped. Hall got them moving quickly, not wanting to waste any time.

Retracing their steps, Hall looking at the Settlement Stone before they turned the corner and entered the tunnel, they were happy to get back to the meadow and the warmth of the sun. The wind hit them full force, Pike digging his talons tighter into Hall's shoulder. He thought he should give some kind of pep talk, go over strategy, talk plans. But he had nothing to offer.

The mountain was two or three miles of open ground away from the edge of the town. It was a nerve-wracking hike over the relatively flat, knee-high grass. There were several small clusters of trees scattered throughout the meadow, a couple small streams that were easy to jump across. Far to the south, the edges of a forest were visible, the mountain creeping north and sheltering the trees and coming within a mile of the town itself.

Hall hoped to get a better view of the plateau and standing stones as they got closer, but the angle was wrong. The flat land was too high up and turned away from their approach. He could see the tops of the stones, and that was it. The higher plateau was closer to them, but so high up the side of the mountain that nothing was visible.

A good place for a lookout tower, Hall thought. He cursed himself for letting his thoughts drift back to town planning. He forced himself to focus on the upcoming confrontation.

Only about a hundred feet from the meadow, the plateau was accessed by a wide path. Two large pillars, carved stone totems, sat on either side of the path, which had been carved out of the mountain itself.

The totems were about five feet tall, two feet in diameter, and worn down by wind and rain. They looked to have once been stone trees, representatives of the World Tree itself. Now they were just cracked and broken. The path was smooth, hard-packed dirt, about five feet wide. It ran up the steep side of the mountain, switchbacking in a couple of places. The mountain had been carved and cut to make the path but it still looked natural and part of the mountain itself. The tight turns and steepness would prevent any mounts from climbing.

Spreading the party out, putting distance between them, Hall led the group up the side of the mountain. He kept Pike out of the sky. The dragonhawk could have scouted ahead but could also have warned anyone that they were coming. The bird was not natural to this area and would look out of place. There had been no animals, birds, or chipmunks, or anything, that they had seen. The entire meadow was quiet. Another reason not to have Pike in the air.

Hall regretted having Pike flying overhead yesterday but it was too late. He hoped that a strange bird seen in the air once would be dismissed.

Cresting the path, he stepped onto the plateau and paused,

taking it in. The ground was dirt and exposed stone rising up on a slight angle. Thirty feet wide at this point with the path continuing beyond. The flat plateau extended to the northeast, around the curve of the mountain. He could make out the first of the standing stones beyond, the noise of the two waterfalls loud and overwhelming, something Hall was thankful for.

Stepping away from the edge, spear in hand, Hall started toward the first stones. They were arranged like an arch, a gateway. Two stones set vertically into the ground, six feet wide with that side facing Hall and the path, about six to eight feet between them. Laid across the top was a thin slab. All the stones were smooth, perfect, untouched by wind or rain. Not much could be seen beyond the gate of stones which were set where the plateau curved around the mountain.

The grass, in patches around the exposed stone, was green with a few plants. As he got closer to the stones, Hall saw the patches start to change from green to brown and dying. The moss, which was green, now took on a purple tinge. It looked sickly, dying.

Hall paused at the stones, off to the side of the opening. He looked back at Leigh. The Druid looked toward the stones, back to the ridge that led away from all this and back toward the stones. Hall could see the inner fight that Leigh was waging. Duty and responsibility won out.

She nodded at Hall.

Taking a tighter grip on his spear, Hall stepped through the stone opening.

————

Before him was a long meadow, not that wide and maybe a quarter mile long. The waterfall from the higher plateau was midway down, cascading down the rock face into a small pool that turned into the stream that continued to another pool and then flowed to the waterfall that fell to the lower meadow. Small groves of trees filled the space, wide open spaces around and between them. Around the central pool was a circle of standing stones, sets of two vertical stones with one laid horizontal, the top of a tall tree above.

There was no noise beyond that of the waterfalls. No birds flying, no animals running around the grass. The whole thing was peaceful but just felt wrong.

Groves were supposed to be peaceful. Places of serenity, but there was always activity. There were always Custodian Druids, visiting Centaurs or Satyrs, or some other forest creature, always wild animals roaming the Grove.

Here, there was nothing.

Just the wrongness.

It wasn't just the colors of everything. Where there should have been greens and browns, there was purples and grays. Instead of the color of life, there was the color of corruption. Moss grew everywhere, shades of purple, climbing up the trees and hanging from the branches. The trees were all drooping, branches hanging lax. The bushes and smaller trees were thin, leaves gone, sickly-looking things.

Hall felt sick as he walked deeper into the Grove. He checked his stats and saw no changes, no debuff, but he still felt it. His stomach churned, his head hurt. He just felt wrong.

"No. Oh no," Leigh said as she stepped through the stones. She started to cry. "I should have come sooner. This is my fault…" her words trailed off as she collapsed to the ground crying.

"What happened here?" Sabine said, coughing and gagging.

"It's corrupted," Leigh said, gasping it out between sobs. "The Grove has been desecrated."

They all looked out across the landscape, fighting back the feeling of wrongness.

"Can it be saved?" Hall asked.

"I think so," Leigh said, forcing herself to stand up. "Yes, I can do it."

QUEST COMPLETE!

You have escorted Leigh, Druid of the Tree, to the Lost Grove on Edin.

THE LOST GROVE

Reward: +500 Druids of the Tree Renown, +500 Alliance with Leigh, +20 Experience

"What do you need from us?" Hall asked.

He had never really cared about the mission of the Druids, never truly understood what they did. He had only cared about the quests and the experiences and rewards. But looking at this Grove, at what had been done to such a special place, he had to fix it. He had to help bring it back to what it should be.

"We have to find out why it got corrupted and what happened to the Custodian."

THE CORRUPTED GROVE

Leigh, Druid of the Tree, has asked your help is discovering what has corrupted the Grove on Edin.

Find the Source of Corruption 0/1
End the Corruption of the Grove 0/1
Reward: +1000 Druids of the Tree Renown, +1000 Alliance with Leigh, +500 Experience

ACCEPT QUEST?

Hall didn't hesitate in accepting the quest. Glancing at

Sabine and Roxhard, they nodded. They had accepted as well. They all tightened grips on weapons and staffs.

"Be alert," Hall said. "We don't know what's ahead."

He started forward, the others spread out around him. He thought about having Roxhard take the point but wanted the Dwarf to be able to use the *Battle Rush* ability to start the fight off. The ability wasn't usable if the Dwarf was engaged. Hall as a Skirmisher was no tank, but he could take some damage if absolutely needed and *Leap* out of the way when Roxhard charged in. His leather light armor wouldn't allow him to take many hits, but he could hold an enemy's attention for a short time if needed.

They walked through the trees, avoiding touching anything. The grass, mostly moss, was springy under their feet. Each step sank into the wet and slippery surface. They pushed on deeper into the Grove, coming up to the circle of Standing Stones.

Hall paused, listening, looking around. He thought about sending Pike up but held the dragonhawk back. Taking a deep breath, mentally preparing himself, Hall stepped through the stone and into the Grove itself.

———

The Branch of the World Tree was easily thirty feet tall and the trunk almost six feet around. It was called a Branch because the lore said this tree was a splinter of the World Tree that was broken off when Hankath was fractured. Each island had a at least one Branch of the World Tree, and it was those Branches that kept the islands floating and anchored in relation to each other.

This tree was once white with hints of gold and silver in the branches and bark. It would have been beautiful. Full, lush, branches reaching high into the sky. Now it was sickly, looking more like a weeping willow than the oak that it was. The bark was gray, cracked. The branches all drooped and many were without leaves. The silver leaves that should have shined were now purple and black, lacking any luster at all.

It sat on an island of grass and dirt, the thick roots exposed, in the middle of a pond. The island was about twenty feet around, the pond was another ten feet from shore to store. A path of large stones stood an inch or two above water, leading from the shore to the tree. Each was two or more feet in size, a foot between. The waters of the pond moved swiftly with the current, the water pushed by the waterfall.

Hall circled to the left, motioning Roxhard to the right. They moved to where they could see the entire island. Aside from the tree, there was nothing. He saw there was another path of walking stones on the other side of the island.

"By Abnoba," Leigh exclaimed, shocked.

She pointed to the tree.

Hall focused on where she pointed, finding what had caught her attention. About midway up the trunk, ten feet or so off the ground, was a black spike sticking out of the tree. What looked like blood, dark sap, leaked out around the nail.

"What is that?" he asked.

"A Demon's Nail," Leigh replied.

THE CORRUPTED GROVE

Leigh, Druid of the Tree, has discovered a Demon's Nail spiked into the World Tree. It is undoubtedly the source of the corruption.

Find the Source of Corruption 1/1
End the Corruption of the Grove 0/1

"What is a Demon's Nail?" Sabine asked.

She walked to the edge, studying the black spike. It was small from where they were, barely visible, but they could all feel the darkness radiating from the small object.

"When a contract is struck with the Dark Man, to sign the deal he gives the person a Nail to drive into the object they held most dear. It is a sign of the person accepting the dark powers," Leigh explained. There was an edge to her voice, an anger that Hall had never heard before.

The one person that the Settlement Stone had counted, it was the Grove's Custodian. The person that was entrusted with the care and safety of the World Tree had been the one to corrupt it.

"The Dark Man," Roxhard asked. His eyes were fixed on the tree and the spike. Instead of looking around, studying the land and searching for threats, the Dwarf was fixated on the tree.

"Feardagh," Leigh spat on the ground as she said the name.

A name they all knew. A demon, a follower of Balor the Corrupt. The one that was responsible for the fracturing of the world. The Dark Man was chaos, anarchy.

Sky Realms Online had no true Gods, no true religion. The various races called on Spirits in place of Gods, for the same purposes. Some argued that the Spirts were Gods, just not called that. For the most part, as it didn't affect gameplay, no one cared.

Now, apparently, it appeared that the spirits and the demons did affect the world.

"Can we remove it?" Sabine asked.

"I don't..." Leigh began, pausing, studying the nail, thinking of all that she had heard about such things. "I don't think so. I think only the corrupted can."

"Or killing the corrupted," Sabine stated.

"Yes," Leigh said, steel in her voice, determination and resolve. "That would destroy the Nail."

"Let's move," Hall said, leading them out of the standing stones to the east, away from the mountain side.

They crossed the pond and saw the meadow stretching out, a forest beyond along the bottom of the far mountain. A brook meandered across the meadow, coming out from under the mountain and turning into the small pond.

A stone bridge arced over the brook. There was no railing, the stones tight fitting, covered in moss. Thin, barely wide enough for one person to walk across, Hall hesitated at the bottom. The brook was only about ten feet wide, the water moving fast and rapidly over the rocks. It looked deep, thick with purple plants. Placing one foot carefully on the bridge, he started the slow walk across.

They gathered on the other side facing into the far side of the Grove. The trees were thicker, the corruption worse. The mountain curved back to the cliff, ending the meadow and the forest, a wall of stone that contained the corruption. Dark, large shadowed shapes could be seen moving beneath the trees.

"Moss Shamblers," Leigh said, pointing at the shapes. "Guardians of the Grove."

"Connected to the Grove," Hall asked, watching the seemingly random movements of the shadows, knowing the answer.

"Yes," Leigh answered. "They'll be corrupted as well."

"Can we avoid them?" Roxhard asked.

"No. They'll come to the aid of the Custodian."

Leigh had come to the same conclusion that Hall had. The Custodian had been the one to corrupt the World Tree.

"So, we need to kill them all," Hall stated.

"We'll lose the element of surprise," Sabine said, shaking her head, finger raised and trying to count the moving shapes.

"I don't think we ever had it," Hall said. "Tell us about the Shamblers."

CHAPTER THIRTY-ONE

HALL STABBED OUT WITH HIS SPEAR. THE TIP CUT INTO THE Corrupted Moss Shambler, pushing through and poking out the other side. There was no budge to the creature's health bar, the strike doing no damage. Hall cursed and jumped back as the long arm swung out. He ducked and felt the pressure wave as the limb barely missed connecting.

It would have done significant damage if it had hit.

The Shamblers were strong even though they did not look it. A giant pile of roots and moss, plants and vines, held together by the magic of the Grove. They stood eight feet high, incredibly wide. Hunched over, the arms hung down to the ground as they walked on thick tree stump-like legs. They shambled, sliding more than walking, which is how they got their names. No neck, the head just grew out of the shoulders. Two bright red eyes, large orbs, with drooping tendrils framing the face. The creature made no noise as it moved, just the sound of the legs sliding across the ground.

He could feel the heat behind him, waves coming off the burning Shambler.

It had been the first they had come across, and their plan

had worked. Being a creature of moss and vines, stabbing it would do no good. Only blunt weapons or magic would harm the Shamblers. Or slashing as Roxhard had discovered when he started cutting chunks off with his axe. The Shambler was too large, too tough with too much Health, for that to be an effective strategy. They hit too hard.

They had prepared torches, finding the driest and least rotted wood they could. Hall and Leigh each carried one as neither had magic or weapons that would harm the Shamblers. The plan was for Roxhard to hold the creature's attention while they worked to light it on fire. Sabine would stand back and fire *Shadowbolts* at it.

A good plan that was working on the first one but when a second came bursting out of the trees, Hall had to drop his torch and attack with the weapon at hand. His spear.

He had hoped to do some damage or at least slow it down. The long weapon did neither. And worse, the burning one was not dead yet, occupying both Roxhard and Sabine. They could not leave until it was dead, and the wet creature was slow to burn.

Hall turned the Shambler, leading it away from the others. He could see Leigh behind it, with Angus, looking for a way to attack. She held her magical cudgel in hand waiting for her chance. Pike hovered over the cow.

He backed up, feeling a tree behind him. His spear still stuck in the creature, and he struck with the flat of his blade, dealing no damage to the creature but prompting a retaliation. The arm swung out, but Hall was in too close and easily ducked. The limb slammed into the tree, shaking the trunk, cracking the bark. The Shambler's arm snapped, the roots holding it together breaking. The front part bent forward.

Dumbly, the creature lifted the arm or tried to. The hanging part was too heavy, causing the limb to drag on the ground. That was when Leigh struck.

She swung her Epic level weapon, the *Ironwood Shillelagh Of Thunder*, with as much might and momentum as she could. The weapon's end slammed into the back of the Shambler sending bits of moss, root and vine into the air like a small explosion. The Shambler turned at the attack, ignoring Hall and focusing on the one that had done some damage.

Pike flew up, hovering in front of the creature, and opened his mouth in a screech. A bolt of lightning shot out, striking the Shambler in its face. Smoke curled up from the few bits of dried roots. The creature stumbled back, what was once its face now gone. Burned and destroyed.

Leigh swung again. The cudgel slammed into the Shambler, more of it exploding outward from the impact. Again, she hit the creature, this time the impact was followed by a deep boom, and almost half of the Shambler's chest disappeared. The creature stumbled back, disoriented and unable to move. The magic of Leigh's cudgel had activated.

Hall took advantage of the stunned Shambler. He jumped up onto its shoulders, reaching down and holding on to a root growing out of the top of its head. Taking his sword, he started chopping at the shoulder joint, pieces of root and vine falling away.

The creature moved, and Hall jumped off, the Shambler's arm falling away.

"Its leg," Hall shouted as he landed.

He quickly scrambled to the side as Leigh swung at the Shambler's closest leg. More parts of its body exploded at the impact, leaving a gaping hole. The Shambler shifted, leaning, as it tried to take its weight off the destroyed leg.

Angus charged, slamming into the Shambler's chest. Off balance, it fell backward. The small cow reared up, falling back to the ground and slamming his front hooves onto the Shambler's chest. The weight and impact pushed large holes into the creature.

Hall lined up with the Shambler's head, where he thought it connected to the body, and swung down. He used his sword like an axe, hacking at the thick roots. Bit by bit, he cut into the head, slowly hacking it off. It stopped moving, and Hall stepped off.

SLAIN: *Corrupted Moss Shambler*
+20 Experience

A shared kill, they didn't earn that much experience.

Roxhard and Sabine stepped back from the Shambler they had finished off. The Dwarf was breathing hard, flexing his right arm and holding the left limply. *A Shambler must have hit him*, Hall thought, as Leigh stepped over to Roxhard to heal. She laid her hands on his arm and activated the spell. He smiled at her touch.

"This isn't going to work," Sabine said, pointing at the Shamblers. "Just two of the things took a lot out of us."

"I agree," Hall replied, crouching down next to the one he had killed. He poked through the body with his sword, seeing if there was any loot on them.

He felt the tip hitting something hard in the middle of the Shamblers chest. Ripping aside the vines and roots, he reached down and pulled out a hard object about the size and shape of a softball. It had skin like that of a nut and once had been smooth but was now pitted and cracked. It was black, feeling foul to the touch.

Success!
You have harvested: Corrupted Shambler Heart

Skill Gain!
Herbology Rank 2 +.3

He held it out to Leigh.

"What has the corruption done?" Leigh gasped, staring at the object. "That was once beautiful. A perfect golden seed, taken from the Branch itself."

"Want it?" Hall asked.

"No, keep that foul thing away from me," she said, stepping back from it.

With a shrug, Hall placed the object in his pouch. He had no idea what it was, or what it could be used for, but he'd gotten a skill gain from it so there was some use for it. Just no time to find out now.

"What do we do?" Roxhard asked.

He was looking through the trees at the shadows farther back, the other Shamblers. There were a lot of them.

Hall stood up, spear in hand, watching the Shamblers movement. There was a pattern to their movements he realized, not just random wanderings. They weren't on patrol, there were too many gaps that he could see.

"We can slip by them," he said with confidence.

"I thought we were worried about them attacking us when we got to the Custodian," Sabine asked.

"We are," Hall replied and shrugged. He had no other ideas or options. "We go forward and deal with the Shamblers if it comes to that, or we go back." He turned around and looked at the party.

"Forward," Leigh said, holding her cudgel. Angus shook his head and mooed, stomping his hooves to get some loose Shambler vines off.

"I follow you, boss," Roxhard said.

Sabine shrugged. "What the hell, why not?"

"Good," Hall said and smiled. "Forward it is. I really want to meet my new neighbor."

———

The Corrupted Moss Shamblers were a shell of their former shelves. They behaved nothing like the ones that Leigh had described. Those had some free will, the ability to think. These were basically automatons. They moved in their pattern unless provoked or something came into their attack radius.

Hall tested the theory out on the first one they came across once they started moving again. He tossed a rock, a slimy moss-covered thing, at the Shambler. The projectile got within five feet, and the Shambler moved quickly, batting at the rock. Once the threat was eliminated, the Shambler started moving again.

He didn't want to push the radius, so he kept ten or more feet between them and a Shambler at any time, making sure they were always moving behind the creatures. He kept them bunched up, dangerous to be sure, but it kept their profile small and easier to move through the rings of Shamblers.

And that's how the creatures were organized, a loose ring through the forest. Layer after layer. Someone's idea of a defensive position. But someone that really didn't know what they were doing.

Hall also liked how far apart the rings of Shamblers were placed. Twenty feet or more between them, and the last ring was thirty feet from the inside edge of the trees.

The forest ended in a small clearing backed up against the cliff. Purple-colored grass with a few rocks covered in moss spread out from the trees to the sheer face of the mountain. A small opening was set into the face of stone, dark inside. The clearing was empty.

They stopped just inside the last tree cover, Roxhard watching the Shamblers barely visible behind them. Hall studied the cave and the clearing, looking for signs of anything. The Custodian had to be inside the cave, and Hall had no interest in confronting anything in a possibly confined space.

He would have loved to have been able to scout out the cave, but it was too dangerous to make the attempt.

Instead he opted for the direct approach.

"Charge on my signal," he told Roxhard, directing the Dwarf and Sabine to stay hidden.

With a nod to Leigh, the two of them stepped out of the tree cover, Pike and Angus staying behind.

"Follow my lead," Hall whispered to Leigh. "Hello," he called out, loudly, his voice echoing off the cliff.

They stood waiting for a minute or two. Nothing happening, and Hall was about to call out again when the shadows around the cave opening shifted. They watched as a figure stepped out of the cave.

The clearing was in the shade, the afternoon sun blocked by the mountain and the Grove itself, which seemed to be in constant twilight, but the figure held a hand up to shade its eyes from the light. It seemed to shamble like the guardians in the forest, moving slowly and a little stiffly. The clearing was only twenty or thirty feet deep so they were able to get a good look as the figure moved away from the rock face.

Tall, a frame that suggested an Elf and male. Standing well over six feet if he had stood upright, the man was dressed in a thick brown and unmarked robe with the hood pulled up. The hood framed his face, the features lost in shadow, and the edge of the hood was caught up on two antlers growing from the man's head. Each was bone white, the right one ending in six points, the left was broken off a couple inches from where it grew out of his head. In his gray-skinned hand, he held a gnarled staff, the top end broken off and ending in jagged splinters.

"Who are you?" he growled, his voice hoarse and rough. "Why did you come here?"

Leigh gasped, shocked, and Hall glanced down quickly, hoping she was able to keep her composure. The man across from them didn't look like much, stooped and broken, but Hall could feel the dark power radiating from him.

Identify gave him no information. His level was too low or the Elf's level was too high. Or a combination of both.

Skill Gain!
Identify Rank 1 +.1

"We were sent from the Grove in Cumberland," Hall said. "They had not heard from you and were worried."

"The fools," the man grumbled and chuckled, a dry and raspy sound. "I am fine. Now, begone," he said and made a shooing motion.

He turned back toward the cave when Leigh spoke, drawing his attention. Hall cursed.

"You're Vertoyi," she said, tone just shy of accusation. "The Custodian of this Grove."

The broken Druid turned back. He focused on Leigh, studying her, realizing what she was.

"The Elders sent you to report on me," he said, laughing. He said it arrogantly. "A little whelp like you?" He laughed harder, coughing but still laughing. "The bastards," Vertoyi barked, angry now. His mood shifted back and forth, and Hall knew the man was insane. "This is how they honor me? Me?! They send a whelpling to spy on me? How dare they? Well, girl," he growled, his arms waving at the Grove around them. "What do you say? What will you report to your masters? Will you tell them how beautiful my Grove is?"

"Beautiful?" Leigh screamed, outraged. "You have defiled this sacred place. You have corrupted it and made the Branch diseased."

Vertoyi took a step back, shocked at her outburst. He had really expected her to approve of the Grove, Hall realized. The Custodian looked from Hall to Leigh, past them and into the trees. For a second, Hall saw recognition. The Druid was seeing the Grove for what it truly was, but then the fleeting look was gone. The eyes were angry, the Druid growling.

"How dare you?" he screamed back at Leigh. "I have done nothing but care for this place. I have given it my all and made it beautiful and powerful. Just like I will to all the Groves in all the world. The Elders are fools, and I will make them see. Or they will die," he finished simply, no longer as angry.

Hall braced himself. This was it, he knew.

"But you will die first," Vertoyi stated and pointed at Leigh.

"Now," Hall yelled, pushing Leigh down and out of the way as a storm of splinters shot toward them.

CHAPTER THIRTY-TWO

HALL KNEW THERE WAS ONLY ONE WAY THEY WERE GOING TO win this, and that was to hit the Custodian hard and fast and often.

The plan lasted all of a couple seconds.

Vertoyi's *Splinter Storm* was twice as wide as Leighs, the shards twice as long. Hall barely got out of the way as he fell down opposite Leigh. He felt the wind of the splinter's passing just inches from his skin. He knew the spikes that Vertoyi shot out would penetrate his leather armor with no issue.

He heard Leigh grunt, hoping it was just from hitting the ground. She didn't scream or cry out in pain, so he hoped she had not been struck by the splinters.

There was the sound of booted feet on ground, stomping rapidly, and Hall felt the rush of Roxhard as the Dwarf barreled toward the Custodian.

Hall turned on his side, starting to stand back up, watching the blur that was Roxhard charge toward the seemingly unprepared Custodian. Roxhard ran and ran and slammed full speed into a wall of earth that appeared out of nowhere. Vertoyi stood behind it, arm upraised, sneering. Roxhard hit with a loud crack and bounced backward where he slammed hard into the ground and lay unmoving.

Hall cursed.

"Roxhard," he barked and pointed as Leigh started to get up from the ground.

She didn't appear hurt and headed toward the still unmoving Dwarf, crouching and keeping low. Hall saw the movement to his side, Sabine moving that direction. There were two of her, the *Shadow Self* spell already activated. She raised her hand and pointed, a dark streak of purple lightning shooting out toward the Custodian.

With a lazy wave of his hand, his hood fallen back to reveal a face streaked with hatred, he moved the *Earth Shield* into the path of Sabine's bolt. Her *Hexbolt* struck the shield, but instead of dissipating against it, the dark lightning wrapped around the mound of mud and grass. It streaked over the top, around both sides, and met on the opposite side before continuing and slamming into Vertoyi's chest.

The Custodian staggered back a step, the *Earth Shield* collapsing, as the streaks of lightning wrapped around his body. He grunted in pain but raised a hand and pointed at Sabine. He tried to speak but a spasm of pain wracked his body.

"It won't last long," Sabine yelled. "His resistance is high."

Hall knew they were lucky the spell was affecting Vertoyi at all.

He drew the javelin from over his shoulder, took aim, and let it fly. Vertoyi saw it coming, tried to raise a shield from the earth but only managed to get it three feet high. The dark purple bolts of lightning around his body flared and faded a bit, a few less bolts. The javelin slammed into the Custodian's shoulder, pushing the man back.

The Corrupted Druid's Health bar barely dropped.

"Keep the *Hexbolt* on him," Hall ordered, moving away from Sabine to make it harder for Vertoyi to target them both.

He ran through what he knew of ta Druid abilities, what spells the Custodian would have access to, wishing he knew the Elf's Level. The *Earth Shield* meant Vertoyi was at least level six but most likely higher. A Custodian of a Grove would be high level.

This was a Boss fight.

And they didn't have the advantage of a Wiki with strategies. He wasn't even sure if they would respawn if they died. Would Leigh? She was an NPC. Would she follow the normal laws and respawn where she started? Would he have to travel all the way back to Cumberland to find her again?

Would she even know who he was?

Hall did not want to find out.

They were not going to lose this fight. None of them were dying.

Hall knew he was lying to himself.

Vertoyi's eyes were filled with hate and madness. Pure white in the gray face. Not the normal dusky gray of the Elves but a more muted and ashen colored, like all the life had been drained from him. His hair was pure white, not the earth tones Hall was used to. Whatever deal Vertoyi had made with the Feardagh it had changed him. The Custodian was no longer an Elf.

Reaching over, struggling against the weakening streaks of lightning, Vertoyi pulled the javelin out of his shoulder. He glared at Hall, mouth moving as if talking but no sound coming out. Raising a hand, dozens of wood splinters shot out from the jagged end of his staff.

Hall activated his *Leap* ability and jumped into the air over the splinters. He landed closer to Vertoyi and leaped again. Pointing the end of his spear down, his arc brought him down almost on top of the Druid. He stabbed downward, aiming for the shoulder, but a gust of wind slammed into him. Hall was sent spinning, losing his spear, and dropped to the ground hard.

He struggled to get up, cursing himself for forgetting about the *Gust of Wind* ability that Druid's had. That was their one advantage in this fight, he knew, and he kept forgetting to use it. Most boss fights were against creatures created specifically for that encounter. They had their own abilities and skills, but Vertoyi was a Druid. He was a specific class, which meant he had those abilities and skills.

Hall just had to figure out how to use that knowledge before it was too late.

He pushed himself up, body groaning in protest, watching as Angus and Pike joined the fight. Vertoyi swung his staff, shrugging off a *Shadow Bolt* from Sabine, and cast *Splinter Storm* again at Pike. The dragonhawk barely swerved out of the way, flying higher and looking for an opening. Angus charged and slammed into a hastily erected *Earth Shield*. The cow stopped abruptly, shaking his head to clear the stars.

Vertoyi must have had some ring or item that sped up casting times, Hall realized. There was no way he could cast these many spells this quickly without some enchantment.

The last of Sabine's *Hexbolt* faded from the Druid, who laughed, long and wicked. Hall saw Sabine raise her hands to cast it again, the drawback of the ability being that it could not be stacked, but Vertoyi was quicker. Raising his hand, palm out, Vertoyi barked a single word, and a long bolt of lightning shot out. It slammed into Sabine, striking in the middle of the two images.

She screamed. Her second image flickered and disappeared. Sabine herself fell to one knee, smoke rising from various burns over her body. She was gasping in pain, trying to catch her breath. Her Health was down to 25% from one strike.

Hall stood just out of reach of Vertoyi, moving around to

make targeting harder. He glanced over to see Leigh turning from Roxhard, her beautiful features angry. The Dwarf was up, shaking his head to clear it, and at three quarters Health. The impact into the *Earth Shield* and rolling along the ground had done some damage. Leigh was staying low still, trying to make her way toward Sabine. At her level, the best thing Leigh could bring to the fight was healing.

Roxhard's face was angry, set in stone. The Dwarf was mad. An embarrassed fourteen-year-old boy. Hall had to focus that rage before Roxhard did something stupid.

He stabbed out with his spear. Vertoyi turned and casually waved his hand, a gust of wind blowing through the clearing. The spear was torn from Hall's hands, flying and landing hard against the cliff. It had done no damage.

But the distraction was enough.

Roxhard slammed into the Custodian from the side. Not as fast or as hard as before but with enough impact to knock Vertoyi down to the ground. Standing above the Custodian, Roxhard swung his axe down. The blade was met with a thin *Earth Shield*. The Dwarf growled, yelling a war cry, and kept swinging.

Hall leapt into the air, drawing his sword. He landed next to Vertoyi and swung. He struck a glancing blow along the Custodian's already wounded shoulder. The Elf cried out in pain and roared in outrage. Roxhard hammered on the *Earth Shield*, part of it now blocking Hall's attacks. They both kept swinging, keeping the Custodian occupied and unable to cast another spell. Each blow took off a small amount of Vertoyi's health. They were wearing him down, a little at a time, but they could not let up. A slip and Vertoyi could blast them away.

The Custodian tried to rise, his face a mask of anger, pushing against the unrelenting assault from Roxhard and Hall. A purple streak of lightning slammed into him, sending bolts cascading around his body. Vertoyi fell to the ground, his body spasming.

Hall took his vision off Vertoyi, seeing Sabine standing up but leaning against Leigh. The Druid's hands still glowed, still healing the Witch. Hall was starting to think they might have a chance. Vertoyi's health was dropping. Slowly, but it was dropping.

Something shifted in Vertoyi. He struggled up, pushing against them with his *Earth Shield*, making Hall and Roxhard step back. His body shook with spasms from the *Hexbolt* but he somehow managed to move against it. Veins pushed out on his skin, which was pulled tight against his skull. A spot of black grew in Vertoyi's white eyes.

"Enough," he growled, spitting out the word between spasms of pain from the *Hexbolt*.

He barked a single word and the ground shook.

Small stones fell from the mountain, followed by larger ones. Hall fell back, trying to keep his balance. Roxhard was thrown back as Vertoyi surged forward with his *Earth Shield*. The Custodian kept his balance as his magical earthquake shook. Leigh stumbled, Sabine's weight falling on her, and both went down in a heap. Angus mooed, legs spread wide as the cow fought to stay steady.

"You fools," Vertoyi shouted, somehow standing up.

The ground still shook and Hall finally fell, landing hard and trying to avoid the rocks that were falling from the cliff. A good sized one slammed into his shoulder, his arm going numb. Roxhard rolled on the ground, unable to stand against the movement of the earth. Vertoyi pushed out his arms, the crackling bolts of Sabine's *Hexbolt* breaking apart.

"I am no mere Druid," he yelled, turning from one to the other, full of contempt. "I am the greatest Druid. When I am done with you, I will prove it to the world."

Vertoyi raised his hand high, the broken topped staff in his right hand. He uttered three simple words, quick words, and the sky above them darkened. Hall tried to turn away, but could not. As the ground still shook around him, unable to stand, he watched the storm clouds gather. Dark gray clouds, lightning cracking around them, filled the sky. The bolts got stronger, faster, the cracks following quickly. He watched as a bright streak of light shot down toward them.

The bolt slammed into the ground, an explosion of dirt and rock, the pieces falling down around them. The ground stopped shaking as bolts of lightning shot out from the impact zone. They streaked about the clearing, each striking one of the party members.

Hall felt the impact. His body stiffened, jerked, and spasmed as the electricity coursed through every vein and bone. He felt the burning, his nerves shrieking. He tried to scream but no sound came out.

The pain seemed to last an eternity but it was over quickly.

The lightning faded, and Hall dropped to the ground. He was panting, having a hard time catching his breath as his heart raced a mile a minute. Groaning, he looked up from where he was on his hands and knees. Roxhard writhed in pain on the ground. Angus was unmoving. Pike lay on the ground, his wings jerking as the dragonhawk tried to move. Sabine was unmoving, smoke drifting up from her body. Leigh was down, trying to get up. Smoke rose across Hall's vision, and it took him a second to realize it was coming from his body.

In the corner of his vision, he saw his health meter blinking rapidly. There was barely any of the bar left.

And standing in the middle of the clearing, slowly rising to his full height, was Vertoyi. Laughing.

Hall tried to get up, the pain intense, every part of his body screaming in protest.

He gasped, grunting in pain, as a booted foot slammed into his side. He fell against the mountainside, small pebbles still falling. Though small, the impacts still felt like boulders five times their size. He tried to push away from the mountain, but the kick caught him again. Blackness creeped in on the edges of his vision. Hall fought to stay conscious, watching his Health drop even more, the bar still blinking red.

The Custodian didn't kick hard, it was the accumulation of everything. The lightning, the hits he had taken, the rocks and now the kicks. Hall could feel his Health bar dropping, each single point of life disappearing, ticking down to when it would be zero, and he would die.

He tried to cough, harsh sounds escaping and spitting up blood. He thought his lung was punctured, ribs fractured. Sabine still had not moved, Roxhard had stopped rolling on the ground. The Dwarf was trying to sit up. Vertoyi glanced that way and casually swiped his hand in front of him. Hall felt the wind tear down across the face of the mountain and slam into Roxhard, sending the Dwarf rolling across the ground. He came to a stop and didn't move.

"No," Hall tried to yell, the words coming out ragged and around coughs.

Vertoyi turned back toward him, sneering.

"You shall be first," he said, walking toward Hall.

The Custodian pointed the broken end of the staff at Hall, smiling.

Hall closed his eyes, not wanting to see, but knowing he would feel each one of the dozens of splinters that were going to be shot at him.

CHAPTER THIRTY-THREE

He waited for the pain.

Hall wanted to fight, to get up. He wanted to buy time for the others to get away. Hoping they would run when he was killed, knowing it would not happen. He cursed himself for bringing them into this unprepared. He had still been treating it all like a game, like he would have if still playing. Death was no big deal. It was part of the game and part of how all Boss fights went.

This was different.

The pain was too real. It was too much. There had always been pain in the game, just light taps when struck. Just enough to know it had happened. But safety measures had been put in place. Those were gone.

It was just him and the pain. Worse than anything he had ever experienced.

But he still fought, still tried to get out of the way.

"Goodbye, fool," Vertoyi said, laughing.

"NO!"

The word was followed by Vertoyi yelling in pain and anger.

Hall opened his eyes, painfully shifting to look past the Custodian.

Leigh was up on one knee, leaning to the side with one arm supporting her. Small splinters were sticking out of Vertoyi's back, a dozen or so, most stuck in the folds of his heavy robe.

"Child," Vertoyi said calmly. "Why do you insist on fighting for them? The Elders care nothing for you. Nothing for me. They just care about themselves. They are liars. Using us for their own amusement."

"You are the liar," Leigh growled, standing up.

She was hunched over, clearly still in pain. Hall didn't need to see her Health bar to know she was near the end.

Run, he thought. *Get away*.

"It is you," Leigh screamed. "You are the liar. Look what you have done to this Grove!"

Hall watched Vertoyi pause, look around the clearing at the rot and the corruption. He shook himself, as if clearing his head and removing an image.

"I have made it stronger. Nothing can destroy this place now. From here I will spread my teachings to the world. I will make it stronger."

"You will bring it death," Leigh said and collapsed to a knee again. She was breathing heavy, weakening.

"Jealous," Vertoyi said and stalked toward her, angry. "You are as jealous as the Elders. They sent me here, alone, to this empty place because they were jealous. And afraid." He stopped a couple feet from her, pointing at her, almost jabbing at her with a bony finger. "They were afraid of what I could do. They were afraid of my power."

Hall felt himself breathing a little easier. Each breath still hurt, bad, but he could see his Health slowly regenerating naturally. His Vitality was gone. He was not regaining any, but at least he still had some Energy and slowly more Health.

There might still be something he could do if Leigh could stall Vertoyi longer.

"Power you got from the Corruptor's servant," Leigh spat. "What did the Dark Man promise you in exchange for your soul and the destruction of the Grove?"

"More lies told you by the Elders," Vertoyi said, calmer, speaking like a teacher to a student. "The Feardagh and his master, Balor, do not want to destroy. They want to build. To improve on our beautiful world. To take the wonder of nature and make it better."

Leigh stared up at Vertoyi, anger and accusation in her eyes. Her face was etched in pain, her breathing ragged, but the anger was there. The only thing keeping her going. Her gaze seared the Custodian, the force of it making him step back.

"You are blinded by your false power," she said, not screaming, resolute, her words having great weight.

"My power is real," Vertoyi said. "I will…"

"LIAR!" Leigh shouted, interrupting him and standing up to her full height. Somehow, she made herself get up. Still more than a foot shorter than the Elf, her presence was more than his, stronger than his. "For years I tried not to follow the teachings, to not become a Druid. I didn't think it was what I wanted. But now, seeing what you have done, it is all I want. I hope the Elders can forgive me for my failures. I have let them down. I have let the Grove down. I have let myself down." She took a step forward, stumbling but standing. Vertoyi backed up a step. "But no longer. I will not let you destroy this Grove."

"I have not destroyed-"

"STOP IT," Leigh screamed, the words echoing in the clearing.

Hall managed to sit up, leaning against the cliff. He could see shadows gathering in the trees. The Corrupted Moss

Shamblers approaching. Not at Vertoyi's call but at the commotion and the unleashed magic.

"Stop lying to yourself," she said, hearing the noises of the Shamblers

She turned, seeing the dark purple forms lumber out of the trees, two of them. They stopped at the edge, waiting for a command.

"Is that your idea of helping the Grove?" she asked, pointing at the Shamblers.

Vertoyi stared at them, his head tilted, as if seeing them for the first time.

"Why are they rotting?" he asked quietly.

He looked around the clearing again, the same look as before when it seemed he was viewing the reality. This time, he didn't lose focus on what was in front of him. This time, he remained seeing the corruption.

"The seed," Leigh said, stumbling and falling to the ground again. She looked at Hall, pleading. "Show him the seed."

It took Hall a couple seconds to understand what she meant. A Shambler shifted, and Hall remembered the object in his pouch. Vertoyi looked back at him, not with anger or fear, but curiosity.

"What seed?" the Custodian asked.

Hall reached into the pouch and pulled out the seed. He held it in his palm, arm stretched out toward Vertoyi.

The Custodian stared at the seed, stepping close and leaning down. Hall's eyes darted around for his short sword. If he could grab it and stab the Druid, land a critical strike, he could end this. Hopefully. But the sword was nowhere near and Hall thought himself still too weak to move fast enough. He watched Vertoyi's eyes change. A new color appeared in the white, the irises' taking on a green tone as the Druid looked at the seed.

"What is that?" he asked.

"A seed from one of those," Hall answered weakly and pointed at the Shamblers.

Vertoyi looked back at the creatures and then again at the seed. The white started to fade from his eyes. There was blue there now, starting to reappear.

"But it should be golden," the Druid said quietly. "Not cracked. Why is it cracked?"

The Druid looked back at the motionless Shamblers.

"Did this make those?" he asked.

He stood up, taking the seed with him. Holding it in one hand, the broken staff in the other, he walked over to the Shamblers. They did not move, just rocked back and forth. Hall used the cliff face behind him to help stand up, to help keep him up. Vertoyi studied a Shambler, looking from the seed to the creature.

Without warning, quickly, Vertoyi reached into the Moss Shambler's chest. The roots and vines did not stop him, there was no magic called or summoned. The Custodian just reached into the creature and pulled his arm back out. In his hand he now held two seeds. The new matched the other, cracked and corrupted.

The Moss Shambler shook, its great body shifting and writhing. It fell apart, just collapsed into a pile of roots, moss and vines.

Vertoyi paid no attention to it. He just studied the two seeds.

"I did this?" he asked.

"Yes," Hall answered, loudly and clearly.

He watched as Leigh pulled herself toward the motionless body of Angus. She reached out toward the animal, trying to touch him.

Vertoyi dropped both seeds, stepping back like they were hot, as they rolled around on the ground. His eyes followed them, turning to the last Shambler, passing over the creature and stopping on the forest and the trees.

"What have I done?" he said, walking past the Shambler and into the forest, leaving them behind.

Hall braced himself, searching the ground for a weapon, expecting the remaining Shambler to attack. It did not. It did not move, just shifted, the body in motion even if it did not take a step.

Skill Gain!
Polearms Rank 2 +.2

Skill Gain!
Small Blades Rank 2 +.2

Skill Gain!
Thrown Rank 2 +.1

Skill Gain!
Light Armor Rank 2 +.2

He pushed himself off the cliff, taking a hesitant step. First one, then another. Slowly, a single small movement at a time. Put his foot down, steady himself, move the other. Leigh had made it to Angus, and a glow was coming from her hand where it touched the cow.

Angus' breath had been ragged, the chest moving up and down in a stuttering rhythm. Now it changed to somewhat normal, slow and deep, but the cow was breathing regularly at least. Hall stopped next to them, looking down at the motionless form of Pike laying nearby. He could not see any movement to the dragonhawk's chest, no flutter or twitch of a wing or feather.

Hall wanted to crouch down next to his companion, to

hold the small dragonhawk but he was afraid to. He did not think he would be able to get up. Leigh crawled over to Pike, laying a hand on the bird. She looked up at Hall and smiled, small and weak, but it was a smile. Hall took that as a good sign.

She waited a minute, a long minute, as her Energy recharged enough before casting the spell. Hall watched the glow spread from the Druid's hands and over Pike. He held his breath, waiting. There, a small movement. A feather twitching and then breathing. The bird still did not move, but Pike was breathing.

"Thank you," Hall said.

Leigh smiled, looking weak and tired.

"Your turn," she said.

Hall shook his head.

"The others first."

He reached down, bracing himself, and helped Leigh to stand up. Steadying herself, she moved toward Roxhard and Sabine, slowly but steady, and gaining strength with each step.

Hall looked toward where Vertoyi had gone. There was no sign of the Druid, the Shambler still motionless. It made Hall uneasy. Vertoyi seemed to have come out from whatever spell the Feardagh had put on him. Not a spell, Hall amended, but the Druid's own choice. Even though he seemed sane now, there was no counting on it. The same with the Shambler. It could move at any time.

They had to take advantage of this opportunity before they lost it.

He hurt still. Every nerve in his body was tingling, on fire. Every muscle was tight, contracted. Every bone was bruised. His right arm was numb, shoulder bruised from the rocks. Every breath was painful through the punctured lung and fractured ribs. He knew he needed healing badly and bandages would not work. Not for these wounds.

Reaching down to the potion pouch on his belt, he felt around until he recognized the cork and pulled out a Light Healing Potion. Good for only Twenty Health over a period of ten seconds, it would be better than nothing. Pulling the cork out with his teeth, spitting it on the ground, he tipped the small vial of green liquid into his mouth.

Immediately he felt the magic of the liquid coursing through his body. Some of the pain went away, bit by bit as it healed over time. The majority of it was still there, still painful to breath and walk, but his Health bar was no longer blinking red. He hadn't bothered to use the potion during the fight because it would not have mattered. Light Healing wasn't going to help them in this fight.

He made a mental note to find out where to get the more powerful potions from, or figure out how to make them. If this was an example of the fights they would be encountering, they would need the potions badly.

Roxhard was sitting up, holding his head in his hands. Leigh was next to Sabine, her hands on the Witch.

"What happened?" Roxhard asked.

"We got our asses handed to us," Hall replied.

"Why are we still alive?"

"Leigh talked him down," Hall said, moving back toward Pike, who was struggling to stand up.

He reached down and gently picked the dragonhawk up, cradling the bird tight against his chest. Angus mooed quietly from where he lay on the ground. Hall reached out and scratched the cow behind the ears. Angus gave him an odd look, wondering what Hall was doing, but tilted his head so Hall could get at the spot better.

"Glad you're both still with us," he said to the animals. "You three," he added to Roxhard, who nodded. "And you four," he said as Leigh helped Sabine to stand up.

The Witch was wobbly, burn marks across her exposed skin. She was angry.

"Where is that bloody Druid?"

Hall pointed into the woods.

"Let's not go that way," Sabine muttered, eyeing the motionless Shambler.

"No other choice," Hall said. "It's the only way out."

———

They waited until Leigh had regained enough Energy to cast *Nature's Touch* healing on all of them again, including Angus and Pike. They had all gathered their weapons that had been dropped, adjusted loose armor, and drank what few Light Healing potions remained while waiting for Leigh to recharge between castings.

Hall set them moving before they were all at full strength. He wanted out of the clearing incase the Shambler started moving or Vertoyi came back, as mad as ever. They moved slowly, eyes constantly looking for more Shamblers. There were some, unmoving like the one in the clearing and easily avoided.

Pike rode on top of Angus, crouched down, trying to smooth his feathers. Some of the green tips were still blackened. They all still bore marks from the lightning attack and Vertoyi's beatings. Vitality had been extremely slow in coming back and even Leigh's healings could only do so much.

Halfway through the forest, Leigh stopped. The others hesitated, looking back at her quizzically. She was looking at a tree, hand reaching out to touch it. Running her fingers along the bark, Leigh gasped in shock.

"What is it?" Sabine asked, impatient to get out of the forest.

"Something's changed," Leigh said, unsure of what she was seeing. "I don't know what but there has been a shift."

"Good or bad?" Hall asked, looking toward where the Grove was. He had an idea of what had caused the shift, and it could have gone either way.

Leigh removed her hand, looking at her fingers, brushing the tips against her leather skirt.

"Good, I think," she replied but paused. "I think. It's hard to tell because the corruption runs so deep."

Minutes later, they reached the edge of the forest and looked out across the meadow. The standing stones were there, the Branch peeking out above the edges. They saw nothing else.

Hall exchanged a glance with Leigh. She nodded.

"You two head back to town," he said to Roxhard and Sabine. "Gather our gear, and if we're not there in an hour-" he paused, looking toward the Grove. "If we're not there thirty minutes after you, then run. Get as far from here as you can."

Roxhard looked like he was going to protest but Sabine pulled at him. She didn't hesitate. Reluctantly, the Dwarf followed, casting looks back.

Hall ignored him, waiting with Leigh until she was ready. Standing straighter, she started walking toward the pond. Hall followed with Angus and Pike, tightening his weary grip on the spear.

———

Stepping through the stones, they reached the edge of the pond. They still saw nothing, no movements or shadows. Hall led them across the stepping stones and onto the small island. The Branch dominated, and Hall could see a change in the tree. It was still dull, pitted, and cracked, but there seemed to be some life it now. He couldn't tell what it was, a feeling more than visual, but the tree was different.

And for the better.

Moving slow, cautiously, they made their way around the great tree and stopped.

Sitting with his back against the tree was Vertoyi.

He looked thinner, more emancipated, but stronger in some way. There was life to the Custodian where before there had been just madness. He wore a contented smile on his face, head leaning back against the tree with his eyes closed.

Hall saw a line of sap running down the trunk and behind the Druid. He traced the line up with his eyes and pointed, catching Leigh's attention.

"Wasn't that where the Demon's Nail was?" he asked.

The Nail was no longer there, removed. A small hole in the trunk remained, a black scar in the bark.

She nodded, crouching down in front of Vertoyi.

One hand still held the broken staff, the other was laid across his leg, palm up. In that palm was a black ash. The Nail, Hall guessed, assuming that was what happened when the deal was rendered null and void. It had taken the last of Vertoyi's strength to pull it out of the tree.

Quest Complete!

You have discovered that the Grove's Custodian, an Elf named Vertoyi, had become corrupted, and desecrated the Grove through his dark power. You have managed to end the corruption of the Grove and the corruption of Vertoyi.

THE CORRUPTED GROVE

Find the Source of Corruption 1/1
End the Corruption of the Grove 1/1

Reward: +1000 Druids of the Tree Renown, +1000 Alliance with Leigh, +500 Experience

You are now "TRUSTED" with Leigh.
She is grateful for your aid and friendship.

Leigh went to stand up when Vertoyi coughed. She almost fell back while Hall gripped the spear, shifting it so he could stab down quickly.

The Custodian's eyes opened slowly and he blinked, trying to focus.

"What is your name, child?" he asked, staring at a point over Leigh's shoulder but somehow still able to see her. His voice was no longer as rough. It was softer but weak.

"Leigh," she answered, kneeling on the ground in front of him.

"Thank you," Vertoyi said, a small sad smile across his face. "You have saved me and the Grove."

She didn't say anything, unsure what to say to the obviously dying Elf.

"I was a fool," he said, coughing, in almost a whisper that Hall had to strain to hear. "Jealous of the Elders, angry. I was easy prey for the Feardagh."

He stopped talking, overcome with a coughing fit. The rasping sounded painful but Vertoyi still smiled, his unseeing eyes bright. Hall felt the sun breaking through the strange miasma that had shrouded the Grove. A beam fell across Vertoyi and the smile deepened.

"The Grove will need a Custodian," he said, his eyes turning and focusing on Leigh. "Someone strong to undo the corruption I have caused. It will take someone special, someone dedicated. Will you be that someone?"

"I cannot," Leigh replied, not moving, tears flowing down her face. "I never wanted this. I never wanted to be a Druid. I cannot care for a Grove."

"But you can," Vertoyi said with confidence, his words soft

and encouraging. "You proved that today when your words broke me out of my confusion."

"I am not worthy," Leigh cried. "There are others."

"The Grove chooses you," Vertoyi said with a deeper cough, raspier.

His head fell back, his eyes closed. He reached up with his free hand, the black ash falling away and disappearing on the wind. Hall watched as Vertoyi touched his forehead, tracing a pattern across the skin. He pulled his hand back, and Hall saw that there was a small glowing object held between two fingers. It was a seed, a small one, glowing bright.

Vertoyi's hand fell limp, still clutching the seed. His chest stopped moving, no breath escaping his lips.

Hall pulled up his Settlement menu and looked at the Population listing. It said one. No longer two, just him. Vertoyi was dead.

Leigh stared at the seed in Vertoyi's hand. It still glowed, brighter than before. Pulsing, a call.

"You don't have to take it," he said.

"I know," Leigh answered, her voice full of conviction, and reached out. "But I want to."

She gently took the glowing seed from between Vertoyi's fingers. She held it up, turning it every which way, examining all the sides. She looked up at the Branch, the piece of the World Tree, the reason that her order of Druids existed. The reason that the world still existed and Edin floated in the sky of Hankarth.

Smiling, tears running freely down her cheeks, Leigh placed the seed against her forehead. There was a bright flash, blinding, and when Hall's vision cleared the seed was gone. There was not a mark on Leigh's forehead, nothing to indicate she had gained some great knowledge or power.

But there was a change to the Grove. The purple of corruption was no longer as bright, hints of greens and browns appearing. They were small, fighting hard against the corruption, but Hall knew they would get stronger with time.

He looked up at the tree. Silver was appearing at the ends of the leaves, the cracks and pits starting to heal.

Opening the Settlement menu again, he saw the population was back at two.

"Come on," he said, reaching a hand down to Leigh. "Let's go back to town, neighbor."

CHAPTER THIRTY-FOUR

"Neighbor?" Leigh asked as she stood staring at the large tree.

"The Settlement Stone," Hall explained. "It shows a population of two. It was Vertoyi and me, now it's you and me. Apparently, the Grove is in the confines of the settlement."

"So, we'll be seeing a lot more of each other," she said, glancing at him with a coy smile.

"Yeah," he said and was glad. "As long as you call me Lord Hall and pay your taxes," he added. "Your Grove is in my lands."

Leigh rolled her eyes. Hall laughed. It hurt to laugh but at that moment he didn't care.

Together they walked across the stepping stones, crossing under the standing stones. They made their way across the meadow toward the thin part of the cliff where the entrance stones were. They saw two figures standing on the edge.

Roxhard and Sabine.

"I thought I told you to head to town," Hall said.

"Yeah, well," Roxhard started to say and shrugged.

"We didn't," Sabine said simply. "We got the quest

completed prompt and stopped, figuring it was safe enough. What happened?"

Hall motioned to Leigh and let her explain. She did, quickly. It didn't amount to much. She was the new Custodian and wasn't quite sure yet what that meant.

"You're going to fix all that?" Sabine asked, motioning to the corrupt Grove behind them.

"I hope so," Leigh answered, looking over her shoulder.

Her face dropped as she realized the monumental task ahead of her.

"You can do it," Roxhard said.

Leigh turned back and smiled.

"I don't know about the rest of you but I need some serious rest," Hall said.

They all nodded.

"And food," Roxhard added.

———

Hall lay on his bedroll, blanket pulled up, staring at the rotted ceiling above him.

They were in the same building as before, where they had left their gear. A small fire, a quick meal, some more healing, and they had all laid down. There was no watch. Not this night. Hall had gone back and forth. They weren't in truly safe territory but he felt safe enough.

And they all needed the rest.

But it wasn't coming for Hall.

He didn't know why. He was tired. His body ached. He wanted to sleep but it wasn't coming.

Instead, he was staring at the ceiling.

A ceiling that belonged to a building in his village.

His village. He was wondering if he had made a mistake.

He didn't want to be a leader, let alone a mayor or governor or whatever he was now.

Which was nothing. Not at the moment. And he could control what happened. He didn't have to rebuild the village, expand it or find citizens. They could fix up enough housing for just them and make it a just a base of operations.

But he knew himself. He wouldn't stop there. He had already been thinking about what rebuilding Skara Brae would mean, what the town would need.

He opened up the Settlement Menu and started looking through all the options. He looked through the text on government and was surprised to see there were options. He had expected there to be only the one. It appeared that the Lord of the town could control how much power they had over the day to day operations.

Rank II Settlement Available Forms Of Government

Mayoral: The Lord of the Settlement, or chosen representative, is the sole voice of rulership. There can be a council that assists but they would be advisers only. The Mayor is responsible for all final decisions.

Lord's Council: The Lord and chosen representatives, chosen by election or appointment, make the decisions together. The council has a say in the decisions but the final decision is up to the Lord. The Lord can follow the council's advice or chose another direction.

Town Council: A council of representatives, chosen by election or appointment, which can but does not need to include the Lord, make all decisions by vote. The majority vote wins and decides the final decision. The Lord can override if they so choose but would most likely not as they appoint the council to run the day to day operations of the settlement.

Hall liked the last option. He had no desire to deal with the day to day operations of running a village. He just wanted the village and to make it grow and turn into something. At the same time, he still wanted to be free to adventure.

He spent about an hour looking through the menus, seeing what was there and getting an idea of what his next move would be.

That scared him. He was thinking long term.

Getting up, careful not to disturb anyone, Hall headed for the front opening of the house. Pike did not move from where he lay curled up next to Angus but the cow did raise his head. He saw it was Hall and lay back down, going back to sleep. Hall walked outside where it was darker down below the ground. He made his way around to the nearest set of stairs.

The moon shone down, providing light now that he was out of the shadows of the buildings. It was a bright night, and he could see the edge of the island not that far away. He started walking in that direction.

He stopped about five feet from the edge. Close enough that he could see the edge, the grass growing and tufts of dirt hanging over with nothing below, just held up by roots connected to the rest of the meadow. It was a jagged line, the edge of Edin. Sharp points, long and thin pieces extended out and in. It appeared as if the rest had just been snapped away.

As it had.

Hall could see some of the other islands. Darker shadows in the dark of night. The stars were above, some blocked by higher islands.

Previously, before the glitch, he had not been a long-term planner. He played, he leveled, he did dungeons. He didn't think about what the best build was, what path he should follow to be the best at endgame. He just played.

He had known others that planned everything out. They plotted their path of progression from Level 1 to max level, knowing what they needed for equipment and skills to be the best at endgame. The problem was that the endgame had always been changing. It was a moving target. New content was added on a regular basis, just as people got bored with the old.

But now Hall realized he needed to plan long term. He needed to think about where to go and how to get there, especially if he was going to grow Skara Brae.

He needed to be smart about it.

It wasn't just about him. Not anymore.

He wondered when he had finally accepted that this was truly his life. He had believed them to be stuck in the game, there was no other real choice but to think that way. But in the back of his head he had thought there was always a chance. When had that changed?

Why had it changed?

Hall sat down on the grass, feeling the ever-present wind passing along the meadow. It felt cool against his skin, refreshing. He looked over his shoulder, surveying the land between the ridge and the mountains, the land that was now his.

It was rugged, unwelcoming, but it was his.

He looked up at the stars and smiled.

It wasn't like the previous life was anything special.

But this one? This new life?

It could be something very special.

Epilogue

HE PULLED THE KNIFE OUT, FEELING THE BLOOD SPLASH ONTO his gloved hand. Cursing, the thrust messier than he had wanted, he stepped back and let the body fall to the ground. It landed with a thud that sounded like it could be heard for miles around.

Looking down both ends of the long and dark alley, Davit waited in the deeper shadows, ears alert for any sound. There was none. No running feet, no cries of alarm.

He bent down and carefully but quickly searched the body. A Gael shopkeep, this one a tailor. Just another body. This kill made an even half dozen. Ever since Auld and that Skirmisher, Hall, dismissing him, Davit had been forced to move from city to city. A growing trail of bodies behind him.

That group had been the only other Players he had seen. Just him and a lot of NPCs.

Even here, in Cold's Ridge, a port town on the island of Huntley, there were no other Players. He had finally managed to leave Auld, killing another NPC to get the money to book passage. Davit had wanted to return to Cumberland, start fresh, but unable to, he had instead chosen Huntley as a destination. He had hoped to find another group of Players, others to join up with. Others that could protect him.

He didn't want to kill, not really, but he was good at it and they were just NPCs, after all. They'd respawn, and if they didn't, not a big deal. Before the glitch, before getting trapped here, he had killed NPCs every chance he got. Had driven the ex-girlfriend crazy. He had fun with it. No harm, no foul. Now was different. There were consequences. Armed and angry consequences.

Guards.

It wasn't fair. He was a Player. They were NPCs.

And this dead NPC was poor.

Only twenty silver and nothing else of value.

Pocketing the money, Davit left the alley and stepped out onto the hard-packed dirt of the streets. Cold's Ridge lived up to its name. There was a light covering of snow across the frozen ground. He could see his breath in the air. Hunching down, pulling his arms in tighter, Davit started walking down the street. There were few people out, drunks mostly. Nights in the Ridge, as the locals called it, were cold and windy, and the smart people were inside already.

He made his way through the dark streets, taking random turns in case he was being followed. There were not that many Bodin in Cold's Ridge, so he stood out. There were not that many Bodins in most cities or towns. There had been before, when there had been more Players, but not now. He stood out. Too much for his liking.

Davit hated being a Bodin. He had never liked it.

He turned down the street that led to the abandoned house he was staying in and stopped. Out front were four armed guards and what looked like two men. All turned toward him as he stepped into the light from one of the few street lamps in the small town.

"That's him," one of the men shouted, pointing. "That's the Bodin."

"You there," a guard said as all four turned and started his way.

The numbers against him, Davit turned and ran. He slipped and stumbled on the icy ground, hearing the running boot steps of the guards close behind. He cursed, grunting as he slammed into the corner of a building, turning into an alley.

A dead end.

Drawing his two rapiers, Davit turned and faced the open end of the alley. The guards drew their weapons, stepping into the alley two abreast.

"You're under arrest for theft and murder," one of them said.

He wondered how he had messed up, how they had found him. It didn't matter. He'd have to kill the four guards and leave Cold's Ridge. There were no airships tonight, so it was into the wilds of Huntley and make for one of the other ports. Level four now, the idea of being in the wilds wasn't as daunting.

The alley worked in his favor, only allowing two of the guards to approach at a time.

Fifteen feet, ten feet, the guards approached with caution.

Sounds of fighting, grunts of pain, came from the front of the alley. The two guards turned at the commotion, and Davit attacked. He took a couple steps and slid across the ground using the icy surface to his advantage. He stabbed with one blade, sliced with the other. The guard screamed in pain as one rapier sliced his hamstring, the other stabbing into his lower back. Slipping and sliding, falling, Davit pushed up with the blades, catching the guard in the back and using the momentum to make the guard fall to the ground behind him.

Jumping up, he turned to the second guard only to find a

sword stabbing into the man's chest. The guard fell back without a word.

Davit could barely see the owner of the sword. He was tall, a Wood Elf, that was all the detail visible in the dark alley.

"Boss wants a word with you," the Elf said, no threat in his voice, just friendliness.

Davit realized the Elf was a Player.

Any reluctance and caution he might have felt fled. Davit was excited to see another Player and one that had quickly, and without hesitation, killed town guards.

Walking out of the alley, the Elf following, Davit saw the bodies of the other guards. Both looked to have their heads crushed, the bodies leaning awkwardly against the walls. Smiling, wanting to laugh, he stepped out onto the street. Lamps gave pockets of light against the dark, and standing in one of those pockets was a large man with a female Norn, a Shaman, and a female Elf, a Skirmisher, standing behind him.

A Nord, the man was easily six inches over six feet and a couple hundred pounds. He wore brigandine armor with no sleeves. His muscled arms were covered in lines of blue and black tattoos. Leather bracers, leather steel studded gloves, leather pants with sewn in metal plates and armored boots. He held a large flat-headed war hammer in one hand, a large shield over his back. The only item he wore against the cold was a wolf's fur cloak. A Warden.

He was clean shaven except for a patch on his chin that grew long down his chest and was braided. The sides of his head were tattooed and shaved clean, a thin line of hair on the top that was braided and ran long down his back.

The Norn was tall and thin, gaunt. Pale white skin and shining silver hair. She wore the robes of a Shaman and hung a step behind the man. The Skirmisher leaned on her spear, a purple dragonhawk on her shoulder. Dressed in leathers, she had black hair with deep purple streaks. She was smiling.

"NPCs," the man grunted and spit on the ground. "Don't they know their betters when the see them?"

Davit glanced back at the Elf, who moved back toward the Nord and Skirmisher. Both were Players. In the light, Davit could see the Elf's features. Long green hair, some of it pulled into a top knot. Bright green eyes and blue swirling tattoos. Davit thought he recognized him. Possibly from the Laughing Horse Inn on that first day? Cuthard or something like that.

"Who are you?" Davit asked, focusing on the Nord Warden, the obvious leader.

"One like you that knows how things should be. The NPCs should be kneeling to us. We are Players. We are their betters. We should be ruling this world, and we shall start with this miserable town."

"Who are you?" Davit asked again.

"Iron."

NAME: HALL
RACE: HALF-ELF
CLASS: SKIRMISHER
LVL: 3
XP: 1060 | **NEXT LVL:** 1300

UNASSIGNED STAT POINTS: 0
STATS:
BASE ADJUSTED TOTAL:
Health
36
0
36

Energy

54

0

54

Vitality

18

0

18

ATTRIBUTES:

BASE ADJUSTED TOTAL:

Strength

11

0

11

Wellness

13

0

13

Willpower

10

0

10

Agility

16

4

20

Intelligence

11

0

11

Charisma

10

0

10

Attack Power

1

2

3

Spell Power

1

0

1

Protection

2

9

11

Attack Speed

-3 sec

-1 sec

-4 sec

Spell Resistance

0

0

0

Carry Capacity

30

0

30

ELEMENTAL RESISTANCES:

Air

0%

Fire

0%

Earth

0%

Water

0%

RACIAL ABILITY:

Limited Night Vision

CLASS ABILITIES:

Rank Value

Evade

1

Leap

1

Leaping Stab

1

Shared Vision

SKILLS:
Combat
Light Armor
2
11.4

Polearms
2
12.7

Small Blades
2
12

Thrown
2
10.9

Activity
Identify
1
2.2

Triage
2
10

Environment
Camouflage
1
0.5

Stealth
1
1.5

Survival
2
13.2

Tracking
1
2.3

Professions
Cartography
2
15.6

Herbology
2
14.5

Skinning
2
11.7

Reputation (Faction)
Druids of the Grove —1300 (Known and Friendly)
Kingdom of Essec — 1600 (Known and Friendly)

Reputation (Alliance)
Guard Captain Henry —1300 (Friendly)
Watchman Kelly — 800 (Known)
Merchant Dyson — 700 (Known)
Druid Leigh — 3600 (Trusted)

––––––

This concludes Grayhold, but don't worry, the second book in Sky Realms Online picks up the story, and the fun has just begun!

––––––

- Forced to live this new life, is Hall ready to be the Lord of Skara Brae?
- Can Hall become the leader his companions need him to be?
- Will responsibilty as Lord and Custodian prevent Hall and Leigh from developing a relationship?
- How else will Sky Realms Online surprise Hall and the others?
- Who is Iron?

Silver Peak preorder coming soon!

About Troy Osgood

**LitRPG: the genre I always wanted to be writing in
but didn't know it until recently.**

I'm a relative newcomer to the genre, discovering it in the last
year or so, but this is where I should have always been.

I've been gaming for decades. Started with an old Atari
2600. I've never been a FPS or RTS fan, it's always been RPGs
for me. Contra, Metroid and my personnel favorite Legend of
Kage all hold a special place but first and foremost have been
RPGs.

In 2001 I discovered MMORPGs with Ultima Online (I
was a Trammy on Chesapeake for a number of years) and then
moved on to Final Fantasy XI and then World of Warcraft
from Beta to a couple of months after Wrath of The Lich King
expansion came out. Pretty much daily.

Life got in the way and I stopped but always kept my love

for the games and went back to UO and WoW multiple times through the years well dabbling in others (mostly Lord of the Rings online). I've backed Kickstarters for a couple MMO and normal RPGs but just don't have the time to play as much.

And I wish I had more time to read all that is available, but I do what I can. This writing thing seems to get in the way.

It was during the leveling my Dwarf Warrior on Antheron (2nd character I had taken to max level, first was a Tauren Hunter on Illidan) that I had the idea of writing down my guild's adventures through Azeroth; turning the quests and raids into stories.

I never got around to it, but that was when I first got the idea of writing GameLit/LitRPG, even though I didn't know what it was at the time.

And that brings us to now.

I've published some sci-fi (space opera) and fantasy (sword and sorcery), and when I discovered the litRPG genre I started developing what would become Sky Realms Online. At the same time, Aethon Books was looking to publish some books in the genre. I submitted to them and the rest is history.

This is a world I want to be writing in for a long time. Grayhold was the longest, and most fun book I've written (the sequel Silver Peak beats it). I love the world of Hankarth and have so many stories to tell. If you couldn't tell, I created the class/skill system in SRO as a combination of UO and WoW and the Skirmisher is a homage to my favorite MMO class of all time: the Dragoon from FFXI.

LitRPG is a genre that I am really enjoying, and plan on being in for a long time with regular releases.

That of course, depends on if you want to keep reading. I hope so as I have huge plans for Sky Realms Online: at least nine books with some spin-offs, side-quests and lots of other fun stuff. And those're just the current ideas. The world, and the characters could go far beyond that.

I'd like to thank **Steve Beaulieu** and **Rhett Bruno** at **Aethon Books** for everything they've done. Awesome team to work with. I'm so impressed with everything they did, and SRO wouldn't be what it is without them.

Check out all the other books from Aethon. You won't be disappointed. My editor, **Ilse Davison**, did a great job and, well, the amount of edits was high (thanks to my bad habit of double spacing), but what she found helped a ton.

The cover by **Jackson Tjota** is absolutely beautiful and damn does Pike look awesome. Even better than I imagined.

SRO: Grayhold is the first of my books to make it to audio and I couldn't be happier with the results. **Pavi Proczko** knocked it out of the park.

None of this would be possible without the love and support from my beautiful wife and daughters. Thank you **Kat**, **Heaven** and **Paisley**. I love you all so much.

And thank you for giving Sky Realms Online a try. I look forward to this journey with you. Please leave a review on Amazon and Goodreads and spread the word.

See you in the next book,

Troy

Newsletter: https://www.ossynews.com

FROM THE PUBLISHER

Thank you for reading _Grayhold,_ book one in Sky Realms Online.

WE HOPE YOU ENJOYED IT AS MUCH AS WE ENJOYED BRINGING IT to you. We just wanted to take a moment to encourage you to review the book on Amazon and Goodreads. Every review helps further the author's reach and, ultimately, helps them continue writing fantastic books for us all to enjoy.

If you liked _Grayhold_, check out the rest of our catalogue at www.aethonbooks.com. To sign up to receive 3 FREE books from some of our best authors as well as updates regarding all new releases, visit www.subscribepage.com/AethonReadersGroup.

SPECIAL THANKS TO:

ADAWIA E. ASAD
JENNY AVERY
BARDE PRESS
CALUM BEAULIEU
BEN
BECKY BEWERSDORF
BHAM
TANNER BLOTTER
ALFRED JOSEPH BOHNE IV
CHAD BOWDEN
ERREL BRAUDE
DAMIEN BROUSSARD
CATHERINE BULLINER
JUSTIN BURGESS
MATT BURNS
BERNIE CINKOSKE
MARTIN COOK
ALISTAIR DILWORTH
JAN DRAKE
BRET DULEY
RAY DUNN
ROB EDWARDS
RICHARD EYRES
MARK FERNANDEZ
CHARLES T FINCHER
SYLVIA FOIL
GAZELLE OF CAERBANNOG
DAVID GEARY
MICHEAL GREEN
BRIAN GRIFFIN

EDDIE HALLAHAN
JOSH HAYES
PAT HAYES
BILL HENDERSON
JEFF HOFFMAN
GODFREY HUEN
JOAN QUERALTÓ IBÁÑEZ
JONATHAN JOHNSON
MARCEL DE JONG
KABRINA
PETRI KANERVA
ROBERT KARALASH
VIKTOR KASPERSSON
TESLAN KIERINHAWK
ALEXANDER KIMBALL
JIM KOSMICKI
FRANKLIN KUZENSKI
MEENAZ LODHI
DAVID MACFARLANE
JAMIE MCFARLANE
HENRY MARIN
CRAIG MARTELLE
THOMAS MARTIN
ALAN D. MCDONALD
JAMES MCGLINCHEY
MICHAEL MCMURRAY
CHRISTIAN MEYER
SEBASTIAN MÜLLER
MARK NEWMAN
JULIAN NORTH

KYLE OATHOUT
LILY OMIDI
TROY OSGOOD
GEOFF PARKER
NICHOLAS (BUZ) PENNEY
JASON PENNOCK
THOMAS PETSCHAUER
JENNIFER PRIESTER
RHEL
JODY ROBERTS
JOHN BEAR ROSS
DONNA SANDERS
FABIAN SARAVIA
TERRY SCHOTT
SCOTT
ALLEN SIMMONS
KEVIN MICHAEL STEPHENS
MICHAEL J. SULLIVAN
PAUL SUMMERHAYES
JOHN TREADWELL
CHRISTOPHER J. VALIN
PHILIP VAN ITALLIE
JAAP VAN POELGEEST
FRANCK VAQUIER
VORTEX
DAVID WALTERS JR
MIKE A. WEBER
PAMELA WICKERT
JON WOODALL
BRUCE YOUNG

CPSIA information can be obtained
at www.ICGtesting.com
Printed in the USA
LVHW110223101219
640002LV00001B/90/P